# STRICTLY
# BUSINESS

## NATHANIEL CLARK

Copyright © 2020 by Nathaniel Clark.

Library of Congress Control Number: 2020916136
ISBN: Hardcover 978-1-6641-2715-9
Softcover 978-1-6641-2714-2
eBook 978-1-6641-2713-5

All rights reserved. No part of this book may be reproduced or transmitted in any form or by any means, electronic or mechanical, including photocopying, recording, or by any information storage and retrieval system, without permission in writing from the copyright owner.

This is a work of fiction. All of the characters, names, incidents, organizations, and dialogue in this novel are either the products of the author's imagination or are used fictitiously.

Any people depicted in stock imagery provided by Getty Images are models, and such images are being used for illustrative purposes only. Certain stock imagery © Getty Images.

Print information available on the last page.

Rev. date: 08/27/2020

To order additional copies of this book, contact:
Xlibris
844-714-8691
www.Xlibris.com
Orders@Xlibris.com
746089

# Karma

I stand in a place I know all too well . . .
Alone and miserable, this has to be hell.
Maybe I pushed you away, or maybe you ran . . .
All I know is you're gone, and that wasn't planned.
It's funny how things changed since I last was home . . .
No visits, no letters, no one answering the phone.
I'm stranded in this place and wondering why . . .
I treated you good, but you left me to die.
I guess that was then—it's all in the past . . .
Good deeds go undone, and nice guys finish last.
I know that you're gone, but it still feels bizarre . . .
I should've been prepared—everyone leaves when things start to get hard.
You said that you loved me and would always be by my side . . .
But when I needed you the most, it was you I could not find.
I'm not even mad anymore, just really hurt . . .
It is what it is—I guess I got jerked.
What keeps me going is that life isn't out of my hands . . .
Very soon I shall rise, then I'll shine again.
History repeats itself, so those who left will try to come back . . .
But this time I'll be wise—it'll be me who turns my back.

# Acknowledgments

I would like to thank anybody that has ever been in my life, whether it has been good or bad. No matter what kind of relationship, friendship, or association we had, you have helped me grow as a man. I am who I am today because of my life as a whole, not in part. The good, the bad, and the ugly have all made me a better person today. Thank you very much.

# Note from the Author

This book was not written to glorify the street life. This book was written to open eyes and give people a real look at life in the streets. My hope is that this tale may be able to save someone who is on the wrong path or considering going down the wrong path. Life in the streets is barbaric and unapologetic, and the more you live it, the more of it you become. Most kids in impoverished communities are taught at a young age to be leery of police, not to trust or respect women, and are exposed to levels of violence that most people can't even fathom. Many are programmed for failure before they are mature enough to choose the type of life they want to live. Kids are taught to sell drugs before they understand the effects that drugs have on a person or the community; they are taught to be violent and kill before they have an understanding of how precious one's life truly is. Youth are being taught that jail is cool and school is for fools. This book shows the reader exactly how things turn out for those of us who choose to live by the code of the streets.

This book is fictional, but there are many real-life instances and truths written in these pages. There are people who live these ways daily, whether it be a parent who lost their child to the streets, the person who took a life now living in a cage for the rest of their life, or those who commit egregious acts due to their love of money or drugs. This book is a look inside the mind of those who live life in ways that many can't or won't understand or relate to.

Well . . . maybe after reading this book, you'll have a better understanding of what life is like for those of us who have chosen this path. There is much to be learned from us even if it's what not to do. I don't expect for many of the readers to agree with or respect this way of thinking or acting. I just hope to shed some light on why people think and act these ways. Not everyone in these environments turns out like the characters in my book, but many do. So instead of complaining about crime, drugs, welfare, etc., become a part of the solution. Help educate the youth. Show them that it's okay to love one another; expose them to how life can be if you get an education and work hard because, believe it or not, many children in impoverished communities don't get to see that. The people they see with nice things and respect are drug dealers and those who take what they want with guns.

People don't see the all outcomes to the street life . . . until now. This book is a tale that gives the reader all sides of the streets—the good, the bad, and the ugly. I have been living the street life since I was a child. I have never done anything but stick to the code of the streets. What has that gotten me? Nothing but a long criminal prison record. The money . . . gone; some was stolen from people I trusted the most. The rest was spent on lawyers, commissary, etc. The houses, apartments and cars . . . gone; lost all of those when I came to jail. Friends and romance . . . don't make me laugh. Everyone is your friend when you have something they want. As soon as things got real, all my so-called friends disappeared as did the women.

I'm thirty-six, and I have spent half of my life in prison. I don't have any friends. I don't trust anybody. I only see the worst in all situations and people, and I have an extremely deep hole that I have to try and climb out of because of past poor decisions. This is my reality due to the life I chose to live. I wrote this book because this is the only life I have known; however, I've learned that a certain flower is capable of being grown in complete darkness. Like that flower, I am choosing to blossom from this darkness and show the world that something beautiful can come from this. As I mature as a man, I see where I went wrong, and I hope that by sharing these things with you, it can stop another person from following in my footsteps.

There is nothing cool about our children being raised by someone else while we are in prison or dead. There is nothing pleasant about being locked in space smaller than a bathroom with another man for eighteen hours a day, having to smell his farts, hear him urinate, and be an arm's length away while he defecates. There is no going home when a child is sick or a loved one dies. There is no twenty-four- or forty-eight-hour pass home when your sibling or child graduates. There's no reset button once you start this journey. No, this is life for those of us who choose to live the street life.

What's more saddening is that prison is one of the better outcomes, considering the many other tragic endings that some of us meet. There is no glory in being permanently paralyzed because you were shot. There's nothing tough about being in a box, six feet in the ground, dead either. These are the unfortunate realities of people who choose to live life like I have.

I'm not trying to make anyone feel sorry for these lost souls. I'm just trying to help people see why they are this way. No one is born evil or mean. Life makes them this way. Knowing why can help prevents it from occurring in the future. Just as those souls were lost, I believe with the proper love and understanding, those lost souls can be found. Despite what the movies or rap songs may say, there is no pot of gold at the end of this rainbow, just a cage in the mountains or a box in the ground. I share what I know because I now believe that everyone deserves a chance to live. This is a lonely life filled with pain, paranoia, and regrets.

People often ask what prison is like. I'll answer that in the most honest and accurate way I can. Being in prison is like being dead but still getting to see how everyone you love goes on without you. Let that sink in.

Read this book. Digest what happens and why. Understand that there are people who live and think like this, then ask yourself, "Do I really want to be a part of this world?" If your answer is yes, you deserve everything you get from this point on. Thank you for listening.

# 1

The road to life can be a rough one; Reds knew this firsthand, but he was not deterred by what life had thrown his way. Reds would take the pile of shit that life had given him and make a beautiful garden out of it.

Reds's situation was a bad one. His mother, Betty, was a heroin addict. Although Betty didn't neglect Reds physically, she showed him things that no child should have known. Betty showed Reds how to be a hustler. Betty hadn't lost all her dignity though. She mainly supported her habit by boosting. Betty quickly showed Reds the ins and outs of the game. She had an older daughter, Stacy, whom Betty had given to her mother to raise while she ran the streets. Betty had learned from that mistake and refused to make it twice. Betty saw Reds as her meal ticket, a guaranteed check every month, despite the fact that by keeping Reds around only corrupted him.

Betty never called anyone when she had Reds. Reds's father, Rob, wanted to raise Reds. Rob was an addict also, but he got his life together when he found out that Betty was pregnant. Rob didn't want Reds to turn out like him. He wanted better for his son. Betty wasn't having it though. She felt like she was entitled to at least one of her children. After all, she was the one who gave birth to them. Betty figured that she deserved something for all that pain during labor. So instead of trying to have someone talk her out of her second born, she decided not to let anyone know. Betty took little Reds from Chester County Hospital and headed to Philly.

Betty had not the slightest clue as to how to be a mother, so she wasn't. Betty and Reds were friends. That relationship would soon enough lead to them being partners in crime. Once Reds was old enough, Betty taught him to steal and help her con people for money. Because of this, Reds no longer looked at the world as being filled with people; he saw the world as being filled with victims. Betty would give her drugs to Reds and tell him to put it in his underwear. Betty told Reds that because he was so young, his underwear was his "secret hiding place," meaning no one could touch or look there. Reds learned the game quick. He didn't really have a choice. If they didn't make money, they didn't eat, and Reds loved to eat.

Betty had so many hustles that it was impossible for them not to eat though. There was the "sleep and swap," which meant that Betty would take a man to a hotel room and sleep with him. Reds would already be hiding under the bed when she got there. As Betty would "entertain" the john, Reds would crawl from under the bed and steal his money. Then there was the "distraction detail." In this con, Betty would take Reds to the department stores and gather up all the nice clothes. When she was ready to make her escape, Reds would go to the security guard at the door and take him to the other side of the store while Betty made her getaway with the clothes. Once Betty stashed everything in the car, she'd come back and get Reds. They'd then take their merchandise to the projects in North Philly and sell it.

These were just a few of her tricks. Reds learned at an early age that he had to use his head to survive. He also learned to say no to drugs. Betty didn't hide anything from her son. She told Reds that she was hooked on drugs—medicine was what she called it.

"Don't ever use this stuff. It makes you weak," Betty used to tell Reds. "You don't ever wanna be weak. You're mommy's strong lil' man."

"Why do you do it, Mommy?" Reds asked.

"Somebody tricked me into doing it. Now I can't stop or I'll die. But nobody can ever trick you because you know now," Betty said.

Reds nodded his head like the good student that he was.

On Reds's twelfth birthday, he and Betty went to the Gallery Mall to do some boosting. Reds was taking more than he normally would have because it was his birthday and he felt he deserved it. Betty always told Reds, "If you want somethin', you gotta go get it 'cause ain't nobody gonna give you shit!"

So that's exactly what Reds was doing, spoiling himself. Betty was dope sick, so she was being sloppy as well. If one of them had been paying attention, they would have seen the security people approaching them.

When Reds and Betty attempted to walk out of the store, they were rushed by security. Betty had warrants for everything, from drug sales to identity theft all the way down to retail theft. Betty knew she was done, so she told the police that she made Reds steal the stuff because she was dope sick. Betty also taught Reds to never talk to the cops, so he didn't speak. All he kept saying was, "I'm a minor. Talk to my mom," which is what she told him to say.

Betty gave the police her mother's, Annabell, phone number, and the police called her. They informed Annabell that she needed to come up pick her grandson or he'd be taken to a juvenile detention center. Annabell had never gotten a chance to meet her grandson. Betty would call from time to time, but she never took Reds to see any family. Betty feared that if she took Reds around any of them, they'd try to keep him. Reds's grandmother was more than happy to go get Reds.

Reds stayed with his grandmother for two weeks and visited his father on the weekends. On the third weekend, Annabell asked Rob to keep Reds.

"I can't handle that boy. He's too much for me," Annabell said.

So Reds moved with his father, who quickly learned that Reds was no ordinary twelve-year-old. Rob was a street-level dealer, who had gotten hooked on his own product shortly after meeting Betty. He cleaned himself up when he heard that Betty was pregnant, but he never got a chance to be a father to Reds because Betty had taken him to Philly as soon as she left the hospital. Rob had no idea of the type of things that Betty had taught Reds, but he wanted to try and teach him to do things the right way. Rob signed Reds up for football, basketball, and track in order to give him something positive to do with his time. The problem was that Betty's damage was already done and irreversible.

While practice was going on, Reds would sneak into the locker room and coach's office and rob them blind. After having several conversations with Reds, Rob understood the type of things Betty had been teaching their son. Every time they would go into a store, Reds would steal whatever he wanted. Even when Reds had money, he would steal.

"Why are you stealin' when you got money?" Rob would ask.

"Why pay when I can steal? That's just wastin' money," Reds replied.

These were the type of conversations Rob and his son would have. Rob understood Reds's position. Reds was so open about what he was doing because he hadn't been taught that what he was doing was wrong.

After two years of trying everything, from beatings to grounding, Rob finally gave up. Reds had gotten kicked out of school for beating up one of his teachers. When questioned about his behavior, Reds gave his father a dose of his own medicine.

"Why in the hell would you hit one of your teachers?" Rob asked.

"He made me mad," Reds replied.

"So you think it's cool to hit people when you get mad?" Rob said.

"I don't see why not. You hit me when you get mad," Reds said.

Reds was no dummy. He knew exactly what he was doing. It would be impossible for Rob to scold him for something he had taught him. Rob knew the game, and it was obvious what direction his son was headed. Reds had broken his father's spirits; Rob simply gave up hope that his son would do the right thing. Although he gave up hope, he didn't give up on Reds. Rob didn't condone what Reds was into, but he couldn't stop it. So he laid down some very simple rules.

"This is how the real world works. You can do whatever you wanna do, *but* if you get caught doin' wrong, you have to pay the consequences. So I'm not goin' to keep bein' mad at you all the time. Do what you want, but if you get caught, accept your punishment. I won't bitch about what you do, but you can't bitch about what I do if I catch you," Rob said.

That conversation just made Reds stay alert. Reds knew that if he got caught, he'd be punished. Reds liked his father's "don't ask, don't tell" policy.

Even though Reds didn't live with his grandmother, he was still in contact with his big sister, Stacey, who lived with Annabell. Stacey was ten years older than Reds. Stacey always knew that she had a little brother, and now that he was around, Stacey spent a good amount of time with him. She knew that Reds was a handful, but that was still her baby brother and she loved him whether he was right or wrong. Although Reds was a problem child, he loved his family very much. It was the streets that he would terrorize.

Reds had been living in West Chester with his dad for three years now. Stacey had recently moved from Coatesville to West Chester to be closer to Reds. West Chester is right outside of Philly, located between Chester City and Coatesville. Although West Chester isn't a big city, it's very close to three cities, so there's nothing slow about it. In the borough of West Chester, things are just like any other hood. There isn't as much violence as some of the big cities, but that's about it.

When Stacey moved to West Chester, she moved into Sidetrack. It was an apartment complex or projects as some would call it. They called it Sidetrack because it was located on the side of the railroad tracks. There were a few major drug areas in West Chester, and Sidetrack happened to be one of them. Chestnut Street, where Reds lived, was one of the other ones. Reds had become interested in the drug game not long after he moved to West Chester. He saw the way the drug dealers lived, and he wanted to be like them. Reds would often be paid to be a lookout for the drug dealers, but out of respect for Rob, nobody would give him any drugs.

When Reds turned sixteen, he got his first drug pack. It came by way of Stacey's boyfriend, Mike. Mike, like all the other hustlers around Reds's way, took a liking to Reds. After being constantly harassed for a year, Mike gave Reds his first pack. They sat at Stacey's kitchen table while Stacey was at work, and Mike broke everything down.

"Look, lil' nigga, I'm givin' you a $120 pack. Off that, you keep $50 and give me $70," Mike said.

"Damn, why it ain't $60 a piece?" Reds asked.

"'Cause I gotta reup. Now stop askin' questions, and go get that money, youngin'," Mike said.

Mike wasn't a hustler; he was a stickup kid. Mike got all his drugs, or work as it's often called, from the people he robbed. He'd then give the drugs to Reds to hustle. Being that Mike was the type of person that he was, he showed Reds how to clean, load, and shoot a gun. Mike also sold Reds his first gun, a .380, for $150.

Mike wasn't big time; he just did what he did to get by. Because of that, he didn't have a constant supply of drugs for Reds. Reds, on the other hand, was dedicated to getting money. He basically lived on the block and started to accumulate a lot of customers. The downside of Reds and Mike's relationship was that Mike couldn't keep Reds with enough drugs to sell.

After a long night of hustling, Reds came in the house and was about to go to sleep, but Rob asked him to walk with him to a diner and get some breakfast.

On their way to the diner on Market Street, a black Land Rover pulled up on them. A slim brown-skinned man rolled down the window.

"What's up, cuz?" he yelled.

"Oh shit, when the fuck they let you out?" Rob responded.

J.R. parked the truck and hopped out. Reds couldn't help but notice how fly J.R. was. J.R. wore a pair of Iceberg jeans, an Iceberg shirt, a black leather Avirex jacket, and a brand-new pair of tan construction Timberland boots. It was 1999, every hustler that was getting real paper was wearing Iceburg. J.R. was also wearing a huge Cuban link chain with an iced-out Jesus piece. The chain and medallion hung down past J.R.'s privates. Reds also noticed an iced-out Rolex watch on J.R.'s wrist.

"This is your cousin, J.R.," Rob explained to Reds.

"What's good, lil' cuz?" J.R. asked as he dug in his pocket and pulled out a $50 bill for Reds.

"I was good, but now I'm better. Thanks, cuz!" Reds said with a wide Kool-Aid smile on his face.

As Reds looked at his cousin, he told himself that he wanted to be just like him. Rob and J.R. talked for a minute. J.R. explained that he had finally gotten his day in court and was found not guilty on the murder charge he was fighting. J.R.'s pager started going off as they were conversing. J.R. looked at the number on his pager.

"A'ight, cuz, I gotta go, but I'll be in touch," J.R. said. "Take it easy, lil' cuz. I'll catch you around."

As Reds and Rob sat at the diner and ate, Rob filled Reds in on who J.R. was and what he was about.

"Damn, Dad, J.R. seems cool as shit," Reds said.

"I love him to death, but that nigga is a fuckin' monster," Rob said. "I think Satan himself would be afraid of that nigga."

"Why you say that, Pop?" Reds asked quizzically.

"J.R. looks like a drug dealer, but he's not. He's a cold-blooded killer. He works for some major nigga, kills people just as fast as he'd shake their hand. He must be gettin' paid well though. Nigga stay laced. They say he paid the lawyer $75,000 to beat that murder rap. And it don't look like it hurt his pockets either. See how that nigga's rollin'?" Rob said.

After Reds and his dad ate, they headed back home. Right as Reds was dozing off, Mike paged him. He put 120 after his number, which meant that he had a pack for Reds. When Reds saw this, he wasn't so tired anymore.

As Reds posted himself on the corner, a fiend came up and asked for a $10 rock. Reds spit the dime into his hand and was about to give it to the fiend when the fiend dug in her panties and pulled out a sock full of pennies.

"What the fuck is that?" Reds asked in a confused tone.

"It's $10," the fiend said flatly.

"That shit don't look like $10 to me," Reds responded.

"I'm sayin' it's all pennies, but them shits spend just like dollars," the fiend stated.

"Fuck it. Give it here," Reds said as he extended his hand.

When Reds grabbed the sock, he noticed it had fecal stains on the bottom.

*WAM!* Reds smacked the fiend as hard as he could with the sock full of change. She went down instantly, and change flew everywhere.

"Bitch, get cha dirty ass the fuck outta here," Reds said angrily.

As the fiend was leaving, Mike was coming up the block. When he finally reached Reds, he gripped him up.

"What the fuck you hit that fiend for?" Mike asked.

"She tried to buy a dime with all pennies. Then, the sock that had the pennies in it had shit on it," Reds explained. "Now get the fuck off me!"

Mike let Reds go then explained to him that he can't treat fiends like that. "They the reason you gettin' money. How you gonna treat them bad? They feed you. If you treat your customers bad, they gonna fuck with somebody else. Always remember, if it wasn't for them, it wouldn't be no you," Mike explained.

Reds locked that lesson in his memory bank, then he gave Mike some advice of his own. "Hey, Mike, you like my big brother and all, but I don't like people puttin' their hands on me. Don't do that shit again," Reds warned.

"Listen to you! You my lil' nigga! Don't fuck up no more, and I won't put my hands on you," Mike said.

# 2

It was late night, and Reds was posted on the block. It was getting cold, so Reds went home to grab a heavier coat. He figured that since Chestnut Street was sort of dead, he'd stop by Stacey's. He would give Mike the money he owed him, and hopefully there would be more money on that side of town for him to make.

As Reds opened Stacey's door, Mike whispered to him, "Don't turn on the lights."

"Why the fuck is you sittin' in the house with all the lights out?" Reds asked.

"I'm watchin' them two bitch-ass niggas on the corner gettin' my money," Mike said.

"I repeat my question. Why are you doin' it in the dark?" Reds repeated.

"'Cause I don't want 'em to see me watchin' 'em. They don't know that they got my money either," Mike said.

"I'm not sure I follow you, at least on the last part," Reds said.

"I robbed them niggas like three months ago and told 'em not to come back out here. I guess my word don't hold no weight," Mike said.

"Why do you care if they grind out here? You don't even hustle," Reds said.

"Fuck them niggas. They ain't from out here. They takin' money from my niggas that's hustlin' out here. They takin' money that you could be gettin'. So I lay 'em down, and if I get any drugs, I'll give it to you, which I get parts of too. More money for you, more money for me. It's a win-win situation," Mike said. "Is it real cold out there?"

"A little bit. You can see your breath," Reds answered.

Mike walked out of the room. When he returned, he had a bucket of water in his hand.

"Come on, lil' nigga. I need you to hold me down," Mike said.

"What the fuck is the bucket for?" Reds questioned.

"You'll see. You got cha gun on you?" Mike asked.

"You know it," Reds sang like O-Dogg in *Menace II Society*.

Reds and Mike walked up to the two guys from out of town. Mike had his hood up and his head down. Right as they got close to the two, Mike and Reds both drew their weapons.

"I thought I told you bitch-ass niggas you can't grind out here," Mike barked.

"Aww shit!" the tall one said out loud.

"Come on now. Y'all know the routine. And I wish one of you stupid-ass niggas would do somethin' dumb so I can push ya shit all the way back," Mike said with authority.

The two guys that were on the corner walked behind the building with Reds and Mike. Mike payed close attention to Reds. He was happy to see that Reds was calm as could be. Reds didn't say a word. He just kept his gun on his target.

*This lil' nigga is really built for this shit,'* Mike thought to himself.

Once they got behind the apartment building, Mike told both of the two out-of-towners to strip.

"Come on, dog. It's cold as shit out here," the fat one said.

Without any sign, Reds was on him, smacking the fat one in his head with his gun until he started bleeding. Then just as fast as he started, he stopped.

"He said take ya fuckin' clothes off," Reds said as he caught his breath.

Mike just stood there, watching Reds like a proud father. Mike was very impressed with how Reds was acting. Both of the out-of-towners stripped down to their boxers and socks. Mike handcuffed both young boys to the fence that separated the apartment building from the railroad tracks. Once he gathered their clothes, he threw the bucket of cold water on them.

"Oh shit! Aww, man, don't do this, homey! It's cold as shit out here!" the tall one said.

"Think about that shit next time you faggot-ass niggas come out here to get some paper," Mike said.

As Mike started walking away, he heard one of the out-of-towners complaining. Mike turned around as Reds was aiming his gun at the tall one.

"Yo, what the fuck is you doin'?" Mike said as he ran over and grabbed the gun from Reds. "We ain't tryna turn no robbery into a homicide." Mike wrapped his arm around Reds and started walking away, glad that he turned around when he did. "What's wrong with you, lil' nigga?" Mike asked as soon as they got back in Stacey's house.

"Ain't nothin' wrong with me. Fuck them niggas! They think shit's sweet out here, so I was gonna show 'em it ain't," Reds said.

"That's what's wrong with you, lil' niggas—you ain't got no value for human life. I see you gonna be a problem. Don't make me regret that I gave you that gun," Mike said.

Reds didn't say anything. He sat there quietly and broke down the stuff that was taken from the out-of-towners. *This nigga be out here robbin', and he's soft as duck shit,* Reds thought to himself.

The summer had come and gone, and Reds continued to work for Mike. Things were okay, but Reds was very ambitious and kept telling Mike that he needed more drugs. The problem was that Mike had stopped reporting to his parole officer and now had a warrant. Mike couldn't be out so much anymore, so things had slowed up.

Reds sat down with Mike one day and told him that because things were slow, he planned on branching off and doing his own thing. Mike acted like it was cool, but deep down, he felt like Reds was turning his back on him because he was down.

Once Reds and Mike parted ways, it took Reds a few days to find a new supplier. Reds was walking through town when J.R. pulled up on him.

"Hop in, family," J.R. said.

J.R. took Reds to lunch at New Haven's, a cheese steak spot.

"I've been hearin' ya name a lil' bit out here. I want you to be careful," J.R. said. "I also heard you was fuckin' with Mike. Watch that nigga. He's a snake."

Reds explained that he and Mike were no longer dealing with each other anymore and why.

"Let me drop somethin' on you, lil' cuz. Only a sucker hustles for another man. You takin' all the risk, you should get all the money," J.R. said.

"I don't got a connect," Reds said.

"Look no further, lil' cuz. I gotchu," J.R. said.

J.R. took Reds to his apartment and gave him a digital scale and an ounce of cocaine.

"Never buy nothin' that's already cooked. You're losin' money that way," J.R. said. "A true hustler knows how to cook his own shit. When you cook your own shit, you control how potent the work is and how much extra you are gonna get."

"One problem: I don't know how to cook," Reds said.

"Have no fear. Big cuz is here," J.R. said. "I can teach you how to cook if you want."

"Hell yeah, let's get to cheffin'," Reds said.

J.R. pulled out an empty salsa jar, a spoon, a fork, and a box of baking soda. "Now hand me the scale," J.R. said as he started boiling a pot of water. "I'm gonna tell you what to do, but you are actually gonna do it. After we cook this batch, I'm gonna give you a quiz. If you pass, you can have the work and everything you learned free of charge. If you don't pass, you owe me $1,000. Deal?"

"Abso-fuckin'-lutely!" Reds said knowing he'd pass.

J.R. told Reds exactly how to cook coke into crack. When he was finished, J.R. asked Reds to recite what he had just learned.

"Let me show you what you just told me," Reds said.

Reds grabbed the jar, crushed the coke, added ten grams of baking soda, some water, then cooked it. J.R. was shocked.

"Damn, lil' man, you gotta photographic memory," J.R. said. "Now you got the game. Once you get done with that, come holla at me, and I'll introduce you to my man Nice. He'll be your new connect, and he'll charge you $900 an ounce," J.R. said.

"Sounds good to me. Now if you'll excuse me, I gotta chop this shit up," Reds said.

Reds chopped the whole thirty-eight grams into little pebbles. He had a long tube of M&Ms in his pocket. He quickly dumped the M&Ms out, then filled the tube with crack.

"What the hell is you doin'?" J.R. asked. "Them shits look like dollar rocks."

"They are. I ain't takin' no shorts. Whatever the fiends got, I'm takin'. I'm measurin' everything by eye. I can give out somethin' for $2 if that's all they got. Plus, if the cops try to grab me, I can just throw all these lil'-ass rocks all over," Reds confidently said.

"I see you gonna be a major threat to these niggas out here. Prepare for the hate that comes with success," J.R. said as he smiled.

"Cuz, I'm ready for whatever comes my way. I got a fully loaded clip!" Reds playfully but seriously said.

They both laughed.

As soon as Reds got on Chestnut Street, he started telling the fiends that he had that hang-time and was taking all money, shorts and all. The crackheads loved it because they thought they were getting a bigger bang for their buck. Pretty soon, nobody with bags would be able to get any sales when Reds was around. His method of distribution quickly became known as dump.

# 3

J.R. warned Reds about the hate that comes with success. Reds would soon learn exactly what J.R. was talking about. Reds ran through the thirty-eight grams that he had and was ready to meet Nice in no time. J.R. told Reds to meet him at his apartment at three o'clock in the afternoon.

Reds hadn't been in the house in two days. He hadn't taken a shower, brushed his teeth, changed his clothes, or nothing. Reds bounced back and forth from Chestnut Street to Sidetrack, only stopping to grab something to eat from the store. The crackheads had found themselves a new crack king. Reds got an extra ten grams when he cooked the ounce up, so he showed the smokers love. Whatever they were trying to buy, Reds gave them damn near double what they would've gotten if they bought bags.

J.R. heard a knock on the door. He checked the peephole then opened the door.

"Damn, nigga, you lookin' bad. You need to catch up on ya rest," J.R. said when he saw Reds. Reds looked very tired and drained of all energy.

"When they start payin' a nigga for sleep, I'll never get outta bed," Reds responded.

Reds bragged to J.R. about how he hadn't been in the house for two days. "I was knockin' that work off. I don't got nothin' else left," Reds boasted. "I spent a few dollars on food and shit, but I still brought in $2,500," Reds said.

"Food and things?" J.R. said putting emphasis on *things*. "If you ain't go in the house and you still got the same clothes on, what things are you talkin' 'bout?"

"I'm sayin' I got my dick sucked a couple times," Reds said.

J.R. just started laughing. "You too much."

"What, a nigga got horny. What was I 'posed to do? Them bitches suck a nigga's dick like they life depends on it. Last night, I let two smoker bitches tag-team me, best head I ever had!" Reds said with a big smile on his face.

J.R. just laughed harder. He had been Reds's age and knew what it was like to discover what a woman will do to get a blast of that crack rock.

"I guess boys will be boys. What did you do with your money though?" J.R. asked.

"I got it right here," Reds said as he pulled out his money.

"No, where did you stash the money while you was grindin'?" J.R. asked.

"In my pocket, where it's 'posed to be," Reds said, thinking he knew it all.

"That was a bad move, lil' cuz. What happens if the cops run down on you? So what if you get all the crack off you? You still lose all your money. I know you think you superman, but what happens if a nigga catches you slippin' and robs you? And you can be caught slippin'—anybody can. If a nigga got the drop on you, you better respect the shooter and give it up. Your life is worth more than a couple dollars, and that's all you should have on you, a couple dollars. Any time you make more than $100, take it in the house and put it up," J.R. said.

"I see what chur sayin'," Reds said like the good student he was.

"Oh, there's more. I know you ain't think I was gonna let you off that easy," J.R. said. "Your second mistake was not gettin' any sleep. Whether you know it or not, sleep helps keep the mind alert. No sleep in forty-eight hours means your chances of gettin' caught slippin' are greater. Crackheads will always be there. It's okay to let 'em miss you from time to time. They'll just love you more when you come back. You always make the money. Never let the money make you. The key to this game is to make the most amount of money possible while takin' the least amount of risk as possible," J.R. said.

Reds nodded his head and stored that information in his memory bank. Reds paid very close attention to everything that J.R. said. It was easy to listen to J.R. because Reds looked up to J.R. He had all the things that Reds wanted—money, power, and respect. J.R. led by example. That's why Reds followed what he said.

"Thanks for puttin' me up on game," Reds said.

"Oh, there's more," J.R. said.

"Are you serious?" Reds whined like a little kid.

"Hell yeah, I'm serious! Never keep more than seven grams on you at a time. I know you was talkin' 'bout tossin' that shit everywhere if the cops tried to grab you, but just to be safe, only keep seven grams or less on you. That way, if shit does go bad, you ain't got no major case," J.R. said.

"I feel you." Reds sighed.

"What's wrong?" J.R. asked.

"I just feel like a dickhead for doin' so much shit wrong," Reds said.

"Naw, you ain't no dickhead. You are human though, and we all make mistakes. I'm just here to show you your mistakes so you don't make 'em again. Steel sharpens steel. Pretty soon you'll have this shit mastered, and you won't have to hear my mouth," J.R. said.

"Can I ask you a question?" Reds said.

"Shoot," J.R. responded.

"If you got the game figured out, why you ain't hustlin'?" Reds asked in a puzzled tone.

"My job pays a lot more than hustlin'," J.R. said.

"What's that?" Reds pried.

"In my line of work, everything is on a need-to-know basis. You'll hear things about what I do, but nobody knows what I do. Everybody is just goin' off what they see on the news or read in the newspaper. You'll never hear anything about what I do from me," J.R. said.

"Okay, ask you no questions, tell me no lies," Reds said.

"Exactly," J.R. responded.

About an hour later, Nice arrived. Nice was a massive man. He stood about six-foot-six and had to weigh about 250. His voice was very deep, like Barry White's. After J.R. introduced everybody, it was time to get down to business.

"So, lil' homey, what you lookin' to grab?" Nice asked.

"I got $2,500, and I was hopin' to get three ounces," Reds said.

"Damn, this is our first meetin', and you already bargain-shoppin'," Nice said.

"Shit, why not? Worst you can say is no," Reds said.

"Damn, J.R., I dig the lil' nigga," Nice said. "I'm gonna give you the three for $2,500, but from here on in, you only fuck with me. Is that clear?" Nice asked, looking as serious as ever.

"Death before dishonor," Reds said.

"Yeah, I can definitely see that J.R. is rubbin' off on you," Nice said with a smile.

Nice got on his phone. "Three onions to Mingo's, thirty minutes," Nice said then he hung up.

Once Nice hung the phone up, he told Reds to go to Mingo's, a Spanish bodega located near Sidetrack. "Once you get there, tell the guy workin' at the register that Nice sent you. He will then ask you what time it is. You are to say 'three o'clock.' He'll then give you a paper bag with three ounces in it," Nice said.

"So I'm 'posed to give you my money now?" Reds asked.

"That's my man—you can trust him, cuz," J.R. interrupted.

Without hesitation, Reds gave Nice the money and left for Mingo's.

When Reds got to Mingo's, he did as he was told and received what he was supposed to receive. After he got his coke, Reds decided to take J.R.'s advice and go home for some much-needed sleep.

Once Reds awoke, he took a shower and grabbed a bite to eat. After he ate, he went to a fiend's house and cooked the coke. He put seven grams in his M&M tube and took the rest home. On his way out the house, Rob came home. Rob cursed his son out for not coming home.

"My bad, Pop, I was at work." Reds said.

"Where you workin' at?" Rob asked, shocked by Reds's answer.

"You don't wanna know," Reds responded. "But I got some money for you later on tonight."

"Do I want to know where this money is comin' from?" Rob asked.

"I'm good friends with Santa Claus," Reds said.

Rob just shook his head. "The streets only have two ways out, boy—death or jail," Rob said.

"Every now and then, one of us make it," Reds shot back.

"I don't want that stuff in my house," Rob finally said.

"No problem," Reds said as he walked out the door.

Reds was running through crack like it was water. He was also running into quite a few problems. A lot of hustlers were jealous of Reds, so they hated on him. Nobody would do anything to him because they all knew that Reds was like J.R.'s little brother. Instead of doing something to him, people were calling the cops on Reds, giving his description and whereabouts, saying he was selling drugs. Reds was always getting chased by the cops because of this. After the first time, he started stashing his drugs in trash cans and alleyways. Since he didn't have drugs or a lot of money on him, he didn't feel the need for a gun. So if the cops did catch him, they'd just call his dad and make Rob come pick Reds up.

Then there were the females. They were hating on him too. Reds was dedicated to getting money, and he lived by the motto "fuck bitches—get money." Reds would have sex with a few girls from the neighborhood, but as soon as he busted his nut, he was gone. There was no time for cuddling or getting to know a chick. Reds was married to the game. Then there were the girls that he just wasn't interested in. Reds would flee them, which just made them enemies. One of which decided to start a rumor that he was gay. This infuriated Reds, and he swore that if he ever found out who said it, they would die. Only problem was Reds didn't even know where to start looking. He didn't know if it was a jealous dude or a hating chick. He sought out J.R. for advice about the situation.

"That's all part of the game, my man. These niggas are afraid to confront you, so they tell on you. That just means you gotta stay on ya game. Now as far as that gossip shit goes, that's part of the territory too. Look at it like this: as long as they are talkin' 'bout you, you are doin' somethin' right. It's when they stop talkin' that you gotta start worryin'. Let that shit roll off ya back. Fuck 'em. But if you find out whoever said it, you make 'em pay. Show no mercy!" J.R. said.

On top of all the bullshit Reds was going through in the streets, he had problems at home too. Rob didn't like him running in and out of the house or the fact that Reds never went back to school after Rob fought so hard to have him readmitted. Every time Rob would say something to Reds, his answer would always be the same: "When they start payin' me to go to school, I'll never leave the classroom."

Rob knew he was losing his son to the streets, but there was nothing he could do about it. He just sat back and watched his son slowly slip away.

In the summer of 1999, things came to a boiling point. Rob was snooping through Reds's things and found a gun, nine ounces of coke, and some money. When Reds came home, Rob told him that he had to find somewhere else to stay.

"What chu talkin' 'bout?" Reds asked.

Rob explained what he found in Reds's room and told Reds that he wouldn't be disrespected like that. "I ain't gonna have the cops runnin' in here because you usin' my home as a fuckin' stash spot. I told you I ain't want that shit in here," Rob said.

"If you wasn't bein' nosey, you would've never found my shit," Reds said.

"Nigga, is you crazy? This is my mothafuckin' house, and I can go look through whatever the fuck I wanna," Rob angrily said.

"That's crazy. I pay rent, and I can't even get no fuckin' privacy!" Reds shouted.

"First off, you better lower your mothafuckin' voice. I don't give a fuck what you do in the streets. You gonna always be my lil' boy! And I'll put ya lil' ass down," Rob said.

Once he was sure his message had gotten through to Reds, he finished. Reds didn't say anything because even though he thought he could beat his father, he would never raise his hands to him.

"You can get all the privacy that you want in your own home," Rob said.

"Whatever, where is my gun and shit?" Reds asked.

"I'll hold on to that until you find a new place to stay. I know if I give you that shit, you'll just take your ass right back on that corner. Once you are all moved out, you can have your drugs and shit back," Rob said.

Reds quickly found a place and furnished it with the flyest furniture. Reds got his drugs and gun from his dad and was on his way. It was July 1999, and Reds had saved almost $30,000. He had his own apartment, his own car, and things were going well. Most importantly, he had the guidance of J.R.

Reds put everything into selling drugs. He wasn't even entertaining the neighborhood chicks like that anymore. If he got horny, he'd just trick a fiend. He told himself that this was smarter because he didn't have to ever leave the block. But Reds was getting tired of sleeping in his bed alone. He now wanted a girlfriend. There was no doubt that he wouldn't have trouble finding a girl. The problem was finding the right girl. Reds had a "money over bitches" mentality, but all that was about to change.

## 4

It was Fourth of July, and everybody was having a BBQ. Reds had to be fresh today because he knew it was going to be jumping. He took a shower, brushed his teeth, made sure his waves were spinning, then he got dressed. Reds threw on a dark blue pair of Guess jean shorts and a red and white Guess T-shirt. He topped it off with a pair of red and white Bo Jackson Nike sneakers. Next was his jewelry. Reds never really wore jewelry because he was always hustling and J.R. had told him, "No bling while you doin' ya thing."

Reds and J.R.'s relationship continued to grow as Reds accepted J.R. as his mentor. Reds felt that he could trust J.R. He was family, and he always had his best interest at heart. J.R. had so much love for Reds because he was family and because Reds reminded J.R. of himself when he was younger. Nice and Reds's relationship was also blossoming. Nice never had met a person of Reds's age that acted the way Reds did. Reds was the most thorough young kid Nice had ever met. It didn't hurt that Reds was also making Nice a good bit of money too.

For his birthday, J.R. grabbed his little cousin a forty-inch Cuban link chain with an iced-out grenade on it. Nice grabbed Reds a Mavado watch with an iced-out bezel. Reds was thankful for his two mentors and the gifts they had given him.

Reds hadn't worn either of the gifts since he got them in May, so he figured he'd break them out today. Reds planned on going to the cookout in Locus Court (an apartment complex) with J.R. and Nice. He knew they'd be happy to see him so fresh. Reds grabbed his gun, his cell phone, and pager, then gave himself a quick look-over in the floor model mirror.

"Damn, you's a sexy ma'fucka!" Reds shouted.

Reds had a reason to be feeling himself. He had money, a 1997 Buick Regal, a decked-out apartment, swag out of this world, and he was handsome as hell. He stood six feet tall, about 180 pounds, with reddish brown wavy hair, and a baby face. Reds's complexion was what people called high yellow. If he didn't have the "fuck bitches—get money" mentality, he could have easily had any girl in his neighborhood. But today, Reds told himself that he was going to bag something nice.

As Reds was walking to his car, his Star-Tech Motorola began to ring. "Yes," he answered smoothly.

"'Sup, boy?" Rob asked in a raspy tone.

"What's up, Pop? I'm 'bout to shoot over J.R.'s for a minute, then I'm headed over Locus Court for the BBQ," Reds said.

"You got room for an ol' man?" Rob asked.

"I always got room for the man that created me," Reds responded.

"A'ight, what time is you stoppin' by?" Rob asked.

"Give me like an hour or two," Reds said.

"See you then," Rob said before he hung up.

Although Reds and Rob had fallen out when he kicked Reds out of the house, Reds had since patched things up. He talked to J.R. about what was happening, and J.R. told him Rob was right. After some thought, Reds understood his father's position and apologized for bringing drugs in his home. Rob never asked Reds for anything, but Reds made sure his father was comfortable anyway. Even though Reds didn't live with his father, he gave him $500 every month. Every time Reds went shopping, he made sure he got his dad something. Rob told Reds that he didn't have to do any of that, but Reds wasn't hearing it.

"You my dad, and I can buy you whatever I want," Reds would say.

Reds stopped by J.R.'s apartment, and they played a game of *NBA Live '99* on PlayStation and rapped for a little bit.

"Damn, I see you clean up nice. Shinin' like a boss is 'posed to," J.R. said, giving his cousin some props.

"Yeah, you know I had to be fresh today. I know the bitches is gonna be out," Reds said.

"Do my ears deceive me? What happened to 'fuck bitches—get money'?" J.R. asked.

"I got money. Now it's time to fuck bitches," Reds said with a laugh. "Plus, I'm gettin' tired of fuckin' smoker bitches. Don't get me wrong—they got the best head in the world, but I need some pussy. I'm talkin' kissin', layin' in the bed with 'em, and all that. And it ain't no way in hell I'm fuckin' no smoker!"

"I can definitely dig it," J.R. said.

"I'm hopin' I get a bitch that knows how to act so I can wife her. I need a bitch in the bed with me at night. Nigga tired of sleepin' alone," Reds said.

"Okay, now you're trippin'! You just went from one extreme to the other. First, it's fuck bitches. Now you wanna love bitches. Oh, how glad I am that I'm no longer young and confused. Allow me to give you some advice. That wifey shit ain't for niggas like us," J.R. said.

"Why not?" Reds asked.

"'Cause there ain't no time for women when you're in the streets. When the streets call, you gotta answer. Women fuck with a nigga's judgment, and they're demandin' of our time the same way the streets are. Our time is limited with this street shit. You gotta get in and get out. When you got a chick, you don't go as hard 'cause you fuckin' around with her. Stay focused. There will be plenty of time for wives and all that shit when you retire," J.R. said.

"I feel you, cuz, but I need a bitch. I think I can have a chick and still handle my BI," Reds said.

"Hey, if it don't apply, let it fly," J.R. said. "Now let's go get somethin' to eat."

"Word! I gotta make a pit stop by my pop's and pick him up," Reds said.

"No problem, I'll meet y'all there," J.R. said.

Reds pulled up and blew the horn. He didn't want to get out of the car. He was too busy rapping to the DMX album *It's Dark and Hell Is Hot*. When Rob came out the house, Reds turned the stereo down a little. When Rob got in the car, he smacked Reds up side his head playfully.

"Don't be beepin' your fuckin' horn at me, boy," Rob said.

"My bad," Reds responded as he fixed his waves.

"Mind if I smoke a joint? Tryin' to get up an appetite," Rob said.

"I don't think that's a good idea. I'm dirty," Reds said.

"What the fuck you takin' crack to a cookout for?" Rob asked.

"No drugs, just my gun," Reds said.

"Well, drive like you got some fuckin' sense then," Rob said as he shook his head.

Rob knew that Reds was deep in the streets, but he would never stop loving his son. That's what unconditional love is all about, loving a person even if they have flaws.

Things were going good at the cookout. There was a bunch of people there, but one female in particular caught Reds's eye. Her name was Erin. Erin was about five-foot-five, brown skinned, had shiny black hair that came down to her shoulders, and she was pretty as hell. Erin's waist was small, but she was thick in all the right places. Her behind was fat, thighs were thick, breasts were nice and perky, and her smile was beautiful. Erin had on a white halter top that showed off her flat stomach and sexy belly ring. She had on a blue Baby Phat jean mini skirt and a pair of white Air Force Ones. Even though Reds was getting a lot of attention from the females at the cookout, he only wanted Erin's attention. She was the only girl at the cookout that wasn't drooling over him, J.R., or Nice.

All throughout the day, Reds would catch Erin staring at him. Reds was tired of playing games. It was time to make his move. Reds looked over at Nice, who was there before Reds or J.R., and asked him if Erin had come by herself.

"Naw, she came with her man, Mark. But dude is a lame. You can probably pull her still. It all depends on your timin'. I'm surprised you ain't notice, homeboy. He been up her ass all night," Nice said.

"Nah, I wasn't payin' attention to no niggas. Plus, just 'cause a few niggas is in her face don't mean she got a man. Look at all the bitches that been at our table all night," Reds said.

"True, true," Nice replied.

Reds looked over at Erin and caught her watching him again. He smiled and winked at her. She smiled and blew Reds a kiss. Reds no longer cared if she had a man—she just gave him the green light. He walked over to Erin and grabbed a soda out of the cooler that just happened to be sitting next to her.

"How you doin' beautiful?" Reds asked.

"I'm better, now that I'm finally gettin' some attention," she responded.

"I'm Reds," he said.

"I know who you are. My name is Erin," she said with a smile.

"And I know who you are also. I guess that makes both of us pretty popular," Reds said in complete Mack mode.

"So which one of them bitches that was crowdin' y'all table is yours?" Erin asked.

"None of them, I'm single. But I heard that your man was here," Reds shot back, letting her know he knew what was up.

"Unfortunately, here he comes now. But look, I'm cool with your sister. I'll get your number from her and give you a call," Erin said.

"I'd like that," Reds replied.

As Reds was getting up to leave the table, Mark stumbled over and got right in groupie mode.

"Damn, nigga! That's some nice-ass jewelry you got on," Mark commented.

"Thanks," Reds said like it was nothing.

"I might wanna grab somethin' like that. Where you get that at?" Mark asked.

Reds looked Mark from head to toe then started shaking his head. "This way out cha league, homeboy," Reds said as he walked away.

Stacey called for Reds to come over and play a game of spades with her, J.R., and Nice.

"Damn, sis, why you ain't tell me you knew Erin?" Reds asked.

"'Cause I know she got a man, and I don't want you gettin' in no shit over no pussy. Plus, Erin is in her thirties. I think that's too old for you," Stacey said.

"Awwww," J.R. and Nice said, making fun of Reds.

"Damn, last time I checked, my mom was in prison," Reds sarcastically said.

"She is, but your big sister is still gonna look out for you," Stacey said as she grabbed Reds up and gave him a kiss on the cheek.

"Awww," J.R. and Nice chimed in again.

"Yeah, yeah, yeah! That's all well and good, but shorty chose me, and I can guarantee that I'm gon' fuck," Reds said with a devilish grin.

"I don't think so, lil' bra," Stacey said.

"Oh, yes, muddafucka!" Reds said in his best African accent.

The whole card table broke out laughing.

Toward the end of the night, everybody was looking for someone to take home. J.R. had this pretty-ass light-skinned chick named Tania. Nice managed to grab the only white girl that was at the cookout. She was pretty also.

"Okay, Nice, I see you got the only white meat in the house," J.R. stated.

"Can't go wrong with a snow bunny! She's bad as shit and she likes girls. We 'bout to go pick up one of her girls from the university, then we head to my spot. I always wanted to be a director. Tonight's the night. We gon' make a crazy porno. Don't trip though. It'll all be available for your viewin' pleasures tomorrow," Nice boasted as he shook hands with Reds and J.R.

"I'm out, cuz. What you gettin' into?" J.R. asked.

"I gon' fuck the shit out of Maria's sexy ass tonight. Make her talk that gwala-gwala shit to a nigga," Reds said.

Reds grabbed Maria and went to see if his dad needed a ride home. Reds found out that his dad had left thirty minutes earlier with Ms. Pam, an older woman that lived on the other side of town. As everybody was leaving, Mark was asking people if they knew where Erin was.

"She left like an hour ago when you started actin' stupid," Stacey said.

"Ain't nobody ask you, bitch! Mind ya fuckin' business before I slap the shit out cha nosey ass," Mark barked as he got in Stacey's face.

"Why don't chu wait in the car. I gotta go check on my sister real quick," Reds said to Maria.

Maria complied, completely oblivious to what was about to happen. As Reds was going to check on Stacey, he heard her snapping on Mark.

"Mafucka, you crazy if you think you gon' slap me," Stacey snapped. "Ain't nobody scared of you, bitch!"

Reds didn't need to hear anymore. As soon as he got in arm's reach of Mark, Reds punched him square in the nose. Mark went straight down, holding his gushing nose.

"You broke my fuckin' nose!" Mark yelled in pain.

"Yeah, nigga! I'm a man. Hit me!" Reds said.

Reds's adrenaline was beginning to pump, and he was hyped. Reds pulled his gun from his waist and stuck it in Mark's face. "Nigga, if you ever talk to my sister like that again, it's a shootin'!" Reds barked.

Right then, J.R. appeared. "Be cool, cuz," he said.

Reds stood up and asked Stacey if she was cool. Stacey shook her head, letting Reds know she was all right. Stacey was shocked by what her brother had just done. She knew Reds carried a gun, but she had never seen her baby brother perform like he just had. Reds tucked his gun back in his shorts.

"Okay, the show's over people. Let's keep it movin'," J.R. instructed.

Everybody went back to their business, then J.R. put his arm around Reds. "Go home now! When you get there, lock your keys in the car. Call a tow truck, and make sure you remember the nigga's name that shows up. Make the call from your cell phone, and be sure to keep the receipt," J.R. whispered to his cousin.

"Why? What's up?" Reds asked in a puzzled manner.

"Just do exactly what I said," J.R. said firmly.

"Okay," Reds responded.

As soon as Mark noticed it was J.R. who called Reds cuz, he became scared. "Aww, J.R., I'm sorry, I-I-I- didn't know that was ya peoples. I didn't mean no disrespect to them, and I damn sure ain't mean no disrespect to you. I mean that from the bottom of my heart. I don't want no trouble," Mark said then he turned to Stacey. "I'm sorry, Stacey. I'm just a lil' tipsy."

"You's a pussy," Stacey said.

J.R. never said a word. He just stared at Mark, then he turned and left.

# 5

Reds and Maria drove straight to Reds's spot, and he did exactly as J.R. told him to. About twenty-five minutes later, the tow truck pulled up and opened Reds's car. Reds learned the tow truck driver's name by making small talk.

After Reds paid him, he asked for a receipt. Once all was taken care of, Reds took Maria in the house. As soon as she saw how clean Reds kept his apartment, she asked if he lived alone.

"Of course I live alone. Why you ask that?" Reds answered.

"'Cause this shit is fly! You ain't gonna be livin' by ya'self for long," Maria said half-joking, half-playing.

"Oh, you movin' in already?" Reds joked.

"You gonna be beggin' mami to stay here after I put this pussy on you," Maria said with confidence and a smile.

*I hear you*, Reds thought to himself. "Yeah fuckin' right!"

Reds lit some scented candles and put a movie on the big screen television. They sat on his black leather couch and watched *Belly* as they flirted a little bit. About thirty minutes into the movie, Reds started rubbing on Maria's thigh.

"I guess we ain't gon' finish the movie," Maria said with a devilish smile.

"Fuck that movie. It's on tape. We can watch that shit anytime," Reds said.

Reds started kissing on Maria as he let his hands explore her most private parts. Maria felt Reds's manhood. He was rock hard. Maria decided to get right to it. Truth be told, Maria had been watching Reds for about two months now, and she wanted him just as bad as he wanted her, if not more. Maria stood in front of Reds and started to undress.

"Wait a minute," Reds said as he turned the television off. He grabbed the remote control and turned the stereo on. He hit Disc 4 and the song "Pony" by Ginuwine came on.

"Damn, you must do this often. You got the music all ready and shit," Maria said.

"Naw, I pay my sister to come over here and clean twice a week. This just happens to be her favorite CD. I leave it in my stereo for her so she don't be gon' through my shit," Reds said.

"Umm-hmm," Maria said as she took off her shirt and bra. Her breasts were nice and round like two big coconuts, and her dark brown nipples were big and erect. Maria stuck two fingers in her mouth, then she started playing with her nipples as she danced to the music. After a few seconds, she lifted her breasts to her mouth and licked her nipples. Reds stood up, and Maria pushed him back down on the couch. "Stay . . . 'til the show is over," she ordered.

Maria pulled her capris down, revealing her black thong. Then she turned around and shook her plump backside for Reds. Right above the crack of her behind, she had a tattoo that said, "Finger-lickin' good."

Reds was growing more and more excited by the moment; he couldn't wait to get his hands on Maria. He had taken his shorts, T-shirt, and jewelry off and sat on the couch in his boxers. Reds admired the sexy Puerto Rican goddess that stood in front of him. She took her thong off and revealed an extremely fat pussy. Her pubic hairs were shaved into the shape of a triangle. She put her leg on the arm of the chair and popped her pelvis in Reds's face. Reds grabbed her by the butt and pulled her closer. He licked on her inner thigh, sending a chill up Maria's spine. Then he parted her vaginal lips and started licking on her clitoris. Reds poked his tongue inside her warm, wet tunnel from time to time. This drove Maria crazy. Reds stuck his middle finger in her mouth, and she sucked on it for a minute. When he pulled his finger out of her mouth, he gently slid it in her ass as he continued to lick and suck on her clitoris.

"Oh, papi!" Maria screamed.

Reds could tell that she was enjoying what he was doing because she was tooting her ass up to allow his finger to fully go inside her. When he got all of his finger in her ass, she continued to grind harder on his finger.

"Goddamn, papi, you feel so good. Don't stop! Don't stop!" Maria shouted. She grabbed the back of Reds's head and tried to smother him with her fat pussy. "Me voy a venir!" Maria shouted as she came in Reds's face.

Reds stopped for a second and looked up at her with a scowling look on his face.

"I know you didn't just piss on me," Reds said in a serious tone.

"Oh no, papi! I came, baby, muchas gracias," Maria said as she sat on Reds's lap.

Reds quickly recovered with, "I know, baby. I was just playin' 'cause it was so much." Reds started licking around his mouth.

"Let me help you, papi," Maria said as she licked the juices off his face. "I'm sorry for cummin' in your face, papi. I told you I was cummin'."

"No, the fuck you didn't! You yelled some Spanish shit, which I don't understand, then you opened the floodgates. I ain't mad though. You taste good," Reds said as he gave her a kiss. "But we do practice reciprocation in this house. That means it's your turn!"

Maria put up no fight. She started kissing on his neck and licking on his chest, then she made her way down to his stomach and showered it with kisses. Reds lifted himself off the couch slightly so she could take his boxers off. When Maria got a good look at his manhood, she was pleased.

"You big, papi! The night just keeps gettin' better," she said.

"Yeah, I've been blessed. Now get to work," Reds said as he clapped his hands twice.

Maria grabbed Reds's manhood and kissed all over it. She slowly placed the head of Reds's shaft in her mouth and sucked it like it was a lollipop. She then worked all of him in her mouth. Maria made sure she kept it real sloppy, leaving saliva all over Reds's dick and balls. What Reds loved the most was the slurping sounds she was making as she sucked on him. Then she deep-throated him and stared deep into his eyes as she was doing it. When she got to the top of his dick, Maria would flick her tongue on the head, making Reds feel like a million bucks.

*Damn, this bitch is a fuckin' porn star,* Reds thought to himself.

After spending some time on the shaft, Maria started sucking on Reds's balls, leaving them soaking wet. She returned to Reds's penis and continued to suck, but this time, she stroked his manhood with her right hand as she took him in and out of her mouth. While she was doing that, she massaged his balls with her left hand. She slurped and sucked loudly, then she started rubbing Reds's dick all over her face. This was the best dick suck Reds had ever received. As much as he gave the fiends their props, they had nothing on what Maria was doing to him.

"God damn, bitch! Please don't stop!" Reds moaned as his feet started to curl. "Look at me again. I like that. You on some real porn star shit. Oooh yeah, just like that. What the fuck!"

Reds couldn't take it anymore; he was about to erupt. "I'm cummin'! Swallow all that shit! Oh my god! You's a nasty bitch!" Reds yelled out in ecstasy as he exploded.

Maria punched him in the arm after swallowing every drop. "Shut up, puta! I came in your mouth too."

"I think you just sucked the soul out me," Reds said in amazement.

"You can have this every night if you want," Maria said.

"I ain't never had a dick suck that took my breath away," Reds said, completely ignoring her last comment.

"Well, you better hurry up and get cha second wind," Maria said.

"Why's that?" Reds asked.

"'Cause I'm tryna get fucked," Maria said with a dirty look.

Reds grabbed the condoms off the table and threw Maria on the floor. After he got his erection back, he put the condom on and slid inside of her slowly, allowing her to feel every inch of him. Reds pushed himself deep inside of Maria until he couldn't get any more of himself in her.

"Ahe, ahe, this pussy ain't loose. Take it easy!" Maria shouted.

*This pussy definitely ain't loose,* Reds thought to himself.

Reds started slow stroking Maria, but the more she started to get into it, the harder, faster, and deeper Reds would go. Reds flipped Maria over and started stroking her from the back. Maria was into it now, throwing herself back at Reds like a pro.

"Right there, papi! Oooh, that's the spot!" Maria cried out.

Reds kept his rhythm and slapped her hard on her ass.

"Ahe!" Maria yelled out.

Reds remembered that Maria liked it when he put his fingers in her ass, so he put his thumb in his mouth to get it wet. Once he was satisfied that his thumb was lubricated enough, he popped it in Maria's ass and continued to stroke her.

"Oh, papi, I love you! Harder, harder! Oh shit, faster, fas—I-I-I'm cummin'!" Maria shouted as her juices flowed down her leg and all over Reds.

As soon as Reds felt Maria's warm juices running down his balls, he got extra hyped and started drilling her, bringing himself to climax also.

Reds and Maria lay on the floor breathing hard for a few minutes. Maria looked Reds in the eyes and said, "I swear to God, I never been fucked like that before, papi!"

"I'm sayin' the pussy wasn't bad," Reds said, trying to play cool and not let Maria know she had put it on him too. "So you love a nigga, huh?"

"As long as you keep throwin' dick like that, I'll kill a bitch for lookin' at chu for too long," Maria said with a laugh.

Maria and Reds took a shower, then they went to sleep.

When Reds woke up, his phone was ringing.

"Yes," Reds answered.

"What's good, cuz?" J.R. asked.

"Everything right now. Bitch got me feelin' like I hit the lotto," Reds said as he noticed that Maria wasn't in the bed. When he stood up to see if she had left, she walked into the room butt naked with a plate of breakfast. Maria looked just as good naked as she did in clothes.

"I'm glad to hear that you enjoyed yourself last night, but did you do as I told you?" J.R. questioned.

"Of course I did. Now, would you mind tellin' me what that was about?" Reds asked.

"Naw, but you sure you followed every step?" J.R. asked again.

"I'm sure," Reds said.

"A'ight, I'll be home all day if you wanna come chill," J.R. said.

"I'll be through. One," Reds said.

"A'ight. One," J.R. said before he hung up.

Reds and Maria ate breakfast, then they had sex again. When they got out of the shower, Maria popped the question, "So what's up with me and you? Are we exclusive or what?"

*Yeah, I know this bitch is open, talkin' like that,* Reds thought to himself. Reds wanted to yell, "Hell yeah we exclusive," but then he'd be exposing his hand. So he decided to play it cool. "I think it's too early to know that yet. I definitely think you got potential. So if you play ya cards right, it's definitely possible," Reds said.

"I guess that's a good answer," Maria said. "I didn't say nothin' last night, but what was all that about last night with you and Mark? You was on some real gangsta shit."

"Wasn't nothin' gangsta about it. I'm a man, and I don't tolerate disrespect. Nigga disrespected me, so he got what his hand called for. If you want to give what I did a title, that's on you. I was just bein' me," Reds said.

"I ain't even gon' lie. That shit turned me on like a ma'fucka," Maria said as she gave Reds a kiss and grabbed his privates.

"So I guess it worked out for the best. Now let's get you home. I gotta go handle some shit," Reds said as he got up and got dressed.

After Reds dropped Maria off at her house, he stopped at the corner store to grab a newspaper. What he saw on the front page shocked him. In big bold letters, the newspaper read, "MURDER OR SUICIDE?" Underneath the headline was a picture of Mark.

# 6

Reds sat in the car and read what the newspaper had to say about Mark's death. From what the paper said, Mark had been either thrown or he jumped off the railroad tracks. It asked for anyone with information to contact the police immediately. Reds was upset. He knew things were about to get real hot for him, and that meant no money for a while. He felt like he had been set up, and he knew just who to talk to about it.

"Cuz, what the fuck is goin' on? And I ain't tryin' to hear that secretive shit either. I'm really startin' to feelin' like you tryin' to make me the fall guy!" Reds said angrily.

"What the fuck is you talkin' 'bout?" J.R. answered like he was clueless.

"First off, don't insult my intelligence. Now I know why you had me go through all that dumb shit last night. While I was gettin' pussy or waitin' on a tow truck, Mark was gettin' killed," Reds said.

"Mark's dead?" J.R. asked in a shocked tone.

"Come on with the dumb shit, you know that pussy is dead," Reds said, growing more and more angry.

"A'ight, hold on. Mark is dead, and you feel like the fall guy because you think I did it. Is that why you flippin' on me?" J.R. asked.

Reds told J.R. what he read on the front page about Mark's murder/suicide. Reds went on to snap about how people saw him fuck Mark up the earlier that night. "Ma'fuckas saw me put a toaster in dude's fuckin' face, and now he's dead! Who the fuck you think they gonna come at 'bout this shit!" Reds continued to snap.

"I don't know why you bitchin'. It sounds to me like you have an airtight alibi. You can't go to jail for fightin' with a nigga before he died. You have two people who can vouch for where you were last night. Even if the cops do believe a bunch of people who were drunk last night, Mark wasn't killed with a gun. He was pushed or jumped or whatever you said. Tell the cops exactly what you did after you left the cookout and exactly who you were with. Do that, and you'll be cleared as a suspect. You got nothin' to worry about," J.R. said coolly.

"Did you ever think that I might have come out of the house dirty and got grabbed for questionin'? Then what would have happened if they caught me with a burner or some work?" Reds asked, still mad.

"I know you ain't takin' a gun or drugs to the store to buy a newspaper. This is somethin' that you do every mornin', so I know you would've found out about it before you started your day. Last but not least, I didn't do it, so I couldn't have warned you," J.R. said.

"So why have me lock my keys in the car and all that bullshit?" Reds asked.

"I had a feelin'. And you should be glad I did," J.R. said.

"A fuckin' feelin'?" Reds spat.

"Yeah. Rule number one: anytime you're seen publicly beefin' with someone, always keep an alibi for that night. If somebody else sees y'all beefin', and they got bad blood with the person you beefin' with, they'll have the perfect opportunity to get away with murder. When they out the nigga that you was just seen beefin' with, you're gonna be the first person that the cops look at, not them. This is classic get-away-with-murder 101," J.R. said.

"A'ight, cuz, I'm gon' lay low 'til the cops go to my crib and tell my pop they want me. Once I get the word that they are lookin' for me, I'll turn myself in and deal with this bullshit," Reds said.

"Why you sound so down? You have nothin' to worry about," J.R. said.

"It doesn't matter if I have anything to worry about or not. Either way, this shit is gon' fuck up my money," Reds said.

"Aww man, you work too hard as it is. You need a vacation," J.R. said.

"This ain't no fuckin' vacation. This is a fuckin' disaster," Reds said.

"You're blowin' this way out of proportion. Nigga probably offed himself. Only thing he had goin' was Erin, and from what I saw last night, she didn't want 'em no more," J.R. said.

"Suicide huh? Yeah right," Reds said as he walked out the door.

"I love you, cuz!" J.R. yelled out as Reds left his apartment.

As Reds walked into his apartment, his cell phone rang. "Yes," he answered.

"The cops just left here talkin' 'bout they wanna talk to you 'bout a murder! What the fuck you done did, boy?" Rob questioned.

"I didn't do nothin'. I just read the newspaper. I knew this was comin'. Bird-ass-nigga got outta line with Stacey last night, and I had to fuck 'em up. I look in the paper this mornin' and see that he's dead. I'm not even gonna fight with the cops 'bout this shit. I didn't do shit, so I'll turn myself in and answer their questions," Reds said.

"A'ight, come pick me up, and we'll go down there together," Rob said, letting Reds know that he stood behind him.

Reds and his father entered the police station and announced that they wanted to see the homicide detective.

"Good afternoon, Mr. Carter. I'm Detective Morris," the cop said. "Please follow me."

Detective Morris took Reds and his dad into an interrogation room. "Do you wish to have a lawyer present, Mr. Carter?" the detective asked.

"No," Reds said. Reds wasn't going to play their games and let them twist his words up. He planned on giving very short and to-the-point answers then leaving.

"Do you mind if I record this?" Detective Morris asked.

"No," Reds answered.

"Do you mind if I call you Nasir? Or would you prefer if I called you Reds?" Detective Morris asked.

The detective put emphasis on the nickname *Reds* like he had uncovered something by knowing his nickname. Reds was unphased by this.

"Doesn't matter," Reds said coolly.

"Okay, Reds, would you like to have something to eat or to drink?" the detective asked.

"What I'd like to do is answer your questions and get the fuck outta here," Reds said, becoming annoyed with the bullshit.

"Well, Nasir, if you don't know, we are investigating the death of Mark Cristy. As of right now, we are treating this as a murder," Detective Morris said.

"Okay," Reds said.

"Did you know know Mr. Cristy?" the detective asked.

"You already know that I knew him. Can we please stop playin' games?" Reds said.

"Okay, did you have a physical altercation with Mr. Cristy last night?" Detective Morris asked.

"Again, you already know I did," Reds said.

"Can you tell me what that was about?" Morris asked.

"He threatened to slap my sister, so I punched him in the face," Reds said like it was nothing.

"Did you see Mark after that? You know, like later on that night?" Morris asked.

"No," Reds said.

"Did you kill Mr. Cristy or know anything about his death?" Morris asked.

"Absolutely not," Reds said.

"Well, do you have anyone who can verify you whereabouts from when you left the cookout until about six this morning?" Morris asked.

"Actually I do. I left the cookout with a woman whose name and phone number I can provide you with. We went back to my place, and I locked my keys in the car by accident because I was so excited to fuck the shit outta her. I called West End Towing, and they sent a man named Tony to come open my car. I took my lady friend in the house, and we had sex all night. We woke up, she cooked breakfast, and we had more sex. Then I dropped her off at her place around noon," Reds said.

"That almost sounds rehearsed to me," the detective said.

"Nah, I just have a knack for details," Reds said.

"Okay well, if everything checks out, it should be fairly easy to clear you as a suspect. That is something you should be grateful for. Please don't go too far until I inform you that you have been cleared as a suspect," Morris said.

As Reds shook the detective's hand and was preparing to leave, the detective asked, "Oh, could I ask you just a few more questions about the cookout? You know, since you have such a knack for detail."

"Shoot," Reds said.

"Do you know a man by the name of Jermaine Richers a.k.a. J.R.?" Morris asked.

Reds stomach immediately began to bubble, but he showed no outward signs of his nervousness.

"That's my cousin," Reds said calmly.

"Was he at the cookout?" Morris asked.

Reds already knew the detective knew the answer to the question. Lying would only make J.R. look guilty. "Yeah, he was at the cookout. He was the one who pulled me off Mark and told me to chill," Reds said.

"Did he seem mad or happen to mention doing anything to Mark?" Morris asked.

"'Do anything,' what does that mean?" Reds asked. It was his turn to play games now.

"Doing anything like violence, harm, etc.," Morris answered.

Reds took notice that his demeanor had changed. Reds could tell that this guy really wanted J.R. bad. "Naw, he didn't mention anything to me," Reds said.

"Listen kid, we know J.R. is a cold-blooded killer. We also know that that you shoved a gun in Mark's mouth last night. So I guess your knack for detail isn't so good because you forgot to mention that. We also know that you are making a good bit of money in the pharmaceutical business. Did you by any chance pay J.R. to take care of your dirty work? How do you young kids say it . . . Is J.R. your shooter?" Morris asked.

The detective now was extremely close to Reds as if he could smell a lie if Reds told one. Reds's nervousness intensified greatly, but he never showed it. During their days of theft, Betty had taught her son to never let others see you sweat. This lesson was paying off at this moment. Reds maintained his composure.

"I don't know where you got that idea from, but you are wrong about both things. I am not a drug dealer, and I did not pay my cousin to do anything. J.R. wouldn't hurt anybody," Reds said.

"Listen, punk, I'm homicide! I don't give a fuck about you selling drugs or carrying guns. I don't get involved until the guns are actually used. I'm the death police, kid! This is what I care about!" Morris yelled as he pulled out a folder with six pictures in it.

The first was of Mark's disfigured body. There was also a picture of a badly burned man, a separate picture of a badly burned woman, a picture of a man with his throat slit, a picture of a man with three gunshot wounds to his head, and last was a picture of a man who had been decapitated. Reds's mind began to race.

"We're not sure about Mark yet, but we know for sure that your cousin did these other ones. Still think he's a nice guy?" Morris asked.

"Well, Detective Morris, it sounds to me like you are talkin' to the wrong person. If you know that my cousin committed all these heinous crimes, why are you talkin' to me? You should be locking him up. I'm sorry, but I can't help you with Mark's death or any other death for that matter. But you seem like a smart cop. I'm sure you'll solve these cases," Reds said.

Detective Morris was very passionate about his job, and he took it as an insult that Reds was talking to him the way he was. "You think this is a fuckin' game, you little punk!" Morris screamed.

No sooner as Detective Morris started to get out of control, Rob stepped in. "Detective, if you disrespect my son again, this interview will be over," Rob said calmly.

Detective Morris checked himself mentally, then he continued. "I apologize, Mr. Carter. It's just that I want this monster off the streets. If you're afraid of J.R., we can protect you. I can put you and anyone else in your family in witness protection. Not only can we provide safety, we can also give you immunity if you had a part in any of this. Our main focus is on J.R.," Morris said, revealing his hand.

"As I've told you previously, J.R. is a kind man, and I don't know anything to tell. I don't need immunity because I didn't do anything," Reds said.

"You know what, kid? I believe you. So since you didn't do anything and J.R. is such a kind person, why don't you agree to wear a wire. Go talk to J.R. about Mark's death and all the other deaths, and if he doesn't know anything, you'll actually be helping him. Once he says he doesn't know anything on wire, it'll clear him as a suspect," Morris said.

Rob wanted to interrupt, but Reds had been handling himself very well. Rob wanted to see how his son would handle this.

"I'm sorry. I'm not interested in doin' any police work. They pay you guys good money to do detective work, not me. You have to graduate from the academy in order to do detective work. Since I didn't, I wouldn't dare attempt a job that requires such skill. I think I'll let you guys handle the cop work," Reds said.

"Okay, smart-ass," Detective Morris said. "If you hear anything, give me a call." Detective Morris then handed Reds and Rob a card with his name on it. "Oh, and we are going to need the address to the apartment that you are staying at. We may need to speak to you again, and we may want you to take a polygraph test," Morris said.

"Well, I live in Sharpless Work Apartment Complex, Apartment 4a. If you need to talk to me, fine. But under no circumstances whatsoever, am I takin' a polygraph test," Reds said.

"Why not?" Morris asked. "Do you have something to hide?"

"Are lie detector tests 100 percent accurate?" Reds questioned.

"No, but—" Morris started to say.

Reds cut him off midsentence, "Well then, you just answered your own question. Are we done?"

"I guess so. Like I said earlier, don't go far. We may need to speak with you again," Morris said.

Morris thought it would be a lot easier to get Reds to talk if he knew something. This battle had proved harder than he had anticipated. He'd wait patiently though. They all mess up in the long run. And when Reds or J.R. did, Morris would be there to slam their face in the dirt.

When Reds and Rob left the police station, Rob had a few choice words for his son.

"It seems as you've chosen the life that you wanna live. I don't agree with it, but you are my son and I love you. I've always told you that if you was gonna do somethin', be the best at it that you can be. It also seems as if you've been taught well. I'm not encouragin' you, but I'm kind of proud of you. It's bad enough that I gotta hear what you're doin' in the streets. I don't wanna ever hear that you're a rat also. If this is the type of life you choose to live, live it accordin' to the rules. You are involved with some very dangerous people, and there are definitely consequences for not livin' accordin' to the rules. So if you ever decide to take the coward way out, stay away from me. I don't wanna die because you chose not to do the job you signed up for," Rob said.

Reds let his father's words sink in. His father just dropped some real heavy knowledge on him. He wasn't offended by what his father just said. After all, his father was once in the streets also. Reds respected his father for what he had just told him.

"You'll never hear that I'm a rat," Reds said calmly.

"Well, in that case, what's already understood need not be said. How 'bout I treat you to lunch?" Rob said.

"Sounds good to me," Reds said. "Listen, Pop, I know you don't like the life that I've chosen to live, but I appreciate the fact that you still stand by me and try to be understandin'."

"Like I said, what's already understood need not be said," Rob repeated.

And with that, the rest of the ride was driven in silence.

# 7

It was around five o'clock in the evening. Reds had decided to stay in the house and get his thoughts together. Reds was upset about this whole situation. There was no way he could even attempt to hustle until this situation died down. The good thing about the case was that without any hard evidence or witnesses, Mark's murder would be ruled a suicide. There was no doubt in Reds's mind that J.R. killed Mark. Reds just didn't know why. If J.R. had killed all those people in the pictures, he was definitely good at what he did. So he'd probably get away with this one too.

Reds was becoming paranoid. He thought that the cops might try to raid his apartment in order to get some leverage on him. Reds didn't keep anything at his apartment except for his gun. He refused to not have a gun around him at a time like this. Things were crazy, and he didn't know what to expect. All he knew was that if someone tried to harm him, he'd be ready. If the cops ran in his apartment and found the gun, it would only get him probation; he wasn't a felon.

As Reds sat in the house in deep thought, his phone rang. "Yes," he answered.

"You okay, boo-boo?" Stacey asked. "I been hearin' shit all day, but Daddy just gave me the scoop."

"I'm good, sis, thanks for askin'. My head is hurtin' though. My fuckin' phone won't stop ringin'. Ma'fuckas all nosey and shit," Reds expressed.

"Well, you know how that go. It's like thirty different stories out here about that shit. And you know Maria is usin' this as an excuse to let everybody know that you was with her last night. I told her to stop runnin' your business. She said she just tryna clear ya name. Bitch talkin' 'bout she thinks she might love you. She don't even know you like that," Stacey said.

"Damn these good looks and great sex," Reds said as he laughed.

"I see you still got your sense of humor, but I ain't tryna hear that shit. You my baby brother," Stacey said.

"Fuck outta here, ain't nothin' these freak-ass bitches ain't already told you. Tell me you ain't never heard that shit before," Reds said.

"I swear you're the most conceited person I've ever met. Bye, lil' brother," Stacey said.

As soon as Reds hung the phone up, it rang again.

"What's good, cuz?" J.R. asked.

"Chillin', not gettin' *no* money," Reds said, putting emphasis on the last part.

"You'll survive—you ain't broke. You tryin' to come through? Nice got the snow bunny from last night on tape. It's a couple other bitches on here too. This shit is X-rated. You gotta come check it out," J.R. said.

"A'ight, I gotta holla at chu anyway. I'll be there in a few," Reds said.

When Reds got to J.R.'s house, Nice and J.R. were smoking a blunt of hydro.

"Smoke this. It'll take the edge off," Nice said as he passed Reds the blunt.

"Nah, I'm good. I don't use the drugs. I just move the drugs," Reds said.

"You always got some fly shit to say. Well, check it—I move the drugs too. But when shit gets crazy, I use the drugs. This tree is fire," Nice said.

"Only thing I'm addicted to is gettin' this paper. The less I use, the more I move," Reds said.

"This nigga thinks he's a rapper! Nah, I respect it though. I swear I find it hard to believe that you're only seventeen," Nice said.

"I'm seventeen, but I'm a old nigga," Reds said with a smile.

"That you are," J.R. interrupted. "So tell me, ol' wise one, where did you go wrong last night?"

Reds let out a long sigh. "You really called me over here to dig in my ass?" Reds asked in a frustrated tone.

"Why wouldn't I?" J.R. responded.

"I guess when I let everybody see me put my gun in Mark's face," Reds said.

"That's one. What else?" J.R. asked.

"I don't know, but I'm sure you're gonna tell me," Reds said.

"Is that an attitude I'm sensin'? 'Cause if it is, I can just keep my thoughts to myself," J.R. said.

"I'm sayin' I'm kinda heated 'cause I ain't gonna be able to get no paper for god knows how long. But go 'head and let me have it. I know you ain't gon' tell me nothin' wrong," Reds said.

"Good answer. Your second mistake was that you gave the nigga a warnin' instead of killin' him. In war, there is no mercy. A warnin' is a sign of mercy. In war, you annihilate your adversary completely," J.R. said.

Reds nodded his head, letting J.R. know that he understood what he was saying.

"You pulled your gun on a man and then showed mercy by not killin' him, leavin' him the opportunity to come back and not be so merciful on you. Good thing he decided to kill himself later on that night," J.R. said.

It was at that moment, that Reds completely understood why J.R. killed Mark. Reds was extremely grateful for what his cousin had done for him. "Damn, cuz, I ain't never look at it like that. Thanks," Reds said.

"Don't thank me. I didn't do nothin' to the nigga," J.R. said as he winked his eye at his cousin.

"I mean thanks for the lesson," Reds said.

"Anytime. Oh, and feelin's are for female. So if you mad, be mad at chaself. You fucked up, and mistakes can be costly. Shit makes you think when it hurts ya pockets," J.R. said.

"Understood," Reds said.

"Niggas be on ya ass 'cause we see it in you. You a boss in the makin'. By the time you hit our age, you'll be retired if you listen to what we say. In a few years, we can all be on an island, doin' the type of shit you 'bout to see on this tape," Nice said.

They all laughed then started watching the tape.

"God damn, that white bitch is a fuckin' beast! I ain't never seen no bitch squirt so much juice out her pussy. She makin' that shit shoot across the room," Reds said after a few minutes of watching the tape.

"Fuck all that. Look at this," J.R. said.

Reds continued to watch in amazement as Nice fucked the white girl. She had herself bent into a human pretzel. While she was getting fucked, she was licking another chick's ass. The blonde chick was getting fucked, and a brunette was squatting her ass in the blonde chick's face. While the brunette was getting her ass eaten, she rubbed on her clit and started squirting all over Nice and the blonde chick. At the end of the video, Nice had the blonde chick sitting on her shoulders and neck with her ass in the air. Nice came in the rim of the blonde's ass, then he grabbed the camera. Another chick came on camera. She looked like she was half white and half Chinese. She stood next to the blonde while the brunette squirted in the rim of the blonde's ass too. The girl that looked half-Chinese took a straw and sucked all the nut and pussy juice out of the rim of the blonde's ass.

"Unbelievable!!" Reds said as he shook his head. "I think I need a drink after that one. Please tell me you got them hoe's phone number."

"Of course," Nice said.

"Well, we might gotta do some tradin'," Reds said.

"What's mine is yours, lil' brah. Since it looks like you gon' have some free time on your hands, we might swing by there and holla at 'em one day," Nice replied.

With that, Reds's mind drifted back to his current problem. "That reminds me, cuz. I gotta holla at chu 'bout the dumb shit the detective was talkin' today," Reds said.

"I already know," J.R. said.

"What chu mean you already know?" Reds asked.

"Lil' cuz, my hand is longer than you could ever imagine," J.R. said.

"How so?" Reds inquired.

"I'm fuckin' the chief of police—bitch love a nigga. Soon as the interview was over, Detective Morris took the tape to Chief Luther. She listened to it, then Morris's bitch-ass gave her his take on the situation. Basically, they graspin' for straws. It'll be ruled a suicide within two weeks. Oh, and you did real good with the detective," J.R. said. "I'm proud of you."

"Word," Reds said as he absorbed what J.R. had just told him.

Reds sat in silence for a minute. He came to the conclusion that his two mentors were the real deal. *If I take what these two niggas is offerin', plus my own skills, I can be better than both of these niggas before I'm twenty-one*, Reds thought to himself. That thought sounded really good to him.

# 8

It had been weeks since Mark had been killed. Reds was growing restless from just sitting around. He thought about just hitting the block and hustling, but he knew it wouldn't be wise. Something told Reds that as soon as he tried to start hustling, the cops would be right there waiting for him. So instead of hustling, Reds took part in one of his other most favorite activities.

As Reds sat back on his couch with his eyes closed, his phone rang. "Yes," Reds answered.

"It's safe for you to start workin' again," J.R. said.

"Say word!" Reds said, getting hyped.

"Word!" J.R. said with humor in his voice.

Reds jumped up and quickly regretted it. "Ouch!" Reds shouted. "You bit my shit!"

"That's your fault—ain't nobody tell you to jump up like you was crazy," Maria said as she wiped her mouth.

"What?" J.R. asked.

"Nah, cuz, I wasn't talkin' to you. But listen—I'm'a hit chu later," Reds said as he pulled his pants up.

"A'ight, one," J.R. said as he hung up.

Reds looked at Maria. "Somethin' just came up. I gotta go handle somethin'. Hurry up and get dressed. I'll take you home," Reds said.

"Why don't I just stay here and clean up a lil'?" Maria suggested.

"I like my idea better," Reds responded quickly.

"Why you keep frontin' like you don't like me bein' around? I been here with you for the last two weeks, treatin' you like a king, and now I gotta go? What about all my shit? All my makeup and clothes are here. I'm sayin' what the fuck!?" Maria said in an upset tone.

*Damn,* Reds thought to himself, *I done let this bitch suck and fuck her way in the crib.*

"Listen," Reds said. "I dig you, but I don't know if I'm ready for all that relationship shit! I'm young, and I need my space. So even though I like you, I don't trust you all up in my shit when I ain't here."

"That's really fucked up! I'm good enough to sleep with and pamper you, but I'm not good enough to live with you," Maria said with tears in her eyes.

"I just fuckin' met chu! And I damn sure ain't tell you to move all your shit in here. You tryin' a lil' too hard to lock a nigga down. I told you from the jump to just be cool. This shit you pullin' right now ain't cool," Reds said.

"Fuck you, Reds! Just let me get my shit, and I'm outta here," Maria said, then she paused for a second to see if Reds was going to try to stop her. When she saw that Reds was unfazed by her last comment, she stormed off. As Maria gathered her belongings, she cussed Reds out in Spanish.

Reds wasn't sure of everything she was saying, but he knew he was getting cussed out. When Maria was finally ready, Reds realized how much stuff she had in his apartment. Honestly, he couldn't be mad at Maria. He was the one that begged her to stay with him when he didn't have anything to do. He was the reason that Maria brought a lot of her stuff to his apartment. But now that Reds had something to do, he was discarding Maria.

Maria pulled five gym bags of clothes to Reds's car. She also had a bunch of shoes, hair spray, and a bunch of other feminine products. Maria asked Reds to open the trunk and help her put her things inside.

"Oh, now you wanna be civil? Just a few minutes ago, I was a bunch of mothafuckas and bitches. I might not know a lot of Spanish, but I know when I'm gettin' cussed out. So since you think I'm an asshole, allow me to show you how much of an asshole I can be. Walk, ya stupid ass home!" Reds said as he got in his car.

"Stop playin'," Maria said as she looked at Reds like he was crazy.

"Do I look like I'm fuckin' playin'?" Reds asked as he shut the car door.

"My house is far as shit! I can't carry all this shit there! It's impossible!" Maria yelled.

"I guess you gonna have to make two trips. But you should be good—it ain't 'posed to rain 'til later," Reds said with a smirk.

"Come on, papi, stop playin'," Maria said, hoping Reds was joking.

"Bitch, just a few minutes ago you said 'fuck me' or somethin' to that effect. So fuck you too!" Reds said as he started the car up.

Maria started yelling in Spanish and throwing things at Reds's car. Reds just turned up the music and pulled off, leaving Maria standing there looking stupid.

Reds decided to go to Sidetrack first and see what was what. Just because the investigation was over didn't mean that Reds didn't have to be careful. He knew the cops would be watching him, so that gave him an advantage. There was no doubt about the fact that Reds was jumping back in the game head first. He would just have to be cautious.

When Reds finally got to Sidetrack, the fiends flocked to him. By word of mouth, Reds found out that a few people had tried to fill his shoes and sell dump. They were unsuccessful because they tried to use his method to rob people out of what they paid for. Reds also learned that people had been talking about him. Some of the talk was good, some of the talk was bad, but a few of the people who had bad-mouthed Reds hustled in Sidetrack. Reds decided to make them pay for their slanderous words.

"Today is double-up Thursday!" Reds told all the fiends. "That means you pay $20 and get $40 worth of product. Let 'em know I'm back and I'm showin' love!"

Instantly, word got out about what Reds was doing, and nobody could catch a sell. Even if Reds left to go drop money off or pick up more drugs, the fiends would wait for him to get back. There were a few people who wanted to step to Reds about what he was doing because he was messing people's money up, but after what just happened to Mark, people were afraid. Nobody was sure if Reds killed Mark, but everybody was sure that if he didn't do it, Mark was killed because of what happened with him and Reds at the cookout.

Nighttime fell, and Reds finally saw Mike for the first time in almost a month. The cowards on the block had devised a plan to get Reds off the block without having to do it themselves.

"What's good, lil' nigga?" Mike asked as he approached Reds.

"I'm straight. It's these other niggas that's out here hurtin'," Reds said with a smile.

"Yeah, I hear you out here shuttin' shit down," Mike said.

"You goddamn right!" Reds said proudly.

"A'ight, well, dig this. You takin' off my plate. I got three niggas out here, and none of 'em can catch a sale 'cause you out here with this double-up shit. That shit stops right now!" Mike said with authority.

"The double-ups would've never started if these bird-ass niggas knew how to keep my name out they fuckin' mouth. And you soundin' like you givin' me an order rather than a request," Reds said, matching Mike's aggression.

Mike started laughing. "Listen to you. You forgettin' who the fuck you talkin' to? What? You think 'cause you my girl's lil' brother you safe? Or maybe 'cause you J.R.'s lil' man? You already know how I get down. I don't care about none of that shit. You might got the rest of these niggas fooled because of what happened to Mark, but I know you ain't have shit to do with that. So to answer your question, yeah, that was an order. I'd advise you to follow it or start gettin' treated like the rest of these niggas out here. I don't got no picks! Mark was a pussy. You don't wanna bring that type of shit my way. Stay in ya league, lil' nigga!" Mike said.

As Mike said the last part, he poked Reds in the head. The truth was Mike was just as scared of J.R. as everybody else, but he felt like he had a pass because he was Stacey's man. But what Mike didn't know was that it wasn't J.R. that he needed to be afraid of.

"My fault, Mike, I don't want no trouble. All that double-up shit is over," Reds said in a defeated tone. Reds cussed himself for not having his gun on him.

"Now you talkin' like you got some sense," Mike said, then he patted Reds on his head like a puppy.

"Just so you know, it's all love. I'm gonna take the rest of the night off," Reds said.

"That's my man. I'm gonna go get my niggas out here ASAP!" Mike said, glad that he ended the situation without having to put his hands on Reds.

Reds walked to his car and drove to J.R.'s apartment. He was furious about what had just taken place. Reds had never felt so disrespected in his life. Mike crossed a line that you just don't cross, and he'd pay dearly for it.

## 9

    Reds got to J.R.'s house, and no one was home. He tried to phone J.R., but he wasn't answering his phone. The Mike situation was a decision that Reds would have to make on his own now. There was no doubt in Reds's mind as to what he was going to do to Mike for the way he disrespected him. Reds just wanted to talk to J.R. first to see how he should go about doing it.

    Reds sat in car and thought of waiting for J.R., but that thought quickly came and went. Reds's emotions had the best of him. He drove to his next-door neighbor's, Juanita, to grab what he needed for the night. As he drove to Juanita's house, he couldn't help but to be happy that he had bought all the guns that he did. Reds had befriended a neighborhood junky by the name of Beaver. He learned that Beaver had recently started a new job working for a cleaning company. This particular cleaning company only cleaned rich people's homes. Like a true crackhead, Beaver found a way to steal some merchandise he could sell. He would make a copy of the people's house key on his lunch break then go back a week or two later and steal all the guns from their homes. Beaver had a few guns left, and Reds was willing to buy them all. Beaver didn't know the caliber of the guns or anything. All he knew was that he could get some crack for them. Reds had bought two .44 Bulldogs and a 9-millimeter with an extended clip and beam. Beaver could have easily gotten $3,500 or better for all three guns. Instead, he settled for only ten grams of crack.

    As Reds thought of his newly purchased toys, he grew excited, he couldn't wait to put them to use.

    Juanita lived two doors down from Reds's apartment. Juanita was cute, petite, and most importantly, Spanish. Reds didn't know what it was, but

Spanish women drove him absolutely crazy. Juanita and Reds had known each other from school and had recently become friends with benefits. Reds believed that if a person couldn't be used, they were useless. He also believed that everyone gets used, it's just your job to make sure you're not abused. He explained this to Juanita, then he offered to pay her rent every month in order to keep a safe in her apartment.

"You use me, I use you. No harm, no foul," Reds said with his charming smile.

As soon as she heard that he was going to pay her rent every month, Juanita agreed. She was far from a broke chick, but she was also far from a dumb chick. Rent in West Chester was high. If Reds would pay her $800-a-month rent, she let him keep whatever he wanted in her home. That just meant she'd have an extra $800 to shop with. After they both laid down some ground rules, Juanita gave him a key to her apartment. Her only request was that he called before he came over. And Reds only asked that she never tell anyone that he kept a safe there. Reds was confident that Juanita wouldn't run her mouth about their business. Juanita stayed to herself, and he had never heard any business of hers in the streets. That's why Reds chose to ask her in the first place.

Reds called Juanita when he pulled in the parking lot of his apartment complex.

"I'm on my way through," he stated.

"I'll be waitin', papi," Juanita said.

After going to his apartment and grabbing a black pair of Dickies, a black hoody, black mask, and a black pair of Timberlands, he headed to Juanita's. When he walked through the door, Juanita was butt naked on her couch. She had on a porno and was masturbating with a huge black dildo.

"Welcome to mi casa," Juanita said in a soft moan. "As always, you can have whatever you like."

"I can't right now, baby. I gotta take care of somethin'. But I can tell you this—that image of you is locked in my head. I'm definitely coming back for a shot of that," Reds said as he tried to refocus.

Reds walked in the room and started to open the safe when Juanita walked in. "Is everything okay, papi?" she asked.

"Yeah, but I need you to go into the other room until I handle this," Reds said politely.

Juanita put up no fight. She calmly walked back into the living room and finished watching her porno. Reds grabbed his .44 Bulldog and loaded it with hollow-tip bullets. He tucked the gun in his waistline and walked out the room. He walked over to Juanita who was still naked and gave her a kiss and told her he'd be back, then he was on his way. Reds was so mad at the way Mike disrespected him that he didn't get sexually aroused as he looked at Juanita's naked body, and she was sexy.

It was about eleven-thirty at night, and Reds was hiding behind two trash cans that were located in between two houses that were on the corner of Matlack and Barnard Streets. He could hear two of Mike's workers, Dion and Tony, talking about how Mike had played him. They gossiped like women and called Reds all types of cowards and suckers. Reds sat in the shadows and grew angrier and angrier by the moment. He made a last-minute decision to kill both of them if they were on the corner when Mike came around. Reds patiently waited for almost two hours before he finally heard the words he had been waiting for.

"I gotta go page Mike and have him bring another pack 'round here," Dion said.

About twenty minutes later, Mike came strolling up. As soon as he came on the block, Tony left to go home and get something to eat. Mike and Dion stood on the corner and talked. As they laughed and joked, Reds emerged from the shadows and turned the corner of Matlack and Barnard Streets into a scene befitting of a horror film.

# 10

Reds drove home and took a shower. He didn't feel bad about what he had done. In his eyes, he did what needed to be done. He put on the clothes that he had on earlier then drove the .44 Bulldog to the Brandywine Reservoir and tossed it in. After he disposed of the gun, he headed back to Juanita's for some sex. Now that he had taken care of what was bothering him, Reds craved Juanita's body. He also needed an alibi for the night. He knew that if worse came to worse, Juanita would ride and say he was there all night.

Around three-thirty that morning, Stacey called Reds. Stacey was crying hysterically. "Mike's dead! They killed my baby! Oh my god, he's never gonna get to see our baby!" Stacey cried.

"What?" Reds asked in a shocked tone. He wasn't shocked about Mike's death; he was shocked about what Stacey said about a child.

"I said Mike's dead! I'm fuckin' pregnant! And I never even got to share the news with him. I can't believe this shit! My baby ain't gonna never have a dad. What am I gonna do?" Stacey cried. "I know you or J.R. can find out who did this. I want them to pay!"

"Yo, watch ya fuckin' mouth! You can't be sayin' shit like that on the phone. I'm gon' make sure you and the baby is good—that's my word! Now where you at?" Reds asked.

"I'm at the hospital," Stacey said.

"A'ight, I'm gonna come and pick you up," Reds said.

"They said I gotta go to the coroner's office to identify the body. I passed out when they told me Mike was dead. Shontay brought me here to make sure I was good. I told her she could leave—I was gonna call you. We gotta go to identify the body," Stacey said.

"I'm on my way," Reds said.

Reds and Stacey got to the coroner's office and were greeted by some white man in a lab coat. He had a picture of the tattoo on Mike's arm.

"Is this his tattoo?" he asked.

"Yes, but I'd like to see the body," Stacey said.

"I'm sorry, but I don't think that's a good idea. He was shot several times with a large-caliber gun, judging by the damage done. He doesn't really have a head. It's basically just neck and shoulders," the man said.

Stacey just started crying in Reds's arms.

"Come on, sis. Let's go home," Reds said.

Reds took Stacey home and spent the night on the couch.

The next morning, Reds's phone started ringing.

"Damn, fam, I got the news a few minutes ago. How's she takin' it?" J.R. asked.

"Not good at all, she's pregnant," Reds said as he let out a sigh.

"Damn!" J.R. said. "I'm on top of shit."

"It's cool. Fall back. I'll holla at chu later," Reds said in a whisper.

"Say no more," J.R. said.

"I'll be through later on," Reds said.

"A'ight, one," J.R. said before he hung up.

Reds stayed with Stacey all morning, but she told Reds that she wanted to be by herself, so Reds left.

Around six o'clock that night, Reds sat on J.R's couch.

"So what's the scoop, cuz?" J.R. asked.

"Shit is definitely crazy right now. I'm still fucked up about Stacey being pregnant," Reds said.

"You didn't know," J.R. said.

"What chu mean?" Reds asked in a shocked manner.

"I know you was behind that," J.R. said.

"How you know that?" Reds asked.

"I told you I'm fuckin' the chief of police. She gave me the rundown about the list of leads because she knows Mike was fuckin' with my cousin. It came up that you and him had words earlier in the night. Then when I talked to you and told you I was on top of things, you said 'fall back.' As soon as you said that, I knew what it was," J.R. said.

"Yo, that nigga violated crazy! Fuck that bitch-ass-nigga. I'm only sick 'cause my sister is hurtin'. I'm gonna make sure her and the baby are good though," Reds said.

"Well, the nigga did so much dirt that they don't know where to start lookin'. Then, there's Dion. They just got him being at the wrong place at the wrong time. She did say that she doesn't like the fact that your name keeps comin' up in murder investigations. I told her you and Mike was like brothers. I don't think they got their sights on you though," J.R. said.

"That's always good," Reds said.

"Plus, the niggas that was out there wasn't too much help either. Whoever did it was smart. They had on a mask. They didn't leave no shells. They used hollows, so the slugs can't be traced, and they didn't leave no witnesses," J.R. said. "I just hope the nigga got rid of the gun anyway."

"I don't see him bein' smart enough to do all that and then keepin' the gun," Reds played along.

"Yeah, you're probably right," J.R. agreed. "I know what though. Nigga literally shot Mike's whole fuckin' face off. Now that's gangsta!"

Reds just laughed as he enjoyed the praise his cousin was giving him.

"Whoever did it don't got nothin' to worry about," J.R. added as he winked at Reds.

Reds didn't say anything. He just shook his head knowingly.

"How you sleep last night?" J.R. asked.

"Good. I was upset about Stacey bein' so hurt, but I got her and the baby, so it's cool. I can do way better for them than Mike could have anyway," Reds said.

"This shit is in ya blood. I didn't think it would bother you, but I got somethin' to take ya mind off shit anyway," J.R. said.

J.R. and Reds arrived at the strip club around eleven o'clock. J.R. told Reds that no matter what was going on in life, pussy would always make you feel better. They were both dressed to impress. J.R. had on some white linen Coogi shorts, a white Coogi button-up shirt, and a fresh pair of black-and-white Prada shoes. J.R.'s head was freshly shaved and his beard was shadowed out. He wore a big chain with diamonds in it and an iced-out Rolex. J.R. told Reds he was treating tonight, so Reds didn't have to bring any money. J.R. had about $10,000 on him and didn't plan on leaving with any of it.

Reds had on some dark blue Versace jean shorts, a white and navy blue Versace shirt, some white and navy blue Air Force Ones, and his Cuban link chain with the Jesus piece.

When they got to the door, J.R. spoke to the bouncer. "Me and my folks is tryna have a good time. Problem is my folks ain't twenty-one yet. We want VIP, bottle service, and no metal detectors," J.R. said.

"Four thousand dollars," the bouncer said sternly.

"No problem," J.R. agreed and quickly gave him the money.

The bouncer removed the rope, and J.R. and Reds walked around the metal detector. VIP was on the second floor. J.R. and Reds were seated, and bottles were served by a butt-naked black chick. She sat the four bottles of Moet on the table, then she started dancing and popping her pussy to Juvenile's "Back That Ass Up."

J.R. turned to Reds and said, "Anything goes in VIP."

Reds's eyes never left the stripper. She was light-brown skinned with long dark hair, had firm C cups, thick thighs, and an ass that looked like two basketballs. Her pussy was shaved bald, and as she rubbed on it, she showed Reds her tongue ring, which glowed in the dark.

"What's your name, sweetie?" J.R. asked.

"Honey," she said as she shook her titties in his face.

Reds couldn't help but to think how much that name suited her. Her skin complexion looked just like sweet honey.

"Honey, do me a favor, baby. Take ya sexy ass to the cash room and bring me back $5,000 ones," J.R. said as he smacked her on the ass.

"Oh, and bring some more bitches with you. The sexiest bitch in here, next to you, that is. Bring $2,500 to me and $2,500 to my cousin."

Honey's eyes got big, then she smiled and rushed off. Honey came back with a tray that had five stacks of money on it. Each stack of money had five hundred one-dollar bills. Honey also brought a chick that looked like Pocahontas with her. She was naked except for a pair of moccasins and a feather in her hair. The Indian-looking dancer also had a tray with five stacks of dollar bills on it. They had a huge bouncer with them. The bouncer was midnight black and had muscles on top of muscles. When the bouncer reached J.R., he spoke. "I can assure you that each tray has $2,500 on it," the bouncer said.

"It's cool, big guy. I don't really give a fuck. We ain't leavin' with none of this money anyway," J.R. said as he handed the bouncer fifty $100 bills.

The bouncer counted the money then turned and left. The Indian-looking chick was about five-foot-ten, and she weighed about 160 pounds. Her legs were long, and her ass looked as soft as drugstore cotton. Her breasts were about a C cup, and she had full lips. As she sat the tray of money down, she looked at Reds.

"What's your name, sis?" Reds asked.

"They call me Tontoe. I'll be dancin' for you tonight unless you want someone else," she said.

"Well, that depends on how well you can keep my attention," Reds said, shouting over the music.

"I think I can keep your attention for one night!" Tontoe screamed with a smile.

Once she said that, she started giving Reds a lap dance. Reds's erection was rock hard as she rubbed her naked body all over him. When Tontoe felt Reds's erection, she turned around and straddled him. Her titties were bouncing in his face, so he licked them as he caressed her ass.

"That's a beautiful chain, and your Jesus piece got so much ice in it," Tontoe said.

"Nothin' but the best for God," Reds said with a smile.

"Fuck talkin', cuz, anything goes!" J.R. yelled across the table.

J.R. told Honey to stand in front of Reds. "You thirsty?" J.R. asked.

"It's whatever," Reds said.

J.R. took a glass and filled it with Champagne, then he threw it on Honey. "Drink up, nigga!" J.R. yelled as he laughed.

Honey started to protest, but J.R. interrupted. "Don't worry, y'all goin' home $5,000 richer tonight," J.R. told Honey.

That was enough to silence her. Honey walked closer to Reds, and he licked the Champagne off her breast, stomach, and legs. When he was finished, he started fingering Honey.

"Ooh, daddy!" Honey yelled as Reds slid his fingers inside of her. Honey squeezed her breasts together and pushed them into Reds's face for him to suck on while he finger-fucked her. Tontoe walked over to J.R. and unzipped his pants. She sucked his dick as he sat and drank from the bottle of Champagne. J.R. hit the bottle hard a few times, then he closed his eyes and enjoyed the warm sensation of Tontoe's mouth. When he opened his eyes, J.R. looked over at his cousin. Reds had Honey standing on one leg while he held her other leg up in the air and ate her pussy. J.R. grabbed a handful of money and threw it at Honey.

"Cuz, *we* payin' *them*! Get cha dick sucked," J.R. said.

After J.R. had nutted in Tontoe's mouth, he handed her some money. "Why don't you go help your girl out with my cousin," J.R. said.

Tontoe tucked the money in her boot and went over to Reds and Honey. While Honey sucked Reds's dick, Tontoe concentrated on his balls. When he nutted, they both licked on the tip of his dick as he came on both of their faces. When that was over, they both left for a minute to go clean up.

"Yo, cuz, I fuckin' love this spot!" Reds said with excitement.

"I knew you would. That's why I brought you here," J.R. said.

As Reds and J.R. continued to talk, Honey came back with a strap-on dildo. When J.R. saw the look on Reds's face, he looked over at Honey and saw the strap-on she was wearing. J.R. immediately put his hand on his gun. Tontoe came right behind Honey and started kissing and rubbing on her body. Tontoe went down on her hands and knees, and Honey started fucking her with the strap-on. J.R. and Reds enjoyed the show that the strippers were putting on. They sat back and watched and threw money at the two strippers.

After Honey fucked Tontoe, she took the strap-on off, and they switched. Tontoe was fucking Honey with intensity, pulling her hair, slapping her ass, the whole nine yards. After about five minutes, Tontoe started eating Honey's ass. Reds was hyped as hell, and J.R. was happy to see his little cousin enjoying himself.

After the show was over, Tontoe walked over to Reds and grabbed his dick. He was hard as hell. She undid his shorts and pulled his dick out, then she sat on it. Tontoe rode Reds like a mechanical bull.

"Yee-yee-yee-yee-yee-yee-yee-yee-yee!" she yelled out.

Reds couldn't believe what was happening to him. He looked over at J.R. and saw him fucking Honey in her ass with the neck of the Champagne bottle. Reds couldn't help but to smile. All he kept thinking was, *I love this life.*

At the end of the night, both Honey and Tontoe had earned themselves $2,500 apiece. Honey asked Reds and J.R. if they wanted to continue to party after the club shut down.

"Hell yeah!" Reds excitedly said before J.R. could say anything.

"Fuck it. My folks wanna keep rockin', we rockin'," J.R. said.

"Okay, let us go change, and we'll be out. What y'all drivin'?" Honey asked.

"We'll be in the forest-green Land Rover," J.R. said proudly.

"Can y'all give us like thirty minutes?" Honey asked.

"Yeah, we'll go grab a bite to eat and shoot right back here. Y'all want us to grab you somethin'?" J.R. asked.

"Naw," both girls said.

Reds and J.R. left to go get something to eat. When Honey and Tontoe got into the dressing room, Tontoe asked Honey, "You sure you wanna keep fuckin' with these niggas? The one with the Jesus piece looks cool, but the nigga with the bald head was on some real disrespectful type shit. I was gonna say something, but he was payin' big money," Tontoe said.

"Girl, I'm 'bout to teach that punk mafucka a lesson. That nigga stuck a bottle in my ass, called me all types of bitches and whores, farted in my face while I was suckin' his dick, then had the audacity to ask what it would cost to let him piss on me! Fuck that. I'm 'bout to have my brother rob them niggas. I know he still got money. I felt it in his pocket. And the jewelry them niggas got on gotta be worth a small fortune," Honey said.

"Fuck 'em then. I'm with it," Tontoe said as she got dressed.

As J.R. and Reds went to get something to eat, J.R. warned Reds, "Make sure you keep ya gun on you, cuz. These stripper bitches be on some grimy shit sometimes."

"Come on, dog, they're bitches," Reds said, ignoring J.R.'s warning.

"Bitches can be worse than niggas, cuz," J.R. said.

"I feel you," Reds said, but he really didn't.

Honey and Tontoe came out of the strip club and walked over to the Land Rover.

"What hotel y'all tryin' to go to?" J.R. asked.

"Y'all spent enough money for one night. I was thinkin' we could shoot to my spot down the Bad Lands. We can show y'all how much we appreciate the money y'all spent tonight. Y'all down with an orgy?" Honey asked.

"Hell yeah!" Reds shouted out.

"A'ight then, we can go to my place, get it in, sleep late, wake up, and do whatever comes to mind," Honey shot back.

"Sounds like a winner to me," Reds replied.

"Okay, follow us," Honey said as the girls walked to her car.

"Man, these bitches is tryin' to show us a good time, and you all on some other shit," Reds said to J.R.

J.R. heard him, but he ignored the comment. J.R. knew Honey and Tontoe were up to no good. He could see it from a mile away. This was a lesson that Reds would have to learn the hard way.

They pulled up on a small side street in North Philly. J.R. and Reds got out the truck and followed the girls to the house. When they got to the front door, Honey acted like she couldn't find her keys. As they waited, a slim light-skinned guy emerged from the shadows with a switchblade.

"Y'all niggas know what the fuck it is! Give it up or get gutted like a pig," he said.

Both of the girls put their hands up. In the blink of an eye, J.R. did some type of karate move and knocked the knife out of the guy's hand with his left hand and drew his gun from his waist with his right. Just as fast as he'd done that, he shot the slim guy in his face twice. Honey and Tontoe started to scream.

"Shut the fuck up, bitch!" J.R. growled as he pointed the gun at Honey's face. "You bitches thought it was sweet, huh?"

"No, no, no," Honey said.

"Okay then, if you live here, open the door," J.R. said.

"I-I-I must've lost my keys," Honey said.

"Sure you did," J.R. said then he looked at Reds. "Cuz, these bitches is all on our dick, and you all on some other shit," J.R. said, trying his best to imitate what Reds was saying in the truck.

"I didn't know nothin' 'bout this shit," Tontoe said, trying to save herself.

"These bitches brought us out here to get robbed and killed," J.R. said to Reds. Then he turned his attention back to Honey and Tontoe and said, "But with a fuckin' switchblade though."

"I swear to God," Honey started to say.

J.R. quickly cut her off. He turned to Reds. "Man, kill these bitches!" J.R. said as he walked to the truck.

*BOOM! BOOM!* Reds shot Honey and Tontoe both in the head, then he ran to the truck. J.R. got back out the truck and shot both of them two more times in the head.

"Next time I tell you to shoot a mafucka, you better shoot 'em more than once," J.R. said as he got back in the truck.

They drove for about thirty minutes in silence. Reds felt stupid for ignoring J.R.'s warning. J.R. could tell that Reds knew he messed up, so he didn't get on him. He remained silent too. When they got to West Chester, Reds finally spoke. "My fault for not listenin', cuz," Reds said.

"I know you be thinkin' I be on some paranoid shit, and I do! But that's why I ain't dead yet. It's always better to be safe than sorry," J.R. said.

"I feel you. But let me ask you a question," Reds said.

"What's up?" J.R. responded

"I thought you always said if I'm gettin' robbed, respect the shooter," Reds said.

"I did, but that ma'fucka had a knife!" J.R. said.

They both burst out laughing as they headed home.

# 11

In a matter of two months, a lot had happened in West Chester. There were the normal drug and robbery arrests, but there were also three unsolved murders that had taken place, and nobody was happy about that. West Chester wasn't known for its murder rate. So now that bodies were dropping, things were getting hectic. The police were all over, and the mayor had ordered the police to implement a stop-and-frisk law. This law would allow the police to hop out and search people whenever they felt the need to. The mayor pleaded with people, via the news, to stay indoors after dark. He also let the people of West Chester know that a reward was being offered for any information leading to the arrests for the murders. Strict orders were given to the police to make it next to impossible for the drug dealers to sell their product. The mayor and the police chief figured that if they stepped on some toes for long enough, they'd get someone to dance with them.

In the weeks after Mike and Dion's murder, Reds stayed indoors a lot. If he wanted to go out, he and J.R. would go to Delaware or Philly. Reds kept his distance from his sister because she lived in Sidetrack, and the cops were always out there. Reds would stop by and give Stacey money every once in a while, but most of their contact was by way of phone. Stacey would go over Reds's apartment every once in a while, but being around her made Reds feel uncomfortable. Reds loved his sister and was saddened by the fact that he was the one who had caused her the pain she was experiencing. Deep down, Reds blamed Mike because if he hadn't gotten out of line, he would still be alive. Despite his feelings though, Reds still carried some guilt.

One thing that killing Mike, Dion, and the strippers did was give Reds a sense of power that he had never felt before. At first, Reds thought that he'd have a hard time dealing with killing another person. He always heard people talk about how hard it was to deal with taking another person's life. But this was not the case with him. Reds had actually been sleeping a lot better at night since the killings. Reds figured that since he was dealing with the murders so well, it must mean that he was meant to do these types of things. He also found it extremely ironic that the first person to give him a gun was the first person that he killed.

Reds now considered himself the total package. He was thorough. He knew how to get money. He got plenty of women, and he now knew he could take it to the point of no return and not think twice about it. Reds was a hustler first, so he didn't look for trouble. He knew from experience that gunplay slowed money up, but God help the person who wanted a problem with Betty's son.

It was early in the morning, and Reds's phone wouldn't stop ringing. "Yes," Reds answered.

"What's good, cuz? You should be up by now—the early bird gets the worm," J.R. said.

"Yeah, but when it's huntin' season, the bird gets shot tryin' to get the worm," Reds said.

"Point taken. But anyway, you tryin' to go to the firin' range?" J.R. asked.

"I was plannin' on catchin' up on my sleep, but fuck it. I'm down," Reds replied.

"A'ight, meet me at my spot in an hour, and we out," J.R. said.

Reds got dressed then stopped at Juanita's to grab his 9-millimeter with the beam on it. Once he got his gun, he headed to J.R.'s.

On the way to the range, Reds explained how hot things had become since Dion and Mike had been killed. The cops were really making everybody pay for not knowing anything. Reds breezed through Chestnut Street a few times and gave some fiends his number. He also gave a few fiends from Sidetrack his number when he stopped by Stacey's. So even though he wasn't able to be out, he was still making money. Reds was actually liking just working off his phone. It gave him a lot of free time. He was one of the few people in West Chester that wasn't really affected by what the cops were doing. The money he was making off his phone was so good, he wondered why he hadn't thought of it sooner. He had clientele from both sides of town now. The plan was genius.

"I knew you'd find a way to do you. A true hustler adapts to anything, and you is one hustlin' mafucka I've bared witness," J.R. said. "Now let's see how good you shoot from a distance."

Reds just smiled because he knew that J.R. had no idea about the 9-millimeter with the beam on it. Once they got inside, J.R. spoke to an acquaintance of his that worked in the firing range, then they bought ammunition and got in their lanes.

"A thousand dollars to whoever gets the most kill shots," J.R. proposed, thinking he had an easy win.

"You family, cuz, I don't wanna take your money," Reds said, setting the bait.

"Is that bitchin' I hear?" J.R. responded.

"Never that. Well, since you wanna do somethin' so bad, make it $5,000, big man," Reds said with a smile.

"Locked," J.R. quickly responded, letting Reds know it was a bet.

As soon as J.R. said "lock it," Reds pulled out his 9-millimete. He had the gun on his waist and the extended clip in his back pocket. After he put the clip in, he squeezed the handle of the gun, and the beam turned on.

"What the fuck is that?" J.R. asked in a shocked tone.

"A true hustler adapts to anything—I believe those are your words. This, my friend, is $5,000 in the bank," Reds said with a big smile on his face. "You didn't think I was gonna come down here and let you take advantage of me, did you?"

"I don't like that shit. I'm 'bout to drop a dime on ya ass," J.R. said, quoting the famous line from the movie *Belly*.

On the way home, Reds got a call from Stacey. She sounded mad and said she needed to talk to Reds ASAP. He told her that he was on his way. Since she sounded upset, when they got to J.R.'s apartment, Reds decided to go straight to go see his sister instead of dropping his gun and money off first.

Reds parked a few blocks away from Sidetrack because he didn't want the cops to harass him if they saw his car.

"What's good, sis?" Reds asked as he strolled in Stacey's apartment.

Stacey was still sobbing and tapping her foot, something she did when she was angry. "Sit down," Stacey said. "Remember when I asked you about the fight that you and Mike had on the night he got killed?"

Reds didn't like where this was going already. "Yeah," he stated.

"You told me that y'all had words, but you made peace by givin' him the block for the rest of the night," Stacey said.

"Yeah," Reds agreed.

"Well, Mike told me that y'all had words, but he also told me that he had to put his hands on you to get you to see how serious he was. When I asked him if y'all fought, he said no. I found that extremely odd 'cause I know you. If a nigga touch you, it's at least gonna be a fight whether you wrong or not. Then I figured that y'all were like brothers and maybe, just maybe, you let it go 'cause you was wrong. But when you told me what happened, you never mentioned Mike touching you. Did you leave that part out so I wouldn't suspect you?" Stacey asked with tears in her eyes.

"Sis, you buggin'," Reds answered.

"Okay, well maybe you can explain this: you also told me that you left around nine o'clock that night and went to Juanita's for the night," Stacey continued on.

"Okay, first of all, I never mentioned Mike touchin' me because it wasn't important. But the rest of what you are sayin' is on point," Reds stated.

"Okay. Well, it's funny 'cause I was talkin' to Kia earlier, and she told me that she heard the gunshots, then the call came over the scanner, so she decided to go outside and be nosey. She told me that she tried to flag your car down to ask you what happened, but you was haulin' ass. That was well past nine o'clock. It didn't hit me until I started to think about it," Stacey said as she started to cry again. "I knew you wouldn't let some shit like that go. I just never thought you would go this far with it. You killed Mike, didn't you?" Stacey was hysterical now. She was crying and shaking.

"Come on, sis, you buggin'," was all Reds could manage to say.

"I can tell by that stupid-ass look on your face that you did it. You never could lie to me, you mothafucka!" Stacey screamed as she jumped up and threw a glass at him.

Reds quickly dodged the glass, but Stacey was already in motion. She rushed Reds and punched him in the face. Reds grabbed her and held her tight. He didn't know what to do, so he just whispered the words "I'm sorry."

"Get the fuck off me! I fuckin' hate you! I want you to fuckin' die!" Stacey screamed.

Reds loved his sister, so he let her go and tried to explain. He had no idea how she had even gotten him to admit it. He didn't plan on telling her.

It just came out. Reds tried to make her understand what had gone down and why he did what he did, but that was useless. Stacey wasn't hearing it. Reds had really underestimated how much love a woman has for her man. Sometimes that love can be stronger than the love she has for her own family. It was Stacey's last statement that hurt Reds the most.

"The cop asked me if I thought you had somethin' to do with this shit, and I told them they were crazy, that you had your ups and downs, but it would never go this far. Well, I guess I was wrong. So you know what I'm gonna do? I'm gonna let the detectives know what happened, and they are gonna take your punk ass away from the streets just like you did Mike," Stacey said, her words dripping with venom. She turned and went for the phone.

"Come on, sis, you talkin' crazy now," Reds said.

"Fuck you! You wanna be runnin' 'round here like you J.R.? Well, you 'bout to see firsthand what it's like to go to trial for murder." She spat.

"I told you I'm gonna take care of y'all! I'll make it better," Reds said with a broken voice and tears in his eyes.

"Oh, now you wanna be a kid again. Don't start cryin' now, tough guy. You just don't get it. This shit ain't no fuckin' game! You can't bring Mike back. You can't be my child's father. You can't be nothin' to me or my baby 'cause your ass is goin' to jail," Stacey said.

What Stacey didn't know was that Reds wasn't crying because of what he had done to Mike. Reds was crying because he knew what he'd have to do if his sister tried to make good on her threat to send him to jail. Stacey grabbed the phone and started to dial the number 9.

"Sis, stop!" Reds pleaded.

Stacey ignored him and pressed the 1 button.

"Sis, please!" Reds cried.

Stacey stopped and looked him dead in his eyes, then she went to dial the last 1 button. Reds punched her with all of his strength in her temple. Stacey went out like a light. Reds then grabbed the phone and hung it up. Reds was looking at his sister lying on the floor, then he started talking to her like she could hear him.

"Why you do that, sis? Why you wanna get me locked up? I'm your brother. How can you choose that bitch-ass nigga over your family? He tried to play me," Reds explained.

As he was talking to an unconscious Stacey, the doorbell rang. Reds gripped his gun as thoughts quickly ran through his mind.

*Shit, did she hit the last button before I knocked her out? Is the cops at the door?* he thought.

He crept to the door and checked the peephole. He was relieved when he saw it was J.R. at the door. Reds opened the door and let J.R. in. As J.R. entered the house, he asked Reds if Stacey was okay. Reds had told him that Stacey was upset before he left J.R.'s apartment. J.R. had stopped by to see how his cousin was holding up. It wasn't until he got all the way in the apartment that he noticed Stacey lying on the floor.

"What the fuck is goin' on?" J.R. asked with a puzzled look on his face.

Reds quickly shut the door and explained what happened.

"Why the fuck would you tell her the truth?" J.R. snapped.

"I don't even know. It just came out. I never could lie to her. Man . . . fuck!" Reds barked as he realized he had really gotten himself in a jam.

"You remember what I told you about mistakes? They will cost you. Well, guess what? You just made a very big mistake. The one thing that you got in your favor is that you have the option to pick how much it's goin' to cost you," J.R. said.

"What chu mean?" Reds inquired.

"I mean you have the power to choose if you are gonna pay for this mistake with your freedom, which would mean your life. Or her life," J.R. said as he pointed to his unconscious cousin. "I will say this: you have a very hard decision to make, and you gotta make it fast."

When Reds remained silent, J.R. spoke again. "I'll offer you this bit of advice. Anybody that will turn you in for a murder and have you locked up for the rest of your life doesn't love you that much. Anybody can be family. They have no control over the fact that y'all have the same blood runnin' through y'all veins. What matters is the amount of love that person possesses for you. If a ma'fucka don't love you, why should you love them? The hard part isn't the decision. That's a no-brainer. The hard part is going to be livin' with what you gotta do," J.R. said.

It was times like this that Reds valued his cousin's wisdom. "I'm not goin' to jail, cuz," Reds stated.

"Okay then, do you want me to handle this for you?" J.R. asked.

"Nah, this is my mess. I'll clean it up. Go 'head and leave," Reds said somberly.

"A'ight, call me," J.R. said as he left the apartment. J.R. knew that the situation his little cousin had gotten himself into was a tough one for even the most heartless person. J.R. was proud of the way his protege was handling it, like a gangster. J.R. wiped his fingerprints off the doorknob and was gone.

After J.R. left, Reds used an extension cord to tie Stacey's hands and feet in a hogtie. He grabbed some rubber gloves from the kitchen cabinet. After Reds put the gloves on, he put tape on Stacey's mouth. Reds tore her apartment up, making it look like a robbery. He took all of the money and jewelry he could find. Once Reds was satisfied that it all looked the part, he turned the radio up full blast. Reds went in the bathroom and shot Stacey in the head. He cried uncontrollably the whole time. Some of his tears were from sorrow, but most were from anger. He cried for him, and he cried for Stacey. He cried because he knew this would crush his father. But most importantly, he cried for his unborn niece or nephew.

Reds turned the radio off after killing his sister and just sat on her couch for hours. He felt absolutely empty inside. Reds had just taken it to a whole new level. He was now sure that any obstacle that got in his way from here on out would be eliminated. Any good that was inside of Reds had died along with his sister and her baby. At least that's how he felt. He made a conscience decision to live in the jungle, and in the jungle, it's kill or be killed. Stacey was going to call the cops, and that would have sent Reds away for the rest of his life for sure or maybe even gotten him the death penalty. She didn't feel bad about what she was going to do to her brother. All she thought about was herself. So that's exactly what Reds had to do, think about himself.

A little after midnight, Reds crept out of his sister's back window and made it to his car unseen. He made a few calls then headed across town to pick up an ounce of weed. Reds didn't smoke, but after the night he just had, he needed something to put him to sleep.

In less than three months, Reds had killed six people; two were family. A monster had been born, and the streets would be wise to be terrified.

# 12

It had been a month since Stacey was murdered. Reds's dad took the death of his only daughter hard. Reds couldn't be of any help to his father because he was experiencing mixed emotions of his own. His sister and her child's death had a different effect than the other murders had on him. Some days he would cry all day while others he'd say, "Fuck her" and just have an attitude. When it was time for Stacey's funeral, Reds and J.R. paid for everything. After the funeral was over, Reds decided to isolate himself from everyone. The family understood. Everybody knew how close he and Stacey were.

It was around noon and Reds was just getting out of bed. A knock came at his door. It was J.R.

"What's good, cuz?" J.R. asked.

"Shit," Reds replied.

"That's what you look like, shit. Take ya ass to the barbershop and take a shower or somethin'. I didn't know this shit was gonna beat you up like that," J.R. said.

"Me neither," Reds responded.

"I told you that you should've let me handle that," J.R. said.

"I had to do it. I wasn't sure that I would've been able to forgive you if you did it," Reds said honestly.

"I can respect that. But check this out—what's done is done. You can't go back in time, family. You my peoples, and I love you, so here," J.R. said as he handed Reds a gun.

"What the fuck is this for?" Reds asked with a confused look on his face.

"I love you, dog. I'd rather see you put one in ya head and get this shit over with than to keep killin' ya'self every day," J.R. said.

Reds sat on his couch and looked at the gun for a minute. What J.R. said made perfectly good sense. Reds let his words sink in.

"Go 'head. Pull the trigger," J.R. said again.

"I don't want to," Reds said.

"I know. You love life too much to kill ya'self," J.R. said. "I just wanted you to realize that."

Reds smiled for a second. "What would you have done if I put the gun to my head?" Reds asked.

"You want the truth?" J.R. replied.

"Always," Reds shot back.

"I would've let you bang ya'self," J.R. said with a serious look in his eyes.

"What!" Reds said in a shocked tone.

"If you don't wanna live, I don't want you alive," J.R. said. "Now get out of this slump and start livin', nigga!"

Reds couldn't do anything but appreciate his cousin's wisdom and honesty. He cracked a smile and got up to hug J.R.

"Yeah the fuck right! This shirt is Versace, nigga, and you smell like the ma'fuckin' wilderness. Go get ya ass in the shower before you start tryin' to hug a nigga," J.R. said as they both laughed.

Once Reds got out of the shower, he felt refreshed. J.R. filled him in on what was going on in Stacey's investigation. "The cops think that Stacey got killed because somebody might've robbed her, thinking Mike left a lot of money there. They're not even thinkin' 'bout chu. Because Mike lived the type of life he did, they don't even know where to start lookin' as far as suspects is concerned. Both cases, his and Stacey's, have pretty much gone cold," J.R. said.

"Good lookin', cuz. I don't know what I'd do without you," Reds said.

"Me neither," J.R. said sarcastically.

"A'ight, well, I'm 'bout to go get my hair cut. I'll catch you later," Reds said.

"You know how to get in touch with me," J.R. said

Reds was learning how cause and effect worked. He now had firsthand knowledge of how a situation that meant nothing to him (the Mike situation) could lead to something that meant the world to him (his sister's situation). This would be just another lesson that he'd have to learn from, and as with all things in life, it would help strengthen his character.

Reds stepped out the door of his apartment and felt the cool October breeze blow on his face. Just as the trees shed their leaves for the changing of seasons, Reds would shed his old skin and allow new skin to grow for the changing of seasons. Stunting season was about to begin. It was time to turn it up a notch.

Reds called his fiends and let them know he was back around and had a batch of straight-drop (cocaine cooked to its purest form, no cut or other additives). Soon things would go back to the way they usually were, at least as far as money was concerned. Reds had to get back to being Reds. He made a decision to stop smoking weed because that's all he had been doing for the last month. Reds felt that smoking weed would only make him vulnerable in the streets. If he was high all the time, he could easily get caught slipping. Reds was one of the few people in the streets that didn't need to get high. He felt intoxicated when he got money—that was his addiction.

Reds sat in his house later on that night and counted out some money. After he finished counting the money, he put it in a bag and was about to drop it off at his safe in Juanita's house. A knock came at his door. He tossed the bag in his room and went to his door.

"Who's there?" Reds asked.

"It's ya baby's mother," Maria said.

"You must got the wrong house 'cause the nigga that live here don't got no kids," Reds said.

"You might not have none that you know about, but now you know, so can you open the door so we can talk?" Maria said nervously.

Reds opened the door and let her in. He had a look on his face that said he thought she was lying.

"Can I have a seat?" Maria asked.

"I don't see the harm in that," Reds said.

"Look, I know we were on bad terms last time I saw you, but we need to put that past us," Maria said.

"Is that what this is about? You wanna get back together?" Reds asked.

"Yes and no, I'm pregnant, and I want us to be a family," Maria said with eyes that looked right through Reds.

"Slow down, Speedy Gonzales! I don't even know if the baby is mine. Plus, this ain't a good time. So this is what I'll do—first thing tomorrow mornin', I'll drop off $300 to your house, and you can get an abortion," Reds said.

"Nigga, fuck you! I'm not gettin' no fuckin' abortion. I'm too far along for that anyway. I should've never came over here. I just thought that you would've liked to know you were gonna be a father. 'Guess I was wrong. And you can keep ya lil' money. I can take care of mines on my own," Maria stated as she rolled her eyes and stood up. She struck a nerve when she made the comment about Reds's money.

"First off, ain't nothin' lil' 'bout my money. Secondly, why you just now sayin' somethin'?" Reds asked.

"Well, you wouldn't answer my phone calls, and the only other family member I knew how to get in touch with was your sister. I didn't want to call because of that shit with Mike happened. I figured it was a bad time for her, so I waited it out. But before I got a chance to holla at her, that shit went down with her. And I just want to say I'm so sorry for your loss," Maria said.

Reds took in what she had just said, and it all made sense, but he needed more time to think things through. "Damn, this is all comin' so suddenly. Give me some time to assess the situation and let me get back to you," Reds said.

"If you don't want to be a part of me and the baby's life, that's fine. I won't take you for child support or anything. I just wanted you to be able to make the decision if you wanted to be a part of our lives," Maria said.

"Breathe easy. If the baby's mine, you don't got nothin' to worry about. I'll handle my responsibilities to the fullest," Reds said.

"Thank you, papi," Maria said as she leaned in and gave Reds a kiss on the cheek.

"But look, I'm on my way out. Do you need a ride?" Reds asked.

"I'd like that," Maria responded.

Reds dropped Maria off and told her that he'd give her a call in a few days. After dropping her off, Reds went about his business as usual. Over the next few days, any time Reds wasn't handling his business, his thoughts quickly drifted to Maria and the baby. Reds was warming up to the fact of possibly becoming a father, especially when he thought of how he'd lost his sister and her baby.

*This is the cycle of life. You lose someone and you gain someone,* Reds thought to himself. He even spoke to J.R. about it, and J.R. told Reds that he thought it was a gift and a curse if the baby was his. The gift would be the baby, and Maria would help fill the void in Reds's heart over the loss of Stacey and her baby. The curse would be that it would definitely slow him up in the drug game. J.R. did tell him that if it was his, he thought Reds was doing the right thing by taking care of it.

Reds also spoke to his father about the situation. Rob wanted the kid to be Reds's for various reasons. First, he wanted a grandchild. He also hoped that a child would slow Reds down. Rob wasn't stupid—people were dying at an alarming rate in West Chester, and all of them were one way or another connected to his son. Rob thought if Reds stayed in the game, it would only be a matter of time before he was burying his son. He also was trying to fill the hole in his heart from the loss of his daughter and grandchild. Rob was very encouraging and told his son to be there for Maria. He told Reds that Maria would need him during the course of her pregnancy, and there would be certain parts that he wouldn't want to miss. He also told Reds that the Lord puts someone in your life every time he takes someone out. Rob had his son gassed up.

Based on his own feelings, along with J.R. and his father's advice, Reds decided to move Maria in with him. Reds decided to make sure Maria was taken care of during her pregnancy. Once she had the baby, Reds would get a blood test, and if the baby wasn't his, he'd part ways. Deep down, after analyzing the situation, Reds was a little confident that Maria was telling the truth. She didn't ask him for any money, and she said if he didn't want anything to do with her or the baby, that was fine—she'd take care of it on her own. Everything was starting to add up, and the closer he got to Maria's apartment, the more confident he grew that he was making the right decision.

Reds knocked on Maria's door. After a few seconds, she answered. "Who's there?" she asked.

"I think it's your baby's father," Reds said with a smile.

The door flew open, and Maria was in Reds's arms, hugging and kissing him. She was so happy that Reds wasn't trying to deny her child. When Reds told her that he wanted her to move in with him, she declined. Maria told Reds that she wanted her baby to have its father, and she was willing to give Reds another chance at a relationship, but it would take time. Maria was seven years older than Reds, and he admired her maturity. Reds told her that he wanted to be at every doctor appointment and promised to be there when she needed him.

Right before he left, Reds apologized for the way he treated her when he made her walk home. That made Maria cry and earned Reds a kiss. He slept better that night.

Over the next month, Reds and Maria became very close. They continuously tested each other. Reds was always offering her money to see if that was her aim. But Maria passed with flying colors every time and declined. Then there was Maria. She called every night and asked for crazy foods like pickles and peanut butter or eggs and marshmallow fluff. She wanted to see if he'd get out of bed or stop whatever he was doing to tend to her. She also wanted to see if he was with someone else. Reds never left her hanging. Whatever she wanted, he would bring to her. And he never sounded like he was busy or with another woman.

They were riding in the car one day, and the cops pulled them over. Reds had an M&M tube full of crack. Maria told him to give the crack to her, and she dug in her panties and placed it inside of her. The cops pulled Reds out of the car and told him that they got a call that he was carrying drugs on him. They searched him then searched the car.

As they both stood outside of the car, Reds in handcuffs, Maria just smiled at her boo, knowing the cops would never find any drugs in his car. After the search turned up nothing, the police let them go.

When they got in the car, Reds thanked Maria for saving him.

"I go extra hard for my man," Maria stated matter-of-factly.

Reds loved the loyalty. "So I'm your man now?" Reds asked.

"Yeah, papi, I'm all yours!" Maria said with a smile.

"So as your man, I'm demandin' some pussy tonight," Reds said with a smile.

"That can be arranged," Maria shot back as she laughed at her man's silliness.

Since they started talking again, Maria wouldn't have sex with Reds. She wanted him to know that she wasn't a whore. They had sex on the first night at the BBQ because she was tipsy. But it wouldn't be so easy this time.

Even though Reds and Maria were officially together, Maria still didn't want to move in with Reds. She had a point to prove; she was trying to show Reds that she didn't need him. Reds had received her message loud and clear. He no longer suspected her of having an ulterior motive. As far as he was concerned, she was a rider, and he wanted to show her his appreciation.

He bought her a diamond bracelet for her birthday, and Maria told him to take it back. "I want you, papi, not your money," Maria said.

It was statements like this that told Reds all he needed to know about his lady—she was a thorough chick. It was also that statement that caused their first fight in a month and a half. She didn't want the gift that he bought her, and he argued with her that he was her man and could buy her whatever he wanted.

"Fine, just because you buy it doesn't mean I have to wear it," Maria said.

Maria had a backbone and didn't just do whatever Reds said because he had money. He loved that about her. Maria was a firecracker, and her swag reminded him so much of his sister.

"I swear you be wantin' me to fuck you up," Reds said jokingly.

"You ain't gonna do shit," Maria shot back.

Reds slapped her playfully on her cheek. She slapped him back just a little bit harder. He ripped her shirt, so she tried to rip his. This was all some sick sort of foreplay to the two of them because this little act led to sex. This was the first time they would do it, but it damn sure wouldn't be the last.

It was now mid-November, and Maria had picked up a little weight, but she wasn't showing too much. Reds would still ask her to strip for him, and she would gladly comply. Little requests like that made her feel sexy. And sexy she should feel—Maria was beautiful even at four-and-a-half-months pregnant. Pregnancy made some women look ugly. Not Maria though, her pregnancy enhanced her beauty. Their sex life was amazing! Maria's pussy would get so wet that it was ridiculous. Her hormones were going crazy, and although she complained a lot, she also wanted to have sex a lot. She was smart. She'd piss Reds off by nagging him then let him relieve his frustrations on her lady parts. She wanted to have sex in store bathrooms, in the car. She would even call him while she was at work and ask him to come through for a quickie. Her favorite thing to do was to call Reds and have him come home or her job only to suck his dick and then send him off.

Reds was head over heels in love with Maria. He brought her around the family and let her chill with him and J.R. It only took one conversation between J.R. and Maria, and she had him on her side too. Maria was pregnant, and she still cooked and cleaned and made Reds really feel loved. She was definitely a keeper.

# 13

It was early December, and Reds was tired of running back and forth from his apartment to Maria's. They spent damned near every night together. Some nights at her spot, some nights at his. This particular night, Reds lay in Maria's apartment, exhausted after a session of mind-blowing sex. Reds looked over at Maria, who was completely passed out. As soon as Reds saw she was sleeping, he started packing her belongings. When Maria awoke and saw Reds packing up her stuff, she asked, "What 'chu doin'?"

"You movin' with me," Reds said without even looking at her. "And don't even think about tryin' to argue with me. You have no say in this."

"S, you're basically takin' me hostage?" Maria asked.

"You fuckin' right," Reds said.

"Ooh, and is sex involved? Am I gonna be your sex slave?" Maria asked with a dirty look on her face.

"You think not," Reds said.

"Okay, baby, you win. But we gotta slow down with the sex. You be just beatin' on the baby. If you keep this up, you gonna make the baby retarded," Maria said.

They both laughed at her silly joke.

"I do want to let you know that I'll do this as long as it makes you happy, and you're doin' it for you, not me," Maria said.

"I'm doin' it for both of us, and no other woman has ever made me happier than you," Reds said.

"So you trust me?" Maria asked.

"100 percent! And now that I'm sure of that, you're comin' home where you belong," Reds said.

Maria got up and jumped into her man's arms. "I love you, papi," Maria whispered to Reds as she kissed his lips.

"I love you too. Now get cha big ass off me before you break my back," Reds said playfully as he slapped her backside.

"Fuck you," Maria said then she slapped Reds's face softly. This started their rough-housing, which always led to sex.

Reds and Maria spent most of the night moving all of her belongings into Reds's house. They left all her furniture in her apartment; Reds's stuff was nicer. Reds truly enjoyed Maria's company and was happy that he moved her in with him. Maria had met Rob, and he loved her too. Reds had definitely made a smart move by letting Maria into his life. He was so wide open that he didn't even doubt that the baby was his anymore. All his doubts about Maria were gone—she had proven to be a thoroughbred. They spent most of their time together, and whenever Reds had to go take care of business, she didn't complain anymore.

Reds loved being there for Maria, but he was starting to notice that running her to doctor's appointments and other places was messing his money up. Reds loved Maria, but he loved money more. He decided to get Maria a car in order to make himself more available to his customers.

Reds walked in the apartment, gave his lady a hug and a kiss, then handed her some keys.

"What's this?" Maria asked.

"The keys to your car," Reds said.

"What? Why you buy me a car, papi? You didn't have to do that. I was savin' for one," Maria said.

"I got plenty money. I can spend a lil' to get my baby a car. Plus, I be missin' a lot of money 'cause I be havin' to run you all around. This gives us both more freedom. You don't gotta wait on me all the time, and I don't have to take you everywhere. Not that I mind, but daddy still gotta get that cash. We'll call this an early Christmas gift, my way of showin' my appreciation for all the cookin' and cleanin' you do," Reds said.

"Okay, what kind of car is it?" Maria asked anxiously.

"A 1997 Honda Accord," Reds responded.

"Can I see it?" Maria asked.

Reds took Maria outside and showed her the car. It was candy-apple red. "Wanna take it for a test drive?" Reds asked.

"Later, but first I wanna give you an early Christmas present," Maria said.

They were standing in the parking lot of their apartment complex, positioned in between Maria's Honda and another parked car. Maria went in her pocket and pulled out two Halls cough drops. She had a sore throat earlier and had bought some from the store. She placed the Halls in her mouth and squatted down and unbuckled Reds's jeans.

"What are you doin'?" Reds asked.

"Thankin' my man," Maria said with a smile on her face.

"You crazy. It's cold out here, and we're outside," Reds proclaimed.

"What? Chu scared?" Maria asked as she placed his penis in her mouth.

"Oh my," Reds said as he instantly felt the tingling sensation of the Halls on his manhood. "Fuck it. Go hard."

The fact that they were outside and could be caught turned Reds on. He looked down at Maria as she took him in and out of her mouth like a pro. She made those loud slurping noises that Reds loved, then she started sucking on his balls. The cool air on his wet penis felt good as he felt Maria's warm mouth on his balls.

After sucking on his balls for almost a minute, Maria went back to his dick. She deep-throated Reds and looked him dead in his eyes with the most erotic look on her face that Reds had ever seen. He couldn't control himself anymore. He released himself in her mouth. Maria swallowed every bit of it.

When she was finished, she zipped his pants up and stood. "The baby needs all the protein it can get," Maria said with a devilish look on her face.

"Why you be doin' this shit to me?" Reds asked.

"Shut up, boy. You know you like it," Maria responded as she slapped his chest.

"Like I—? I fuckin' love it! Especially when you get all slutty," Reds shot back, and they both laughed.

"I'll always be your slut if that's what you want. I aim to please," Maria said with a smile.

"I'm satisfied," Reds responded.

# 14

Reds bought Maria her car right on time. It was two weeks before Christmas, and Reds planned on showing out on the gift side of things. He wanted to give everybody a wonderful Christmas this year. He planned on grinding extra hard so he could do this without having to touch his stash.

Now that Maria had her own vehicle, she could get her stuff done without it interfering with what Reds had to do. Maria still demanded time from Reds, but she gave him more than enough room to handle his business.

Maria had recently learned that she was having a baby boy at her last doctor appointment. She wanted to give Reds the news for a Christmas gift, but she couldn't hold it in. Maria broke down and told him the same night she had found out.

Since the baby was due in April, Reds figured that Christmas would be a good time to buy everything for the baby. For the next two weeks, Reds would spend a majority of his time hustling and shopping. He'd go from store to store and rack up on stuff for his family. This was arguably the happiest time of Reds's life.

Christmas morning was amazing. Reds woke up to Maria's tongue going up and down his shaft. After she finished pleasuring her man, she served him breakfast in bed. After Reds ate, he reciprocated the favor Maria had previously done for him and gave her some head. While he was orally pleasuring his woman, Reds thought of a conversation that he and J.R. had earlier in the week. J.R. was telling him that if he really wanted to turn Maria out, he should eat her ass. Reds thought it was nasty at first, but after the way she had Reds feeling this morning, he decided to try it. Reds let his tongue slide down to Maria's asshole. He could tell immediately that he hit the jackpot. Maria started going crazy. He wanted to tease her, so he stopped after a few minutes.

"No, papi, don't stop," Maria contested.

"Shhhh," was all Reds said.

He turned her over and started making love to her. Twenty minutes and two positions later, Reds had Maria in the doggy-style position. He pounded her hard until he saw white creme oozing out of her pussy and onto his dick. Once he felt her body start to shake and he was satisfied that she had come, he pulled out of her and spread her ass cheeks.

Reds was now eating Maria's ass again as he rubbed vigorously on her clitoris.

"Oh my god, papi! What the fuck are you doin' to me!?" Maria shouted.

Reds said nothing. He was a man on a mission. He kept licking on her asshole like a fat kid licking an ice cream cone. Maria was loving what Reds was doing to her. She reached around and grabbed the back of Reds's head and pushed it deeper in between her ass cheeks while she tooted her ass up. Reds kept licking and rubbing on her clitoris. Maria felt herself about to cum.

"Fuck me in my ass, papi! I'm almost there! Ahe! Ahe!" she screamed.

Reds listened to her and slowly slid his manhood into her tight ass.

"That's it, papi, just like that! Pull my hair," Maria moaned.

Once Maria got used to the way Reds felt in her ass, she started throwing it back. Reds reached around and started rubbing her clit again.

"Fuck me harder! Ooh, papi, cum in my *culo*!" Maria yelled.

Reds's strokes began to get faster and faster as Maria's dirty talk took him to the promise land.

"Touchdown," Reds announced as he erupted inside of Maria's ass.

They both lay in the bed, sweaty and held each other. Maria looked into Reds' eyes. "I guess you pulled out all the stops for Christmas, huh?" Maria asked.

"That's my secret weapon," Reds said with a smirk.

"Well, it ain't a secret no more! Now I know about it, I'll be askin' for a lot more of that," Maria said as they both laughed.

"Your wish is my command, my queen," Reds said.

"Aww, you do treat me like a queen. Baby, thank you," Maria said.

"I'm just treatin' you how you 'posed to be treated," Reds said honestly.

"Well, I know what, after experiencin' this kind of love, you better not never try to leave me," Maria said, "I'll have to kill a bitch."

"I ain't goin' nowhere," Reds said as he got up and got dressed.

"Where you goin'? It's Christmas." Maria pouted.

"I left somethin' in J.R.'s truck. I gotta go grab it. I'll be right back," Reds said.

"Don't be long," Maria said.

Reds ran out front and grabbed two boxes out from under the seat of J.R.'s truck. He ran back up to the apartment and gave Maria her Christmas present. "Merry Christmas, baby," Reds said as he handed her the boxes.

"Aww, you shouldn't have," Maria said with a smile that said she was lying. She opened the first box and saw it was a gold X&O bracelet that was flooded with diamonds. She grabbed Reds and began kissing him passionately. "Thank you, baby! I love it!" Maria said with much enthusiasm.

"You better, but I think you gonna love me a lil' more once you open the other box," Reds said with a smile.

Maria opened the other box and saw an X&O chain with a diamond-encrusted heart hanging from the middle. "You sure do know how to spoil a bitch," Maria said with tears in her eyes.

"Yeah, you know I can't be out here shinin' if my lady ain't shinin' too. We a team, so we gotta shit on 'em together. You a reflection of me," Reds said very coolly.

"Well, it was hard to find you a gift 'cause you got everything. But I managed," Maria said as she got up and walked to the bedroom. She got on her hands and knees and pulled out a black mink coat. "Merry Christmas, papi," she said.

"Oh shit!" Reds said as he ran his fingers up and down the coat. "This ma'fucka nice as shit. Thank you, baby!"

"You don't have to thank me. Shit, that's the least I can do. I had some extra money saved up that I was gonna use for a car. But since you took care of that, I decided to take care of you. I know you like to show ya ass. Now you can really stunt on 'em," Maria said.

"I like the way you think, woman," Reds said as he kissed Maria. Reds took his mink off and looked at his watch. "The furniture store is gonna be deliverin' my pop his furniture in about an hour. Hurry up. Let's get dressed and get over there," Reds said.

"Baby, it's Christmas. Ain't no furniture store gonna be open on Christmas," Maria said.

"I got that all under control. I paid the two workers at the furniture store $500 apiece to deliver the furniture to my dad's today," Reds said.

Maria just stared at her man and smiled. He definitely knew how to get what he wanted.

Reds and Maria got to Rob's house just as the furniture truck was pulling up. Reds and Maria walked in the house and greeted his father. Reds told his dad that the furniture people were outside waiting to take the old furniture out the house and put his Christmas presents in.

Rob was in love with the Italian leather furniture his son bought him for Christmas. In addition to the living room set Reds bought his father, he also got him a big screen television.

"Thanks, boy," Rob said as he hugged Reds and gave him a card with some money in it and a box with a pair of Jordans.

Reds thanked his father, who was laughing at the fact that his son didn't even count the money. He just threw it in his pocket like it was chump change. Rob also gave Maria a card with $100 in it and a $500 gift certificate to Toys "R" Us.

"Thank you, papi," Maria said as she kissed Rob on the cheek.

"What? You tryin' to take my woman?" Reds said jokingly.

"Nigga, go 'head with that nonsense! That's my daughter and grandbaby," Rob said as he threw punches at his son's arm and chest.

Rob thought it would be nice to get Maria a gift, being as to how she didn't have any family in West Chester. All her living family was in Puerto Rico. Her mother, who lived in West Chester with Maria, had lost a battle to cancer two years earlier.

"Are y'all stayin' for dinner?" Rob asked.

"Do bitches sit down and pee?" Reds responded.

"Boy, shut up," Maria said as she smacked him upside his head.

"And everybody wonders why I'm so violent. I gotta be to survive 'round y'all," Reds said with a smile. "But look, I gotta go give J.R. his Christmas gift real quick."

"What chu get him?" Rob asked.

"I took his truck four days ago and got TVs, rims, and a system put in it," Reds said, only telling half of his gift.

"I'm sure he'll like it," Rob said.

"Take a look. The truck is outside," Maria said.

Everybody went outside so Rob could check the truck out.

"Damn, that ma'fucka is clean," Rob said.

Reds drove to J.R.'s and parked out back. He was supposed to have J.R.'s truck back three days ago. J.R. had been calling him, but Reds just ignored his calls.

"You know I should fuck you up for takin' my truck hostage," J.R. said.

"My fault, cuz! Look, I fucked up, and I knew you'd be mad. But before you start trippin', I just want you to know that I'm'a get it fixed," Reds said in a serious tone.

"Get what fixed? What the fuck happened to my truck?" J.R. snapped.

"I let Maria drive it to the store, and she crashed the front end," Reds said, holding back his laughter.

Reds knew that J.R. was going to be livid about his truck being smashed up.

"What! Listen, cuz, I love you to death. But as soon as Maria has the baby, she's gettin' shot. I ain't got no rap. Now, I'm gonna go put my sneakers on and meet you outside. I want a fair one," J.R. said as he walked back in the house.

"I can respect that. I'll be out back," Reds said.

J.R. came out back and saw his cousin standing next to his truck.

"I know you don't celebrate Christmas, but you know I had to get you somethin'," Reds said with a smile.

J.R. looked at the truck and could tell that it had been washed and detailed. Then as he got closer, he saw that his truck was sitting on twenty-inch rims. "Okay, okay, good fuckin' lookin', fam," J.R. said as he admired the rims. "I'm glad I don't gotta fuck you up now."

"Nigga, we was 'bout to fight. I don't know 'bout you fuckin' me up, fuck around and might'a got ya ass beat," Reds said.

J.R. threw his hands up, and they play-fought for a few minutes. When they were both tired, Reds announced, "It gets better."

He showed J.R. the TVs in the headrest of the truck and the system. "And I know a nigga that do stash boxes. Got you the ill stash spot," Reds said.

Reds put the heat on high, turned the radio to a certain station, then flicked the high beams on. As soon as he did that, the compartment where that passenger side air bag was located came open. J.R. looked at the brand-new .50-caliber Desert Eagle handgun that lay where the air bag used to be. He pulled it out and saw it had a beam on it.

"Never lose a bet 'cause of poor shootin' again," Reds said.

"First of all, I didn't lose 'cause of poor shootin'. I lost 'cause you can't miss when your shit got a beam on it. But it's still a good look, cuz," J.R. said.

"No doubt. All the love you done showed me, it's only right I return it," Reds said.

"Come on in. I got somethin' for you too. It ain't no Christmas gift, but a gift nonetheless," J.R. replied.

They walked inside, and J.R. gave Reds his gift. When Reds saw that his gift was wrapped in black tape, he knew exactly what it was. Reds was holding a kilo of cocaine.

"This a bird?" Reds asked.

"Great minds think alike. I figured I'd give you the gift that keeps on givin'," J.R. said.

Reds was at a loss for words. He just grabbed J.R. and hugged him. "I love you, cuz," Reds said.

"No fuckin' doubt," J.R. responded. "You my lil' brova, but I'm'a still need like $15,000 back off that. I had to take care of somethin', and the coke was in the house. Didn't cost me nothin', so I ain't gonna charge you up. I just wanna make a lil' somethin'."

"I definitely don't got no problem breakin' you down. If I eat, you eat," Reds said. "You know how we do."

After some small talk about drug dealing and what-not, Reds asked J.R. if he wanted to come to his dad's and eat. J.R. had plans with his mom, so he declined.

Reds called Juanita's house, but she wasn't home. He was glad because they had been fighting a little bit. Juanita was in love with Reds, and she secretly wanted to be with him. When she saw that he had moved Maria in with him, the petty fights and arguments started. It wasn't nothing serious, just little smart remarks about Maria. Instead of her being herself around Reds, like she normally was, Juanita always seemed to have an attitude when Reds came through. He knew what it was about—Juanita was hurt. He figured that in time, she'd cool off and be fine. He still trusted that she wouldn't try nothing crazy though.

Reds dropped the kilo off in the safe then headed home to spend Christmas with his family.

When Reds got back to his dad's house, Rob and Maria were just finishing up the food. Reds sat on the couch and watched football. Maria finally kicked Rob out of the kitchen and took over. Rob joined his son in the living room and enjoyed the football game.

"I'll tell you what, boy—you let this one get away from you, and I'm'a kick ya ass," Rob said, referring to Maria.

"She ain't goin' nowhere, Pops. I got this one in the bag," Reds said. "Plus, I'm askin' her to marry me in March right before she has the baby."

"Smart man," Rob said.

They all sat in the house for the rest of the night and ate, laughed and joked. All in all, it was a wonderful day for everybody. As Reds sat on the couch with Maria lying in his lap, he couldn't help but think, *I could get used to this.*

Reds kept hustling hard for the week that followed Christmas, making all the money he spent back. He had devised a plan that was a sure winner. He told all the fiends that he was going back to bags, but he promised his customers that they'd be the biggest bags anyone had ever saw. Reds put 500 grams of cut on the kilo that J.R. had given him, and that gave him 1,500 grams of crack after it was all cooked up. He was selling half of a gram for $20 and taking no shorts. He'd make $60,000 of the kilo, pay J.R. his $15,000, and pocket $45,000. It was an instant hit.

Reds knew that the coke wasn't as good as what he normally had because he was using more cut, but he knew he'd still move it quickly. He was sure of this because he knew the way addicts think—they'd rather have quantity over quality. They were getting a half of a gram for $20—who could complain? Reds got no complaints. Instead, he was praised like he was a god.

Reds was now working only off his phone, so he didn't have to worry about anyone hating on him or the cops harassing him. Nobody really saw Reds too much anymore, but he was getting money like never before. Life was good.

# 15

It was New Year's Eve. Reds and Maria were preparing for a night on the town. They were meeting J.R. and Nice at the Star Social Club, a neighborhood hangout. J.R. and Nice had just finished cussing Reds out on the phone because he was bringing Maria. Reds made a lame excuse about him needing a designated driver because he planned on getting drunk. But everybody knew why he was bringing Maria—he was sprung. Maria caught Reds at a very vulnerable time in his life. That's why he had fallen so hard and so fast for her. Maria made him forget the pain that he was going through. Reds knew this also, but it was okay because Maria seemed to be just as in love as Reds was.

Reds and Maria pulled up just as a car was pulling out right in front of the club. Maria told Reds how much she liked the way J.R.'s truck looked, so a few days later, Reds got twenty-inch rims and TV's for his Regal. Reds and Maria pulled up with the system quaking. Jay-Z could be heard for blocks as he rapped the words to "Dope Man," a song off his new CD.

They turned heads as they got out of the car. Reds had on a pair of blue Rocawear jeans, a black Rocawear shirt, and a brand-new pair of black Timberland field boots. He wore the black Rocawear leather coat along with a Cuban link chain that had an iced-out Jesus piece hanging from it and a Movado watch that had diamonds all around the bezel. Maria was looking fly also, even at five months pregnant. She had on a pair of black Dolce & Gabbana slacks, a tan and black Dolce & Gabbana sweater, and a pair of black and tan Jimmy Choos. She had her jet-black hair straightened, which hung down to the middle of her back. She had on the X&O necklace and bracelet that Reds bought her for Christmas and no makeup except for lip gloss. Maria looked stunning as she walked to the front door like she was on a runway. Maria didn't look like she was brought into this world through a vaginal cavity. She looked like she fell out of the sky.

Reds caught himself about to shoot some Spanish guy when he heard him tell another guy that Maria had a fat ass. He stopped for a second then decided to take what was said as a compliment and not disrupt their night up.

Once they got inside, they saw J.R. and Nice sitting with a table full of women.

"Oh yeah, I'm glad I came with ya ass tonight," Maria said, referring to all the women around J.R. and Nice.

Reds walked up to J.R. and Nice and gave them both some love. J.R. and Nice were shining like they were supposed to. J.R. wore a pair of dark blue Coogi jeans, a multicolored Coogi sweater, and a black pair of Gucci loafers. J.R.'s chain and watch were flooded with diamonds also. Nice had on a white, red, and green Coogi hoody, a dark blue pair of Coogi jeans, and a pair of red, white, and green Gucci loafers. Nice wore a platinum chain, bracelet, and pinky ring, all of which had plenty of diamonds in them.

"God damn, lil' nigga, you clean up nice!" Nice said.

"Why not?" Reds replied coolly.

"Respect, respect," J.R. acknowledged.

They all conversed amongst one another, then Maria came over and spoke to J.R. and Nice. She gave Reds a long kiss then walked off to do some mingling of her own. Even though she was doing her own thing, she kept a watchful eye on Reds. Maria knew that women were just waiting for a chance to try and steal Reds from under her, and she wasn't having that.

Everybody was enjoying themselves, but they were also prepared for danger if it arose; Reds, J.R., and Nice were all carrying guns. Even Maria had a box cutter in her Fendi bag.

After being social for an hour, Maria decided to go sit with Reds. Her heels were killing her feet.

*Don't make no damn sense,* Maria thought to herself as she looked at Reds, J.R., and Nice. They bought the bar out and had three booths filled up with bottles, and they were only giving out bottles to females. All three were drinking, but Reds was demolished. Maria came over and sat on Reds's lap, claiming her territory. Nice walked over.

"Whoo-pish," Nice said as he made a motion like he was throwing a whip.

"Fuck you, nigga!" Reds said jokingly.

"How's that piss taste?" J.R. asked.

"Fuck you talkin' 'bout?" Reds asked.

"Maria's the dog and you the tree. She's markin' her territory," J.R. said as he and Nice got a good laugh.

"Leave my baby alone! Y'all just jealous," Maria said as she gave Reds a kiss.

"Jealous of what?" J.R. asked. "Watch this." J.R. hit Nice on the arm and said, "Pick one."

Nice pointed to this gorgeous light-skinned chick. J.R. leaned in close enough for Maria to hear what he was about to say. "This is a game called 'pick 'em and pull 'em.' One person picks the girl. The other person pulls the girl," J.R. said.

J.R. called the chick over to the table and whispered something in her ear. Then he palmed her ass as she started licking on his neck.

"I can't be jealous, sis. It's too much pussy in here, and I can have any one I want," J.R. said.

"I don't be playin' that game, baby," Reds chimed in.

"Sure you don't," Maria shot back as she rolled her eyes.

"Matter of fact, watch this," J.R. said as he walked up to the DJ booth and grabbed the mic. "Me and my peoples is havin' a sexiest-panty contest. As soon as the ball drops, take off ya pants and shake ya ass. The winner—matter of fact, fuck it—everybody who dances will get plenty of money. Y'all know we got it."

As soon as the ball dropped, the DJ started playing "If I Could Be Your girl", by Beenie Man and Mya. There were about twenty women dancing seductively in their thongs, booty shorts, and revealing panties. Reds, J.R., and Nice were throwing money on the girls. Reds gave Maria some money to throw on the girls too. She was a sport. She took the money and threw it along with them, but she still wasn't feeling it. Maria knew that if she hadn't come, Reds would be picking a few of the women that were shaking their goods in his face to have sex with. Maria just couldn't believe how much a chick would degrade their self to get a few dollars, then they wonder why guys be so disrespectful toward women.

Maria had decided she had seen enough and got up to use the bathroom. When she returned, she saw this pretty white girl in white laced panties all in Reds's face. Maria walked right up on her. "Beat it, snowflake," Maria said in a warning tone.

The white girl didn't even look at her. She kept her gaze on Reds.

"Why don't you wait your turn, hun'," the white girl said.

Maria was about to tell her that she was Reds's baby's mom when the white girl turned around and noticed Maria was pregnant.

"Damn, bitch, you pregnant! He don't wanna see your big ass in no panties. Why don't you go find your baby's daddy," the white girl said.

Reds was about to interject, but before he could say anything, he saw Maria make one quick hand motion. Reds felt something warm on his face. At first, he thought Maria threw a drink in the girl's face. Then he saw the white girl's face was oozing blood. Maria hopped right on the white girl like a lion on a gazelle. She grabbed the white girl and cut her three more times before Reds could get Maria off of her. The white chick was on the ground, holding her face while Reds had Maria gripped up.

"Chill, baby! You buggin' the fuck out!" Reds shouted.

J.R. walked over and took the box cutter out of Maria's hand. "Calm down, killer," J.R. said to Maria.

Maria was still flipping out and threatening the white girl.

"Damn, cuz, I like her. Beautiful and a gangsta, can't beat that! She got any sisters?" J.R. said to Reds between laughs.

"This shit ain't funny! And it's all your fault!" Reds said as he tried to control Maria.

J.R. just smiled and said, "Happy New Year!"

Two bouncers started coming toward Reds and Maria. J.R. stood in front of them and put his hand under his shirt. "What? I wish one of you niggas would. I know where both y'all live. We got this," J.R. announced.

Both bouncers stopped dead in their tracks. They both knew J.R. and what he was about. Although both of the bouncers were huge, neither of them were bulletproof. They both backed off and directed their attention to the white girl.

Nice was the only one of the three that wasn't drunk. He ran over to Reds. "Get cha shorty outta here before the cops come. I'm'a take the white bitch to the hospital and give her some bread so she stays quiet," Nice said.

"Good lookin', fam," Reds replied.

Reds took Maria home and cussed her out for the stunt she pulled in the club. Normally, he would've thought something like that was cute, but Maria was pregnant. He let her have it nonstop for about twenty minutes.

Every time she tried to talk, he'd tell her to shut the fuck up and keep on flipping out.

When he was finally finished, Maria explained herself. She told Reds that she had to fight for everything she ever had in life, and when she saw that white chick in his face, she felt like she had to fight for him. Reds couldn't help but to feel her explanation. He felt bad for going in on her the way he did when all she was doing was trying to prove her love for him.

As always, this argument was followed by love making. Oh, what it was like to be in love.

# 16

It was the first day of the year 2000, and Reds had his first hangover. He had become sober as soon as Maria tried to kill the white girl in the club, but the alcohol was taking its toll now. Reds's head was pounding, and he was dizzy. He climbed out of bed and went to the bathroom for some Aspirin.

When he returned to the bedroom, he had to stop and admire the beautiful woman that lay in his bed. She had on nothing but a T-shirt, which left her naked lady parts exposed. Maria looked so peaceful as she lay on the bed in a deep sleep. Reds's thoughts quickly drifted to how his lady acted the night before. He walked over to the bed and licked his hand, then he smacked Maria's behind as hard as he could.

"Ouch!" Maria yelled as she jumped up. "Why you smack me like that?"

"I got a mean-ass headache 'cause of you!" Reds responded. "So you gon' get up and take care of me. Massage my temples."

"No, you got a mean-ass headache 'cause you drank too much last night," Maria said.

"Yeah, well I couldn't enjoy that either thanks to you, a.k.a. the Spanish Slasher," Reds said with a smile.

Reds lay on the bed, and Maria rubbed his temples until he dozed back off.

When Reds woke up around noon, he checked his pager and called his customers back. After a few phone calls, Reds was getting dressed and headed out of the house. Maria questioned Reds about where he was going.

"I'll be back. I gotta go handle some shit," Reds said.

"Hurry up and come back. I still gotta make up last night to you," Maria said.

Now she was talking Reds's language. She knew she had messed up and was willing to kiss some behind. Reds couldn't wait to get back.

Reds arrived at one of his customers' house and was immediately upset. Bugsy, a loyal customer, had company, which was a big no-no in Reds's book. Reds hated for people to be around when he came through for two reasons. One, they might be cops. Two, because a desperate fiend would try to rob you if they have no other way to get high. Reds wasn't afraid of being robbed. He just liked to avoid a problem if he could. Reds knew that if some junkies robbed him for some coke, he'd have to kill them. Then that would lead to a whole other set of problems. He was very aware of the cause-and-effect law now—something small could cause a very big effect.

Reds saw Apollo, Bugsy's brother, as soon as he walked in the house. Apollo was a crackhead too, but he had just come home from prison and was huge. Apollo stood about six-foot-six and weighed about 250 pounds—most of it was muscle. Reds, never one to back down, asked, "What the fuck is he doin' here?"

"Oh, he cool, that's just my brother, Apollo," Bugsy stated like it was nothing.

"I don't give a fuck if he was Jesus Christ himself. What's he doin' here? You know I don't play that shit," Reds snapped.

"Hold up, lil' nigga, how the fuck you tellin' my brother who he can have in his house?" Apollo interrupted.

As soon as Apollo got in the conversation, Reds kicked himself for not having his gun on him. He knew it was about to be a problem. "First of all, only speak to me when I speak to you. Second, I'm a grown-ass man, not no lil' nigga," Reds barked as he pointed to Apollo.

Bugsy could tell that the situation was about to escalate, so he interjected in attempt to defuse the situation. "Come on, guys, calm down. This is all one big misunderstandin'. Apollo, can you please give me and my friend some privacy," Bugsy stated.

"No problem, bro. But you better teach your man some manners before he gets knocked the fuck out," Apollo said aggressively.

"Who gonna get knocked the fuck out?" Reds asked in a shocked tone.

"You, ma'fucka!" Apollo barked back.

"Listen here, gang, you knock me the fuck out, you'll be dead before the street lights come on," Reds said confidently.

No sooner those words left Reds's lips than Apollo's massive first landed on Reds's jaw. *WAM!* Apollo put Reds to sleep like a baby.

Almost two minutes later, Bugsy was waking Reds up. Reds had no idea what happened. Bugsy was explaining that he tried to stop his brother and apologized to Reds. Reds's pride was hurt. Not only had he been knocked out, but he was also knocked out by a crackhead. What he failed to realize was that crackhead or not, Apollo was still a man. Reds gathered himself then was headed out the door. Bugsy asked for the $100 worth of crack he paged Reds for. Reds took the $100 from Bugsy and told him to be glad he wasn't dead just for being Apollo's brother. Reds left Bugsy's house and jumped in his car.

Reds's first stop was Juanita's to grab his .380. He drove around West Chester, looking for Apollo. Reds had a stash box in his car, but he was so mad that he just drove around with the gun on his hip. Reds wasn't thinking clearly. As soon as he saw Apollo, he planned on killing him on sight. Reds turned onto Matlack Street and was headed toward Sidetrack when he saw lights flash behind him. Reds was so caught up in his thoughts that he didn't realize the cops were behind him until he saw the lights.

"What did I do, Officer?" Reds asked.

"Step out of the car, Mr. Carter," the cop ordered. "We got a call that you were involved in a robbery."

As the first cop was explaining what was going on, two more cops pulled up. One cop was pulling up behind him, and the other was driving against the one-way street they were parked on. It was then that it hit Reds—not only did he have the gun on him, but he also never put the coke away either. He was so caught up in trying to get revenge that he had got caught slipping. Reds knew what he had on him was a state sentence for sure.

He knew he didn't rob anybody, but he also knew the procedure. If the cops pull you out of your car, you're getting searched. Reds was determined not to get caught with the gun and coke. He stepped out of the car as if he were going to comply. As soon as the cop told him to put his hands on the hood of the car, Reds took flight. He flew between two parked cars and ran down the sidewalk. Both of the cops that had just pulled up hopped out of their cars and chased him along with the cop that had pulled him over.

Reds was running so fast that his feet were barely touching the ground. He made a left on Miner Street and ran toward the railroad tracks.

"Freeze! Freeze! Stop running!" the police officers yelled.

Their orders fell on deaf ears. Reds kept it moving. The closest cop to him was the one that pulled him over, and he was about twenty yards away and getting tired. Reds checked over his shoulder as he made a right onto the railroad tracks. He was confident that nobody would be able to see him throw anything on the tracks, so he tossed the crack and the gun. Reds ran all the way to Sidetrack and cut through a hole in the fence. He was now inside of Sidetrack, so he stopped running and attempted to walk into a nearby apartment building.

As he was getting close to a building, five cop cars came swarming in the court. The cops knew exactly who Reds was, so they ran right up on him. They jumped out of their cars with their weapons drawn.

"Get the fuck on the ground, Nasir!" one cop yelled.

Reds just put his hands up, confident that he no longer had any felonies on him. "You got it," he said as he got on the ground.

He was placed under arrest and taken to the police station, where he was processed. Reds wasn't really worried. He knew he didn't rob anybody, and he knew the cops didn't see him throw anything. Since he wasn't caught with anything, the best they would be able to get out of him was resisting arrest. That only carried a year probation, tops.

Officer O'Reiley, a tall, skinny cop, entered the interrogation room first. "We gotcha this time, kid," he stated.

"Whatever. From this point on, I'd like to exercise my right to remain silent," Reds said.

Officer Collier, a short, stocky cop, came in the room next. "Did you tell him the good news?" Officer Collier asked his partner.

"Nah, I thought I'd let you do the honors," O'Reiley said.

"We found your gun and drugs, kid," Collier said with a smile.

As soon as the cop said that, Reds had to use the bathroom. He became instantly nervous, but he remained quiet. He was aware that at this point, there was nothing he could say that would get him out of this. At least nothing he was willing to say.

"You're lookin' at ten years easy, seventeen with a gun and drugs. The juvenile courts will certify your young ass with no problem," Collier said.

"That means you're goin' with the big boys," O'Reiley chimed in.

"Holy shit, O'Reiley! I forgot about the robbery charge! That's another five years minimum. The good news is that you're young. So you'll get out around thirty-two," Collier said.

"Listen, kid, we don't want to see you waste your life in jail. If you help us out, we can help you out. Whatta ya say?" O'Reiley said, playing good cop.

Reds was very street smart and knew how this kind of thing worked. He had been schooled on what to do if he ever got arrested, and that was exactly what he was going to do. Reds just sat there and looked at the cops like they were stupid.

"Hey, if you wanna be a tough guy, go right ahead. But trust me, you don't want to go upstate, kid. They'd eat you for breakfast," Collier said.

"We know who you are and the kind of people you hang around. You give us some info on a murder on something, and we can have you back home in no time," O'Reiley said. "Maybe even get you in witness protection. That way, you don't have to worry about anybody trying to retaliate on you."

Reds said nothing. He just made a motion with his hands like he was running a zipper across his lips. This made the cops mad.

"Fuck this punk kid! If he wants to be a gangster, let 'im. Take his ass to juvie," Collier said as he and his partner walked out of the room.

Reds sat in the interrogation room quietly for almost an hour. As he sat in the room, his mind wandered. Did the M&M tube have his fingerprints on it? What about the gun? And what was this robbery the cops were talking about?

Right before Reds got in the van to be taken to juvie, Officer O'Reiley asked Reds if he changed his mind and wanted to talk to them. Reds said nothing. He just climbed into the van and sat quietly, waiting to be transferred to Lima Detention Center.

Reds was processed at the detention center then was given two affidavits. One was for robbery, the other for drugs and a gun. Reds learned from reading the affidavit that the robbery charged stemmed from when he took the $100 from Bugsy.

*That ra-ass-nigga!* Reds thought to himself. All this dumb shit happened because he called the cops over $100. Again, Reds thought of cause and effect. Reds was angry.

He was taken to his room on the top floor. The counselor on Reds's floor was a guy named Dave. Dave was thirty years old and tried his hardest to be cool with the kids. Dave didn't recognize Reds by his name, but as soon as he saw Reds's face, he knew who he was. Dave liked to party a lot. He recognized Reds from the New Year's party the night before. Dave knocked on Reds's door.

"What's good, baby boy?" Dave asked as he walked in the room.

"Nothin'. Who you?" Reds asked in an annoyed tone.

Reds's face was sore, and he was mad about being locked up. He definitely didn't feel like being bothered right now. Reds planned on staying in his room until he got certified as an adult, then he'd make bail.

"Yo, I'm your counselor. You need a phone call or somethin'?" Dave asked.

"You fuckin' right," Reds responded, instantly becoming a little more cheerful.

"They call you Reds, right?" Dave asked.

"Yeah. How you know that?" Reds asked suspiciously.

"I was at the party last night. Y'all niggas was doin' it. Shit, I thought you was grown. How the fuck you get in the Star?" Dave questioned.

"Money talks, and I got plenty of it," Reds boasted.

"A'ight, listen, superstar, I used to hustle and all that, so I respect how you get cha money. All I ask is that you respect how I get mines. You take it easy on me, I take it easy on you. Don't be in here fightin' 'cause if y'all in here fightin', I gotta do paperwork. All I want is my eight hours, and that's it. So I'm gonna let chu rock out on the phone. I know you probably got shit to handle," Dave said. Dave showed Reds how to dial out of the detention center on the phone then left. "I'll get with you when you're done," he said on his way out the door.

"No doubt," Reds replied.

"Just make sure you tell ya peoples that I looked out for you. Maybe y'all throw some of that money my way next time."

Dave's last remark was said in a joking manner, but Reds knew he was serious. Nobody in this world did favors for nothing. Reds ignored the comment and jumped right on the phone. His first call was to Maria.

"Hey, baby, where you at?" Maria asked.

"I'm booked," Reds said in a somber tone.

"Booked? What chu mean booked, like in jail?" Maria asked. "Oh my god! What happened?"

Reds told her about the coke and the gun but said nothing about the robbery or getting knocked out. "Don't worry, baby. The judge will probably certify me later this week. As soon as they do that, I'll be home," Reds assured her.

"What chu need me to do?" Maria asked, immediately jumping into ride mode.

"Right now, I just need you to be at the detention center every night at six. My visits is from 6:00–8:00 p.m. every night, Monday through Friday," Reds explained.

"I'll be there," Maria said. "Do you need underwear and toothpaste and stuff?" Maria asked.

"Yeah, bring all that shit. I also need you to bring me some sweatpants, T-shirts, and shit," Reds said.

"Do you need any money?" Maria asked.

"Nah, I'm good. They feed us here. But I need to see you tonight so I can talk to you more. Now, I'm'a let you go. I gotta call my dad and J.R.," Reds said.

"I love you, papi! If you need anything, call me, and I'll take care of it. You don't gotta bother your dad or J.R. about nothin'. I got chu! I was there when it's good. I'm gonna be here for the bad. And we'll be together when it's good again," Maria said.

That statement took all Reds's worries away. He knew he had a rider on his side. "I love you so much, mami," Reds said, then he hung up.

Next, Reds called J.R. He told J.R. what was going on. Most of which J.R. was already aware of—he had just gotten off the phone with Chief Luther. J.R. let Reds have it for being so reckless. Reds explained that he was mad about what happened with him and Apollo. J.R. didn't know about what Apollo and Reds had gone through, but he did now. Reds knew that Apollo's fate would be sealed once he told J.R. what happened, and that's exactly why he told him.

*Fuck it,* Reds thought. *If I ain't the one shootin', then I'm the one liable.* Reds went on to explain why he took the money from Bugsy. J.R. wasn't really trying to hear Reds's excuses though. Reds had messed up point blank, period.

"Did you already pay Jimmy like I told you to?" J.R. asked.

Jimmy Dennis was J.R.'s lawyer. J.R. told Reds to make sure he retained him just in case something like this ever happened and Reds needed a lawyer.

"Yeah, I been took care of that," Reds said.

"They probably gonna certify you. I know you got bail money," J.R. said.

"No fuckin' doubt," Reds responded.

J.R. asked a few more questions he already knew the answer to, which was pissing Reds off. "Why you keep askin' shit you already know the answer to?" Reds barked.

"'Cause you runnin' 'round doin' a bunch of other shit I thought you were too smart to be doin'. I might as well see what else I was wrong about," J.R. snapped back, putting Reds in his place.

"Listen cuz, I'm havin' a real bad day," Reds said as he took a deep breath.

"Look, I'm gonna do what I can from out here. If you need somethin', holla," J.R. said.

"I need to get outta jail," Reds said.

"Workin' on it," J.R. said. "One."

Reds called his dad and told him what was going on. To his surprise, Rob already knew. Bugsy and Rob knew each other from the neighborhood. Out of respect, Bugsy paid rob a visit to let him know what went down. Bugsy told Rob that the reason he called the cops on Reds was because he wouldn't let Apollo rob Reds after he knocked him out, then Reds turns around and took his $100. Bugsy, never one to want any trouble, decided to call the cops. He thought the cops would just take the $100 back from Reds, then Bugsy would tell them he didn't want to press charges. Bugsy told Rob that he just wanted his money back, and he would drop the charges. As soon as Bugsy told Rob that, Rob gave him $100.

Rob went on to tell Reds that Bugsy wouldn't be showing up to court. Reds was mad that Bugsy had the audacity to ask for his money back after all the trouble he had just caused Reds. Yeah, Reds was wrong, but street people just don't call the police.

"Thanks, Dad," Reds said.

Reds wanted to make his dad feel like he had helped, but the truth was Bugsy and Apollo would be dead by the end of the week. Reds could have called J.R. and stopped it, but he wasn't. They caused him a lot of stress, so they would pay for it with their life.

# 17

Friday night came, and Maria was at the detention center for her daily visit with Reds. Since the first night Reds got to the detention center, Maria was at every visit. Today, Maria had a message from J.R.

"He told me to tell you that you good," Maria said.

Reds knew exactly what that message meant. Bugsy and probably Apollo were both dead.

"A'ight," Reds said with a big-ass smile on his face. Reds was very appreciative to have someone support him the way that J.R did. Because of this, J.R. would always have Reds's loyalty. A lot of people talk about how much love they have for another person, but when it's crunch time, most people are nowhere to be found.

"What's that 'posed to mean?" Maria asked, referring to the message that J.R. sent.

"Did he tell you what it meant?" Reds asked.

"No, he said you'd know what it meant," Maria said.

"So if he didn't tell you, he must not want you to know," Reds said.

Reds loved Maria with all his heart, but he had seen people he never thought would tell start talking. There was no way he'd give Maria something to tell because he knew if a mother would tell on her own child, Maria would tell on him. Reds quickly changed the subject, and they carried on with their visit like they did any other visit—boo loving.

The next morning came around, and Reds's lawyer, Jimmy Dennis, came to see him. Dennis was, hands down, the best lawyer in the area. He had a lot of pull in the courtroom, and he wasn't afraid to play dirty if he had to. Jimmy was the type of lawyer that would do anything to get his client off as long as the money was right. Jimmy didn't have a problem telling his client that he could beat the case if nobody showed up or if a witness forgot their story. He'd give these bits of advice with a wink and a nod. Jimmy was just as bad as the people he defended, if not worse.

"How ya doin', kid?" Jimmy asked with a huge smile.

"Smilin' that hard, you must have some good news. And if you got good news, I'm great," Reds answered.

"Well, that depends on what you call good news. The victim of your alleged robbery was killed last night, along with his brother. It's a good thing you were in here, or you'd be a prime suspect. Mr. Brown, the man that said you robbed, was shot in the back of the head twice, execution style. His brother was found in the same room. His head had been smashed in with what the police call a blunt object, and both of his hands had been broken. Because of this, they have no other choice but to throw the robbery case out. They no longer have a victim," Jimmy said.

"I definitely consider that to be good news," Reds said. He looked on as Jimmy pulled out a bunch of papers and handed them to Reds.

"This is your motion to suppress. What it says is that they pulled you over because you were allegedly involved in a robbery. If no one shows up to court to say you robbed them, they don't have any probable cause to have pulled you over. Too bad, sorry for their luck, and try again later," Jimmy said with a sarcastic frown.

Reds just smiled at his lawyer's joke. He liked Jimmy's style.

"Two more things. First, on Monday morning, you'll be taken to court and certified as an adult. That means you'll be given a bail, which means that you'll be going home, I'm assuming."

Reds cut him off, "You fuckin' right."

"Secondly, I got a call from a Detective Morris from the homicide division. He'll be here shortly to talk with you. He said he has a few questions about the murders that happened last night. It's my advice that you remain silent. We'll let him ask all the questions while we listen. That means we'll see what direction they are headed in, but they get nothing out of us. I'm here, so I'll talk for you. These dumbass cops can't solve a crime unless somebody helps 'em. We, my friend, never help the cops," Jimmy said.

"I understand that, Mr. Dennis," Reds said.

"You can kill that mister shit," Jimmy said. "Just call me Jimmy or Dennis, but no mister in the front."

"Understood," Reds said.

"One more thing, I don't want you talkin' to anybody about your case. Matter of fact, don't talk to anybody about anything important. You're on a great team, but this team is one of the most hated in the area. These motherfuckers will try anything to get you or J.R., so watch yourself," Jimmy said.

"I'm aware of that. And trust me, I don't even plan on coming out of my room until I go to court," Reds assured Jimmy.

At eleven o'clock sharp, Detective Morris arrived at the detention center. When he joined Reds and Jimmy at their table, he pulled out a recorder, then he spoke. "Good morning, this is Detective Morris interviewing Mr. Nasir Carter. Along with Mr. Carter is Jimmy Dennis, esquire."

"Okay, Mr. Carter, now that we've gotten the formalities out of the way, I'd like to ask you a few questions about a double murder that occurred last night," Detective Morris said.

As soon as the detective said that, Jimmy spoke up. "Just for the record, this is Jimmy Dennis speaking. I'm Mr. Carter's attorney. I've advised Mr. Carter not to say anything, and he agrees that would be best at this time, considering that he was under the custody of the state when this horrific act occurred. He'd hate to throw your investigation in the wrong direction because of an uneducated guess," Jimmy said.

"Well, we think the deaths may have had something to do with Mr. Carter's arrest. It seems that everybody that has a problem with this kid is dying. That's a hell of a coincidence, and I don't believe in coincidences," Morris said.

"As I just told you, my client knows nothing about any murders that have occurred in West Chester or anywhere else for that matter," Jimmy said. "But we do hope you find the monster that killed Mr. Brown and his brother."

"Is this the role you wanna play, kid? 'Cause I'm tellin' you, you will lose this battle," Morris said, growing angry.

"This meeting is over. If you'd like to charge my client, go right ahead. But always remember there are consequences even for the police. We will file a harassment lawsuit so fast, we'll break records. We are sorry that we can't be of any assistance in this matter. If my client hears something, we will contact you immediately," Jimmy said with a smile.

"You know, Jimmy, you are a piece of shit just like the scum you represent," Morris said as he turned his recorder off.

Once the recorder was turned off, the detective looked Reds square in his eyes. "I gave you a chance, kid. Now the gloves are off," Morris said as he left.

Once the detective was gone, Jimmy leaned in close to Reds. "I love pissin' that asshole off," Jimmy said.

Reds just smiled. He felt like he was untouchable. What Reds failed to realize was that nobody was untouchable. Even some of the greatest gangsters of all time had to face the music sometimes. Guys like Jimmy were just around for damage control. Jimmy was a man that could provide shelter from the rain, but that didn't mean that you wouldn't still get a little wet.

## 18

Early Monday morning, Reds was taken to the juvenile courthouse. As he had already been informed, he was certified as an adult. The district attorney said Reds was a very sophisticated criminal. He brought up the several murders that had recently occurred in West Chester and told the judge that the West Chester police were sure that Reds had a role in every one in one way or another. The DA carried on for almost a half an hour about how dangerous Reds was.

When he was finished, Jimmy told the judge that everything the DA had just said was purely speculation. Jimmy didn't really fight because he knew it was a no-win situation. On top of that, Reds wanted to be certified so he could make bail and go home.

After Jimmy finished, the judge told Reds that his charges and the DA's accusations were serious then certified him as an adult.

Reds was taken to the adult district courthouse and was arraigned. Reds's bail was set at $15,000 for the robbery and $15,000 for the drug-and-gun case. Dennis told Reds that his preliminary hearing would be in two days. He informed Reds that he would get the robbery charge dropped at the preliminary hearing and get him 10 percent for the drug-and-gun charge, which meant his bail would only be $1,500.

"Fuck all that. I can pay the $30,000 right now," Reds said.

"Come on, kid, be smart. You come from a poor family. If you try to pay that bail in cash, they'll be all over your ass. Don't give 'em any more ammunition than they already have. On top of that, large cash or financial transactions means the feds and the IRS start snooping around. It's only two days. You'll be fine. I just need you to be patient," Jimmy explained.

Reds agreed with what Jimmy was saying. It made perfectly good sense. He just had his sights set on getting out right away. "You right. I'll just have to sit tight," Reds said.

Reds was processed in Chester County Prison then taken to K-Block, which was intake. Because Reds was only seventeen, he had to be housed by himself. Reds put his sheets on his bunk then went to sleep.

When the gates were opened for lunch, he went out on the tier. He saw a bunch of guys he knew from the neighborhood. They gave him soap, deodorant, and all the essentials he needed to be clean. Then the questions started coming. Everybody wanted to know why he was in jail. Reds kept it very simple.

"They grabbed me on some bullshit," Reds said. "But good lookin' on the soap and shit. Now I gotta go take a shit." Reds quickly went to his cell and put a sheet on his gate.

The doors were opened again at one o'clock for block-out. Reds ran to the phone and called Maria. He explained to her what was going on. He told Maria to go down to apartment 4a. "Knock on the door and tell her it's me on the phone," Reds said.

"Who the fuck lives in 4a?" Maria asked.

"It's a homey of mines. She's good peoples. But she got somethin' for you," Reds said. He had to talk in riddles because he knew the phones were recording.

Juanita answered the door, and Maria introduced herself. Juanita, of course, knew who Maria was, but she didn't give her an attitude. Juanita let her come inside then took the phone.

"Hello?" Juanita asked.

"Hey, ma. Listen, I'm sorry I had to send my baby mom to ya spot, but this is an emergency. I'm out Chester County Prison."

"What happened?" Juanita asked, genuinely concerned.

"Some dumb shit, it ain't 'bout nothin'. I'm 'bout to make bail on Wednesday. But in order for me to do that, I need you to let my baby mom into the room and give her the same privacy that you'd give me," Reds said, hoping Juanita wouldn't trip.

"Sure, no problem, boo. Just make sure you stop by and holla at me when you get out," Juanita said.

Reds didn't know if Juanita had slipped when she called him boo or if she had done it purposely, but he was glad that was all she said. He just hoped Maria didn't catch it and start asking a million question. "Thank you, baby! And I want you to know that I don't mean no disrespect by sendin' my baby mom to ya spot. It was the only way," Reds said.

"I understand," Juanita said. "Okay, here's your girl back."

Juanita gave Maria the phone then told her to follow her. She took Maria in her bedroom and showed her where the safe was at then walked out the room. "I'll be in the front room when you finish," Juanita said.

"I'm in her room," Maria said.

"Okay, did she show you were it was at?" Reds asked.

"Yeah," Maria answered.

Reds then gave Maria the combination to his safe.

"Holy shit, papi, you got—" Maria started to say.

"Shhh! Remember, these phones is recordin'," Reds reminded her.

"Sorry, but damn, I didn't know it was like that," Maria said. Maria was staring at $75,000 in cash, a half a kilo of crack, and five guns.

"A'ight listen, take out $2,000 and come bail me out at the district courthouse on Wednesday," Reds said.

"Okay, baby, I'll be there," Maria said.

"My visits are from one to three tomorrow," Reds said.

"I can't make it. I work from eight to four all week," Maria said.

"A'ight, I'll see you on Wednesday then," Reds said. "Look, the phone is 'bout to run out of time. I'll call you again tomorrow,"

"Okay, papi, I love you," Maria said before she hung up.

Maria packed all Reds money and the crack in a trash bag, leaving on the guns in the safe. She carried it out of Juanita's house and put it in her car. She came back after she put the bag in her car and talked to Juanita.

"I heard you call Reds boo on the phone. I know the type of life he lives, and women come with that. So I'm not mad, but I do want to know if y'all were fuckin'. If you were, I plan on tellin' him that was very disrespectful of him to send me here," Maria said. She was feeling guilty about what she had planned and was looking for an excuse to make her feel better about herself.

"No, we been cool since school. He just pays my rent, so I let him keep his safe here. He's not my type," Juanita said with a straight face.

"Okay, thanks. Reds told me to get everything out of your apartment. He thinks they might have been watchin' him, and he doesn't want any heat to fall on you if they come here," Maria said.

Maria went back to the apartment and packed everything of hers. She loaded her car up that night and headed for the turnpike. Her destination, somewhere down south.

Maria didn't know who the father of her child was. It could have been Reds, but it could have also been two other men. She just chose Reds because he was getting the most money out of the three. Her plan was to get as close as she could to Reds and gain his trust. This way, if the baby wasn't his, she could take his money and be gone in the wind before he got a blood test. Since the other two potential fathers were from Philly, she'd have them tested first. If one of them was the father, that would be her cue to get out of dodge. If the other two weren't the father, she'd live happily ever after with Reds.

All that went out of the window when she saw all of that money. Her greed kicked in. She now knew where the safe was at, and it wasn't likely she'd be able to get to it again. All she could do was think of how she'd kick herself in the ass if Reds turned out not to be the father and she didn't take the money when she had the chance. After briefly thinking it over, Maria decided not to chance it. She packed up the money and coke and left. She thought about taking the guns too, but she didn't like them, so she left them for Reds.

The next night, near the end of block-out, Reds tried to call Maria's cell phone, but she didn't answer. He kept trying for the remainder block-out with no luck. He was sitting in his cell earlier in the day and thought, *How's she gonna post my bail if she gotta work?* He wanted to tell her to give the money to his dad and have him post the bond if she couldn't make it. *Maybe she took the day off. I hope she don't have my ass waitin' 'til she gets off work to post my shit,* he thought.

Reds didn't get any sleep that night. He was worried because Maria didn't answer her phone. *Maybe the battery died. Maybe she left it in her car or at work or somethin'. I just hope she's okay,* Reds thought to himself.

Wednesday morning came, and Jimmy did everything he promised. Due to the lack of a witness, the robbery charge was thrown out. Normally, they make you come to court three times before they throw the case out, but Jimmy had spoken to the judge before they went into the courtroom and told him that the witness was deceased. Once the judge confirmed this, he tossed the case out.

Next was the drug case. The cop that chased Reds came to court and lied; he said he saw him throw the gun and drugs. That case was bound over to the big courthouse for trial. After the hearing was finished, Jimmy asked for Reds to be granted 10 percent on his bond. The judge granted it, and just like that, Reds's day in court was over.

Once Reds got outside of the courtroom, he was taken to a room where he was allowed to make a call for bail. He tried Maria, and to his surprise, the phone was turned off. Reds was pissed. He hung the phone up and was about call J.R. when the sheriff came in the room and told him he was needed in the courtroom once again.

When the sheriff took Reds back in the courtroom, Reds noticed that Detective Morris was in the courtroom.

"What the fuck is he doin' here?" Reds asked Jimmy, referring to the detective.

"They're trying to pull some bullshit," Jimmy said with a disgusted look on his face.

"Your Honor, we are formally requesting to have Mr. Carter denied bail. I have a detective here today that will testify that the West Chester police are in the process of charging Mr. Carter with at least one murder, maybe more."

"Objection! You can't talk about what he's gonna be charged with later. Talk about it when you charge him!" Jimmy yelled.

"Order in the courtroom!" the judge yelled as he banged his gavel. "Objection overruled! You may proceed."

"The Commonwealth fears that if Mr. Carter is given a chance to make bail, he will flee and complicate our attempts to bring him to justice. Furthermore, we feel he is a huge danger to the community," the DA stated.

As soon as the DA stopped talking, Jimmy rose. "Your Honor, the police have it out for my client because of who he's related to. Mr. Carter is not a threat to anyone. If they had anything on my client, he would have been charged already. There is no reason for my client to be denied bail. He's only a kid—he's harmless. Even if what they have charged Mr. Carter with today is true, he didn't try to shoot the police. He ran and threw the gun—that doesn't sound like a killer to me," Jimmy said.

"Your Honor, please don't let this kid's age fool you. Mr. Carter is a high-level drug dealer with the means to flee the area. If we are right, do you want that on your conscience?" the DA asked.

"Again, pure speculation. And the Constitution says that you act according to the law, not your conscience," Jimmy added.

The judge sat for a minute and thought. "You are right, Mr. Dennis. I have to follow the law, not my conscience," the judge said.

Jimmy turned to Reds and gave him a big grin.

"And the law says that no man shall be denied a bail unless he is charged with murder. Despite what the police and district attorney say, Mr. Carter has not been charged with murder. But from what I hear, he may be charged very soon. There is no statute of limitations on a murder, so I can understand the police taking their time. It also makes sense that any person with the financial backing to do so would run."

"Your Honor, everybody's talking about my client having all this financial backing. Let's not forget he just needed 10 percent to post a $15,000 bail," Jimmy interrupted.

"Please don't interrupt me again, Mr. Dennis. This is my courtroom, and when I stop speaking, you can start. Now, as I was saying, there is speculation that Mr. Carter has financial backing. So what I'm going to do is raise his bail to $1,000,000 cash," the judge said.

Dennis jumped out of his chair and started yelling, "This is an outrage, Your Honor! One million dollars is a ransom, not a bail."

"This will ensure he doesn't go too far. If you don't like it, file a motion for a bail reduction," the judge said.

Jimmy turned to Reds. "They're playing dirty now. All I can do is file for a bail reduction every week until they lower your bail."

Reds just sat in his chair quiet. He was furious at what they were doing to him, but there was nothing he could do.

"Your Honor, if my client is under investigation for the things they say he is. I'd like for him to be transferred to Delaware County Prison. Once word gets out about what's going on, if he's in Chester County, there will be plenty of jailhouse witnesses lying on him, saying he told them things he did not. I'm also afraid that my client could be in danger. You never know who's gonna try to retaliate," Dennis said.

"That's a reasonable request, Mr. Dennis. I will grant it. Your client shall be transferred to Delaware County Prison," the judge said.

"Thank you, Your Honor," Jimmy said humbly.

"I ain't scared of nobody doin' nothin' to me," Reds said.

"It's not about that. I don't want you in Chester County. You are too vulnerable to snitches in there. Too many people know who you are. I'll have you placed on a maximum-security block and have you put in a single cell. Remember, don't talk to anybody about anything! There's also one more perk. J.R. can be of a lot of assistance to you in Delaware County. He'll fill you in," Jimmy said.

Reds went back out of the courtroom and asked if he could be allowed a call to tell his family not to bring the money for bail now. He was given another phone call.

Reds tried to call Maria again. Her phone was still off. He tried to call the nursing home where she worked. They said Maria hadn't been to work all week. It was then that it dawned on him. Reds had just been robbed.

# 19

Reds arrived at Delaware County Prison and was placed on unit 8, D Block. Reds was taken to the counselor's office and given a phone call. He called J.R. "Cuz, I'm in Delaware County," Reds said.

"I know. I talked to Jimmy about a half hour ago," J.R. said.

"These pussies is on some bullshit! But I got a problem just as big right now," Reds said.

"What's that?" J.R. asked.

"I think Maria robbed me," Reds said in a low tone.

"What?" J.R. asked in a shocked tone.

Reds told J.R. what happened and why he suspected Maria robbed him. J.R. didn't think what Reds was thinking was correct. "Cuz, you got a thorough chick on ya side. Before you get to jumpin' to conclusions, I'm'a call the hospitals and make sure she ain't hurt," J.R. said.

"You do that, but I got a bad feelin' that she ain't in no hospital," Reds said. Reds didn't think Maria would do something like rob him, but once he spoke to the lady at Maria's job, he got a gut feeling.

As Reds's thoughts drifted, J.R. snapped him out of it "Yo, I know Dennis told you I help you out in DCP. You know I just did a bid out there while I was fightin' my body. I got a gang of guards in pocket. What block is you on?" J.R. asked.

"8-D," Reds responded.

"Okay, that's my old block. I'll have somebody drop you somethin' ASAP," J.R. said.

"As far as Maria goes, go by my dad's and have him give you the extra key to my shit. Go by my house and see what you find," Reds said.

"I got chu, and I'm'a make sure that package lands in a day or two," J.R. said.

"A'ight, I'm'a holla at chu," Reds said.

"A'ight, and don't call 'til you get the package," J.R. said before hanging up.

Reds went back to his cell and lay on the bed. His thoughts raced, and he was stressing hard. Reds wanted to go to sleep, but his mind wouldn't allow him to do so. If what he was thinking was true, he had lost his money, his girl, and his freedom all at once. He couldn't help but think, *They say all bad things come in threes.*

Reds was sure that the only way he was going to get out of prison was if he beat the gun and drug charges. He saw how they were playing, and he didn't like it one bit. Reds played dirty in the streets, but they played dirty in the courtroom. As he sat on his bed in his cell, Reds couldn't help but think, *I hope they don't charge me with a fuckin' body.*

Reds stayed in his bed for two days. He didn't come out to eat or shower. Every time the doors would open for block-out, Reds would come out and try to call Maria. Every time her phone went straight to voicemail, he became surer that he had been bamboozled.

Thursday rolled around, and a guard came to Reds's door with a package. It was a thirteen-inch television. Later on, that day, Reds got some mail. He prayed it was from Maria, but it was from J.R. He sent Reds $1,000 and a brief letter. "None of her shit was in the apartment," was all the letter said.

Reds immediately wanted to go right back to sleep. He sat in the cell for the rest of the day and analyzed the situation. How could he have been so foolish to fall for Maria's game? All Reds had ever seen in life was women that were scandalous. Reds's mother was a swindler who put men, drugs, and the streets before him; his sister put a man before him, and every other girl he had ever dealt with before Maria was only concerned with money and/or his street status. How could he be stupid enough to think that Maria was different?

What Maria had done would scar Reds for life, and shape the way he treated women forever. Reds now thought that all women were disloyal and untrustworthy. The truth was not all women were disloyal and untrustworthy; just the ones that Reds surrounded himself with were. If Reds changed the places he looked for females and the type of females he was looking for, maybe he would find someone who was worth having his heart. Maybe one day Reds would figure that out. But for right now, what Maria had done to Reds would officially make him a womanizer.

Later on that night, around midnight, Reds heard a tap on his door. It was another guard. He opened Reds's door and handed him an open bag of chips. "It's a phone and a charger in there. Keep both of them on you at all times. When they do regular cell searches, they don't search you. As long as you stay out of the limelight, they won't be doin' no searches where they strip you. J.R. told me you was his peoples. He'll tell you when y'all talk. If you need somethin', holla at me only. I can be trusted. My name is Smiley," the guard said as he extended his hand.

Reds shook his hand and thanked him.

"I'll bring you somethin' to eat on the nights I work. J.R. paid me to make sure you good, so you'll be straight. I'm gonna put you up on game. It's a lot of young hood niggas and bitches that work here. Money talks, and if you fuckin' wit' J.R., I know you got bread. You can get whatever you want in here, street food, phones, drugs, pussy, you name it. All you gotta do is holla at me, and I'll hook you up," Smiley said.

"A'ight. Well, look, I don't need nothin' else right now. I just need to holla at my cousin, so I'm'a holla at chu later," Reds said. He was shocked by what he had just heard about what goes on in the jail, but all that was far from his mind right now.

"Look, in like another hour or so, I'm'a bring you a cheesesteak, salt, pepper, ketchup. Is that cool?" Smiley asked.

The thought of a cheesesteak made Reds realize that he hadn't eaten in days. He instantly became hungry. "Yeah, that'll be great," Reds said with a smile.

Reds called J.R., and they talked about a few things. First, Reds wanted the scoop on what was up with his apartment.

"Ain't too much to tell. I went through, and all of her shit was gone. No shoes, no clothes, no nothin'. I called the hospital, and they said she wasn't there. So it's definitely official—she gotchu," J.R. said.

Reds just took in a deep breath.

"Cuz, if I catch that bitch, I'm'a burn her fuckin' face off," J.R. said through clenched teeth. "What did she get you for?"

"Seventy-five thousand dollars, a half-brick, and like five guns," Reds said.

"Ouch!" J.R. said. "Yo, I hope I catch this bitch!"

"Dog, she ain't stupid. She long gone. She knows how niggas get down," Reds said. "I'm 'bout to get some sleep. I'm'a hit chu tomorrow."

The next night, Reds had J.R. go to Juanita's. After talking to her, he was no wiser than he was before. He knew that Maria got him, but nothing more. He had J.R. check the safe.

"Ain't nothin' in here but the burners," J.R. said.

Reds had just learned another important lesson of the streets—trust no one. He was also learning that in the streets, the test often came before the lesson.

# 20

Six Months Later

Reds didn't like it, but he was getting used to being in jail. The courts were playing games as far as his case was concerned, and he was drained emotionally and mentally. Reds didn't get his hopes up anymore when it came to court. Instead, he just rolled with the punches. The bright side to his situation was that J.R. and Nice were handling any and everything that Reds needed.

If Reds had to be in jail, he was glad it was Delaware County. He was getting visits on a regular basis, having sex with female guards. He had a cell phone, plenty of money on his books, and even smoked weed from time to time.

Reds had a suppression hearing that had just passed, and he felt good about it. If they played fair, the case would be thrown out. But Reds wasn't dumb enough to think that they'd do that. He figured they'd pull some sort of stunt like they had several times before and deny his motion.

It was early in the morning, and Reds's cell was opened. The guard told him that he had a legal visit. Reds brushed his teeth and got dressed. When he got to the visiting room, Jimmy greeted him.

"I got bad news, my friend," Jimmy said in a somber tone.

"What's new? That's all we seem to be gettin' nowadays," Reds said as he exhaled deeply.

"We lost the suppression hearing," Jimmy announced.

"What the fuck am I payin' you for? Ain't nothin' went my way since I been booked. When the fuck is somethin' good gonna start happenin'?" Reds snapped.

"Let me remind you that things could be very much worse than they are. From what I hear, you are living pretty good in here," Jimmy said, then he waited a minute for his words to sink in. "I am the reason you are in this jail, my friend. And because you have me as an attorney, you are about to get some inside information from the courthouse. One of my friends at the DA's office tells me that they don't have anything on you as far as the murders go. That's why they're so mad. The detective seems to think you are very much involved in at least three murders. So since they can't prove anything, they are trying to fuck us on the drug-and-gun case. They figure they will get as much time out of you for this case as they can. Their hopes are that they'll have a case built up by the time you are released on this. It's my personal opinion that if they haven't charged you with a murder by now, they never will."

"Well, I guess that news was better than what I been gettin'," Reds said.

"Listen, buddy, I like you. And since I like you, I'm gonna give you some personal advice. Get comfortable for a while. This court thing is a long process. You wanted to play in the big leagues. Well, this is a part of that. Jail comes with the lifestyle you chose. And if you are anything like what these people say you are, a few years is nothing for what you've done," Jimmy said.

Reds just nodded his head, acknowledging that Jimmy was right.

"Now listen, the DA is offering you a five-to-ten-year deal."

Reds became irate at the thought of doing five to ten years. "What! Man, fuck that! I'm not takin' that shit," Reds spoke sharply with his face showing his anger.

"I didn't say you were taking it. I said they were offering it. I can get him down to probably two and a half to five years," Jimmy said.

"I don't want no fuckin' deal!" Reds said in an irritated voice.

"I understand that, but I'm not a miracle worker. I can't just snap my fingers and get you out today. The cops are saying they saw you throw the gun and drugs. We don't have a win at trial. But I don't want you to take the deal. My suggestion is that you go to trial. When we lose, you'll probably get seven and a half to fifteen years. We'll be fine in the appeal courts. Once we get it out of the local court's hands, we'll start to get some rhythm. That car stop was definitely illegal. Our problem is that they want you so bad. It may take a few years, but I'll have you back on the streets without a record. There is also a bonus. I hear you're living like a king in here. I can pull some strings and have you stay down here while you're fighting on appeal. If you gotta do the time, you might as well be comfortable. Whatta ya say?" Jimmy asked.

"You got the law degree and the connections. Whatever will get me home fastest, I'll do," Reds said. Reds didn't like what he was hearing, but he had to take the good with the bad.

"Attaboy! We start trial next week. I'll have the trial over in a day. We won't do anything but object. We'll start on the appeal the same day. And I'll even cut you a break. I'll only charge you $10,000 for your appeal," Jimmy said.

"A'ight, I'll have the money dropped off next week," Reds said.

"Don't worry. Time will fly. I know how this jail is ran. That's why I got you down here. With the guys you got on your side, you're basically on the streets anyway," Jimmy said.

Reds went back to his unit and waited for Officer Croft to open the door to his block. Once he was taken to his block and the handcuffs were taken off, Croft told Reds to go into the hallway.

Croft was fine as hell. She stood about five-foot-eight, had light-brown skin, full lips, and a baby face. Even though she had on a uniform, Reds could tell she had nice-sized breasts, and her pants always hugged her thighs and ass like biker tights. Reds and Croft talked all the time. Reds made advances toward her all the time, but she wouldn't give him no rhythm on that level.

"What up, Reds?" Croft said in a sweet tone. "What cha lawyer talkin' 'bout?"

"Nothin' I'm tryna hear. I'm probably gonna have to do a bid," Reds said.

"County or state?" Croft asked.

"I'm gettin' state time. But since my lawyer is gonna be comin' to see me so frequently, he's gonna have it set up so I can do my time here. Fuck it. It ain't 'bout nothin' though. I still have my appeal. Plus, I got the best lawyer money can buy, so I'll be home soon," Reds said with confidence.

His comment turned Croft on—she loved a man with confidence. "Oh well, that's not so bad. At least you'll be here with me," Croft said with a smile.

"I ain't tryin' to be here with you. You don't play fair. I been tryin' to holla at you, but you shoot a nigga down like I'm a bird or somethin'," Reds said.

"You might get some play if ya fan club wasn't so big. Yeah, these bitches be talkin'. If you tryin' to fuck with me, you gotta leave these other bitches alone. I ain't tryin' to catch nothin' another bitch gave you. These bitches be fuckin' anybody with a couple dollars. I don't get down like that," Croft said.

"So if you don't get down like that, I don't gotta pay for the pussy?" Reds asked.

"Not if you act right," Croft replied. "I like ya conversation when you not tryin' to get in my pants. Plus, I know some people that know you out there. They say you thorough as shit."

"Who you know that knows me?" Reds asked.

"Just know that I know people," Croft replied with a smile.

"Okay, well if that's the case, consider my fan club reduced to one," Reds said, letting her know he was willing to play ball.

"I'm 'bout to get moved to third shift. It's gonna be just me and Smiley over here at night. So if you bein' good, I'll give you a treat," Croft said as she licked her lips.

"I hope you a woman of ya word 'cause I'm lookin' forward to that treat," Reds said with a smile.

Later that night, Reds called Nice.

"What's good, my nigga?" Nice asked.

Reds told Nice what Jimmy said about his case then said he needed $10,000 for his appeal.

"Don't sweat it. I'll take care of it this week, lil' bro. Jimmy is worth the money. If he said he can get you out, he will. Oh, did Nikki holla at chu?" Nice asked.

"Who's Nikki?" Reds asked.

"She works out there. Her last name is Croft," Nice said.

"Oh, that was your work?" Reds asked as it all started to make sense to him.

"Nah, she knew who you was already. I just put in a good word for you," Nice said.

"Yeah, she holla'd. I'm definitely tryna fuck though," Reds said.

"Yo, that bitch real clingy like on some fatal attraction-type shit. Be careful," Nice warned.

"Nigga, I'm in jail! She can be as clingy as she wants. As long as she comin' off the pussy, all is well," Reds said with a smile.

As Jimmy promised, Reds's trial was over in a day. He was sentenced to seven and a half to fifteen years and was allowed to remain in Delaware County until his appeal was over.

Two weeks after his trial was over, Nikki started working control on third shirt. Reds had her on his team as soon as they had sex. They were talking on the phone every night and having sex every time she worked. Reds's time in Delaware County was flying.

## Three Years Later

In April 2003, Jimmy kept his word. He came to the prison and told Reds that the Supreme Court had ruled the car stop illegal. The drugs and the gun were thrown out. Without that, the Commonwealth had to throw the case out. Reds would be going home within a week.

Reds went into his cell and called J.R. He told him that he would be home soon.

"You already know niggas is throwin' ya lil' ass a party," J.R. said.

"Nigga, I ain't little no more. I been workin' out. Nigga definitely got his weight up," Reds shot back.

J.R. and Nice made sure that Reds wanted for nothing while he was incarcerated, but one thing that neither of them would do was go see him. It's an old street superstition not to go to prisons to visit people. Guys in the streets stay away from prisons like vampires stay away from garlic. J.R. hadn't seen Reds since 2000, and Reds hadn't sent any pictures. He wanted to surprise everybody when he got out. The only people that saw him were the females that would come visit him.

"Yo, I'm'a call Nice and give him the good news," Reds said.

"Oh shit, damn, I forgot to tell you Nice got indicted yesterday. I don't know all the details yet. When I get off the phone with you, I gotta call Jimmy and see what's up," J.R. said.

"Damn, well, I'm gon' let you go. Find out what's up with Nice. I'll hit chu later," Reds said as he hung up.

Reds got off the phone, and his mind began to wonder about Nice. He hoped his man was gonna be all right. Reds told himself that if Nice did get booked, he'd make sure he looked out for him. How could he turn his back on someone who showed him nothing but love while he was down?

Reds's mind quickly drifted back to his upcoming release. Reds felt like he was mentally ready to get back on the streets. He had learned a lot from his situation. He also did a lot of reading while he was down. He studied books like *The Art of War*, *The 48 Laws of Power*, *The Master Strategist*, and many other books along those lines. Reds was learning to win with his mind. Most times, if you could out think your opponent, you'd never have to engage them in battle. The Maria situation was a perfect example of outthinking your opponent. She robbed Reds blind, and she did it effortlessly because she used her mind. He appreciated the lesson that came from that particular situation. Because of that, when he caught her, she'd die quick and painlessly. Reds came to jail over $100. He acted impulsively, and it cost him three and a half years out of his life. He promised himself that he'd never be so foolish again. Reds would always think before he acted if he could help it.

He had been preparing for his release for quite some time now. It was time to turn it all the way up and take it to a new level.

# 21

Right after breakfast, on Thursday morning, the guard buzzed Reds's door. "Carter, you outta here!" the guard announced.

Once Reds got sentenced, he had to take a cellmate. He had chosen Tone to move in the cell with him. Tone was fighting a murder, so Reds knew he'd be there for a while. On top of that, Tone was a quiet dude that minded his own business. Since they had been in the cell, Reds and Tone had become really close.

When they told Reds to pack up, he left everything with Tone—pictures, commissary, cell phone, weed, cigarettes, everything. "I'll keep the phone turned on for you, my nigga. And you already know if you need sometin', all you gotta do is holla. I'll call you tonight and give you my number," Reds said as he shook Tone's hand.

Reds walked out of the doors to the prison in two pairs of boxers, a T-shirt, socks, and shower shoes. J.R. was sitting in the parking lot in front of a 2002 Lincoln Navigator. The truck had twenty-inch spinning rims and a quaking system. As always, J.R. was fresh. He wore a pair of all-white Air Force Ones and a gray and black Sean John sweat suit. A rose gold chain with plenty of diamonds hung from J.R.'s neck, and a rose-gold bracelet hung from his wrist.

J.R. smiled as he saw Reds emerge from the prison. The two embraced as if they hadn't had any contact in years. J.R. was glad to have his right-hand man back on the streets again. And Reds was glad to be back with his older cousin.

"You definitely got cha weight up," J.R. said, referring to Reds's muscular frame.

"I see you got cha weight up too! When you make all these upgrades? New jewels, new truck, etc., etc.," Reds said.

"Yeah, '02 was a good year," J.R. responded with a smile.

The closest place to take Reds shopping was Granite Run Mall, but since Reds wasn't dressed to be walking around the mall, J.R. took him to Sixty-Ninth Street.

When they got inside City Blue, J.R. handed Reds $5,000. "Don't spend it all in one place," J.R. said with a playful grin.

Reds immediately went into balling mode.

"Why you dressed like that?" one of the female employees asked as Reds shopped.

"I just came home, baby. I couldn't fit my old clothes," Reds said.

The female just smiled as she looked at Reds's muscular frame. Reds left City Blue with about twenty bags and the female employee's number.

His next stop was Foot Locker. Reds grabbed a bunch of sneakers and a couple pairs of Timberland boots. Before Reds left Sixty-Ninth Street, he made sure he grabbed a cell phone.

On the way back to West Chester, they stopped and got something to eat.

"Yo, ain't nobody seen that bitch Maria?" Reds asked as he ate some shrimp fried rice.

"That bitch gone without a trace," J.R. said. J.R. then started filling Reds in on what was going on.

Reds had been gone a while. Even though Reds had the phone, J.R. didn't really like to talk on the phone unless he had to. So Reds only called him when he needed something.

J.R. gave Reds the latest on Nice's situation. "I don't know what it is, but somethin' ain't right. I can't really put my finger on it, but I know somethin' is wrong. He fired Jimmy yesterday. Nigga talkin' 'bout he wanna lawyer with more federal pull. Jimmy told him he could handle the job, but Nice fired him anyway. We been rockin' with Jimmy since day one. I honestly think that he fired Jimmy because he doesn't want me to know what he's doin'. Nice knows if he starts workin' with them boys, and Jimmy is still his lawyer, it'll get back to me. On top of all that, he's home. Nice got plenty of money for bail, but he was just indicted on running a criminal enterprise. They wouldn't let that nigga post bail so easily, not with a charge like that. They'd wanna know where the money came from," J.R. said

Reds nodded his head in agreement.

"Nigga called my spot last night, talkin' reckless as shit. I don't know if he's just nervous or what, but that nigga was completely outta character last night. Nice is always in control. Last night, he was anything but in control. I don't have no solid evidence, but he knows way too much. I can't risk it. In the game we play, mere suspicion is always enough. Nice gotta go," J.R. said.

Reds didn't speak at first. His mind was racing. Reds thought about how Nice had supported him while he was locked up. Reds told himself that the only reason Nice was being so supportive was because of J.R. who had also brought them together; now he would tear them apart. Regardless of the situation, Reds's loyalty would always remain with his cousin. He knew that if the shoe was on the other foot, Nice would do the same thing.

"I'll take care of it," Reds finally said.

"I didn't tell you 'cause I want you to take care of it. I'm just fillin' you in," J.R. said.

"I know, but if he's talkin', you'll probably be the first person they look at if he turns up dead," Reds said.

J.R. didn't say anything because Reds had made a good point.

"My only question is, how the nigga know ya business?" Reds asked.

"Me and Nice came up together. We used to get money together. I got locked up for a shootin', and while I was booked, he blew the fuck up. When I came home, he was in Philly doin' his thing. He planned on takin' over different corners and needed a person to do the dirty work. He's the reason I have everything I got. And I'm the reason he got most of what he got. This ain't no easy decision for me, but I'm always gonna love me more than I love another. Anyway, a lot of people got killed, getting him those corners. After that, I just became his enforcer. He pays me to keep niggas in line and handle any problems that occur," J.R. said.

It suddenly became clear to Reds why J.R. wanted to get rid of Nice. If what J.R. was thinking was true, Nice could have him on death row. They sat at the table for almost two hours and plotted out Nice's assassination. When they left the restaurant, they had the perfect plan.

J.R. dropped Reds off at his dad's house and told him he'd pick him up in a little bit so they could go car shopping.

Rob was glad to see his son. He went to see Reds every other week while he was locked up. But it felt good to have his son home again. Reds sat in his dad's house and enjoyed his father's company. Reds's room was in the same condition as it had been when he lived there.

"I'm gonna need to stay here for a month or so if that's cool with you," Reds said.

"I don't have no problem with that," Rob said.

"You know I'm gonna be doin' my thing," Reds said.

Rob just gave him a look that said, "You gotta be kiddin' me."

"I promise, I won't bring anything in here. I could have J.R. grab me an apartment, but he's done so much for me already. I don't want to be too much of a burden," Reds said.

Rob wasn't thrilled about hearing that Reds would be hustling again, but he knew there wasn't anything he could do about it. He also knew that Maria robbed Reds blind. "Take your time, son," Rob said, "and be careful."

Reds unpacked all his clothes and took a shower. He left Delaware County with a check for $17,300. He had so much stuff in the county that he didn't even have to go to the store most of the time. He just saved most of the money that J.R. and Nice sent him. Thanks to J.R., Reds didn't have to spend a dime since he had been home. He told J.R. that he wanted to go shopping for a car with the money he left the jail with.

Around four o'clock, J.R. knocked on Rob's front door. He came inside and talked for a while, then he and Reds left to go get his car.

When they got to the car lot, Reds saw an all-black 2001 Monte Carlo. "I like that ma'fucka right there," Reds said as he pointed to the car. He looked at the price on the car. "That's outta my range," Reds said.

"You can talk 'em down to $17,000," J.R. said.

"Yeah, but I only got $15,000 to spend. I need the rest of the money I got for pocket change," Reds said.

"You really think I'm gonna make you spend all ya bread on a car? Whatever the car cost, I'll pay half," J.R. said.

"Good lookin', cuz," Reds said with a big smile.

"That's what family's for," J.R. responded.

J.R. showed Reds how your family was supposed to act. He made Reds want to be a part of what he was doing. What most people fail to realize is that when you show a loyal person unconditional love, they'll always give it right back. This was the kind of bond that J.R. and Reds had built, a bond built on unconditional love. This was the type of bond that would be impossible to break.

After the car was paid for, Reds told J.R. that he had to go see an old friend. "I'll hit chu up later," Reds said. "I need some new pussy."

"You go handle that," J.R. said.

Reds drove straight to Juanita's apartment. Juanita had kept in touch with Reds over the years. She told Reds in the beginning that she'd ride his time out with him, but if she did, she wanted to be his girl when he came home.

"Maria fucked it up for all y'all. I'm comfortable just bein' friends with benefits from here on out. So don't put your life on hold for me. Do you 'cause when I come home, I'm damn sure gonna do me. That shit with Maria hurt too much for me to ever go through again. I'm good," Reds had said honestly.

"I would never do that to you," Juanita had said.

"Nobody will. They'll never get the chance," Reds had responded.

After Reds and Juanita had that conversation, she kind of fell off. They still were on good terms, but Juanita moved on. They still talked on the phone on a semi-regular basis, and she'd even come visit him every once in a while. She told Reds that she started dating, but she promised that she'd never forget about him. Reds knew that Juanita's man worked the 2:00–10:00 p.m. shift. That's exactly why he stopped by her house after two. Reds didn't care that she had a man. He just wanted to fuck.

Reds knocked on Juanita's door and was greeted with a huge hug and kiss. Juanita told Reds to come in. She had on a pair of tights and a wifebeater.

"When the fuck they let chu out?" Juanita asked.

"Today," Reds replied.

"I thought you had a seven-and-a-half-to-fifteen," Juanita asked.

"I did, but I beat the case on my appeal," Reds responded.

She leaned in closer to Reds and hugged him again. "I'm so glad you're home," Juanita said.

"So am I," Reds said as he started to kiss Juanita's neck and rub on her firm ass.

Juanita wanted to resist, but Reds's touch felt too good. She had a man, but she had been in love with Reds for years. She looked deep in his eyes with passion. "That feels so good," Juanita said.

"This will feel even better," Reds said as he took off his shirt and pulled his pants down, revealing his rock-hard erection.

"You 'bout to fuck up a happy home," Juanita said.

"I'm not makin' you do nothin' you don't wanna do," Reds said as he pulled off her wifebeater and started sucking on her breasts.

While Reds was locked up, he got turned on to reading sex novels. He learned from reading the novels that most women liked rough sex even if they've never had it. They just didn't know that they liked it because they had never tried it. Reds tried it out while he was in the county. He used to be very aggressive with Nikki. They'd be fucking, and he'd choke her, slap her, spit on her, all kinds of degrading shit. Nikki told Reds that she liked it, so that was the only way he'd fuck her. A lot of what he was doing to the women stemmed from the way he felt about them. Maria had done him dirty. So had his sister, and he saw his mother do things sexually that no child should ever see a mother do. Reds thought all women were backstabbing whores, so he treated them this way during sex. He didn't often tell women how he felt about them, but he showed them every time he had sex.

Reds took Juanita in her bedroom and pulled her tights off. Juanita didn't have on any panties; her pussy was shaved bald. Reds pushed her on the bed and started eating her pussy. He stuck two fingers inside of her while he licked on her clit. He sucked on her pussy and finger-fucked her until he felt her body quiver, and she came.

"I want you inside me, papi," Juanita moaned softly.

"Shut the fuck up, bitch!" Reds said as he flipped her over and started eating her ass.

Juanita was shocked by the way Reds was talking and manhandling her, but she liked it. She felt like he was taking it even though she was giving it to him. "Ohhhh my god, this feels so good!" Juanita moaned.

Reds was licking her ass and rubbing her clit.

"I'm . . . I'm . . . I'm cummin'," Juanita moaned loudly. "Oh yes, just like that, boo!"

Reds flipped her back over and put her legs up on his shoulders. He started long-dicking her. Every time Reds pushed inside of her, he rammed himself deep inside of her.

"Oh yeah, beat it up," Juanita moaned.

After a few minutes of that, Reds picked Juanita's petite body up and threw her off the bed onto the floor.

"Ouch!" Juanita screamed in shock. "What the fuck is you doin'?"

Reds dove on top of her, held one of her legs up, and slid himself back inside of her.

"Shut the fuck up, bitch," Reds said. "You wanted this dick! Take it!"

He was pumping away inside of her, then he let her leg go and started choking her. Juanita didn't know what was going on, but she liked this. She felt absolutely powerless. She had men try to be rough before, but never like how Reds was being.

"Fuck me! Fuck me!" Juanita gasped.

Reds took one hand off her neck and slapped the shit out of her. "You love this shit, don't chu?" Reds asked. Reds could see the look of shock and excitement in Juanita's eyes. "Fuckin' whore!" Reds barked.

Juanita was feeling like she never felt before. She was at a loss for words. She just shook her head yes. Reds pulled himself out of her, then he flipped her over once again. Juanita was amazed with how strong Reds was.

*This nigga is an animal,* she thought to herself. *What the fuck happened to him in jail?*

Reds now had Juanita face down, ass up. His hand was on the back of her neck tightly. He fucked her hard from the back. He slapped her ass hard and yanked on her hair as she screamed out in pleasure and pain. Reds slowed his strokes and put his thumb in his mouth. Once he was satisfied that it was wet enough, he gently slid his thumb in Juanita's ass while his dick slowly went in and out of her pussy.

"Fuck me harder like a slut. That's right! Slut-fuck me! It's yours!" Juanita yelled as she felt herself start to orgasm. She couldn't believe what she just said to Reds. He had her saying shit she couldn't believe she was saying. She had never acted like this during sex. Reds made her feel comfortable talking like that. He made her feel like she could let go and not be ashamed.

Juanita came several times, but it was Reds's turn now. As he felt himself about to release, he pulled out of Juanita and turned her around, so she sucked his dick.

"Open up," Reds said as he grabbed the sides of her face. Reds started thrusting into Juanita's face furiously like he was fucking a pussy. Occasionally, he'd go too far down her throat and make her gag. "Don't throw up on this dick," Reds growled.

He pumped away until he came. Juanita spit his semen into a cup after Reds pulled out of her mouth. She didn't mind Reds cumming in her mouth, but she didn't like to swallow. They both lay on the floor next to each other, sweating.

"Yo, jail changed you! I ain't never been fucked like that in my life.

You was on some Tarzan, 'knock a bitch out and take it' type shit," Juanita said as they both laughed.

Reds and Juanita both lay in her bed, sleeping comfortably. They were awakened by Juanita's phone ringing. Juanita looked at the number before she answered.

"Hey, baby," Juanita said.

She was obviously talking to her man. He must have asked what she was doing. "Oh, nothin'. I just got finished workin' out. I was layin' here, thinkin' 'bout chu," Juanita said.

As soon as she said that, Reds climbed on top of her. Juanita smiled at Reds as her boyfriend talked on the phone. Reds opened Juanita's legs. She mouthed the word *no*, but didn't put up any other type of fight. As she talked to her boyfriend, Reds slid himself inside of her. Juanita let out a moan. "Ummm!"

Her boyfriend must have asked what she was doing. "I told you I was thinkin' 'bout chu. You want some phone sex," Juanita asked as in a very sexual tone as Reds slid in and out of her. "Okay, I love you too. Hurry up and get home, daddy."

It was when Reds heard what Juanita said to her man that he thought to himself, *I'm in another man's bed with another man's bitch, and after all that just transpired, she talks to him without the slightest trace of guilt in her voice.* Reds pulled out of Juanita and got dressed. *Bitches ain't shit,* Reds thought to himself.

Reds went to J.R.'s after his session with Juanita. He wanted to talk to his cousin about some plans he had. "With Nice gone, I'm'a need a new connect," Reds said.

"I can't think of nobody offhand, not nobody that would be able to cover ya orders. A lot of niggas be frontin' like they got it but only be grabbin' like nine ounces," J.R. responded.

"Fuck it, I just gotta throw my line out and see if I get a bite," Reds said.

"I ain't did no hustlin' for years. I don't have no outlets," J.R. said.

"That might not be a bad thing. I was thinkin' 'bout tryin' somethin' new anyway," Reds said.

"I'm sure this gonna be good," J.R. said.

"I'm tryin' to fuck with the e-pills. I was kickin' it with a nigga from Jersey while I was booked. He said his people got the e-pills on smash out there. I asked 'em 'bout prices, and he said it depends on how much I'm grabbin'. But if I get a lot, they cheap as hell," Reds said.

"Is the nigga official? You know how niggas be lyin'," J.R. questioned.

"You never know 'til it go down, but it's worth a shot. Nigga was always gettin' visits, always had his own, and he was makin' moves. A few people vouched for 'im too," Reds said.

"If you think the risk is worth the reward, holla at the nigga and see what he talkin' 'bout. But I don't want chu goin' up there without me, just in case them niggas try some sucka shit," J.R. said.

"Sounds good to me. He 'posed to get out next week. Matter of fact, they havin' block-out right now," Reds said as he pulled out his cell phone. "I can get the nigga on the phone right now."

Reds and Tone chopped it up for a couple minutes, then he asked him to put Sticks on the phone. A few minutes later, Sticks got on the phone. "What's poppin', Reds?" he asked.

Reds told him that he needed to holla at his peoples.

"Look, I fucks with the green. So I don't have to be out there for you to make the move. I'll call my folks and tell 'em you gonna be callin'. As long as I give the go 'head, they gonna fuck with you," Sticks said.

"I can dig it, but I ain't in no rush. I'd rather wait 'til you get out though. I'll call once you home," Reds said.

"Well, I'm out next week. Take down this number and call it next weekend. We can all meet up," Sticks said.

After Reds took the number, it was set. Reds and J.R. would meet Sticks and his peoples in East Orange, New Jersey.

## 22

Friday night came, and Reds's party was packed. There were naked strippers serving drinks. They had a wet wifebeater contest, a cutest thong contest, and an oral sex contest in which Nice, J.R., and Reds were judges. Iesha, a pretty brown-skinned chick with a full set of lips won the oral sex contest. She made Reds cum in thirty seconds. Some of the other girls were hating, blaming Reds's premature ejaculation on his recent release from prison, not Iesha's head.

"Them bitches just hatin' on my girl Iesha. I was in the county fuckin' bitches every night. My stamina definitely ain't the issue. It's a lotta chick's in here that can vouch for my stamina. This bitch just got the mouth of a god. Iesha should be givin' lessons in colleges around the world. Every woman in the world should know how to suck dick like that," Reds announced.

"Them bitches can't do it like me," Iesha said as she counted her $500 cash prize.

Reds stepped off the stage and saw a familiar face, Erin.

"I see you still doin' big thangs," she said.

"Why wouldn't I be?" Reds responded with pride. "You ain't lookin' so bad ya'self."

"I'm just came over to express how jealous I am," Erin said.

"What chu jealous for?" Reds asked.

"I'm feelin' a lil' neglected. I feel like I should be gettin' more attention than these other bitches," Erin said.

"I'm sayin' you can get all the attention you want when the party is over," Reds said. "I've had a thing for you for a while. So I definitely wouldn't mind givin' you all the attention you want."

"That means you comin' home with me?" Erin asked.

"I think that can be arranged," Reds responded as he undressed Erin with his eyes. He couldn't wait to see how she looked in her birthday suit.

Erin wore a dark blue pair of Armani jeans that hugged her hips, thighs, and backside, a white Armani shirt that hugged her top half beautifully, and a black pair of Prada heels. Her hair was in micro-braids, and pulled back in a bun, showing off her pretty face. As Reds admired her beauty, he grew more anxious at the thought of physically enjoying her body. As those thoughts raced through his mind, Reds saw Coco, one of the strippers that were serving drinks.

"Come here, Coco," Reds said as he flagged her down.

Coco walked over, and Reds introduced her to Erin. "Her glass stays full for the rest of the night," Reds told Coco.

Reds then turned to Erin, "Drink up! It's on the house. You gonna need to be drunk so it won't hurt as much," Reds said.

After he said that, Reds walked away, leaving Erin and Coco both standing there with a smile on their faces. Reds was hoping his plan worked. He needed Erin to get as drunk as she possibly could.

As Reds searched for Nice and J.R., he felt someone grab his arm. He turned around and saw Nikki standing there, looking sexy as hell. She had her hair straightened and wore little makeup. She had on a pink Baby Phat sweat suit that fit her body well and a pair of white and pink Air Force Ones.

"So you get outta jail, now you don't know nobody. Nigga, you called me every day when you was in the county. Why you ain't called since you got out? I been here all night waitin' to see if you was gonna come and holla at me. But you too busy gettin' ya dick sucked and all that other dumb shit. What the fuck was that shit about?" Nikki asked with a major attitude.

"You bitches fuck me up!" Reds said as he laughed. "Okay, you held a nigga down while I was in the county, *but* I was locked up! You was out here goin' clubbin', fuckin', suckin', and doin' you. Now I'm home, I'm 'posed to play myself and wife you? You sound stupid!"

"Ma'fucka, I wasn't fuckin' no niggas 'cause you asked me not to. Yeah, I went clubbin', but—"

Reds cut her off midsentence. "I asked you not to fuck no other niggas that was in the county 'cause I didn't want other niggas hatin' on me. I don't know what you was doin' out here," Reds said.

"I'm tellin' you! I wasn't fuckin' with no other niggas," Nikki said.

"God told Eve not to eat that forbidden fruit. As soon as she thought God wasn't lookin', she ate the ma'fuckin' fruit. If a bitch won't listen to God, why would I think a bitch is gonna listen to Reds?"

"That's some real fucked-up shit, Reds. You's a real piece of shit," Nikki said.

"I've been called worse for less," Reds said. "Don't be mad. You did you while I was booked. Now it's my turn to do me. But if you don't have a problem with that, we can get together sometimes, and do us."

"I can't fuckin' believe you," Nikki said.

"Me neither, but you enjoy the party. Drinks is on the house," Reds said as he walked away.

Reds walked up to J.R. and Nice. "Remind me to kick ya ass later," Reds told Nice.

"Kick my ass for what?" Nice asked with his hands up like he was being robbed.

"For puttin' that stalkin'-ass guard bitch on me," Reds said.

"My bad, baby boy, but I had to get that bitch off me. I figured I'd be killin' two birds with one stone. I'd get you some pussy and get her off my ass," Nice said.

Reds listened to what Nice had just told him. He thought Nice just put in a good word. He didn't know Nice used to fuck her. *Bitches ain't shit*, Reds thought to himself. Reds thought of something J.R. had told him a long time ago: "You can never wife a bitch while you in the game. You'll never have enough time for them both."

That statement was so true because here was Nikki was tripping, demanding time like she was wifey. The truth was Reds just hadn't gotten around to calling her yet. He had just come home and was trying to get situated. He would have told her that, but she was bugging like he owed her something, so he let her have it. Reds didn't feel like he owed any chick anything. Reds also wasn't really feeling the fact that Nice had put a crazy stalker on him. If Nice knew she was clingy like that, he should have never tried to put her on him. But Nice did because it was convenient for him. Reds was starting to understand that when you are in the streets, people only want something to do with you when you can do something for them. Everybody is suspect and always expect the unexpected. That was what life had taught him.

At 2:00 a.m., Erin was completely wasted. She staggered over to Reds. "Let's go sexy," she said.

"I gotta drop my cousin off at his house, then I'll meet you at cha spot. Take ya sexy ass home and get ready for me," Reds instructed.

"The key will be in the mailbox," Erin told Reds. "I'll be in the bed waitin'."

Reds nodded and walked over to Nice. "Yo, I got a mission for us."

"If some pussy is involved, you already know I'm with it," Nice said.

"I got two bitches from Widener University that's tryin' to smut. J.R. already got somethin' lined up, so I figured me and you can fuck 'em, switch 'em, then ditch 'em," Reds said.

"That sounds good. Plus, I gotta holla at chu 'bout somethin' on the way up there," Nice said.

"A'ight, follow me down Adams Street. I'm gonna drop my car off there and ride up with you," Reds said.

Once Reds knew what was up, he walked over to J.R. and hugged him. "Thanks for the party, cuz. I couldn't have thrown a better joint myself," Reds said. "I'll call you tomorrow. Me and Nice 'bout to go fuck these bitches from Widener."

"Be careful," J.R. said.

Nice was standing right there while they had this conversation, but he was oblivious to what was really being said.

"Nigga, you know I'm'a be careful. I ain't fuckin' nothin' without strappin' up," Reds responded.

Nice gave J.R. some love, then they headed out.

Reds made sure he and Nice left in separate vehicles. That way, nobody could say they saw them leave together. J.R. was inside, helping clean up. He'd stay there for at least an hour or more, so his alibi would check out. Reds would park in front of Erin's house, hoping his car would be seen there all night. He planned on blasting his music, so one of the neighbors would wake up and notice his car for making the noise. He would also be able to use Erin as an alibi. Reds would make her believe he was there all night. She was so drunk that she wouldn't know if he was or not. Everything was in place. All Reds had to do was pull this off smoothly.

Earlier in the day, J.R. gave Reds a 9-millimeter to use as the throwaway gun. All night, Reds acted as if he was a little tipsy, but he was very much on point. He told everybody that he was drinking vodka and cranberry, but he was really just drinking cranberry juice. Nice wasn't on point at all. He had no idea he was a marked man.

On the ride to Chester, Nice explained to Reds that since the feds were on his ass, he planned to fall back. "I know that bitch got you for ya stash, so this is what I'm'a do. I got ten bricks right now that I'll front chu. Just give me back $22,000 of each joint. Once you run through them, I'll introduce you to my connect. All I want in return is a check. You'll be gettin' birds for $17,000. All I'm askin' for is $1,000 of every bird, you know, for givin' you the connect," Nice said.

*Damn! Why the fuck this nigga gotta be a rat?* Reds thought to himself. "I'm with it," Reds said. "I really wanna thank you for the opportunity too. You and J.R. been like big brothers to me."

Reds wished he could wait until he got the bricks, but J.R.'s freedom was at stake. There was also a possibility that Nice could be trying to set Reds up too. They talked a little more on the ride up about this and that. What Reds found strange was that not once did Nice ever mention even the possibility of doing time for his recent indictment.

They pulled up on a dark street, right around the corner from the college. Reds pretended to be talking to the girls on the phone. "Yeah, we right 'round the corner in a white Jag. Is we goin' to a hotel, or y'all dorm? A'ight," Reds said as he hung up the phone. "They comin' right now. We goin' in they dorm."

Reds got out of the car. Nice followed. As Reds got out of the car, he took the 9-millimeter off his waist and slid it in his front pocket. They stood outside the car, and Reds described the fictitious women to Nice.

After a few minutes, Nice asked, "Where the fuck is these bitches?"

"There they go right there," Reds said, pointing in the other direction.

Nice looked in the direction that Reds had pointed. As soon as Nice turned his head, Reds drew his 9-millimeter and fired. *BOOM! BOOM! BOOM!*

Nice was dead before he hit the ground. Reds took everything out of his pockets, then he checked him for a wire. Once he was satisfied that Nice wasn't wired for sound, he slipped into the darkness. Reds caught the Septa bus back to West Chester. When he got to Erin's house, she was knocked out cold, just like he planned.

*Another job well done,* Reds thought to himself.

Erin woke up the next morning and saw Reds doing push-ups. It had become a ritual of Reds's to do five hundred push-ups as soon as he woke up. When he stood, he saw Erin staring at him. When Erin got a look at Reds's pumped arms and chest, she became moist.

"You look even better without clothes on," Erin said.

"I wish I could say the same thing 'bout chu, but I haven't seen you without clothes yet," Reds said. "How 'bout you take ya clothes off and we take a shower?"

"That could work," Erin said as she undressed. "What time did you get here last night?"

"I came in at like two-thirty. You was out. Since you looked all peaceful, I figured I'd let you sleep, and do somethin' nasty to you when you woke up," Reds said.

Erin crawled her naked body to the edge of the bed and pulled Reds's boxers down.

"Oh, you ain't tryin' to take a shower?" Reds asked.

"I like a lil' salt on my meat," Erin said as she grabbed Reds's sweaty dick and placed it in her mouth. "Ummm," she moaned as she took Reds in and out of her mouth.

"I love a nasty bitch," Reds moaned.

Erin stopped sucking Reds's dick and told him to lie on the bed. She climbed in between Reds's legs and began to suck his dick again. After a few minutes, she sucked on his balls, then she went a little lower. She licked Reds's ass for a minute. Reds had never experienced something that felt so good in his life. He was so caught up in the feeling that it didn't even register what was going on. Once he realized it was his ass she was licking, he wanted to tell her to stop, but it felt too good. Reds just lay in the bed in a state of bliss.

Erin went back to sucking his dick then his balls. Reds thought that her next stop would be back to his ass. *I can't let this bitch violate me again. Something that feels that good gotta be forbidden,* Reds thought to himself. He had to act fast to stop her. Reds pulled Erin up to his face and rolled on top of her.

"I want that pussy," Reds said. Reds slid himself inside of her.

Erin wasn't doing anything. She just lay there. Reds dug himself deep inside of her, still nothing. Her pussy was tight, so he knew she wasn't a whore, and his dick was far from little. Reds could tell by some of the faces that she was making that she was feeling something. She was wincing, but it was like she was afraid to make noise. Reds put her legs up so he could dig in deep.

"Oh no, nigga, you ain't killin' me," Erin said.

"Well, if you feelin' somethin', why don't you make some noise?" Reds said in an irritated tone. One thing that Reds hated was a dead fuck, and that's exactly what Erin was.

"Oohhh!" Erin moaned.

Reds slapped her hard in her face, trying to get her to get into it. "Shut the fuck up bitch!" Reds barked.

He could tell as soon as he did it, she wasn't feelin' it. She had a look of shock on her face.

"Hold the fuck up! What the fuck was that?" Erin snapped as she held the side of face.

"Rough sex," Reds said like it was nothing.

"This ain't no fuckin' porno, nigga. Don't do that shit again. I ain't one of them freak-ass white bitches you be fuckin'. I don't like that shit," Erin said.

That moment killed the whole mood. Reds didn't even want to finish having sex with Erin. It was like having sex with a corpse. He stroked a few more times then acted like he came. He got dressed and acted like he got an important phone call so he could leave.

*I guess all bitches don't like rough sex,* Reds thought to himself. He didn't really care though. The only thing Erin did that Reds liked was lick his ass, and he would never let that happen again. It felt amazing, but it made Reds feel violated at the same time. He just didn't like the thought of another person's tongue in his ass. He didn't mind licking a woman's ass, but his ass was off-limits. That was a seal that wasn't supposed to be broken.

## 23

Reds talked to J.R. the day after he killed Nice to let him know that everything went smoothly. As always, J.R. already knew Nice was dead. Jimmy called him about an hour before Reds stopped by and gave him the news. Jimmy told J.R. that Nice was killed during what appeared to be a robbery, but the feds were asking questions because Nice was a federal informant. Jimmy told J.R. that he made some calls and found out that Nice had cut a deal to give up his connect in Florida. Neither Reds's or J.R.'s name was mentioned.

Reds was glad to hear that Nice was working for the opposition; now he knew he made the right decision by killing him. It made Reds feel good to have knocked a dirty player out the game. Everybody in the streets knows that a snitch anywhere is a threat to a criminal everywhere. Reds was taught to play for keeps, and that's exactly what he did. Reds would put something down without the slightest bit of hesitation. If that's what it took for him and his peoples to live the good life, so be it.

"This shit with Nice is a valuable lesson," J.R. told Reds. "In the streets, you're here today and gone tomorrow. And it's normally a nigga close to you that'll cause your downfall. When you're gone, all you have to be remembered by is your name. Never tarnish your name for nothin'. I want you to give me your word that if I ever give you a reason to doubt me, you'll out me. You family, I love you with all my heart, but believe me—if I ever doubt you, I'm'a out chu. I mean no disrespect by that. I'm just tellin' you the truth."

Reds thought long and hard about what his cousin had told him before he spoke.

"I give you my word," Reds said.

Reds took the next couple of days to get his plans together. He wanted to make the transition from crack to Ecstasy. Ecstasy was a completely different type of hustle. Reds wouldn't have to be in the streets—he could play the party scenes and college campuses. Reds only planned on dealing with females, so he could only imagine how much sex he was going to be having while in his new line of work.

Reds analyzed things while he was in jail. He knew that everybody wanted to be a boss. But not many people knew what came with being a boss. When you're a boss, you're a target for the police, the stickup kids, people looking for handouts, etc.

Reds also knew that he was blessed with the ability to be able to think for himself. Most people are followers—they need to be led. They'll follow you off a cliff if that's where you lead them. Reds was a born leader; he knew it would be easy to get people to follow him.

Reds was tired of doing all the work. While Reds was locked up, he read a quote in a book that said, "To the man who doesn't have to do any of the work, nothing is impossible." It was time for Reds to sit back and get rich while everybody else did all the work. He wasn't greedy. He would let everybody eat. If his plan worked out right, he'd be able to double his money with every new purchase of product without having to lift a finger. Reds would allow his flunkies to look like the boss while he stayed in the background and got rich. He just needed the right connect and some workers. The plan was perfect. All he had to do was put it in motion.

It was Friday, and Reds would be going to New Jersey tomorrow. It was time for him to talk to his first worker, Juanita. Reds didn't want Juanita selling anything. She would be his driver in addition to providing a place for him to stash his product just as she had done before. Reds went to Juanita's apartment. He knocked on the door.

"Who is it?" Juanita asked.

"It's Reds," he replied.

She opened the door "I was wonderin' when you was gonna call me," Juanita said.

"I've been busy," Reds responded. "But look, I need to holla at chu 'bout some paper. Is this a good time?"

"Yeah, come on in," Juanita said.

"A'ight look, I need somebody to drive me and my cousin to New Jersey a couple times a month. I'll pay for the rental car and all that. I gotta go up there to pick up some e-pills. Once we get the pills, me and my cousin is gonna be catchin' the train back to West Chester. You'll drive the pills back, and we'll meet chu back here. I'll pay you $500 a trip," Reds said.

"Why is y'all catchin' the train back?" Juanita asked.

"I don't want the cops to get crazy if you get pulled over. If you get pulled over by yourself, they won't suspect anything unless you actin' funny. If you got two black men in your car, they might wanna search. Dig me? It's all about takin' the least amount of risk," Reds explained.

"I don't know how I let chu talk me into this kind of stuff. I'm only doin' it 'cause last time you had somebody else do somethin' for you, you got robbed. I don't wanna see that happen again," Juanita said. "Call me when it's time to go. But I can only do it on the weekends. I work durin' the week."

"That's fine. Are you sure you don't gotta talk with ya man first? I don't want him to not be feelin' it, then you change ya mind on me," Reds said.

"You ain't gotta worry 'bout that. He's gone," Juanita said.

"What chu mean gone?" Reds asked.

"I mean he's not my man anymore. I kicked him out the same night I gave you some pussy. I realized he wasn't the man for me," Juanita said.

Reds just smiled. *I got shorty on smash,* Reds thought to himself. "A'ight well, we takin' our first trip tomorrow," Reds said.

"I'll be ready. Matter fact, why don't you just spend the night here," Juanita said with a sexy grin.

Saturday morning came, and Reds woke up, did his push-ups, then woke Juanita up. She was lying in the bed naked. Reds bit her softly on her butt. "Wake up, sunshine. We got moves to make," Reds called out.

Juanita didn't even wanna fuck after the session they had the night before. While Juanita got ready, Reds went to pick J.R. up. They doubled back to Juanita's, then she followed them to the train station. Reds parked his car at the train station, and he and J.R. hopped in the car with Juanita.

When they pulled into the McDonald's on Central Avenue, Reds called the number that Sticks had given him. Reds talked to a guy named Lil' Man. Lil' Man told Reds that Sticks had spoken highly of him. Reds got right to business and told Lil' Man where he was. Lil' Man agreed to meet him.

Twenty minutes later, Sticks and Lil' Man walked in the McDonald's.

"What's poppin'?" Sticks asked as he shook Reds's hand.

Sticks formally introduced Reds to Lil' Man. Reds could see why they called him Lil' Man. He was only about five feet tall. Sticks, Reds, and Lil' Man all sat at a different booth, leaving Juanita and J.R. sitting alone.

"So how much you gonna charge me for the thousand pills?" Reds asked.

"$3 a pill," Lil' Man answered.

Reds was pleased with his answer. He planned on paying around $5 a pill. "Okay, I'll take a thousand pills. This is only a trial run. If the pills is fire, I'll grab five thousand next time," Reds said.

"If you buy five thousand, I'll take a dollar off each pill. Only catch is that you gotta buy at least five thousand every time," Lil' Man said.

"That's understandable," Reds said. "These ain't no single stacks, is they?"

"All you gonna get from me is triple stacks," Lil' Man said proudly.

"That's what the fuck I'm talkin' 'bout," Reds said with a smile.

Lil' Man went on to tell Reds that he'd be getting pills called Starburst and T-Mac's. Reds was liking everything he was hearing so far. He just hoped it didn't end up being too good to be true. There was a chance that they'd get back to West Chester and some or all of the pills would be fake. Reds knew that in the streets, you had to be willing to take chances if you wanted to succeed.

There was always one question that Reds would ask himself—was the risk worth the reward? In this case, it definitely was. If the pills were fake, Reds would only be losing $3,000. He took $5,000 out of Nice's pockets after he killed him, so he really wouldn't be taking a loss. But if the pills were good, Reds would be clearing $7,000 profit. The best part was that Reds would make the $7,000 without having to lift a finger. Reds liked his odds in this particular situation.

Lil' Man made a phone call. "I need a thousand. Make 'em half and half. Meet me at the McDonald's on Central," he said.

Ten minutes later, a skinny but cute brown-skinned chick came in and sat with them. She had a book bag slung over her shoulder. She talked to Lil' Man with a thick Jamaican accent for a minute, then she got up and ordered some food. When she got up, she left the book bag sitting with them.

"Your pills are in the bag. If you'd like, you can go in the bathroom and count 'em," Lil' Man spoke.

"No need. I don't think y'all would play no games over $3,000. You'd have to be some real broke-ass niggas to do that," Reds said.

"Come on, Reds, you know me better than that," Sticks said.

"There's ten bags with a hundred pills in each bag. That's my word," Lil' Man said. "These pills are fresh, so as soon as you take 'em, you're gonna have to take a shit," Lil' Man said.

Reds handed him a wad of cash. "Wanna count it?" Reds asked.

"If you didn't have $3,000 to spend, my peoples would have never gave you my number. I trust that it's all there," Lil' Man said.

"I should be back in a week," Reds said.

"We gon' make a lotta money together," Lil' Man said.

"I hope so," Reds said.

He gave Juanita the book bag and told her to jump right on the highway and head home. He and J.R. would get a ride to the train station with Sticks and Lil' Man.

Reds and J.R. got to the train station in Exton and hopped in Reds's car.

"You trust shorty with ya pills?" J.R. asked.

"Her mom lives in Union Court. Her brother and sister got an apartment together out by the hospital. She knows I know where they live at. I don't trust her, but I don't think she's that stupid. She heard stories 'bout a nigga," Reds said.

"I heard that," J.R. said, proud of his cousin's way of thinking.

"With Nice gone, how you lookin' on the money side of things? If shit ain't right, we can get this money together," Reds offered.

"I appreciate the offer, family, but I'm good on the money side of things. Matter of fact, fuck good. I'm grrrrreat!" J.R. said like Tony the Tiger. "I think I'm'a retire."

Reds laughed at J.R.'s Tony the Tiger imitation then said, "Sounds like a plan. But if I ever need you—"

"If you ever need me, I'll be there," J.R. interrupted.

Reds dropped J.R. off then headed to Juanita's. Juanita gave Reds an extra key to her apartment the night before. Reds sat in the house, watching television for almost a half an hour before Juanita came home. She handed Reds the book bag as she sat next to him. Reds pulled out $500 and gave it to her.

"Thank you, baby," Juanita said as she put the money in her pocket.

"No, thank you," Reds said.

"You know I always got chu," Juanita said with a smile. "But you know how to thank me."

"Yo, you a fuckin' nympho! I never seen nobody that likes to fuck more than you," Reds said.

"What can I say? I'm a man eater," she said with a laugh.

"You a fuckin' freak! I'll be back later. I need you to put these up for me. I'll bring a safe when I come back," Reds said. Reds kept one of the sandwich bags of pills and gave Juanita the other nine. He didn't really trust Juanita, but after what he went through with Maria, who could blame him? Reds just told himself that he would never give her something that he couldn't afford to lose.

"This must mean you payin' my rent again?" Juanita asked with a smile.

Reds just laughed. "Yeah, rent on me."

Reds's next stop was West Chester University. He met a beauty named Tyesha who went to school there. He met her at Burger King. She was eating by herself, so he just sat down and joined her. After talking for a while, he got her number. Reds had spoken to her a few times since, but today would be the first time they got together. When she told Reds she attended the university, he immediately saw earning potential in her. Reds knew that most college kids were having financial troubles, and they liked to party. Reds would use this to his advantage. He could give them a way to fix their financial situation and party at the same time. He figured he could use this same technique on strippers, but for now, his attention was on Tyesha.

Reds knocked on Tyesha's door.

"Hey, sexy," Tyesha said as she opened the door.

Reds gave her a hug then went inside. Tyesha was a petite chick. She had a cocoa complexion with hazel eyes; her breasts were the size of large grapefruit. She had a nice bubble butt for her size, and her smile was beautiful and radiant. As soon as Reds went in, he started running game. "I was just in the area, so I figured I'd stop by," Reds said.

"I'm glad you did," Tyesha said.

"So what's good? Any parties tonight?" Reds asked.

"This is a college campus—there's parties every night," Tyesha said.

"Do anybody be havin' any good e-pills?" Reds asked.

"It's this guy named Rico. He be havin' 'em sometimes," Tyesha said.

"Triple stacks?" Reds questioned.

"Naw, double," Tyesha said. "You ain't gonna find too many people with triple stacks 'round here."

"So how much he be chargin' for the pills?" Reds asked.

"$20," Tyesha responded.

Now it was time for Reds to bait her in. He remembered the first phone conversation they had. He asked Tyesha where she was taking him for their first date. She told Reds that she didn't have money to take him anywhere but Burger King. Reds would offer her a chance to make some money now.

"So if I told I know somebody that got triple stacks for $20, what would you say?" Reds asked.

"I'd say you're bullshittin' or the pills are trash," Tyesha responded.

"The pills are official," Reds shot back.

"Who would do that?" Tyesha asked.

"You," Reds said as he pulled out the bag of pills and threw them to her. "These are called Starburst. Sell 'em for $20 a pill. You take $10 and give me $10 off every pill. That's a $1,000 for each of us. The best part about this lil' deal of ours is that you never have to pay for anything up front. How long will it take you to move those hundred pills?" Reds asked.

"Don't play with me," Tyesha said with a big smile that let Reds know she was with it.

"I don't play, baby girl. I know you could use the money, so I'm helpin' you out. In return for my good deed, you'll pay me half of everything you make. One hand washes the other. What chu say?" Reds asked.

"I say hell yeah," Tyesha said. "I can move at least a hundred pills a day. Probably more on nights when I go to parties."

"Didn't you say this was a sorority house?" Reds asked as he got an idea.

"Yeah," Tyesha answered.

"Okay, I want you and your sorority sisters to throw a party seven nights a week. Whoever shows up gotta buy one pill to get in. Once they get in, keep sellin' 'em. As people start drinkin' and dancin', they'll buy more. If people are payin' $20 for double stacks, you'll shut shit down sellin' triple stacks for the same price," Reds said.

"I gotta talk to my sorority sisters 'bout the parties, but I'm definitely tryin' to make some money," Tyesha said.

"If they willin' to throw parties every night, I'll deck this whole place out. Let everybody in the house see a lil' somethin' off what's goin' on. If everybody is eatin', everybody is happy. Whatever you work out with them is on you. They answer to you. You answer to me. All I ask is that you keep our business between us," Reds said.

"A'ight, I'll call you tonight and let chu know what's up," Tyesha shot back.

"Sounds good. Oh, and don't say nothin' over the phone that you wouldn't say in front of the police," Reds warned.

"Nigga, I'm from the hood, Riverside Projects! I know what to say and what not to say on the phone," Tyesha said with a laugh. "So these pills is mine, right?"

"I gave 'em to you. Go ahead and get money," Reds said. "Call me later."

Later on, that night, Tyesha called Reds. "Hey, boo, I gotta headache. Can you bring me a bottle of Aspirin?" she asked.

Reds understood exactly what she was asking for. He was just shocked at how fast she moved the pills. Reds took another hundred pills to Tyesha, and she gave him $1,000. She told Reds that everybody liked the pills. She also advised him not to go too far—she'd be calling soon.

It was Sunday night, and Tyesha had run through five hundred pills. Whoever said money is the best motivator damn sure wasn't lying. It had only been a little more than a day, and Tyesha had made $10,000, half of which went to Reds. When Reds dropped off the fifth bag to her, she asked him to double her order from a hundred to two hundred.

In less than a week, Tyesha went from Old Navy and sneakers to Dolce & Gabbana and heels. Tyesha was one hell of a hustler. She had the sorority house doing big numbers. She told Reds that only one of her sorority sisters was willing to help her move the pills, but nobody objected to the house being decked out or parties every night.

The last time Reds talked to Tyesha, she looked like she was about to pass out. Reds told her to get some sleep. She said she had been up for three days, hustling.

"Let cha sorority sister take over for a while," Reds said.

Tyesha put up a fight. Reds told her that he wouldn't give her any more pills if she didn't get some sleep. She finally agreed and told him she was gonna let her sorority sister knock the batch he just given her off.

Reds loved Tyesha's drive-though. He had a good feeling about her. They could do big things together.

## 24

By Wednesday, Reds had to go see Lil' Man. Reds asked Juanita to call in sick and take him to Jersey. Juanita told Reds she couldn't call off work, so he offered her $1,000 to take him, which Juanita quickly accepted. Reds took $10,000 to Jersey and saw Lil' Man.

Just as they had before, things went smoothly. Once Reds and Juanita met back up at her apartment, she told Reds that he didn't have to pay her if he spent the day with her. Reds couldn't argue with a deal like that. He and Juanita stayed in the house all day, and to Reds' surprise, he actually liked hanging out with Juanita.

Thursday morning, Reds met Tyesha at the Burger King around the corner from the university. She gave Reds $2,000. Reds had a surprise for Tyesha. She had proven to be hungry as far as money was concerned. So Reds decided to give her a boost of confidence. He wanted to do something to let her know he thought she was doing a good job. Even though he didn't trust her, he wanted her to think he did.

"You been doin' ya thing, girl. So as a show of confidence, I'm gonna give you a thousand pills this time. As always, the split is fifty-fifty, $10,000 for me, $10,000 for you. You cool with that?" Reds asked.

"How I'm gonna argue with that?" Tyesha responded.

She was grateful for what Reds was doing for her. Her confidence had been through the roof since she started getting money. She wasn't a bum chick before she met Reds, but she damned sure wasn't on the level she was on now. Tyesha was from Riverside Projects in Delaware. She was always a cool chick, but she was a cool-ass broke chick. She was working at McDonald's in order to get through school.

In the short time she had known Reds, Tyesha had come up. Tyesha no longer had to wear sweatpants and T-shirts everywhere. She had designer clothes now. She didn't have to walk everywhere; she bought a car. She didn't have to live off ramen soups anymore—she ate wherever she wanted. Tyesha was broke when she met Reds, so it was only natural for her to be truly appreciative for the money Reds was putting in her pocket.

She looked at Reds like a big brother in certain ways. She also found him to be extremely attractive as well.

As they sat and talked, Tyesha told Reds about this guy from campus. "So I been tryna holla at this nigga for a second, but he been too busy. Well, since I got the best e-pills around, everybody is on my dick. Now all of a sudden, he got time for a bitch. So I had this nigga come to the sorority house with me and my sisters, then we trained 'em," Tyesha said proudly.

"'Trained 'em' as in everybody fucked 'em?" Reds asked with shock.

"Hell no! 'Trained 'em' like I had him eat everybody's pussy in the house on tape. Then I had 'em lick my ass. Then I kicked his stupid ass out," Tyesha said with a laugh.

Tyesha felt comfortable talking to Reds about things like that. She knew he liked her because he approached her when they first met and told her. But since they were getting money together, Tyesha thought Reds might not want to mess that up. She understood and didn't want to mess it up either. She did, however, want to have sex with Reds. So Tyesha told him stories like the one she just had because she wanted him to know that she was capable of having sex without any attachments. Her plan worked beautifully.

Reds got a good laugh out of her story. He thought of all the times men degraded women. It was hilarious that a man would let a woman play him like that just because she was getting money. "Damn, you got a nigga jealous," Reds said.

"Jealous for what?" Tyesha responded.

"I'm tryna get trained! I'll sling this dick on tape, but I ain't eatin' no pussy or no ass," Reds said.

"All you gotta do is ask. You keep a bitch paid. Ain't nothin' you could ask for that I wouldn't do. How 'bout a fivesome? Me, you, and three of my sisters," Tyesha said.

"Goddamn, now that's what I call a dream come true," Reds said in excitement.

"But there's one condition: I'm fuckin' you first by myself," Tyesha said.

"That was gonna happen anyway," Reds said. "So when we gonna make this happen?"

"We can do it now," Tyesha said.

This was something that Reds loved about Tyesha. She was down for whatever, whenever.

Tyesha and Reds went back to the house.

"I'm 'bout to stunt on these bitches," Tyesha said.

"What chu talkin' 'bout?" Reds asked.

"I'm'a fuck you in front of everybody. I'm not lettin' nobody join 'til next time. Is you cool with that?" Tyesha asked.

"That's just promotion for me. Why wouldn't I be down with it?" Reds responded.

They went upstairs, and Tyesha showed Reds where her room was. He got undressed while she went and filled her sisters in on what was going on. Tyesha came back in the room and took her clothes off. Reds sat on her bed in his boxers and enjoyed the show.

Tyesha was built like she ran track. Her ass was tight, and her breasts were perky. Her stomach was flat, and her hips were crazy. Tyesha's pubic hairs were trimmed closely. She walked over to Reds and started to kiss on his chest. She then made her way down to his stomach. Reds's manhood began to harden. Tyesha noticed the bulge in his boxer briefs. She took his underwear off and got a pleasant surprise.

"Damn! You workin' with somethin'," Tyesha said pleasantly. Tyesha placed Reds' manhood in her mouth and worked her magic.

"Ummm, that's a girl. Put all this dick down ya throat," Reds moaned.

Tyesha was trying to deep-throat Reds, but she couldn't—he was too big. After several attempts, she gave up. Her eyes were watering, and she had slobber all over her chin.

Reds looked at Tyesha's face and was instantly turned on. He loved it when things got sloppy during oral sex—that was sexy to him. Tyesha lifted up Reds's shaft and started sucking his balls. Reds was excited now and ready to get to it.

"Stand up. I want you to put one leg on the bed and lean over a lil'," Reds instructed.

She followed his orders, and Reds slid himself inside of her. Tyesha's pussy felt good. She was tight as hell and wet as a waterfall. On top of that, she knew how to fuck. As Reds fucked her from the back, she threw the pussy back. Her pussy felt so good that Reds pulled out and took the condom off.

"I need to feel all this," he said.

"Any way you want it, baby, just don't cum inside me," Tyesha warned.

Reds slid back inside of her. His first few strokes were slow. He wanted to fully enjoy himself. Gradually, he started to speed up and hammer her.

"Oh shit, that feels sooo gooood! Oohhh yeah, beat this pussy up," Tyesha moaned loudly.

Reds was feeding off her words. She had him hyped now. Reds was throwing himself in her, and Tyesha was going crazy. Reds didn't know if she was being loud because of the sex or if she was trying to let her sorority sisters know the show had started. He didn't care though. Tyesha's energy had him in a zone. Reds heard a noise behind him, so he turned his head, but he never stopped stroking Tyesha. He saw two of Tyesha's sorority sisters standing in the doorway. Tyesha's door was wide open. Reds was pounding on Tyesha, but she continued to throw it back.

"That's right. Throw that pussy at me, bitch!" Reds grunted. He pulled out of her and flipped her over on her back. Reds went to the other side of the bed so he could see the doorway. There were now three girls there, all of which were cute. Reds was going to give them exactly what they wanted—a show.

Reds put Tyesha's legs in the air, then he grabbed her waist and slid back inside of her. He hammered away at Tyesha like he was trying to drill through her all the while talking dirty as he intensely stared at her sorority sisters.

"Tell 'em how much you love this dick," Reds barked.

"I love it!" Tyesha cried out as Reds aggressively pumped in and out of her.

Reds was sweating now, which made the scene look even better. The girls were in a trance as they watched Reds do his thing. There wasn't a dry set of panties in the house.

"This nigga is a fuckin' beast," one of the girls said.

As Tyesha started to moan louder, Reds started to choke her.

"Shut the fuck up, bitch, and take this dick!" Reds barked. He could tell that Tyesha was shocked by the fact that she was being choked. He gave her a second to let it sink in. "Yeah, you like this, don't chu?"

Tyesha shook her head yes. Reds pushed himself as deep as he could go inside of her. "Oohhh my god! I can feel it in my stomach!" Tyesha moaned.

Reds pulled out of her and lay on the bed, his erection pointing straight in the air like a rocket.

"He gotta big dick," came from the hallway.

Tyesha climbed on top of Reds and started riding him backward. She was squatting up and down on him as she held on to his ankles for support. The sight of Tyesha's pussy and ass in his face, bouncing up and down on his dick, took Reds there.

"I'm 'bout to cum!" Reds shouted.

Tyesha hopped off Reds. He was looking at her, waiting to see what she was going to do next. He was about to get mad—he wanted to nut. Tyesha grabbed a jar of Vaseline off her dresser. She put Vaseline on the top half of Reds' dick, then she climbed back on top of him. This time, she let Reds go in her ass. Tyesha was very careful with this. She allowed Reds's head to go in slowly, then she moved down about a quarter of the way. Then she took about half of him in her ass. She bounced up and down on the top half of Reds's dick until she got a rhythm.

She was facing Reds now and braced his chest for support. Once she got her motion down, she sped up. She moaned loudly, "Ahh, aahhhh!! Cum in my ass, daddy!"

Reds' excitement level was through the roof now. He looked at the women in the doorway then at Tyesha, then he erupted in Tyesha's ass. Her pussy was so wet that it dripped on his stomach.

"I ain't know you had a shot like that," Reds said.

"You ain't do too bad ya'self," Tyesha said. "I'll tell you what though, that dick brought the best outta bitch."

They both laughed. Reds heard clapping coming from the doorway. All Tyesha's sorority sisters were clapping their hands and whistling.

"You got a card? I might gotta call you. You fuck like a porn star," the short one said.

Reds looked over at Tyesha who was smiling hard. She knew she'd be getting her props after this, and that's exactly what she wanted.

# 25

Over the next month, Reds and Tyesha became super tight. They both kept their promises to each other. Reds spent a little over $10,000 upgrading the sorority house. He bought them a pool table, a hot tub, and a sixty-five-inch flat screen television. Tyesha kept her promise and gave Reds his fivesome. Tyesha and the three sorority sisters that watched him have sex with her did the deed. Reds was shocked when they actually agreed to let him tape it. Tyesha truly was his personal genie. They started in the hot tub and ended up in the living room. Tyesha and her sorority sisters were rolling (high) on e-pills, and Reds was drunk. That was a night that Reds would never forget.

Reds damned near lived in the sorority house. Tyesha had him having sex with just about every chick that came through the house. Tyesha didn't tell anybody who Reds really was. She just said he was some rich kid whose dad left him a bunch of money. So everybody knew he had money, but nobody knew where it was coming from.

A lot of good had happened in the last month. But as the saying goes, "the sun doesn't shine forever." Reds was starting to see that Tyesha was letting her hustling and partying interfere with her school. On top of that, she was getting too high. Tyesha was always high, and she never went to class. She only had three classes, and she had dropped two of them already. Reds warned her that if she failed out of school, she'd be messing their money up. She told Reds she had everything under control. Tyesha had lost a considerable amount of weight since Reds had known her. She was already petite. Now she was starting to look malnourished. Reds didn't even have sex with her anymore. He just had sex with the other chicks in the house. Tyesha asked Reds why he never wanted to have sex anymore, and he was brutally honest.

"I got major love for you, Ty, so I'm'a keep it real wit' chu. You startin' to look sick. I'm around, so I know it's 'cause you gettin' too high. But if I didn't know any better, I might think you had somethin'. Look at chu, baby. You done lost like twenty pounds since I've known you. Slow down. Gettin' too high is gonna be ya downfall," Reds warned.

Reds had to stay on top of Tyesha. She was his cash cow. If she got kicked out of school, she wouldn't be allowed to live on campus, and the thought of that hurt Reds's heart. He was sure she'd still make money if she wasn't in school, but not like she would be making if she was in school. Tyesha had made Reds $60,000 in the last month. Reds planned to grab ten thousand pills on his next trip, and Tyesha was his only worker. She was doing so good that Reds didn't even need to look for more workers. She had things on lock. It was imperative that Reds kept Tyesha on track.

Tyesha heard what Reds was telling her, but she wasn't listening. She thought she knew it all. She was a little hurt by the comment Reds made about her looking sick, so she said, "Fuck him," and she made her mind up that she would go somewhere else for sex.

Tyesha met E at the Granite Run Mall. They exchanged numbers and were keeping in touch. She thought E was cute. He was about her height, slim but muscular, and had a curly hair. E was Puerto Rican and black. He had light skin and emerald-green eyes. Tyesha thought he looked like the rapper Peedi Crakk. E was from Chester. He came by the sorority house a few times and partied. When he came through, Tyesha was rolling as usual and in a good mood. He watched her move pills and count money all night. E liked Tyesha, but he liked money more. He immediately went into scheme mode.

When the party was over, Tyesha took E up to her room, and they had sex. When they were finished, Tyesha wanted to show-off for E, so she pulled out all the money she made for the night and told him she had to go put it up. E didn't know exactly how much it was, but he knew it was a lot. When she came back in the room, E picked her brain.

The Ecstasy had Tyesha's guard down. She was feeling great and was very loose with her information. She bragged about how she was a boss and how much money she made. Tyesha wanted to be a boss. She was now about to find out the price of being a boss. She had made a crucial mistake of revealing too much to the wrong person and ignored the old saying, "bitches can get it too."

It was about 9:00 a.m., and Reds was getting dressed for his aunt's funeral. He wasn't too close to her, but he was going to pay his respects anyway. The funeral was nice except for the part when his crackhead cousin started acting a fool. His cousin, Toni, made a spectacle of his aunt's funeral. Toni was just coming home from rehab and had supposedly found the Lord. She made it a point to cry louder than anybody else. But the real show started when she went up to the casket to say her last good-bye. Toni started acting like she caught the Holy Ghost, then she fainted. When everybody looked at her like she was crazy, Toni jumped back up and tried to get in the casket, screaming, "Take me with you!"

J.R. and Reds sat in the back of the funeral and had a good laugh. That was all they could do. It was shameful—the lengths a person would go to steal another's shine even in death.

After the funeral was over, everybody gathered in the basement of the church to eat. Reds's cousin, Shontae, came over and sat with him and J.R. "Hey, cuz," she said warmly. "Good to see you finally home."

"Good to be home. How you been?" Reds asked as he gave her a hug.

"Great! Me and my man moved to Altoona. Shit's lovely out there," Shontae said.

"Where the fuck is that at?" J.R. asked.

"It's right by Penn State University," she answered.

"What took you out there?" Reds pressed on.

"Well, you know my man, Reem, be movin' that dope," Shontae bragged. "Bundles is goin' for $200! It's a hustla's paradise out there. Coke is $150 a gram. Shit, even regular weed is $10 a gram. They don't even got no syrup or wett [PCP] out there."

"What's the price for triple-stack e-pills? Reds questioned.

"Thirty dollars a pill," she answered.

"Damn, that's nice," Reds said as he turned to J.R.

J.R. nodded his head in approval.

"So I was thinkin', you might be able to help Reem," Shontae said.

"I don't play wingman for nobody," Reds said.

"I know that's right," J.R. said with a laugh.

Now her true agenda was starting to come to light. If she didn't need Reds for something, she would have never disclosed this information to him. Reds knew she was doing more than just making casual conversation.

"I don't mean help like that. One of my homies told me that you was real tight with this chick from the university. I heard she got the best e-pills in town," Shontae said.

"Yeah, that's my buddy," Reds said.

"Okay. If you can plug Reem in with her, he'd plug you into the coke scene out Altoona. Y'all won't be competition to each other. I know all you fuck with is the coke, and all he fucks with is the dope. Plus, he wanna bring the e-pills out there," Shontae said.

"I don't know if shorty sells weight. I don't deal with her like that. We just cool. But give me ya number, and I'll let chu know somethin' soon," Reds said.

She gave Reds her number, then she got up to leave.

"Oh, cuz, one more question," Reds said to Shontae.

"What's up?" she asked.

"Why Reem ain't just come holla at me?" Reds asked.

"He ain't no pussy, but he's a lil' leery of y'all. But don't say nothin' though—he'll kick my ass," Shontae said.

"Ain't nothin' to be scared of over here," Reds said.

"Yeah right, feed that shit to somebody that don't know no better," Shontae said as she walked back over to Reem.

"I'm tellin' y'all this bitch got crazy bread! I'm'a be bloody if we let this one slip. She mad loose with her shit. If we don't hurry up and get her, somebody else will," E explained to his brothers, C and Kurupt. "I watched her make like $5,000 at one party. This bitch is big time. I know she got money!"

E passed the blunt to his brother. They were smoking a three-time loser, which consisted of weed, wet, and crack. E and his brothers were stickup kids. They were small time though, sticking up street corners and dice games. If they got $1,000, they considered it a good sting. So Tyesha was looking like a Brinks truck to them.

E and his brothers were all young. E was the oldest at twenty. They were all foolish and trigger happy. They were always hungry for a stickup, and Tyesha was looking like a steak dinner. This was just what Reds had warned Tyesha about—getting too high would prove to be her demise.

"I'm tellin' you it ain't even no guns in the house. It's all college bitches. We ain't gonna find another job this easy," E said.

"Let's get this money then," C said.

"Fuck it. I'm in," Kurupt said.

It was around three in the morning; Tyesha was rolling and couldn't go to sleep. She had just finished cleaning up. Her sorority sisters were entertaining guests in the hot tub. Tyesha wanted to go get in the hot tub with her girls, but she didn't want to cock-block. Tonight, everybody had a dude except for her. She thought of calling E and seeing if he wanted to come over. As her mind drifted, her phone rang. She looked at the caller ID, and to her surprise, it was E.

"Hello," Tyesha said.

"What chu doin?" E asked.

"I was just thinkin' 'bout chu. I can't get no sleep, and I'm horny as hell," Tyesha said.

"Well, I guess it's a good thing that I'm outside," E said.

"What? You ain't outside," Tyesha said.

"I was thinkin' 'bout chu too. So I had my brothers bring me down here. I know y'all party all night, so I didn't think you'd mind," E said.

"Nah, I don't mind. I'm on my way out front right now," Tyesha said.

She hung her phone up and went outside. E and his brothers were smoking the last of another three-time loser. They were all high as a kite.

"What y'all smokin' on?" Tyesha asked as she gave E a kiss.

"It's all gone," E said as he threw the last of the blunt on the ground. "Let's go in the house. We gotta talk."

"Okay, but can't you at least introduce me to your brothers," Tyesha said.

"You can meet them after we talk," E said.

Tyesha was wondering what the hell E wanted to talk to her about. She was hoping he wasn't trying to cut her off. Reds's comment about her looking sick had her real self-conscious.

Tyesha walked in the house with E. His brothers followed behind them. When they got inside, Tyesha told E's brothers that they could watch television or play pool until she finished talking to E. Tyesha took E up to her room and shut the door. E stood in front of the door.

"So what's up?" Tyesha asked.

"Where's the money?" E asked in a very serious tone.

"What?" Tyesha asked. She thought E was playing.

"Bitch, I said where the fuck is the money," E barked as he pulled his gun off his waist.

Tyesha was so scared that she almost peed herself. She wanted to scream, but she thought E might shoot her. She looked in E's eyes and saw nothing but emptiness. "E, just calm down," was all she could think to say.

Unfortunately, that wasn't the right answer. All that did was send E into a rage. He smacked her with his gun, putting a knot on her forehead. "Bitch, you think I'm playin' with ya stupid ass?" he said as he repeatedly struck her with his gun. "Who the fuck is in the house?"

"My sorority sisters are down in the hot tub with three guys," Tyesha cried.

E and his brothers had been listening to their favorite rapper while they were in the car. The combination of drugs and music had them all in an aggressive state of mind. He grabbed Tyesha by her hair and dragged her downstairs to his brothers. E had Tyesha lying on the floor in the living room.

"Her sorority sisters are downstairs with some niggas. Go handle that," E said.

Kurupt went downstairs and shot all three of the guys that were in the hot tub. He kept his gun pointed at all three girls and told them to go upstairs.

Tyesha started to panic when she heard the gunshots. *Why the fuck did I ever start hustlin'?* she thought to herself. *I was doin' fine before I met Reds's ass. These niggas is gonna kill me. If I make it out of this, I swear I ain't never gonna sell another drug in my life. Please, God, help me.*

Tyesha's sorority sisters came upstairs topless and crying.

"Shut the fuck up and lay down!" E barked.

Tyesha's sisters lay on the floor, but they couldn't stop crying.

"Where the fuck is the money, bitch?" E asked Tyesha.

"It's upstairs in the laundry room. The pills and the money are at the bottom of a Tide soap powder box," Tyesha cried.

E ran upstairs to look for the money and drugs. When he ran upstairs, Kurupt walked over to Tyesha and pulled her sweatpants down. She didn't have any panties on. Kurupt stuck his fingers inside of her.

"I heard you got that wet-wet," Kurupt said.

Tyesha was crying and scared, but she wasn't about to let them rape her. Tyesha did the first thing that came to her mind. She defecated on herself. Kurupt damn near threw up. He smacked Tyesha hard with his gun. As she lay there bleeding, Tyesha knew death was certain. She knew where E lived, and there was no way he was leaving her alive after this. Tyesha was now sorry she ever got involved with the street life. She thought about her family for a second. She knew she was about to die, and there was nothing she could do. She was now learning the cost of being a boss. Now, it was no longer cool to be a boss bitch. A lot of times, people only see the drug dealers riding high. The money, the cars, the jewelry, that's the fun part. What people fail to realize is that everything that goes up must come down. And sometimes when it comes down, it doesn't land—it crashes.

"Fuck that. One of y'all bitches is givin' me some pussy!" Kurupt said.

He walked over to one of Tyesha's sorority sisters, Natasha. Since they were in the hot tub, she had on bikini bottoms. Natasha's bikini bottoms happened to look like a thong. Even though she was lying flat, Kurupt could still see enough to make his penis get hard. "Hold me down, cuz," Kurupt told C.

He ripped off Natasha's bikini bottoms. She begged him not to rape her. Kurupt paid her no attention. He pulled his pants down and began raping her. All the girls lay there crying and feeling sorry for Natasha, but there was nothing that any of them could do. Natasha cried as Kurupt penetrated her at gunpoint.

E came back downstairs.

"Bitch, it's only $6,000 and five bags of e-pills up there," he said. "I know you got more than this! You forgot you told me what chu was workin' with."

"I went shoppin', and I just reupped. That's all I got. I swear!" Tyesha pled. Tyesha wasn't lying. She was spending her money just as fast as she was making it.

"You must think I'm stupid! You think this shit is a game? Shoot that bitch!" E said to Kurupt.

*BOOM!* Blood and brains splattered all over the place. Tyesha turned her head and started screaming. One of her sisters had just been slain in front of her eyes.

"Shut the fuck up or another ma'fucka gon' get shot!" E barked.

"Where's the rest of the shit?"

"I swear, I don't got no—" Tyesha tried to say.

*BOOM!* E shot another one of her sisters in the head. Tyesha started to throw up.

"Bitch, I'm not playin'," E told her.

The brothers were so high that they weren't paying any attention to the noise they were making. All three of them were in their own little world. Tyesha knew that she and Kareemah were the next to be killed. She figured she wouldn't make it easy for them. C had pulled Tyesha's pants up when she defecated on herself because it looked nasty. Tyesha jumped up and ran for the door.

All three brothers started shooting. Tyesha was shot dead before she even got close to the door. C then turned his gun on Kareemah who was hysterical and shot her in the head. As the last shot was taken, Kurupt noticed flashing lights outside the house.

"Awww fuck, the cops is outside!" Kurupt screamed.

E said nothing. He ran to the back door. C started rapping some gangsta lyrics he had written in juvie. This hyped his brother up who chimed in with him. They were rapping the lyrics to one another. They were both running off a narcotic heart. They ran out of the house with their guns blazing.

There were about twenty cops in front of the house. C and Kurupt were killed almost instantly. E ran out the back door, gun in his hand. He was so high that he didn't even see the cops lying in the shadows. As soon as he got off the steps, E was shot five times in his legs. He was subdued and taken to the hospital.

The police then went inside the sorority house, which now looked more like a slaughterhouse.

Reds woke up around noon. Instead of going to get a newspaper, he opted to just watch the news. As soon as he turned on the Channel 6 news, he saw a reporter standing in front of the sorority house.

"I'm standing in front of a West Chester University sorority house where nine were murdered and three were injured; two of which were police officers. The police aren't releasing many details as of this moment. We do know that five of the people that were killed were students. This area hasn't seen this kind of violence since the string of murders that occurred in 1999 and 2000. I'll have more at 6," the reporter said.

Reds called Tyesha's phone about ten times, but got no answer. He was hoping that she was in class and just couldn't get to the phone. Then reality kicked in. Nine people had just been killed at her sorority house. She damn sure wasn't in class. Reds called J.R. and filled him in on what he knew. He asked J.R. to call Chief Luther and find out if one of the people killed was Tyesha.

About an hour later, J.R. called back and gave Reds the bad news.

"Fuck!" Reds yelled as he hung up the phone. The sun had just stopped shining for Reds.

## 26

Over the next few weeks, Reds learned the details of what happened to Tyesha. Between the students on campus and E, the police knew everything. People around the campus told police that Tyesha was selling e-pills. Word was, she was the largest supplier on campus. The police knew of the parties they were throwing and all. One thing the cops didn't know was that Reds was behind all this.

Reds was sad about what happened to Tyesha, but he was happy that she didn't run her mouth about him. Then there was E. Once he sobered up and realized what he had gotten himself into, he started talking. He told the police that all he remembered was going to the sorority house to rob Tyesha. That was all the cops needed. They filled in the rest of the blanks. They were saying that it was a robbery gone horribly wrong because of the combination of drugs taken by E and his brothers, which was basically right. E was trying to plead insanity, so he was agreeing with what the cops were saying. As far as the cops were concerned, the case was open and shut.

Reds promised himself that he would do all he could to avenge Tyesha's death. She was his first student, and he blamed himself for her death. He didn't know if he was hurt because they were intimately involved or because Tyesha was making him so much money. Maybe it was a combination of the two. Reds didn't like feeling guilty, so he made a mental note to himself not to have sex with any more of his workers.

Through the newspaper, Reds found out that E was being held in Delaware County Prison because his case was so highly profiled. Reds knew exactly where he'd be at, 8-D. Reds called Tone and told him that he needed a job done. He gave no explanation—he just told Tone that he had

$10,000 on E's head. He asked Tone if anybody on the block was fighting a murder or about to get sentenced for one.

Tone told Reds about this guy named Monster. He said Monster was kind of slow. He had taken a deal for life because they were trying to give him the death penalty. "This is the crazy part—the nigga already got a death sentence," Tone said.

"What chu talkin' 'bout?" Reds asked.

"This nigga took a deal for life because he was afraid of the death penalty, but he got full-blown AIDS," Tone said.

As soon as Tone said that, Reds formed a diabolical plan, one that could only work if Monster was on board. "I wanna talk to this nigga ASAP," Reds said. "Don't tell 'em who I am though."

"A'ight, call back around eight o'clock. That's when his side comes out for rec," Tone said.

"I'll call you then," Reds said before hanging up.

Life had a way of working itself out, and E was about to pay for what he did to Tyesha.

Around a quarter after eight, Reds called Tone from a pay phone. Tone put Monster on the phone.

"I got rap star money, and I am aware of your situation. I can at least make you comfortable for the rest of you days in jail," Reds said.

"You got my attention," Monster said.

"There's a nigga on ya block named E. He's the one that killed all them people in West Chester," Reds said.

"I know who you talkin' 'bout," Monster said.

"I don't know if you got the scoop or not, but I got $10,000 on his head. But there's a catch—I don't want 'em dead," Reds said.

"Ten thousand dollars just to fuck 'em up?" Monster asked.

"Absolutely not. I want him to die slowly. I hear that you got full-blown AIDS. I want you to rape 'em," Reds said.

"Damn, I don't really get down like that, but for $10,000, I will. How do I know I'm gonna get my money?" Monster asked.

"Give me an address to someone you trust. I'll drop the money off tonight," Reds said.

Monster gave Reds the address to his mom's house. She lived in the Gardens, a project in Chester. After Reds got the address, Reds asked if Monster had kids.

"Yeah, they live with my mom," Monster said.

Reds instructed Monster to go get some mail from his kids. He came back to the phone a few minutes later, and it was verified by Tone that the address on the letter from his kids was the same address he gave Reds.

"I'm showin' good faith by givin' you the money up front. As you can see, I don't play no games. If you don't uphold your end of the bargain, I'm gonna have ya kids and moms rocked. I don't mean any disrespect by this. I'm just tellin' you what chur gettin' into before you get into it," Reds said.

"I gotcha. I can handle that, lil' nigga. It'll be done by the end of the week," Monster said.

"Enjoy your money," Reds said before he hung up.

After Reds dropped the money off to Monster's mom, he rode around and thought. Reds was seriously considering taking it back to the streets. He figured that college kids hustling at the level he'd have them hustling would make them sitting ducks. Even the ones that were street weren't as street as he needed them to be. Most of the kids on campus didn't even own a gun, and if they did, Reds doubted they would use it. College kids had too much going for them and would be easy to break if the cops got a hold of them. These were things Reds hadn't thought of before. But after a loss, you always end up back at the drawing board, and hindsight is always 20/20.

Reds knew that the streets were where the real money was at, but he also knew that's where all the nonsense was at. *I guess I gotta take the good with the bad,* Reds thought to himself. He was now sure what direction he was headed in, and he knew the perfect place. He just had to knock the rest of the e-pills he had off, then he'd be ready.

Reds had just grabbed ten thousand pills. Tyesha had only taken a thousand off his latest batch. Reds hustled his ass off for the next month and moved all the pills by himself. He was in clubs, strip clubs, college campuses, and in the hood. Reds was drained from all the ripping and running, but it all paid off. He got rid of all nine thousand e-pills.

His birthday was in a week, and Reds needed to catch up on his sleep. For the next few days Reds would let his body rejuvenate, then it was on.

After two days of sleeping and two days of just lying around his house, Reds was ready to get back in the swing of things. He called his cousin, Shontae. Reds told her he'd be in Altoona on Friday, his birthday. She told him to call once he got to Altoona, and she'd give him directions to her house.

Reds had almost $200,000 in his stash. He wanted to do it big for his birthday, so he decided to spend some money. Reds liked his Monte Carlo, but he really wanted a truck. He went to a dealership in Philly and met a guy named Carl. Reds had his eyes set on the Cadillac Escalade pickup. They had just come out, and Reds could see himself sitting in one.

Carl talked like he was from the hood, and he had a little swag with him. Reds explained that he had the money for the truck, but he couldn't account for where the money came from.

"This truck is $60,000, but I can mark it down to $52,000. If I hook it up so that shit looks legit, I get to pocket the $8,000 difference," Carl said.

"A'ight," Reds agreed.

An hour and a half later, Reds was driving off the lot in a brand-new Escalade pickup truck. Reds drove straight to the customs shop and got twenty-two-inch rims and a system for the truck. That cost him another $15,000. His next stop would be Norristown, to the Jewelry Factory. Reds bought himself a forty-two-inch rose gold chain and a rose gold medallion of a shining sun. The medallion was covered in canary-yellow diamonds. After talking deals for thirty minutes, Reds got both for $20,000.

*Now I'm shinin' on these niggas like I'm 'posed to,* Reds thought to himself as he drove back to West Chester.

Right before Reds got to West Chester, Juanita called him. She told him to come by. There was somebody that he needed to meet. When Reds got to Juanita's apartment, she was sitting outside, talking to a short fat man in a nice suit. Reds was curious about who this man was because Juanita said he needed to meet him.

Reds jumped out of the truck feeling like he owned the world. His clothes were sharp, his jewels were bright, and his truck was brand-new.

"Okay, I see somebody is stuntin'," Juanita said as she gave him a hug and a kiss.

"So who's this man I need to meet?" Reds asked.

Juanita turned around and made the introduction. "Reds, this is my cousin, Los. Los, this is my boo, Reds," Juanita said.

As Reds shook Los's hand, he could tell Los was somebody. Los had this aura about him that said he was important. When Reds shook Los's hand, he looked him square in the eye and shook firmly. Because of this, Los immediately like Reds.

"I've been tellin' my cousin 'bout chu for a minute. I finally caught him at my mom's house and talked him into meetin' you," Juanita said. "I'll let chu two talk. I'll be inside."

"I don't have a lot of time, but my cousin really campaigned for you. She obviously thinks the world of you and thinks I can help you. I will make you a proposal, and if you're smart, you'll take it. I hear you're making a lot of money. I can make you a lot more money. There is nothing I can't supply," Los said.

"What's ya prices?" Reds asked after a long silence.

"For what?" Los asked.

"Coke, dope, weed, and e-pills," Reds said.

"Eighteen thousand dollars for a kilo of cocaine, seventy-five thousand for a kilo of heroin, a dollar a pill for the Ecstasy, and four hundred per pound of weed," Los said. "I don't have any customers in this area. My cousin seems to think you are worth dealing with."

Reds was waiting for the cameras to come out, and somebody say that this was a joke. "Are you fuckin' serious?" Reds asked.

"As I have told you, I don't have time for games. I am a very busy man. Everything I have is the best. It comes straight off the boat. To show you, I will give you your first order up front. You pay when you're finished with the first order. From then on, you will pay up front. Some people would say that you just got lucky. I don't believe in luck. Luck is when opportunity and preparation meet. So I ask you, are you prepared to seize this opportunity?" Los asked.

"Definitely," Reds said.

"Congratulations. You just left high school and went straight to the pros," Los said with a smile and a pat on the back.

"I need you to give me a few weeks to get everything together. I don't wanna get the shipment and just sit on it," Reds said.

"I can respect that. My cousin will get in touch with me when you're ready. She will also continue to transport for you. Her fee will be $5,000 per trip," Los said.

Reds felt like he was being told what to do, but how could he argue? If it wasn't for Juanita, he would have never met Los. That's fine with me," Reds said.

"I'll be in touch, my friend. Once you get everything moving, I'd like for you to join me at mi casa for dinner. Now if you'd excuse me, I have a plane to catch," Los said as he walked to his 745 BMW.

After Los left, Reds went inside Juanita's apartment. "Why you ain't been said somethin' 'bout cha folks?" Reds asked.

"He's not the type of guy that you can just go talk to. If he wants to talk, he'll talk to you," Juanita said. "I never told you before 'cause I didn't wanna get cha hopes up and he said no."

"I want chu to know that I really appreciate what chu did for me," Reds said.

"I don't know what I gotta do to show you that I'm'a ride for you. I really wanna be with you, Reds," Juanita said.

"I got too much love to lie to you. I can't never see myself bein' with somebody. I got major trust issues," Reds said.

"I know what you been through. I understand. But I'm tryin' to show you I'm not Maria. I'm'a wait it out. I'll be here when you come around," Juanita said.

Reds did love Juanita, but he wasn't in love with her. She had been there from the start, and she was proving that all women weren't despicable soulless whores who were not to be trusted. Even so, Reds would never let her know that. He feared that as soon as he told her how he felt about her, she'd flip the script on him. He decided to switch the subject. "Oh, you know you just gotta raise. I want you to pick up the shit from Los. I'll pay you $5,000 a trip," Reds said like it was his idea.

Juanita thanked Reds even though she knew the idea was Los's. He had already told her that she would be picking up the drugs and how much she would be paid. Juanita just played like she didn't know. A lot of times, men think they are getting over on women, but most times, men only get away with what women let them get away with.

"Again, I really wanna thank you for pluggin' me in with ya cousin. I can't tell you how grateful I am," Reds said.

Juanita started to undress. "Show me how grateful you are," she said.

Reds had made a rule not to have sex anymore with his workers, but Juanita wasn't really a worker. She didn't sell anything. She just drove the drugs from point A to point B. Reds minimized the situation, so he could continue to have sex with her. After all, she wasn't just a worker—she was special to Reds. What she did today showed Reds where her loyalty was. He knew there was a lot of bad people in the world. He always told himself if he found a good person, he'd make sure they stayed in his life. Juanita was proving to be a good person.

After Reds and Juanita's session, he went to J.R.'s to show him his truck. J.R. saw Reds's truck and made a mental note to step his game up. He couldn't allow his little cousin to show him up, and right now, Reds was definitely shining harder than him. Reds told J.R. about Los. J.R.

was happy for Reds. He also told him to hold on tight to Juanita. She was proving to be a rider.

"So was Maria 'til she robbed me," Reds said sarcastically.

J.R. didn't even bother arguing with him. He knew how Reds felt, and he knew he couldn't change it. They talked for a little while, then Reds headed home. He had to figure out how he was going to set up shop. He wouldn't really know how he would do it until he got to Altoona, but he would start brainstorming now.

As Reds pulled up in front of his dad's house, he made a mental note to get his own spot when he came back from Altoona. He and Rob were getting along just fine, but Reds was getting too much money to be living with his dad. As Reds got out of his truck, he got a text message from J.R.

"Dice game in Sidetrack tomorrow at one," the text read.

The next morning, Reds woke up feeling good. He was officially twenty-one today. He planned on going to Altoona later and balling out for his birthday. He had never been to Altoona, but from what Shontae told him, he knew there was money out there. He also knew there was a bunch of new ladies out there. Reds couldn't wait. But first, he had a show to put on in Sidetrack.

It was late May; the weather was warm. Reds threw on a pair of Nike basketball shorts, a wifebeater, and a pair of Gucci flip-flops. He filled his pockets as much as he could with money. It looked like he had a midget in each one of his pockets. He threw his chain on then headed for Sidetrack. Reds would be shooting with dudes from his neighborhood, so he didn't need his gun. Plus, J.R. would be there.

Reds got to the dice game around one-thirty. There were about eight people shooting dice, including J.R. There was also a lot of females outside, lingering around the dice game, being nosey.

Reds drove his truck real slow through the court, blaring Jay-Z from his speakers. He climbed out of his truck. "I have arrived," he announced. His chain was swinging, and his pockets had an erection. Like normal chicks in the hood, they flocked.

"Damn, where you get that chain?" Kawanda asked.

"Fuck the chain. When you grab that truck? It's nice as shit," Tamira added. "Goddamn, nigga, what the fuck you got in ya pockets, mountains?"

"Bitch, get the fuck out that nigga face! He ain't nobody! The truck probably rented and the chain probably fake!" Blocker yelled to Kawanda.

Reds put his nose in the air and started sniffing. "You smell that? Is that the sour stench of hate I smell?" Reds said. "The truck is paid for, the ice is real, and the mountains in my pockets are made of twenties, fifties, and hundreds."

"Nigga, fuck all that. Come over and lose those mountains," J.R. said. He could sense that guys were feeling some type of way. He was trying to get Reds to chill before things got ugly. The summer was just beginning. J.R. didn't want to make it any hotter by killing somebody at a dice game.

"Excuse me, ladies. I gotta go take these niggas' money," Reds said.

Two hours later, Reds was up $7,500. "A'ight, fellas, it's been fun, but I got some shit to take care of," Reds said. "But I don't want nobody feelin' like I won and ran. I'm up about $7,000. I'll bet it all on one shot. Anybody want it?"

"Bet," Blocker announced.

Reds shook the dice, and rolled a 10. "$15,000 to $7,500," Reds said.

Blocker was hoping that Reds's luck had run out. He had the hot hand all day. It was only a matter of time before the dice switched on him, Blocker hoped. Reds tapped the dice two times on the ground and tossed them. The dice landed on two 5s.

"Oh Lord!" Reds shouted. "That looks like a ma'fuckin' 10 to me! In the ma'fuckin' bucks! Reggie from the custom shop wants to thank you. You just paid for my system and rims. I'll be back next week, and you can pay for my suicide doors."

It was one thing that Reds was winning, but he was really pouring alcohol on the wound by talking trash. Everybody knows that you don't talk bad to a man that's losing his money, especially a lot of money. And you definitely don't do it when there's a bunch of women around.

Reds didn't care about the rules though. He was young, hood rich, and he busted his gun. He didn't feel like the rules applied to him. What he never thought about was a man's pride, which has caused more than its fair share of funerals and life sentences. Not enough will make you a coward, and too much can get you killed.

"Naw, nigga, you stuck the dice. Shoot that shit over," Blocker said. Blocker knew that Reds didn't stick the dice. He just was being a sore loser. His emotions were involved, and he decided to test Reds.

"Nigga, you sound stupid. Pay me my bread!" Reds said with authority.

J.R. saw this coming, but he wasn't going to check Reds in front of others. So he sat back quietly and waited for the show to start. One thing was for sure, right or wrong, J.R. was riding with his family.

"I ain't payin' shit! Shoot the shot over," Blocker said.

"Not over $15,000," J.R. said with his hand under his shirt. J.R. had stopped shooting dice a while ago. He quietly made his way to his truck and grabbed his gun.

Blocker understood exactly what J.R. was saying. Blocker paid Reds his money, but only because he felt outnumbered. He wasn't sure if Reds was armed, but he knew J.R. was.

Reds wasn't satisfied though. He felt that Blocker disrespected him, so he got disrespectful. He counted out $1,000 and gave it to Kawanda. "Give that nigga some pussy. Maybe he'll calm down," Reds said.

He then turned, and addressed Blocker. "I already paid for the pussy, Blocker. That means you don't owe her nothin'. This'll be the first time in ya life you ain't have to pay for no pussy," Reds said.

It only made a bad situation worse when everybody started laughing. Then Kawanda took the money and put it in her pocket, making Blocker irate. "Bitch, give that nigga his fuckin' money back! I got plenty bread," Blocker said.

"Fuck what chu talkin' 'bout, nigga? I ain't givin' shit back! Once he gave it to me, it became mine. You don't tell me what to do with mines," Kawanda said in a sassy tone.

Blocker lost it. He punched Kawanda square in the jaw, knocking her out. And that was how the dice game was ended.

It was around five o'clock that night. Reds's phone rang. It was Tone. "Yo, mission accomplished. I told chu homeboy was shot out. He had the audacity to ask me to watch. Talkin' 'bout he needed verification," Tone said as he laughed.

"So what chu do?" Reds asked as he giggled.

"I watched. I had to! Don't judge me," Tone said as they both bust out laughing.

"Yo, you crazy as shit!" Reds said as he tried to catch his breath.

"That shit was extra funny too. He definitely did it. It was blood and shit everywhere! I'm talkin' some real nasty shit. And I think Monster liked it. A booty bandit may have just been born," Tone said.

Reds was laughing so hard that he had tears in his eyes. "Nah, on some real shit, I appreciate you makin' sure it went down, homey. I just came up earlier. You got somethin' comin' ya way. I just need one more thing," Reds said.

"What's that? 'Cause after this, ya wishes is just about all used up," Tone said.

"If you ever see that nigga again, tell 'em Tyesha sends her love," Reds said.

"That I can do," Tone shot back.

Reds felt good that E was suffering for what he did to Tyesha. He'd sleep a lot better tonight.

# 27

Reds had a lot of time to think while driving to Altoona. It was a four-and-a-half-hour ride. Reds knew there was going to have to be a lot of killing when he took over. Nobody was going to just let somebody come into where they were getting money and take over. While Reds was in prison, he was reading books that taught him to win battles with his mind. So if he could find a way to do what he wanted to do without having to kill a bunch of people, he would. But if things didn't go that way, Reds didn't care how many people had to die. As long as the outcome was him being rich, he was fine with whatever happened.

His strategy was basic marketing, beat the dealer. Reds wouldn't sell any weight. He was going to break everything down. Reds didn't plan on being out there, putting his freedom and life in jeopardy. He planned to find workers and let them get money. One of the things Reds learned from dealing with Tyesha was as long as people made good money, everybody was happy. These guys were selling grams of coke for $150. Reds knew how to cook coke into crack. So he could turn every kilo into 1,500 grams and put grams on the street for $100. He'd pay his workers $40 off every gram and keep $60. This would make Reds $90,000 off of every kilo of cocaine after he paid his workers.

Since the e-pills were going for $30, Reds would put his pills on the streets for $15. His workers would keep $5 and give him $10. Reds would pay $20,000 for 20,000 pills, but after he paid his workers, he'd be clearing $180,000.

The weed was going for $10 a gram, so ounces were probably going for $200. Reds would put ounces out for $100. The workers would keep

$40 and give him $60. So off of 100 pounds, Reds would make $96,000 after he paid his workers.

All in all, Reds was looking to clear over a million every flip. He was so excited that he was actually getting aroused. He was truly addicted to money. Reds planned on hustling for one year, then he'd retire at twenty-two.

Reds's thoughts were disturbed by his phone vibrating. He didn't recognize the number, so he pressed talk but didn't say anything.

"Hello," the caller said.

Reds instantly recognized the voice. It was Blocker.

"Fuck you want, nigga?" Reds answered with an attitude. "Ya bitch ain't wit' me."

"I just wanted to let chu know you better start watchin' ya slick-ass mouth. The only reason you got that money today and not a few slugs from my gun was because I got love for J.R. But I'm gonna promise you this: if you ever try to play me in front of my baby mom again, you gonna die. Consider ya'self warned," Blocker said.

"Well, first of all, you don't got no love for J.R., Your faggot-ass is petrified of J.R. Second of all, I can't play you no more than I already did. I fucked ya baby mom back in '99 when you was in the county. Just so you know I ain't lyin', she got cha name tattooed on her panty line. Yeah, I nutted all over that," Reds said as he started laughing hysterically. "Oh, and it gets better! After I fucked her, in y'all's bed, I drove her out to see you. You wouldn't believe what this nasty bitch had the audacity to do— to show her appreciation for the ride, she gave me some head in the whip. Not only did she suck me off, she swallowed every drop I squirted out. Then, about five minutes later, she went inside the jail, and I know you kissed her in the mouth. That makes you a dick sucka!"

"You know you a dead man, right?" Blocker said.

"How the fuck you gon' kill me? And you already dead—you just don't know it yet," Reds said, then he ended the call.

Reds was furious that Blocker had the balls to call him with that stupidity. Reds knew that Blocker wasn't a coward, but he didn't care. Reds felt like he could do or say whatever he wanted to. Reds was talking to Blocker based off of his emotions. Even though he meant every word he said, he still shouldn't have said it. Reds had just revealed his hand to his enemy, which would prove to be a big mistake.

Right before Reds made it to Altoona, he got another phone call. It was from Nikki.

"What!?" Reds barked into the phone.

"Why you soundin' so mean?" Nikki asked.

"I'm just tired," Reds said as he caught himself.

"Well, why don't you come over so I can put you to sleep," Nikki said.

"Nah, I ain't really feelin' you right now. Last time I saw you, you was actin' crazy," Reds said.

"I was actin' crazy, or was it you who was actin' crazy?" Nikki asked.

"Listen, you played ya'self," Reds said.

"How? 'Cause I love you and wanna be with you?" Nikki asked.

"Good-bye," Reds said before hanging up.

When Reds got to Altoona, he called Shontae. She navigated him to Sheetz, a local gas station. Reds parked and waited for her to arrive. Ten minutes later, Shontae pulled up.

"No . . . you . . . didn't," Shontae said slowly. "That ma'fuckin' truck is the shit!"

"Yeah, that's the reaction I normally get," Reds said with a smile.

"I'm glad you drove it up here so I can take it for a ride, but don't ever bring that shit out here again. These cops be on some real racist shit. That truck is gonna draw way too much attention if you tryin' to get money. You should be okay for the weekend though."

Shontae took Reds back to her house. She was giving Reds the basic rundown on the area. From what he was hearing, he had to be real militant because of the police.

Later on, that night, Shontae took Reds to the club Car. The music was horrible, but the females made up for it. Reds was attracting a lot of attention, being a new face. It seemed like every chick in the club was in his face. Reds had on a pair of dark blue Gucci shorts, a white and red Gucci shirt, and a pair of white and red Gucci loafers. His chain was shining like a colored disco ball, and his waves were spinning.

A white girl named Amanda approached Reds. She was very attractive but was dressed horribly. She had on a pair of short jean shorts with a brown South Pole T-shirt, and a pair of rundown black-and-white Reebok Classics. "Hey, cutie, where you from?" she asked.

"I'm from heaven," Reds replied.

"That's a nice one. I never heard that before. Well, since you're from heaven, we're tryin' to fuck an angel," Amanda said as she pointed to her girlfriend who looked like she was black and Chinese.

This girl was about five-foot-three, 115 pounds, and she was petite. Reds liked thicker women, but he'd take a petite chick as long as she was cute. And what this one lacked in breasts and behind, she definitely made up for with looks. The Chinese-looking chick was one of the few women that was dressed pretty decent. She wore a black pair of slacks, a black-and-white silk shirt, and a black pair of heels. She had long black hair, and her smile was welcoming. The dealmaker was that she didn't have a lot of makeup on.

Reds loved natural beauty, and this one was naturally beautiful. When Reds looked over her way, she winked at him. Reds had shots lined up in front of him. He quickly downed the shots and told Amanda to meet him at the end of the night. "I'll be in the parking lot, standin' in front of a truck that looks like it belongs in a video," Reds said.

Throughout the rest of the night, Reds continued to drink shots. He was hammered. Shontae tried to introduce Reds to a few people from the area, but he was too drunk. Reds came to Altoona on business, but it was his birthday—he wanted to enjoy it.

When they called last call for alcohol, Amanda came over and introduced Reds to Mia, the chick that looked black and Asian. Reds pulled out a bunch of money and asked the ladies if they wanted something to drink.

"We've had a little too much already," Amanda said, letting Reds know they were feeling good also.

Reds was drunk, but he knew exactly what he was doing by pulling the money out. Money was a universal language that everybody understood. It didn't matter where they were from, Reds had never met a chick that didn't like money, and he had plenty.

"I heard you and ya girl is tryin' to do somethin' nasty to me," Reds said in a drunken slur.

"We might be," Mia responded innocently.

"Well, I ain't into all the games. I got room for two in my Escalade. Is y'all with me or what?" Reds asked.

"I guess we can hang out," Mia said.

Shontae drove the girls and Reds to her house. Then Mia drove Reds and Amanda to Amanda's house.

Reds was all over Mia as soon as they got in the door. He didn't really care for Amanda, but she was a means to an end, Mia. Reds was kissing and rubbing all over Mia's body. He grabbed her shirt and ripped it open, exposing her perky B cups. He undid her bra and started sucking on her brown pointy nipples. As Reds sucked on Mia's breasts, Amanda took her clothes off and started sucking on Mia's other titty. Once Reds saw how Amanda looked naked, his mind changed about her. She would definitely be getting some attention from him tonight. Amanda couldn't dress, but she looked magnificent without clothes on. Her round D-cup breasts had bright pink nipples. Her pussy was shaved, but she had a light landing strip of hair going down the middle. Her hips were thick, and her ass was nice. To top it off, her stomach was flat.

Reds liked this. He pushed Mia down on the floor, and started eating her pussy. She grabbed the back of his head and pushed it deeper in between her legs. Mia had light-brown skin and had only a handful of ass, but it looked great on her small frame. Her pussy was shaved completely, which showed how meaty her pussy was. As Reds was licking Mia's pussy, Amanda told him to lift up a little bit. She slid between his legs and started sucking his dick while he ate Mia out.

"Don't stop! I'm about to cum!" Mia screamed out as her body began to shake. She came all over Reds's face.

"Can I have a taste?" Mia asked as she stood up.

Reds shook his head yes. His whole face was covered in pussy juice and cum. Mia licked all of her juices off of Reds's face. She then turned to Amanda, who had stopped sucking Reds's dick, and started kissing her.

"Lay down," Amanda told Reds.

Amanda straddled Reds's face and rode it like a wild bull. While Amanda got her pussy eaten by Reds, Mia rode Reds's dick. Reds ate pussy like a champ, so it didn't take Amanda long to cum.

"I want to feel that dick inside me," Amanda said.

"It feels good," Mia told Amanda as she got off of Reds.

Reds put Amanda in the doggy-style position, so she could eat Mia's pussy while she was getting fucked. Reds drove himself deep inside of Amanda's pussy.

"Yes, yes, that's the spot! Oooh, slap my ass," she moaned.

Reds slapped her ass hard. Amanda knew how to fuck, but unlike Mia, her pussy was super loose. It was like she didn't even have walls. After about ten minutes of pounding on Amanda's loose pussy, Reds was ready to get back inside of Mia. He had Mia and Amanda lie next to each other.

Reds finger-fucked Amanda while he slid into Mia's tight love canal. Reds instantly felt the difference.

While Reds was fucking Mia, she would occasionally turn and tongue-kiss Amanda. Reds found that to be very sexy. Reds started choking Mia as he drove short fast pumps into her pussy. Mia was having an orgasm only three minutes after Reds got inside of her. Mia's body started to shake like she was having a seizure. Reds pulled out of her and started face-fucking Amanda. Reds fucked her mouth fiercely.

"You like that, don't you?" Reds said as he pumped away at her face. "Suck this dick, you fuckin' whore."

Reds rammed himself in and out of Amanda's mouth until he came. When he pulled his dick out of Amanda's mouth, some saliva and cum got on her face. Reds emulated the porn stars and rubbed the spit and cum mixture all over Amanda's face with his dick. "You bitches is somethin' special," Reds said.

He wanted to leave, but he was too drunk. He just lay on the floor with Mia. Amanda didn't even go wash her face. She just cuddled up on the floor with Reds and Mia.

*I love a nasty bitch*, Reds thought to himself as he dozed off.

The next morning, Reds woke up and crept out the house quietly. Once he got in his truck, he called Shontae. "Yo, I'm on Sixth Avenue. How do I get back to ya house?" Reds asked.

"Why don't you have one of the chicks show you how to get here?" Shontae asked.

"I fucks 'em, then I ducks 'em. Them bitches is still sleep," Reds said.

Shontae chastised Reds momentarily for his whorish ways, then she explained how to get back to her house.

When he got to her house, Shontae and Reem were just getting out of the shower. Reds sat on their couch and watched television. Shontae came downstairs and made breakfast while Reds talked to Reem. Reds didn't know what it was, but he didn't like Reem.

"Did you ever holla at cha lady friend down the university?" Reem asked.

"Actually, I never got the chance to. She got killed the day after the funeral," Reds said.

Reem didn't know how close Reds and Tyesha were, so he switched the subject. "I'm sorry to hear that. But on a brighter note, I'm'a take you up the projects and introduce you to my man, Sting," Reem said. "Maybe y'all can get a lil' money together or somethin'."

Reds didn't really tell anybody what type of time he was on as far as what he was trying to do out there. But he did hear one thing that he liked—Reem's man ran the projects.

As Reds ate breakfast, he rethought his plan. He could kill a lot of birds with the same stone if he propositioned Sting the right way. From what Reds had heard, Sting already had the projects on lock. This was a plus for Reds. Since Sting already knew how to move in Altoona and he already had workers, all Reds had to do was make Sting an offer that he couldn't say no to. Reds would give Sting the chance to flood Altoona with crack, Ecstasy, and weed. The only thing was, when Reds made his original plan, he didn't have a middle man in between him and the workers. That's what Sting would serve as, a middle man.

The more Reds thought about it, the surer he was about it. If the workers got caught up in some shit, they would tell on Sting, not Reds. Sting would be Reds's shield. Reds would still be able to make everything he had originally planned on making if he played his cards right.

Around one o'clock, Reem took Reds to Fairview Projects. As they walked through Fairview, Reem spotted Sting. "There he go," Reem informed Reds.

Sting was short and stocky. He was brown skinned and wore a large scar down the side of his face. He had on a pair of sweatpants and a wifebeater. He also had a fairly large group of people around him. Reem took Reds over to Sting and introduced them. Reds could tell by Sting's body language that he didn't really like Reem. Reds could understand why—Reem was a like a groupie. He was the type to call someone his man, and he barely knew them.

"What's bangin'?" Sting asked Reds.

"I ain't into all that, fam. But look, let me holla at chu for a second 'bout some business," Reds said.

Reds and Sting walked away from the crowd.

"Look, I don't really fuck with Reem, but he's the only person I know out here other than my cousin, which is Reem's chick. So before we get off on the wrong foot, don't think I'm anything like Reem 'cause I'm not," Reds said.

"A'ight, so what chu wanna holla at me 'bout?" Sting said.

"I think I can help you make some real money," Reds said.

"I don't need no help, blood 'less you tryin' to get some money for me," Sting replied.

"Do I look like a worker? Did you see what I pulled up in? You think I got that from workin' for a nigga?" Reds asked.

"I feel you," Sting replied.

"We all could use a lil' help even if we don't know it," Reds shot back.

"So how you gonna help me?" Sting asked.

His arrogance made Reds want to shoot him in his face right there, but he refrained from acting impulsively. Instead, Reds explained what he was trying to do. "I wanna lock shit down fo' real! I'm tryin' to have four houses. One for crack, one for weed, one for e-pills, and one where we hold money. We use all your workers, but we do it my way. We don't sell no weight. Everything gets bust down. All I ask is $10 off every e-pill, $60 off every ounce of weed, and $60 off every gram of crack. Whatever else you make, you split between you and the workers, however you see fit," Reds said.

"Okay, you got my attention," Sting responded.

"Every house we use to hold shit in, we pay them $1,000 a month. And we switch houses every month," Reds said.

"So what type of weight is you talkin' 'bout givin' me?" Sting asked.

"Twenty pounds of weed, a key of crack, and five thousand e-pills at a time," Reds said.

"Why would you trust me with all that?" Sting asked.

"Who said I trust you? I'm just willin' to take a chance and hope you not stupid enough to fuck it up. I'm not givin' you nothin' I can't afford to lose. But you'd be a fool to rob me. I'm breakin' bread with you, major bread," Reds said.

Sting was getting hyped now. If Reds had all that work to lose, he was a major. Sting wasn't doing bad, but he wasn't doing nowhere close to how Reds was doing. "I feel you," Sting said.

"I'm payin' you 'cause you already established. It would be cheaper for me to eat with you than to beef with you," Reds said.

"I'm sayin' that shit sounds lovely, but it sounds a lil' too good to be true. Let me think 'bout it, and I'll get back to you," Sting said.

Sting was trying to play it cool, but on the inside, he was feeling like he just won the Powerball. Sting was only grabbing nine ounces of coke from his connect. If he started dealing with Reds, he'd be a boss. It was an easy decision, one that Sting already knew the answer to. He just didn't want to seem too anxious. Reds gave him his number and told him to have a decision within two days.

"Time is money, and I don't like wastin' either," Reds said as he shook Sting's hand and walked off.

As Reds and Reem walked back to his Escalade, his phone went off. "Yes," Reds answered.

It was his dad. "Listen carefully, son, don't ask no questions because I can only read what's on the paper. You are to drop off $50,000 at midnight behind the dumpster at Henderson High School. If you don't, the people that kidnapped me will kill me. Don't go to the police, and don't go to J.R. They are watchin' you," he said.

Then right before he hung up, Rob yelled, "Don't pay 'em! They're gonna kill me any—"

There was a smack, and it sounded as if the phone had dropped. Then Reds heard a voice tell his father to shut the fuck up. Reds was positive of who the voice belonged to; it was Blocker.

## 28

Reds sat in his truck and took it all in. Reem could tell that Reds was somewhere else mentally. "Yo, you okay, dog?" Reem asked.

"Yeah," Reds answered. "I gotta hurry up and get back home."

Reds sped through the streets in order to drop Reem off. When he got to Reem and Shontae's house, Reds didn't even go inside and grab his clothes. As soon as Reem got out of the truck, Reds sped off for the turnpike.

As Reds drove home, his mind raced. He was almost certain that he wasn't being watched, or Blocker would have known he was in Altoona. He was positive that it was Blocker's voice that he had heard in the background. Blocker had a high-pitched voice that couldn't be mistaken. Reds was also sure that he'd kill everything Blocker loved then him. Reds knew that his dad was right—Rob would be killed even if Reds paid the ransom. Reds didn't care though; he was still going to pay it. He would do everything in his power to make sure that nothing happened to his father.

As Reds analyzed the situation, he kicked himself in the ass for talking shit to Blocker. After the things Reds said to Blocker, he was certain his father would be killed. And for the very last time in his life, Reds shed a tear.

Reds acted as if the turnpike was a race track. He floored it back to West Chester, making it home in three hours. He drove home and grabbed the money out of his safe. When he got inside the apartment, it was trashed. Reds figured Blocker took his dad once he couldn't get the safe open.

He drove his Monte Carlo to J.R's and explained what was going on. J.R. was irate. Reds told him exactly what he planned on doing and exactly what he wanted J.R. to do. As Reds told J.R. his plan, J.R. knew he did a good job with Reds. Reds's plan was brutal and heartless. West Chester would be a very sad place tonight.

At exactly midnight, Reds dropped the money off behind the high school as instructed. Ten minutes later, he received a phone call.

"Come pick me up! I'm right by—" Rob started to say.

His words were cut off by gunfire. *BOOM!*

Reds heard a single gunshot, then the phone went dead. He was sure that his father had just been executed. Reds didn't even cry. He just went to a very dark place mentally. He closed his eyes and apologized to his father for causing him harm. Reds called J.R. "They killed him while he was talkin' to me on the phone," Reds said.

"Damn, cuz, I'm sorry," J.R. said with compassion.

Reds didn't even acknowledge what J.R. said. There was no time for sorrow now. There would be plenty of time for that once he got revenge. "On with the plan, but don't move until you call me first. I wanna strike at the same time," Reds said.

J.R. pulled onto Walnut Street and parked. He walked to the end of the block; all was clear. J.R. called Reds. "How you lookin'?" J.R. asked.

"I was waitin' for you," Reds responded.

"A'ight, do what chu do," J.R. responded. He hung the phone up and checked the house windows. The first two were locked, but he struck gold on the third window—it was open. J.R. slipped inside and made his way to the first room at the top of the steps. When J.R. opened the door, he saw Blocker's little brother. He was only fifteen years old. Blocker's brother woke up to a hand over his mouth and a gun to his head.

"If you make any noise, I'll blow ya fuckin' head off," J.R. whispered.

Blocker's brother pissed on himself, but he remained quiet.

"When you answer my next question, do it quietly," J.R. instructed. "How many people is in the house?"

"It's just me, my sister, my mom, and my dad," Blocker's brother answered in a soft whisper.

J.R. had Blocker's brother lead him to his sister's room. She was ten years old. J.R. had Blocker's brother wake up his little sister and keep her quiet. Next, Blocker's brother and sister led J.R. to their parents' room. J.R. made the kids lie on the floor, then he turned the lights on. "Rise and shine," J.R. said loudly.

"What the fuck!" Blocker's dad said as he saw a man with a mask standing in his room.

"Oh my god!" Blocker's mom shouted.

"Your children are layin' on the floor. If anybody gets loud, it'll be a bloodbath in here," J.R. said. As he spoke, Blocker's parents heard the kids on the floor crying.

"Just take whatever you want! Please don't hurt us," Blocker's father pleaded.

Once it was understood that everyone would follow instructions, J.R. proceeded to carry out his plan, a plan so sinister that only Satan himself could have thought of.

As J.R. was taking care of Blocker's family, Reds went into action. He knocked on Blocker's baby's mom door. Kawanda checked the peephole and saw Reds. She opened the door, planning to cuss Reds out. Because of his big mouth, she got her ass kicked. But when she opened the door, she was pushed back in the house. Reds pulled his gun out and asked where Blocker was.

"I swear to God ain't nobody here but me and the baby," Kawanda pleaded. She knew that Reds and Blocker had issues, but she didn't know what Blocker had done, and she damned sure wasn't expecting this. Kawanda was petrified.

Reds grabbed her by the hair and walked her to the bathroom. He made her get on her knees, then he shot her in the face with a .45. He grabbed some hair spray and sprayed Kawanda's lifeless body with it, then he lit her on fire. As Reds did this, he heard Blocker's baby crying. Reds walked into the room and took Blocker's son out of his crib and into the bathroom.

Around six o'clock the next morning, Blocker's aunt called him, crying. She said she was in the hospital, then she explained that Blocker's father, mother, brother, and sister had all been murdered. Blocker was hiding out in a hotel, the King of Prussia.

As soon as Blocker received the news about his family, he instantly became dizzy. Blocker knew his family's murder was because of what he did to Reds's dad. Blocker thought that Reds and J.R. would come after him, but he didn't think they would go after his family. Blocker planned on taking Kawanda and the baby and getting out of town. He figured that as long as he never came across Reds or J.R., he would be okay. He didn't think they would go hard like this.

Blocker was instantly sorry for underestimating his opponents. He cried for a while with his aunt, then he pulled himself together. He told his aunt that he'd be at the hospital in an hour.

Because of the way the family was found, the police were looking at relatives as possible suspects. The police told Blocker's aunt that it appeared that everybody was killed in the act of some sort of sexual activity. They were waiting on DNA results to come back now, but they found semen in the mother's mouth and pubic hairs in the sister's mouth. Everyone in the house was found naked, all in the same bed.

Blocker's aunt couldn't believe what she was hearing. After they questioned her, they asked who else would have had access to the house. She immediately told them Blocker. The police convinced Blocker's aunt to call him and get him to come to the hospital.

"If he didn't do it, he has nothing to worry about," the police said.

When Blocker got to the hospital, he was grilled by detectives. They asked him who would have had a reason to harm his family. He couldn't tell them Reds because if he did, he'd be telling on himself. So instead, he told them he didn't know. Then they switched the focus to him, asking where he was last night. Blocker told the police that he was at the King of Prussia hotel all night. He even had the receipt for the room. So for now, he was off the hook. The police told Blocker they would be in touch with him once they checked his story out.

Blocker sat in the hospital with his aunt and cried. He couldn't believe the way that his family had been found. He knew his parents would never do anything to their children like that. He couldn't believe the lengths that Reds and J.R. would go to humiliate him. It was more than enough to kill his family; they have to do them like this.

Blocker tried to call Kawanda to tell her to start packing. Even though they had gotten into a fight over what Reds told him, Blocker still loved Kawanda. And even though Blocker's head told him that Reds was telling the truth about what Kawanda did, his heart and his pride told him that Kawanda didn't do it. Blocker was a mess. He needed to be with Kawanda and his son right now. A situation like this makes you appreciate the ones you love even more.

When he didn't get an answer, he figured that Kawanda was ignoring his calls because he beat her up. Blocker had the ransom money in the car. He decided to drive to Sidetrack and get Kawanda and his son then get out of town. Blocker had his mind made up that Reds and J.R. were going to pay for what they did, but now wasn't the time. It was way too hot.

Blocker drove to Kawanda's house and let himself in. The smell was awful—something had been burned bad. *What the hell did she try to cook?* Blocker asked himself. He called out to Kawanda, but got no answer. He knew she couldn't have gone far—he had her car, and his car was parked out on the side of the apartment. He walked through the house. Nobody was in the kitchen, so he headed for the bedroom. Kawanda's bedroom was located upstairs, at the back of the hallway. When you got to the end of the hallway, you could go right to her room or left to the bathroom.

When Blocker saw there was no one in the bedroom, he walked out of the room. He saw that the light was on in the bathroom. Blocker pulled his gun out and crept to the bathroom. When he pushed the door open, what he saw made him sick. Half of Kawanda's head was missing, and she was badly burned from her neck to her ankles. There was blood and brain fragments all over the bathroom, and the smell was something Blocker would never forget. The sight of Kawanda's body and the smell sent Blocker straight to the toilet to throw up. Blocker had seen dead bodies before, but never anything like this. When he reached the toilet, he saw little feet sticking out of the toilet bowl.

"Aww naw, not my lil' man! No, not my fuckin' lil' man!!" Blocker shouted. He pulled his son's waterlogged body out of the toilet and held him tight. He cried endlessly. Blocker's son had been left in the toilet like feces. Blocker was now starting to understand what type of people he had decided to go up against. He felt like there was no way he could get even with Reds for what he had done, so he broke down and got on the phone.

"I'd like to report a double murder," Blocker told the 911 operator.

"Where are you at?" the operator asked.

"I'm at 201 east Matlack Street, apartment 6a," Blocker said.

J.R. knew that the police would think something crazy when they found Blocker's family. He didn't really care what they thought. He just wanted the humiliating details to get out. It would only be a matter of time before the press had a field day with the details of the murders. J.R. drove past Kawanda's house to see if the police had found the bodies yet, but Sidetrack was quiet. He spotted Blocker's car parked in the parking lot, but Kawanda's car was gone. J.R. watched Blocker's car for almost an hour. He knew Blocker wasn't just sitting in Kawanda's house with the dead bodies, so he took it that he wasn't there.

J.R. wanted to leave Blocker a message. He broke into Blocker's car and popped the trunk. J.R. put the .45 that he used to kill Blocker's family and his little sister's panties in the trunk. J.R. knew that Blocker would find it and would know exactly what it was. He would also know exactly what it meant: "we can get you whenever we want."

Reds and J.R. met back up at J.R.'s apartment. Reds told J.R. not to touch Blocker. "I want that nigga to suffer 'til after the funeral. Once that's over, he's dead, on sight," Reds said.

"Understood," J.R. said. "But right now, you gotta go take everything that's incriminatin' out of ya house. Ya pop just got killed. The cops will be there soon, snoopin' around."

"All I got there is the safe with my money in it," Reds said.

"Go get that the fuck outta there," J.R. said. "And lay low for a while. Ain't no tellin' what this nigga's gonna do once he finds out what we did. He fuck around and tell."

"I don't think he'll tell. He'd have to tell on himself if he tells on me," Reds said.

"You never know what a nigga will do when his back is to the wall, and he feels like he don't got no win," J.R. said. "I don't know too many niggas that wouldn't tell after some shit like this."

"A'ight, I'm'a go handle that," Reds said.

J.R. never told Reds about the message that he left in Blocker's trunk.

Blocker sat in the police station for hours, telling on Reds and J.R. They killed his spirits when they killed his son. He wanted revenge, but he wasn't sure he could get it. If he took J.R. and Reds to war, he might lose and be killed. He couldn't risk it. They had to pay for what they did to his son. So Blocker decided to have them sent to jail. He knew that by telling on Reds and J.R., he'd have to tell on himself. That was fine as long as they went to jail too. Blocker would give his life to take theirs, so that's what he'd do.

But when it was all said and done, Blocker would only be hurting himself. Everything Blocker told the police about Reds and J.R. was hearsay. He didn't give them anything concrete. Blocker didn't see Reds or J.R. do anything, and they never told him they did anything. Blocker told the police that he was certain that Reds and J.R. killed his family because he took Reds's dad for ransom and killed him.

As soon as the cops got that bit of information, they went to the warehouse where Rob was killed and found his body. Rob had been shot once in the head. Once they found Rob's body, the police obtained search warrants for Reds's apartment, Rob's and Reds' cars, Blocker's car, and Kawanda's car. They didn't need a search warrant for Kawanda's apartment because it was a crime scene. But they couldn't get a search warrant for J.R.'s place because they didn't have an address for him.

The search of Reds's apartment revealed nothing. He had taken everything out of his house and went to Juanita's. It did, however, reveal that Blocker had torn the place up, looking for money just like he had told them. When they searched Kawanda's car, they found the money that Blocker said was in there and the gun that he killed Rob with. Then they searched Blocker's car and found the .45 along with his sister's panties.

They also interviewed Kawanda's neighbors to see if they knew anything. One of Kawanda's neighbors happened to be one of her friends. She told the police that Blocker had beaten Kawanda up because she slept with Reds. All the evidence they were gathering went against Blocker and Blocker only.

When the cops reported what they had discovered to Detective Morris, the lead detective, he had just gotten the DNA results back from Blocker's mother, father, brother, and sister's murder. The test revealed that the semen found in Blocker's mom's mouth belonged to her fifteen-year-old son. It also revealed that the pubic hair in Blocker's sister's mouth belonged to her father. Detective Morris wanted Reds and J.R. bad, but this case wouldn't be the one to bring them down. The evidence was telling a different story than Blocker's. And Detective Morris was a firm believer that evidence never lied.

As Detective Morris sat at his desk, he put together the story that the evidence told. Detective Morris thought that Blocker had killed Kawanda and the baby because she was cheating on him with Reds. He figured that Blocker went to Reds's house and intended on killing Reds. Since Reds wasn't there, he ripped the house up looking for money then took Reds's dad to an isolated area and killed him. The detective figured that Blocker then went to his parents' house to plot out his next move. It was then that he caught his parents molesting his brother and sister. That's when he lost it and killed everybody in the house.

Detective Morris figured that Blocker was trying to frame Reds and J.R. because of a personal vendetta. He wanted to believe what Blocker had told him about Reds and J.R., but all he had was Blocker's word and nothing more. Detective Morris would talk to Reds about his father's murder and see if he'd slip up and say something he shouldn't have, but that was all he could do at this moment. Anything more would result in a lawsuit; Detective Morris was sure of this.

Before Detective Morris's shift was over, he had the cops take Blocker to Chester County Prison where he'd be held on seven murder charges. Blocker's plan had blown up in his face. All he did by talking to the police was put himself away for the rest of his life. He must have never heard the old saying "loose lips sink ships" because if one thing was for sure, Blocker's ship had just been sunk.

## 29

Reds sat in front of the television and watched the eleven-o'clock news. He listened as the reporter gave the details behind Blocker's arrest.

*What the fuck is goin' on?* Reds thought to himself when he heard the police thought they found the murder weapon of Blocker's family in his car. Reds drove to J.R's apartment.

"I thought I told you to lay low?" J.R. asked as he answered his door.

"Was you watchin' the news?" Reds asked.

"Yeah," J.R. answered.

"How the fuck they think they found the murder weapon in his car?" Reds asked.

J.R. sat quietly for a second. "Listen, I was tryin' to send the nigga a message. You know, fuck with his mind a lil'. I put the panties and the gun in his trunk to let him know that we could get him whenever we wanted. I didn't know the cops was gonna search his shit," J.R. explained.

Reds sat quietly for a moment; he was furious. "I wanted to watch the soul leave out that nigga's eyes," Reds said.

"I feel you, cuz. I wanted the nigga dead too. But that bitch-ass nigga couldn't handle the pressure and told on himself. So either way, he was goin' to jail. Look at it like this: he's dead while he's still alive. We killed everything he loves, then he gets charged with the murders. He's gonna be in jail for the rest of his life with nothin' and nobody. He can't even get revenge. That's how you kill a ma'fucka! Make 'em suffer for the rest of their life. Anybody can kill a ma'fucka. But when you kill a ma'fucka while he's still breathin', you really doin' somethin'," J.R. said.

Reds thought about what J.R. said. He wanted to be mad at J.R., but he had a valid point. Reds hated the fact that even when J.R. did something wrong, he had a way of making it look right.

"You know the cops is gonna wanna talk to you," J.R. said.

"Yeah, I know," Reds responded.

"Call Jimmy tomorrow and find out what he suggests," J.R. said.

"A'ight," Reds said as he got up to leave.

"And stay outta eyesight. You 'posed to be layin' low 'til we find out what's up," J.R. said.

"I gotchu," Reds said as he gave his cousin a handshake and left.

The next morning, Reds made funeral arrangements for his father. As he was doing this, he realized that burying people close to him was becoming too common.

After finishing up with his father's funeral plans, Reds sat and thought about quitting the drug game. In such a short time, he had lost everyone he really loved except for J.R. This game had cost him more than he was willing to lose.

After going back and forth with his thoughts, Reds decided to get rich or die trying. There wasn't much left for him to lose, so why quit now? All Reds had left was J.R., and he was probably going to be living the street life until the day he died. Reds didn't care if he lived or not. He wouldn't let the streets win. He refused to let the streets take all he loved and leave him to struggle for the rest of his life. The least the streets could do was pay him for all his losses. Reds would either get rich and use his money to help numb the pain or he would die, and he wouldn't have to deal with all the pain. Either way, the pain would be dealt with or at least soothed.

Around two o'clock, Reds called Jimmy. "I think they wanna talk to me 'bout Bernard Harris killin' my father," Reds said.

"Well, you're grieving your father's death. If they already got the guy, they don't need to talk to you," Jimmy said.

"I'll talk to them as long as they don't start their bullshit," Reds said.

"Okay, it's your call. But I'll tell you like I told your cousin this morning, I don't like talking to those assholes. J.R. has nothing to say unless they plan on charging him with something. Now if you still want to talk, meet me at the police station in an hour," Jimmy said.

"I'll be there," Reds said.

Reds and Jimmy walked into the police station and asked to speak to Detective Morris. Detective Morris came out and took Reds and Jimmy into an interrogation room.

"His father just died—play nice. I just want to say that I'm always against talking to you guys, but my client wants to help you any way he can," Jimmy said.

Detective Morris told Reds exactly what Blocker had told him about everything. He wanted to see if Reds's facial expression would change or something that would tell him if there was any truth to what Blocker said. Reds's facial expression remained the same the whole time.

Once the detective got finished talking, Reds spoke. "I did sleep with his girlfriend. I told him that durin' an argument. Now, I wish I had just kept my big mouth shut. I don't know anything about any ransom money or killin' his family or Kawanda and his baby. I mean, that's some real sick shit. Who kills an innocent child? I guess he's sayin' it was me because he wants to get me in trouble. And as far as my cousin goes, I haven't seen him in weeks. I'm sorry, but that's all the help I can be," Reds said somberly.

"Would you mind takin' a polygraph test?" Detective Morris asked.

"See, this is why I voted against this bullshit. Even when you try to help these guys, they turn it on you," Jimmy said. "My client has done nothing but try to be cooperative, and this is the thanks he gets. This meeting is over. And I'm promising you, if you start harassing my client, I'll file suit and have Reverend Jesse Jackson himself up here and on your ass!"

"He knows more than he's telling," Detective Morris said.

"That's your favorite line. And that's exactly why Mr. Richers won't talk to you," Jimmy said as he and Reds walked out of the police station.

After Rob's funeral was over, Reds mourned his father. Sting had called the night before and told Reds that he wanted to get on board. Reds explained that he just lost his father and needed some time. Sting told Reds that he was ready whenever Reds was. Reds also got a call from Los.

"I've heard of your loss, and I would like to offer my condolences. I want you to know that there is no pressure. Take your time to mourn your father. My offer still stands once this passes," Los said.

That phone call told Reds a lot about Los's character. He liked the way Los conducted himself.

After a month of grieving, Reds decided to take a cruise to the Caribbean. Reds left on a Friday and would return on a Thursday. Reds told himself that once he returned from his trip, he'd turn it back up.

As he was leaving, Reds saw the State Police and West Chester Police everywhere. Because of all the recent violence, the mayor had the town crawling with cops. He publicly promised to take the streets back from the hooligans.

*I'm glad I'm gettin' the fuck outta here,* Reds thought as he drove to the airport.

Reds stood at the edge of the cruise ship, and took the view in.

"Isn't it lovely?" a woman's voice asked.

"It is," Reds replied as he turned to see who he was talking to. What Reds saw was an exotic beauty. She stood about five-foot-four, had jet-black hair, green eyes, and the sexiest lips Reds had ever laid eyes on. A white bikini top clung to her beautifully shaped breasts, and the warm summer breeze had her nipples poking through. Her white miniskirt hugged her thick thighs, hips, and plump backside. Her skin was the complexion of beach sand, and although she showed a lot of skin, she left a little room for the imagination. She topped her outfit off with a pair of all-white low-top Air Force Ones. She was definitely Reds's type, and he wasted no time.

Reds extended his hand for a handshake. "I'm Reds. As I was sayin', this is a very lovely sight. I didn't think I would see anything more lovely while on this cruise. I guess I was wrong," Reds said.

"Thank you," she said. "It's nice to know there's still gentleman out there."

"A gentleman I am, but I didn't catch your name, Mrs.———?" Reds said.

"My name is Rosa. And it's Miss, not Mrs. I'm not married. This young lady is very much single," Rosa said with a warm smile.

"Well, that's good to know. I might have to change that one day," Reds said.

"Who says I want you to change it?" Rosa asked as she gave Reds a look that let him know she was up for his game.

Reds and Rosa flirted back and forth for a while. Reds told her some things about himself, and he learned a few things about her. Rosa was Cuban and Dominican. She was also a student at Florida State University. She told Reds that her boyfriend was supposed to come, but he got indicted two weeks ago. "I needed to get away from all the bullshit, so I decided to take a cruise," Rosa said.

"I feel you. I, too, am usin' this cruise as a stress reliever," Reds said.

"Maybe we can help each other relieve some stress," Rosa said with a devilish grin.

"Maybe, if you promise not to lie to me again," Reds said.

"What are you talking about?" Rosa asked.

"Just a few minutes ago, you told me you was single. Then a few minutes later, you told me your man got indicted. I'm a lil' mesmerized by your beauty, but I pay attention to detail. We don't know each other, so there's no need to lie to me," Reds said.

"I'm sorry. I say boyfriend out of habit. We were together for four years. He is my ex now. When he got locked up, I had his phone. Because of this, I found out he had a newborn baby. I'm a good girl, and even though I don't like to leave when a person is down, I had to. He cheated on me, so he doesn't deserve me," Rosa said.

Reds could sense the pain in her words. "Oh, I see. Well, we don't need to harp on that. But I will tell you he was a fool to cheat on you," Reds said.

"Full of compliments, are we?" Rosa said.

"Not really, you're just deservin' of them," Reds said. "I was 'bout to go snorkelin'. Would you like to join?"

"I don't see why not. I get to see the ocean and look at you without any clothes on. I'm in," Rosa said.

Reds knew Rosa was more than interested. He just had to play it cool, and he'd be eight inches deep inside of her by the end of the night.

When they went snorkeling, Reds saw a little more of Rosa's body. She wore these white bikini bottoms that showed off her plump lady parts, front and back. Reds was infatuated with Rosa's body, and she knew this.

As they were putting on their snorkeling gear, Rosa caught Reds undressing her with his eyes. She didn't say anything. She just bent over and gave Reds a nice view of her goodies. Rosa's top came off when she jumped in the water, so she snorkeled topless. Reds watched her more than he watched the fish.

After Reds and Rosa snorkeled, Reds asked her if she wanted to get something to eat. Rosa quickly accepted. She told Reds that she would go get changed then meet him at his room.

Reds was about to get in the shower when a knock came at his door. Reds answered the door with a towel wrapped around him. Rosa stood in front of him with a bag in her hand. "Hey, sexy. My water ain't getting hot. Can I use your shower?" Rosa asked as she began to pout.

"Of course you can. But I might use all the hot water, so you may have to shower with me," Reds said.

Normally, Rosa would make a man wait to be with her, but she was on the rebound, and Reds made her feel at ease. So she'd give in to Reds and let him have what they both wanted. Rosa stepped inside the room and snatched Reds' towel away.

"Damn, boy, I might not wanna get out of the shower," Rosa said as she observed Reds's manhood.

"We can do whatever you want," Reds said with a big smile.

"In that case, I'd like to eat now," Rosa said as she dropped to her knees and put Reds in her mouth. She took Reds in and out of her mouth slowly. She twisted her head from side to side as she sucked his dick, letting her tongue hang out while doing this. She was really turning Reds on.

He watched her for a minute then closed his eyes and enjoyed her mouth. Rosa worked her way down until she got all of Reds down her throat. Rosa had Reds feeling great and moaning loudly. He grabbed the back of her head and pumped slowly in and out of her mouth. Rosa allowed this to go on for a minute, then she pulled her head back, letting Reds's shaft out of her mouth. "My pussy is tighter," she said as she stood up.

Reds took Rosa to the bed and laid her down. He started licking on her neck, then he slowly made his way down to her breasts. He sucked on her nipples, occasionally gently biting down on them. Reds licked his way down to Rosa's love tunnel. Her pussy was smooth and hairless. Reds could tell she had just gotten a bikini waxing. He kissed her inner thighs, building Rosa's anticipation even more. He blew softly on her wet pussy, then he parted her lips and began to suck on her clitoris.

"Oooooh!" Rosa moaned. "Don't stop, right there! Aaahhhh, that's it, right there!"

Reds slid two fingers inside of her while he worked his tongue. This drove Rosa crazy. Reds continued this until she had an orgasm. Rosa pulled Reds's wet face up to hers then kissed him passionately.

"Fuck me, papi," Rosa moaned softly in Reds's ear.

Reds lifted Rosa's legs up and eased his way inside of her. Rosa dug her nails into Reds's back and bit his neck as he dug himself deep inside of Rosa's tight pussy.

"Be gentle. I've only ever been with my ex, and he wasn't that big at all," Rosa said.

Normally, Reds would have thought she was lying, but her pussy was extra tight. She was so tight that Reds couldn't get all of his dick inside of her. After about five minutes, Reds managed to work himself all the way in. Rosa was in pain, but she took it like a champ. It wasn't an unbearable pain; it was a pain that felt good. She looked so sexy as she closed her eyes and bit down on her bottom lip. Reds was delivering long slow strokes to her for about ten minutes, and she was enjoying every second of it.

"Oooh, I'm cumming!" Rosa moaned loudly.

Reds felt his release coming also. "Me too," he grunted.

"Don't cum inside of me," Rosa said.

Reds pulled out of her and jerked off until he came on her stomach. Rosa lay there and looked at Reds. She found him to be so sexy. He lay down next to her. "You fuckin' up my vacation," Rosa said.

Reds loved how she spoke so properly and pronounced every syllable; it was different from what he was used to. "How am I fuckin' up ya vacation?" Reds asked.

"I'm not gonna see all the sights because I don't want to leave this room," Rosa said.

"Oh, we gonna leave, but you'll be here every night," Reds said.

"Okay. Well, now that I have an open invitation, we can go get something to eat," Rosa said.

After dinner, they stood on the deck of the ship and looked out into the ocean.

"Would you come to Miami and visit me?" Rosa asked.

"Of course," Reds said, lying. He knew that he would never talk to Rosa after this trip. He had only known her for eight hours, but Reds really liked Rosa. He liked her a little too much for his comfort. Reds could see himself falling in love with Rosa in no time, and that was a big no-no for him. Reds was deathly afraid of being hurt again, so afraid, that he would push someone like Rosa away rather than see where it would lead.

"I really like you, Reds," Rosa said.

"You're not so bad yourself," Reds said, trying to make light of the situation.

"No, I'm serious. I've never met someone that I just clicked with like I did with you," Rosa said. "I could see myself being with you."

Reds didn't want to spoil the moment. "I could see myself being with you too," Reds said.

"But that's what scares me," Rosa said.

"Why?" Reds asked.

"I'm Dominican and Cuban. All the men in my family are into the streets. I can tell if a person is into that just by looking at them. The only type of men I'm interested in are guys that live that type of life. I had been watching you before I approached you. Your whole style says street," Rosa explained.

"Nah, you misread that one. I'm a workin' nigga," Reds said as he held her tight.

Later on that night, Reds and Rosa went to the club, which was located on the ship.

"Let's dance, sweetie," Rosa said.

"I don't dance," Reds said.

"What? Are you too tough to dance?" Rosa said sarcastically.

"Absolutely not. I'm half white—I can't dance," Reds said with a laugh.

"You so silly," Rosa said.

"How 'bout this? You give me a lap dance," Reds suggested.

Rosa sat Reds down and rubbed her body all over him. Reds raped her with his eyes and felt every inch of her curvaceous body.

The cruise ship asked the passengers to put all their money on cards for security purposes. The policy of the cruise ship was to give black cards to anyone with $10,000 or better on their account. And if you had a black card, you got free drinks for the whole stay. This rule was made in hopes that the people with black cards would get drunk off free drinks every night then go to the casino on board and lose all their money. This was not the case with Reds and Rosa, but they did take full advantage of Reds's black card. Both Reds and Rosa had drinks flowing freely and got completely wasted.

Around midnight, Reds noticed a thick light-skinned chick eyeing him and Rosa. Reds found the woman to be attractive, so he called her over to their table. Reds introduced himself and Rosa and learned her name was Tiff. He asked if she wanted to party with them, and she agreed. Rosa felt a twinge of jealousy. But the liquor had her feeling good, so she let it go and decided to continue enjoying herself.

After Tiff's fourth double shot of Vodka, she got loose. Tiff began feeling all over Rosa to the point it could have been mistaken for molestation. Rosa was completely drunk, but she still looked at Reds for approval. When he gave her a warm smile and the nod, Rosa just went with the flow. Together they gave Reds a hell of a show. After a three-way kiss, Reds got an idea. "Remember earlier, when you said I gave you your first orgasm?" Reds asked Rosa.

"Yeah," Rosa responded.

"Well, I want you to give me somethin' for the first time," Reds said.

"What?" Rosa asked.

"I never had a threesome," Reds said.

"You want me to give you a threesome?" Rosa asked. "With who?"

"Do you think our new friend is cute?" Reds asked.

"With her?" Rosa asked.

"Why not?" Reds responded with a smirk.

"I never been with a woman before," Rosa said.

"Well, you're a woman, so just do to her the things you like done to you," Reds suggested.

"You promise you're coming to Miami to see me?" Rosa asked.

"Cross my heart and hope to die," Reds responded.

"Okay," Rosa said as she gave Reds a kiss.

By the time everybody was ready to go, Tiff had been informed of what Reds was trying to do. She was hammered too and had no objections. As they walked to Reds's room, Reds examined Tiff closely. She was about five-foot-nine, and 160 pounds of beef in all the right places. If Reds had to guess her breast cup size, he would have guessed a double D. Reds was getting hard as he looked at Tiff switching her derriere from side to side. It looked like she had two basketballs in her pants. She had the body of Serena Williams and the face of the rapper Trina.

As soon as they got into the room, Reds got naked. He wanted to jump on Tiff, but he could tell that Rosa was a little uncomfortable. So he decided to give Rosa his attention and let Tiff join in. Once everybody was naked and in the bed, things got started.

Reds slid himself inside of Rosa. As he started stroking her, she started moaning, "Ahhh! Ahhhh!"

"Slide her down a little. You stand up and fuck her," Tiff told Reds.

Once Reds had Rosa in position, Tiff sat on Rosa's face. "Eat this pussy, girl," Tiff said.

Reds continued to stroke Rosa while looking at Tiff's fat ass. After Tiff came, she told Reds she wanted to eat Rosa's pussy. Reds had Rosa and Tiff switch positions. Rosa sat on Tiff's face as Reds gripped Tiff's hips and pushed himself inside of her. Reds could instantly tell Tiff was a whore. It felt like Reds had stuck his dick inside a Hula-Hoop. He didn't complain. He just went through the motions. Before he kicked her out, Reds wanted to see what Tiff's dick-suck game was like. After Rosa came, she got off Tiff and watched Reds do his thing. Reds pulled out of Tiff and was about to tell her to suck his dick.

"Don't stop now, baby. I'm almost there," Tiff said.

Reds wanted to be a good sport, so he went back inside of her. Since she said she was about to cum, Reds started ramming the pussy.

"Whoa! Whoa!" Tiff started yelling like Joey off of the television show *Blossom*.

As soon as she started yelling "whoa" Rosa started laughing.

"Yo, you cool?" Reds asked Tiff with his face broken up.

"Oh yeah, you just beatin' the pussy up," Tiff said.

"A'ight, but you buggin' me out with that 'whoa' shit," Reds said.

He started fucking her again, but she kept saying "Whoa!" Reds was really regretting bringing Tiff back to his room. He finally just stopped and told Tiff and Rosa to suck his dick together. While Reds was getting his dick sucked, Tiff kept slapping his ass.

"Yo, stop slappin' my fuckin' ass," Reds said.

Tiff stopped then went to her bag. "I want you to try something'," Tiff said as she went in her bag. "Do you have some Vaseline?"

"For what?" Reds asked.

Tiff pulled out a butt plug. Reds looked at her like she lost her mind. "What the fuck is that?" Reds asked.

"It's for anal stimulation," Tiff said.

"For who?" Reds responded.

"For you, silly. You put it up your ass while we suck your dick," Tiff explained like it was normal.

"You got the wrong nigga, bitch! I'll beat the shit out chu!" Reds barked as he got up.

"I'm sorry. I didn't mean to offend you," Tiff said.

Rosa could tell that things were about to get ugly, so she intervened. "I think you should go," Rosa said as she stood up.

"I didn't mean anything by that. I—" Tiff tried to say.

Rosa cut her off. "It's time to go."

Tiff got dressed then left. As soon as Tiff left, Rosa bust out laughing, which made Reds laugh.

"What the fuck was that?" Reds asked.

"It was all your idea," Rosa said.

"That bitch was super weird," Reds said.

"Whoa! Whoa!" Rosa said, imitating Tiff.

They both had a really good laugh about it. Rosa walked over and kissed Reds softly. "Just for the record, you'll never get another threesome from me," Rosa said.

Over the next week, Reds and Rosa became very close. Reds was starting to feel like Rosa was his girl. But as they say, all things must come to an end. Reds had mixed emotions about the cruise being over. On one hand, he was really enjoying Rosa's company. On the other, he knew he had to get away from her. It had only been a week, and he really liked Rosa. It was like she was the perfect woman for him, but Reds knew that nothing was perfect. He was just glad he wouldn't have to find out that she wasn't perfect. The only memories he would have of Rosa would be the ones he got while on this trip.

When they got off the boat, Rosa asked Reds to come back to Miami with her for a few days. Reds told her that he had a lot of things to take care of, but he promised that he'd be down to see her soon. They kissed for a long time, then Rosa promised to call him later that day. Reds got in his cab knowing he'd never talk to her again, having given her the wrong number.

*The sacrifices of bein' a hustler,* Reds thought to himself as he waved bye to Rosa.

# 30

The plane landed in Philadelphia airport at 10:50 p.m. Reds was anxious to get home. He needed to relax, and that's just what the trip to the Bahamas did. Not once did Reds think about home. He enjoyed his vacation fully. But now that he was back home, it was time to get back to business.

On his ride home, Reds called Sting. "I'll be seein' you on Saturday," Reds said.

"I can't wait," Sting responded.

After Reds ended the call with Sting, he called Juanita. "Tell ya folks I'm ready," Reds said.

"Okay, are you back from your trip?" Juanita asked.

"I'm on my way back in town right now," Reds told her.

"Why don't you come over, and we can call him in the mornin'," Juanita said.

"That's not a bad idea," Reds said.

The next morning, Reds had Juanita call Los. Los gave Juanita a phone number and told her to have Reds call that number from a pay phone in thirty minutes. Reds got dressed and headed to a pay phone.

"Hello," Los answered.

"It's Reds," he said.

"This line is safe. What is it that you want?" Los asked.

"Ten bricks, twenty thousand e-pills, and a hundred pounds of weed," Reds said.

Los was silent for a brief second. "So you'll owe me $240,000 next time you see me," Los said.

"A'ight," Reds responded. "Is this the number I can reach you at?"

"No, this is a pay phone. Anytime you call me for business, we will talk on pay phones. Juanita will give you my cell phone number. Only call that number to get the number to the pay phone. It will be a different number every time. When you call my cell, ask for someone's phone number. The number I give you will be the number to the pay phone. Always wait thirty minutes before calling," Los said.

"Gotcha. So next time you hear from me, I'll be sending Juanita with $480,000. $240,000 for this trip and $240,000 for that trip," Reds said.

"That's what I like to hear," Los said. "And if you have any problems, call me. There isn't too much I can't fix."

Reds sent Juanita on her way to see Los. While she was gone, Reds sat in her house and crunched numbers. He stood to make $1.4 million off his first shipment. He only owed Los $480,000 to pay for the first shipment and get another. Reds didn't have to worry about taking any losses because he had Sting on deck. If Reds let them sell everything for the prices they were already going for, he would still make the same. So the way he looked at it, he was getting Sting on his team for free. As Reds played with numbers, he couldn't help but to smile at himself. Reds knew he was one smart businessman. As long as he made sure everybody was getting paid, all would be good. At least that's what he thought.

Later that night, Reds drove to Altoona. His first stop was to see his cousin Shontae. "What's good, cuz?" Reds said when Shontae opened the door.

"I'm so sorry about ya dad," Shontae said.

"It's all right. Everything happens for a reason," Reds said.

"I didn't think you was comin' back up here," Shontae said.

"Yeah, I had to take some time to get my head right, but I'm cool now. At least as good as I'm gonna be," Reds said. "But check it. I need a favor."

"What's up?" Shontae asked.

"Do you have any girlfriends that you trust?" Reds asked.

"Hell no! The only bitch on the face of this earth I trust is my mom," Shontae said.

Shontae's mom was Reds's cousin too, but because of the age difference, Reds called her Aunt Pearl instead of just calling her Pearl. Reds was so hyped about getting all the drugs Los was sending that he didn't even think of stashing stuff at Pearl's house. Reds had to get past his excitement and start thinking straight. Pearl was a great person to hold his stash. She was as hood as it got. Reds knew that as long as he paid Pearl, she'd let him keep whatever he wanted in her house.

"I need to go holla at her," Reds said.

Pearl lived in Altoona also. Reds meant to stop by her house last time he was in Altoona but never got the chance to. Shontae gave him the address to Pearl's house.

"I don't know how to get around up here," Reds said.

"It's impossible to get lost. Everything is on streets and avenues, and they're all numbered," Shontae responded.

Reds left Shontae's house and headed to Pearl's house. Surprisingly, Reds found her house with ease. Pearl saw Reds at his father's funeral, but by the time she went to talk to him, Reds was gone.

Pearl was happy to see Reds. They sat in her living room for almost an hour and talked.

"I'll tell you what, baby boy, you can keep whatever you want in here. In return, you keep me supplied with weed. Ain't no good weed up here," Pearl said.

"Is a pound a month good?" Reds asked.

"What? Do babies wear diapers? Hell yeah, a pound a month is good," Pearl said.

First thing in the morning, Reds would have a huge safe put in Pearl's basement. He'd keep everything in there and take his money home when he was ready to reup. He called Juanita later on that night and told her to come see him the next day. They had already talked, and she knew Reds would be calling when he was ready for the drugs. All that was left now was for the drugs to be delivered, and the show would start.

Around noon the next day, Juanita called Reds. "I'm at the gas station on Seventeenth street," she said.

Reds drove to get her. When they got to Pearl's house, Juanita and Reds unloaded five large bags.

"Damn, boy, what chu puttin' down there, bodies?" Pearl asked with a laugh.

"Nah, just some clothes and shit," Reds said.

"Yeah right," Pearl said as she let Reds and Juanita finish.

Once everything was unloaded, Reds gave Juanita a kiss and told her he had to get to work. Juanita wanted to stay, but she knew she'd just be bored waiting on Reds while he ran the streets. Reds walked Juanita out, then he came back in the house. "Here, Aunt Pearl, go buy ya'self somethin' nice," Reds said as he gave her $300. "And when you come back, I'll have that pound of weed for you."

"Now that's how you kick a bitch out the house—give her some money. But you don't promise her weed—she might come back too fast," Pearl said with a laugh.

"Nah, you take ya time," Reds said.

"Okay," Pearl said as she stuffed the money in her bra and left.

Reds drove to the store and bought a couple boxes of baking soda. He went back to Pearl's house and started cooking the coke into crack. Once he cooked three kilos, counted out the pills, and got the weed in order, Reds took Sting his first package. The package consisted of one kilo of crack, ten pounds of weed, and five thousand e-pills.

Sting proved to be one hell of a hustler. Three days later, Reds got a call. "I need to see you again," Sting said.

"I'm impressed," Reds said. "I'm on my way."

Reds drove to Fairview and saw it was filled with hustlers and junkies. Sting had Fairview looking like the projects in the city. Reds called Sting, and he came outside.

"I see you handlin' things," Reds said with a smile.

"Man, I can't lie. This shit is so good, it's sellin' itself," Sting said.

Sting took Reds inside a house, went upstairs, then came back down with a bag full of money. "I believe this belongs to you," Sting said. Sting handed Reds a bag with $119,600. "You wanna count it?" Sting asked.

"If it's wrong, I'll let chu know," Reds responded. "I'll drop another load off tomorrow."

"Music to my ears," Sting said.

Reds left Fairview and drove straight to Pearl's house. He put his money up then grabbed ten more pounds of weed, five thousand more pills, and another kilo of crack. He told Sting that he was going to drop another load off the next day, but he knew he was dropping it right off. Reds just didn't like for people to be able to calculate his moves. Next time, Reds would drop it off two days later. In Reds's line of work, staying unpredictable meant staying free and, more importantly, staying alive.

After he hit Sting off, Reds called Shontae. "You too busy to shoot a lil' pool with family?" Reds asked.

"I'm never too busy for my favorite cousin," Shontae responded.

As they shot pool, Shontae asked Reds if he'd be able to help Reem with an e-pill connect.

"I told Reem that my homey got killed," Reds said.

"You don't got nobody else?" Shontae asked.

Reds thought for a second. He wasn't really trying to be in competition with himself. He also didn't want to deal with Reem—he was a real clown. Reds was sure that if he gave Reem something and he got caught, Reem would tell. "Nah, I don't got no one else for 'em. But if I come across somethin', I'll let chu know," Reds said casually.

They shot a few more games then left.

After leaving the bar, Reds went to the mall, and Shontae went to her mom's house. While Shontae was at Pearl's house, Reem called. A few minutes later, he came through.

"Did you holla Reds 'bout the pills?" Reem asked.

"He said he ain't got no one else," Shontae said.

"Fuck he mean he don't got no one? That bitch-ass nigga got Fairview flooded with pills. I only agreed to let him come the fuck out here 'cause he was 'posed to be givin' me the pill connect. Now, he done came out here and saw it was sweet, he wanna try to keep all the bread for himself," Reem said.

"I don't know, baby. What chu want me to do?" Shontae asked.

"Nothin', but that's some fucked-up shit. If he wasn't ya cousin, I'd fuck that bitch-ass nigga up," Reem said.

Shontae knew that Reem was a coward, so she just let him vent. Nobody in the house believed what Reem said, but that wouldn't stop Pearl from telling Reds. Pearl didn't like Reem. He had a disrespectful mouth, and she knew he hit Shontae from time to time. Pearl also knew that Reds wasn't to be played with. She decided to tell Reds what Reem had said, and she'd add a little extra just to be sure Reem got his ass beat. Pearl figured it would serve Reem right. He liked to hit on her daughter, see how he liked it when somebody hit him.

Reds came by Pearl's house the next day and asked if she wanted to go get some lunch.

"Yeah, I need to talk to you anyway," Pearl said.

On the way to the Chinese buffet, Pearl gave Reds her version of what Reem had said. She told Reds that Reem said: Reds was a bitch. He was going to fuck Reds up, and that he should rob Reds and tell him he couldn't come back to Altoona.

Reds didn't question a word Pearl said, and he was livid over what he had just heard.

"He was really mad at chu. He said that if you wasn't family, he would have killed you," Pearl added.

"He said what!" Reds asked in an outrage.

"Baby, I'm only tellin' you 'cause I don't want to see you get in no shit. I know Reem ain't a real tough guy, but you never know what a person will do about some money," Pearl said. "So just stay away for a lil' while. Let him cool off."

Pearl was only trying to get Reem's smacked around, but she added a little too much. Pearl didn't know exactly how dangerous Reds was, and her last statement sealed Reem's fate for good.

Reds didn't reveal what he planned to do. He just thanked Pearl for her warning. They rode the rest of the ride in silence. Pearl laughed to herself as she thought of Reds smacking Reem around. Pearl was a sweet lady if she liked you, but Lord help her enemies.

Reds planned on talking to J.R. when he went back to West Chester. If J.R. was looking for some easy money, Reds had a job for him. Thanks to Pearl, Reem was a dead man walking.

Sting finished everything in a little less than a month. Reds drove back home, called Los, then sent Juanita on her way. After he sent Juanita off, Reds went to his apartment. When his father first got killed, Reds wanted to move. But the more he thought about it, he was sure he was going to stay. Reds had a lot of memories of his father in that apartment. And since he wasn't doing anything in West Chester anymore, he figured it would be safe for him to keep his money there.

After Reds put his money up, he went to talk to J.R. They had been keeping in touch by phone, but they hadn't hung out much since Reds went to Altoona. J.R. missed Reds. He was like his little brother. J.R. wanted to go to Altoona with Reds and see what it was like. Reds had told him stories about the women out there, so when he offered J.R. $30,000 to kill Reem, J.R. gladly accepted.

"I'll collect when the job is done," J.R. said.

Reds and J.R. talked for a while, then they headed to Altoona. Once they got to Altoona, Reds showed J.R. where Reem lived. Once J.R. saw where Reem lived, he started his job. He and Reds parted ways. Reds drove to Fairview to see how things were. When Reds got to Fairview, he saw lots of flashing lights.

"Nothin' is ever easy," Reds said to himself as he blew out a deep breath. Reds pulled over and called Sting.

"Yo," Sting answered. "I need to holla at chu ASAP."

"Okay, are you in Fairview?" Reds asked.

"Yeah," Sting replied.

"Walk out of Fairview and down the hill. I'm parked right on the side of the street," Reds said.

Sting came to his car a few minutes later. Reds learned that one of Sting's workers was shot. It had been some beef between Fairview and Evergreen Manor, which were both low-income apartment complexes or projects as the locals called them. Sting had things on lock, and other projects were mad, so they shot Fairview up. Since Reds flooded Fairview with drugs, it was the place to be for all except dope fiends. The other projects made it clear that if they weren't getting money, nobody was.

"It's always a broke nigga tryna fuck somethin' up," Reds said.

"So what's up? You got everything under control?"

"Of course I do. Niggas get shot every day in the hood," Sting said. "I should be ready to see you within the next twenty-four hours."

"A'ight, the police gonna be out there for the rest of the night, questionin' ma'fuckas. They probably be out there for the next couple days," Reds said. "So take ya time. Let shit cool off. Niggas sent a clear message. I think you need to send one back. Plus, it'll give the cops somethin' to do."

"I definitely feel you," Sting said.

Things had been going smoothly since Reds came to Altoona. He knew it was only a matter of time until things got complicated. This small war between two projects could mess Reds's money up. So he had to extinguish it before it got out of hand. Reds was going to sit back and let Sting handle things, but he wasn't sure how Sting would do. So Reds changed his plan. Reds would still let Sting run the point, but he'd call the plays from the sideline.

After Reds met Juanita and put everything up at Pearl's, he called Sting. Reds told Sting to meet him at the McDonald's near the Seventeenth Street Sheetz. When Sting got there, Reds was already seated and eating his food. Sting ordered then joined Reds.

"So what's it lookin' like up there?" Reds asked as he munched on a french fry.

"They still up there askin' questions," Sting said. "It don't look like they gonna be leavin' no time soon."

"Yeah, I figured that. Look, this shit is fuckin' money up. We gotta dead it ASAP. I take it you know who's behind this dumb shit," Reds said.

"Yeah, this nigga named Twan. He from the Bronx. Nigga gotta lil' team that be movin' shit in Evergreen Manor. They gettin' money, but nothin' like what we doin'," Sting said.

"I know, but that's why he's such a threat. A nigga with nothin' to lose has everything to gain," Reds said. "I can have this shit solved in a day or two, but just like all my services, it comes with a price."

"How much?" Sting asked.

"At least $50,000," Reds said.

"Goddamn, I can have some lil' niggas from my hood do it for like $5,000," Sting shot back.

"That's up to you. All I can tell you is that if you put that $50,000 up, shit'll get done right," Reds said.

"I think I'm gonna take care of it," Sting said.

"Okay, but since you got it, I want that nigga dead by the end of the week," Reds said.

"That might be a lil' hard. I told you he got a lil' team up here," Sting said.

"Fuck them niggas. If you kill the head, the body dies. You said you had it, so handle it," Reds said.

"A'ight," Sting said as he took a deep breath.

"And I want you to send a message," Reds said.

"What's that?" Sting asked.

"Does he have any family out here?" Reds asked.

"Yeah, he live out here with his baby mom," Sting said.

"Kill him, his baby mom, and the baby," Reds said. "When you're done, stick a $100 bill in everybody's mouth. Ma'fuckas need to understand the consequences of fuckin' with our money. As soon as that happens, niggas will know to leave us the fuck alone. Once niggas know you play for keeps, they stay out our fuckin' way."

Sting sat at the table in silence. Sting had killed before, but Reds was talking about taking things to a whole new level. Sting's back was to the wall. Sting wasn't really trying to kill Twan's baby mom and the baby. But if he didn't do what Reds was asking, Reds might pay a someone $50,000 to handle him.

"Yo, you cool?" Reds asked.

"Yeah, you just a lil' more ruthless than I thought," Sting said.

"You have no idea how ruthless I can be, and you should never have to find out," Reds said. "But in situations like this, you'll see glimpses."

Sting nodded his head, letting Reds know that he understood.

"So are we clear on how things are to be done?" Reds asked.

"Yeah, I got it," Sting said.

As Sting left the McDonald's, he knew that he had to be careful with Reds. Reds was far more dangerous than Sting had initially thought.

Reds phone rang, and the display screen read, "DON'T ANSWER!" Reds ignored the call like he did all the callers who had been listed like that. A few seconds later, his phone started beeping, indicating that he had a message. Reds checked his messages and heard Nikki's voice.

"Why is you bein' such a fuckin' asshole, Reds? All I wanna do is love you, but you tryin' to make me hate you. You need to stop playin' and act like you know. If you keep tryin' to diss me, you gonna be sorry. Consider ya'self warned," she said as the message ended.

*This bitch is crazy,* Reds thought to himself. He drove to Joylin's house. Reds met Joylin at the Island, a club in Altoona. She was Puerto Rican and stunning, which happened to be Reds's type. She was about five-foot-eight and 150 pounds. Joylin had long curly hair and big bright eyes. She was average in the breast-and-butt department, but she was very pretty and had what Reds called thunder thighs.

Joylin and Reds had chilled together on several occasions, and he liked her. She knew her role, and she had no problem playing it. Joylin never questioned Reds or tried to lock him down. She just enjoyed the time she got to spend with him. Because of this, Reds loved chilling with her. When he got there, he watched a movie, got some head, then went to sleep.

Reds had been staying at different women's houses every night. He'd meet a chick, have sex with her, stay there for a few nights, then move on. Reds wanted to get an apartment; he just didn't have the time to get around to it.

Reds woke up to a knock at Joylin's door. He woke her up, and she answered the door. Some dude she was sleeping with had stopped by unannounced. Reds didn't care what any chick he talked to did. All he asked was that they didn't have any guys around while he was there.

Even though Joylin quickly put her male friend out, it motivated Reds to go get his own spot. Reds got dressed then went apartment hunting. He got a newspaper then went looking.

When he found the apartment in Hollidaysburg, he knew it was the one for him. Hollidaysburg was right outside of Altoona. Not much was going on out there. That's exactly why Reds wanted it. He called the landlord then met up with him. Together, they looked at the apartment. Reds paid him, signed the lease, then got his keys.

Reds's next stop was to the furniture store. He bought everything he needed to make his place comfortable. His stuff was to be delivered around three o'clock that afternoon.

Next, he headed to the liquor store. Reds bought $600 worth of liquor. He wasn't an alcoholic, but he figured he'd keep a nice collection on liquor in the house.

As Reds was driving back to the apartment, he got a call from J.R. Reds gave him directions to his apartment. Almost twenty-five minutes later, J.R. knocked on the door.

"I'm glad you're here. The furniture people are on their way. You can help me decorate," Reds said.

"Yo, Altoona makin' you soft. I'm a fuckin' gangsta. I don't decorate," J.R. said with a laugh. "But I did bring you a housewarmin' gift." J.R. gave Reds a pint of ice cream.

"What the fuck is this?" Reds asked as he held the ice cream. He could tell it wasn't ice cream. It was too light.

"Open it," J.R. said with a smile.

Reds opened the container and saw a bunch of red ice with what appeared to be two large leeches on top. "What the fuck!?" Reds said with his face broken up.

"Nigga was talkin' crazy, so I cut his lips off," J.R. said with a chuckle.

"You's a sick ma'fucka," Reds said in between laughs.

"Fuck outta here. You just mad 'cause you ain't think of it," J.R. shot back.

"This is true," Reds said.

"And I know Shontae might take it hard, so I made sure they'll never find 'em," J.R. said.

"Smart man. But look, I don't got no money here. I gotta go get it," Reds said.

"Come on with the insults. I know you got it. Just drop it off by the crib next time you come home," J.R. said.

"That'll probably be within the next week or two. Oh, and take these fuckin' lips back. I don't want these shits," Reds said as he gave J.R. the container back.

"You're a hater," J.R. said as he left.

# 31

To Reds's surprise, Shontae wasn't all that worried about Reem. It had been three days, and nobody had seen or heard from him. Reds saw Shontae at 4-D's, a local bowling alley/ club, she said Reem was missing in action.

"Did you call the jails and check the hospitals?" Reds asked.

"Naw, he probably with some bitch. Fuck 'em. I hope he stays with her. I got all the money, and everything is in my name," Shontae went on to say. "He still got a good bit of dope left. If you want it, stop by the house. That'll teach his ass."

"I might take you up on that," Reds said. As Reds walked away from her, he couldn't help to think how despicable Shontae was. Reds didn't give care about Reem, but Shontae should have. Reem made sure Shontae was taken care of, and good care of at that. For all she knew, he could be in a really bad situation, and all she had to say was, "Fuck 'em. I got all the money, and everything is in my name."

*That's exactly why I fuck these hoes and duck 'em. Ain't none of 'em worth shit. First chance they get, they out with ya shit. These bitches hopin' for my downfall more than these hatin'-ass niggas. All in hopes to find a buried treasure,* Reds thought to himself. *Bitches ain't shit.*

As Reds was leaving the club, Sting called him. "Can you stop by and see me tomorrow? I need you to take me to the drugstore. I gotta fill a prescription. And I got some good news for you too," Sting said.

"Be home all day, I'll be through some time tomorrow," Reds said.

"A'ight, you know where I'll be at," Sting said before he hung up.

Reds drove to Shontae's. He was going to wait to grab the dope, but because dope went bad, he decided to grab it now. He didn't know how long the dope had already been sitting, so he figured he'd give it to Sting tomorrow and see how well it moved. When he got to Shontae's, she gave him a thousand bundles of dope.

"Good lookin', cuz, you know I got chu, right?" Reds said.

"It's cool. That's a gift. But if Reem comes back here, can I tell him you took everything?" Shontae asked. "I'm done with his cheatin' ass. I just need you to have my back if he gets crazy."

Reds knew he wasn't coming back, so he agreed. "Yeah, cuz, I got chu. But I'm still gonna give you some bread tomorrow. I'm'a make sure don't nothin' happen to you regardless. You my peoples," Reds said.

The next morning, Reds dropped everything off to Sting.

"I took care of that situation with Twan," Sting said.

"Did you handle it like we discussed?" Reds asked.

"Yeah, that shit is all over the news," Sting said. "They said Evergreen Manor is swarmin' with police. I sent the shooters back to the hood."

"A'ight, that's good. Yo, it's a thousand bundles of dope in the bag, along with the other shit. Give me back $25,000 off the dope," Reds said.

"Ain't these Reem's bags?" Sting asked as he looked at the dope.

"You don't have nothin' to worry 'bout," Reds said.

"Say no more," Sting said.

They talked for a few more minutes, then Reds decided to leave. He didn't want to hold Sting up from doing his thing, and he didn't like to stay in Fairview too long. No telling when the cops would decide to do a sweep or something, and he didn't want to be there when it happened.

After Reds finished up with Sting, he went to Shontae's. Reds gave Shontae $7,500 for the hundred bricks she gave him.

"I thought we already agreed that you didn't have to pay me," Shontae said.

"We did, but I just want to do somethin' nice for you to show my appreciation," Reds said.

Shontae was at a loss for words. She never had someone do something for her without wanting something in return. She didn't know how to take what Reds was doing. She thought he was trying to tell her something. Shontae associated nice gestures from men with sex. She thought that any time a man did something nice for her, he wanted to sleep with her. Shontae had accepted this a long time ago, and even though she and Reds were cousins, she decided to thank him the only way she knew how.

"Thank you, Reds," Shontae said as she gave Reds a big hug.

The hug made Reds a little uncomfortable. She hugged him tight, so that their privates touched. Then she kissed Reds on the lips. Reds was shocked by what had just happened, but he thought maybe he was tripping and it wasn't nothing.

"Let me make you breakfast," Shontae said.

"A'ight," Reds said as he sat on the couch and turned the television on.

Shontae went upstairs when Reds turned the television on. As he was sitting on the couch, Shontae came back downstairs. She had on a burgundy bra and thong set. When Reds saw her, he was mesmerized by the way her body looked. He knew she had a body and was cute, but he never looked at her like that until now. He didn't really have a choice; she was showing it all. Her high-yellow skin was blemish free. Her hair looked like silk as it hung down over her shoulders. Her eyes were hazel, and her lips were full. Shontae was short and thick as hell. Her thick thighs complemented her plump ass. Her flat stomach made her breasts look even bigger than they were. Shontae's C cups jiggled as she strutted toward Reds. Her thong was see-through, and it revealed her fat pussy, which had just a little bit of hair on it. Shontae looked sexy as hell as she walked up to Reds. Reds's dick was rock-hard.

"What the fuck is you doin'?" Reds asked. Reds had on a pair of sweatpants, and Shontae could see that Reds' dick was hard. Once she saw this, she had no shame. She thought she was right about Reds wanting to fuck her.

"I'm servin' you breakfast," she said as she sat on Reds's lap.

"Yo, you outta order! You my cousin," Reds said. As Reds was talking to her, he was looking at her breasts.

"We're like third cousins. That shit don't count," Shontae said as she kissed Reds's neck.

"But I call ya mom my aunt," Reds said.

"It's okay. She's not your aunt, and I won't tell. Now stop actin' like you afraid of this pussy. I know you want me. I can tell by the way you lookin' at me," Shontae said. Shontae undid her bra and let her breasts out. Her nipples were big and brown. She pushed her breasts together. "Go 'head," she said.

*Fuck it*, Reds thought to himself. *She don't give a fuck. I don't give a fuck neither.*

Reds didn't know where this was coming from, but they were both adults. It was crystal clear what Shontae wanted to do. And now that Reds saw how she looked in the nude, he wanted to do the same thing. Reds took off his wifebeater and started kissing Shontae. He fondled her breasts, pulled her thong to the side, and played with her pussy while they kissed. Shontae's pussy was soaking wet, which let Reds know it was showtime. He took her thong off then pulled his sweatpants down.

"Sit down," Shontae said. "I'm gonna make you fall in love with this pussy."

Shontae straddled Reds and slid on to his rock-hard erection. "Ooohhh!" Shontae moaned. "Do you feel that?" Shontae was contracting her pussy muscles, making them massage Reds's dick.

"Hell yeah, I feel it! You a fuckin' beast," Reds moaned.

Shontae rode Reds until he said he was about to cum. Then she got off his dick and sucked it until he squirted in her mouth. When Reds came, she kept sucking, which made his body start to shake. His dick was very sensitive, and her mouth was making him go crazy. Reds had to push her off so he'd stop shaking.

"You like that?" Shontae asked with a smirk.

"You a fuckin' pro," Reds said as he sat there and looked at Shantae.

"I'm all yours, daddy," Shontae said. "So what are we gonna do?"

"What chu talkin' 'bout?" Reds asked.

"I'm sayin', every boss needs a down-ass bitch by his side. I'm tryin' to be that for you," Shontae said as she bent over and kissed his dick.

Reds became instantly angry. "Hold me down. You sound stupid. Look how you holdin' Reem down? You's a despicable bitch! You bitch's greed knows no limits. You ma'fuckas will do anything to get a nigga with heavy pockets," Reds said. He pushed her off his lap and pulled his pants up. "You disgust me," Reds added.

"Nigga, fuck you! You act like you ain't just fuck me. You ain't no better than me. You only gave me that money 'cause you wanted to fuck," Shontae snapped back.

Then it hit Reds how fucked up Shontae's way of thinking was. He stopped being mad and started feeling sorry for her. "Cuz, I gave you the money because I wanted to let you know that I was grateful for what you did, not 'cause I wanted to sleep with you," Reds explained.

"Yeah right! I been around niggas like you my whole life," Shontae said. "My daddy used to tell me how proud he was of me and how special I was, then he'd come in my room at night and rape me. My uncle did the same shit, couple older cousins, and I can go on and on, nigga. I know what the fuck you wanted, so I gave it to you."

Reds didn't know what to say. He was wrong for fucking Shontae, but she was wrong for initiating it. After listening to what she had just said, he understood her though. He just walked out the house. Most times, men consider women whores or scandalous because of how they act sexually. What most people don't take into consideration is what happened to cause them to act this way. Most times, as with Shontae, that behavior comes from previous trauma.

As Reds predicted, killing Twan worked out for the better. The police knew that it was drug related, but they had no suspects. On top of that, business couldn't have been better for Sting. There was a little suspicion about Sting's involvement in what happened to Twan, but nothing concrete. The cops came around and asked questions, but without any evidence or witnesses, the case would go cold. Sting had no more problems out of anyone else.

Over the next few months, Sting and Reds made millions together. Adding dope to Sting's order turned out to be a great move. The dope was generating the most money. Los was happy, Reds was happy, and Sting was happy. Things couldn't have been better.

Reds even bought Juanita a house for being so loyal. Juanita thought that meant that Reds was ready to settle down. Once again, she confessed her love, and again, she was shot down. But this time, she felt as though she was making progress. Reds actually told her that he loved her too.

"I'm just not ready for a relationship," Reds explained.

Juanita was mad, but she understood in a way. She told herself that she'd wait until he came around.

Reds spent the day with Juanita and shopped. The weather was changing, and fall was coming. Reds grabbed some stuff for himself and bought Juanita everything she wanted. Reds was very grateful for Juanita. He knew that if it wasn't for her, he wouldn't be in the position he was in now. So any chance he got to do something nice for her, he did.

As Reds drove Juanita back home, he couldn't help but think, *All I got is eight more months*. Once next summer began, he was going to quit the game for good. He had spoken to Los about this, and Los gave him his blessings. Los knew that Reds was young and rich. If Reds wanted to quit selling drugs and enjoy his money, that was his right.

"How are you going to keep from going broke?" Los had asked. "You have a lot of money, but you also have an expensive lifestyle."

"I'm gonna start investin' in houses. I also know a few people that is locked up and have their barber's license. I'm gonna open up a shop and let them work in it. I'll collect rent off the chairs," Reds had explained.

Los couldn't argue with what Reds was saying. It sounded as if he had it all figured out.

"I just gotta make it to the end of the summer," Reds told himself as he drove Juanita home.

Reds dropped Juanita off, then he got back on the road and headed to Altoona.

When Reds got to Altoona, the first place he went was to the mall. Reds was pissed—Nikki wouldn't stop calling him, leaving threatening messages.

"I'm tellin' you it's gonna be me or nobody," Nikki would say.

If she wasn't talking like that, she was cussing him out for not calling her. The thought of having J.R. kill her ran across Reds's mind, but he didn't take her threats seriously. She was just sprung, so he decided to change his number.

While Reds was at the Verizon store, he saw Mia. Mia had gained some weight, but it wasn't unusual to see a pretty girl let herself go in Altoona. There was a lot of females that were cute as hell, but they just stopped caring and let themselves go.

Mia lit up like a Christmas tree when she saw Reds. Mia ran over and gave Reds a hug and a kiss. She said she had been looking for him, but he proved to be hard to find. Reds was glad to hear that—he didn't want to be easily found.

"We need to talk," Mia said.

"A'ight, well I'm hungry, so let's go get some Chinese food," Reds said.

They went and got something to eat, and Mia told Reds she was pregnant.

"That's what's up, but what did you need to talk to me 'bout?" Reds asked as he ate.

"I just told you I'm pregnant," Mia repeated.

"Why you tellin' me?" Reds asked.

"Um, you don't remember havin' sex with me without a condom?" Mia asked.

"Come on, sis," Reds said as he exhaled a deep breath. "I met you at a club, took you and ya girl home, and fucked both of y'all. I know that wasn't the first time that happened."

"Actually, it was. I'm not like that. I was drunk, and that was a one-time thing," Mia said.

"Whatever you say. Listen though, I'm'a do you a favor. I don't have the time to do the math and see if it adds up and all that other bullshit. So you just hit the lottery. I'm gonna give you $10,000 to go get an abortion. You can keep the other $9,700, and do as you please with it," Reds said.

"I can't believe you! I'm not having an abortion. I don't believe in that. I'm having our baby, and you're gonna take care of us, or I'll take you for child support," Mia said like she had it all figured out.

"Is you fuckin' retarded? I don't have a job. On top of that, you don't even know my name. How you gonna take me for child support? You ain't gonna get shit from me unless you take that $10,000 and get the abortion," Reds said angrily.

"Did you forget that you told me you were a pharmaceutical tech when we first met. I saw what you drive. You don't get shit like that from workin' at McDonald's. And I might not know your real name, but I got your license plate number. I'll get your name from that. So if you don't pay child support, you'll go to jail," Mia said.

When she said that, Reds knew this whole thing was a setup. The only way she could have gotten his license plate number was if she got it the night of the threesome, which meant that she was planning on doing this. She must have figured that if she got pregnant to a guy with a good job, she'd have it made and live off of child support for the next eighteen years. Reds was really mad now.

"I'm nothin' like these niggas up here. Take the money and get the abortion," Reds said through clenched teeth.

"You're trying to give me $10,000 to get an abortion. You gotta be loaded. I'm having our baby," Mia said.

"You bitches have no shame," Reds said. "You's a stupid bitch." Reds walked away from her.

As soon as Reds got to his apartment, he called J.R. "Yo, this is my new number," Reds said.

"Okay. What, you lose ya other phone?" J.R. asked.

"Nah, these crazy-ass bitches," Reds said. He went on to explain what he was going through with Nikki and now Mia. "I need you up here," Reds said.

"You gotta be kiddin' me," J.R. said.

"Hell no, nigga! You wanna job?" Reds asked.

"I don't turn no bread down," J.R. said. "I'm on my way."

Five hours later, J.R. was knocking on Reds's door. Reds let him in, and they sat down and started talking.

"So let me get this right. You wanna kill a bitch 'cause you got her pregnant?" J.R. asked in disbelief.

"Nah, I want her dead 'cause she's tryin' to trap a nigga for the next eighteen years. I tried to give her a way out, but she wants to be greedy," Reds said.

"Okay, but just for the record, don't ever say that somethin' is wrong with me again. You wanna kill a bitch 'cause she's pregnant. Somethin' is clearly wrong with you. Maria really fucked you up," J.R. said.

"Naw, she showed me that there is only two types of people in the world, predators and prey. And I'll never let a ma'fucka prey on me again," Reds said.

"I feel you," J.R. said.

"Listen though, I don't know how many people she told about her bein' pregnant, so I don't want nobody to find her. If they find her, they might suspect me," Reds said.

"No problem, I'll just bury her next to Reem," J.R. said as if it were nothing.

Reds showed J.R. where Mia lived at. Now that J.R. knew where Mia stayed and had an accurate description of her, it was only a matter of time before Mia's greedy ass would come up missing. Reds left J.R. to do what he does. Reds had explained that there was a white girl that lived with Mia, so J.R. had to be careful. J.R. decided to catch Mia when she was coming out of the house by herself. That would be the safest way. J.R.'s break would come at about ten o'clock that night.

J.R. was about to call it a night when he saw Mia come out of her house. When J.R. didn't see anyone with her, he got out of his car. "Excuse me, miss. Do you live in the tan house?" J.R. asked.

"Yeah," Mia said as she stopped in her tracks.

J.R. could sense that Mia was a little taken aback by his sudden appearance, so he tried to calm her. "Are you Mia?" J.R. asked.

"Yeah, what is it that you want?" Mia asked.

"Reds sent me here. He described the house to me. I was trying to call him on the phone and make sure I had the right house before I knocked on the door," J.R. said. "He asked me to drop off a crib and some money for you to buy baby stuff."

"Oh, okay," Mia said with a warm smile.

"The crib is in the trunk of the car. I'll take it in the house for you. You can carry the bag with the money in it," J.R. said.

"Okay, but we have to be fast. I'm on my way to my girlfriend's," Mia said.

As they walked to J.R.'s car, Mia asked where Reds was at.

"He's workin', but he'll be stoppin' by tomorrow," J.R. said.

"He told me he didn't have a job," Mia said.

"Oh, he got a job. A good job at that," J.R. said. "I'm sure you'll be gettin' all kinds of gifts from Reds."

As J.R. approached the car, he checked the street, all was clear. Mia stood right beside J.R. as he opened the trunk. When Mia saw that the trunk was empty, she looked at J.R., and that was the last thing she saw. J.R. grabbed her and slammed her head into the edge of the car. Mia fell to the ground, unconscious; it was then that J.R. stomped on her neck until he heard a snap. He laid her lifeless body in the trunk of the car. J.R. moved so fast that Mia never saw her death approaching. J.R. shut the trunk then checked the street once more. Satisfied that no one was watching him, J.R. hopped in the car and pulled off.

J.R. was driving down Fourteenth Street when a cop got behind him. He wasn't worried. He was a professional driver. J.R. stopped at the corner and made a right turn, onto Seventeenth Avenue. He was headed toward the gas station when the cop pulled him over.

"Shit," J.R. said to himself as he saw the flashing red and blue lights He was mad because he knew he hadn't done anything. But more than anything, he was mad because he had been caught slipping. J.R. had left his gun in the trunk when he put Mia in there.

"License and registration," the cop said when he approached the car.

J.R. handed the cop his license and the rental agreement of the car, which was proof of insurance and registration. "What seems to be the problem, officer?" J.R. asked.

"You forgot to activate your turn signal back there," the cop said.

J.R. was sure that he used his turn signal, so he just figured he was being pulled over for DWB (driving while black). Altoona had a lot of black people in it, but it was still a very racist place. A lot of the white people in Altoona blamed the blacks for their loved ones being addicted to drugs. Tonight, J.R. had ran across a racist cop who decided to pull over a "nigger" and check to see if he was carrying some drugs.

The cop ran all of J.R.'s information. Everything came back clear, from the car to the check for warrants. The cop returned and gave J.R. his paperwork back. Then the questions started. "Mr. Richers, what brings you to Altoona?" the cop asked.

"I'm visitin' family," J.R. answered.

"Where do they live?" the cop continued.

"I don't understand what any of that has to do with me not usin' my turn signal," J.R. said, clearly irritated.

The cop didn't like J.R.'s tone or his attitude. As backup was arriving, the cop decided to give J.R. a piece of his mind. "Listen here, nigger. I have the badge. That means I ask the questions, understood?" the cop said.

J.R. had become instantly infuriated. He didn't care how many cops were there. If he had his gun on him, he would have shot this racist bastard right where he stood. J.R. didn't even respond to what the cop said. He just clenched his jaw together. *Don't let these ma' fuckas pull you off ya square,* J.R. thought to himself.

"Do we have a problem, Officer Moser?" the other cop asked as he walked up.

"I think this one may be intoxicated, Officer Star," Moser said. "I need you to stand here with him while I search the car for drugs."

"Step out of the car, sir. We're going to do a quick search," Officer Star said.

J.R. knew he was about to have to run. Both of the cops were overweight. J.R. liked his chances. When J.R. got out of the car, Officer Star asked him to put his hands on his head. J.R. went along like he was going to comply. As soon as Officer Star tried to put the handcuffs on J.R., he bolted.

"Stop! Stop!" Officer Star yelled as J.R. sped down the street. Officer Moser immediately drew his firearm and started firing at J.R. He hit J.R. twice in the leg, sending him to the pavement. Both cops ran to the middle of the block and handcuffed J.R. They called the shooting in, and minutes later, the ambulance arrived.

Once they got J.R. inside of the ambulance, he was taken to Altoona Regional Hospital under police escort. Once he was gone, the police started sealing off the crime scene. Another cop checked the car for anything illegal. When he opened up the trunk, he found Mia's dead body looking right at him. "We got a body!" the cop yelled.

The next day, Reds woke up and watched SportsCenter as he ate breakfast. Once SportsCenter went off, Reds turned to the twelve-o'clock news. After he turned to the channel, a reporter was on the television saying, "I've got the latest on a man that was shot by Altoona police and the body that was found in the trunk of his car, coming up at twelve."

Reds was so confident in J.R. that he didn't even suspect it was him. "Who the fuck rides around with a body in the trunk?" Reds said out loud.

The news started with a big picture of J.R.'s face on the screen. "This man, Jermaine Richers, thirty-four years of age, from West Chester, Pennsylvania, was pulled over for allegedly driving while intoxicated. Details are sketchy, but we do know that Richers tried to run from the police, causing him to be shot several times. After he was taken to the hospital, police found a dead twenty-two-year-old woman in the trunk of his car, along with a loaded handgun. Richers is in the Altoona Regional Hospital in stable condition. As soon as doctors release him, he'll be arraigned on murder charges. More on this story at six," the reporter said.

Reds looked at his television in disbelief. He quickly shook off the shock, grabbed his phone, and called Jimmy. Reds explained what he saw on the news. Jimmy told Reds to let him make some calls, then he'd get back to him. Reds hung the phone up and sat in the house, wondering how all of this had taken place. If he knew anything, he knew that J.R. wasn't intoxicated, not with a dead body in the car. Reds's mind was going a million miles a minute. He wanted to go to the hospital and see how J.R. was doing, but he knew better than to do that. Reds knew that Jimmy would be calling the hospital to check on J.R.'s condition. Reds would just have to sit tight and wait for Jimmy to call him with the details. An hour later, Jimmy called Reds back.

"He'll be released from the hospital later today. He'll be taken in front of a judge, denied bail, then taken off to Blair County Prison. I'll know more tomorrow, and I'll be at his next court hearing," Jimmy said.

Reds knew that Jimmy had already been retained, but he offered to pay him additional fees since J.R. was so far away. "Make sure you keep me up to date on everything," Reds said before hanging up the phone.

Reds sat in his apartment and tried to think. Around ten-thirty that night, Reds got a phone call. He didn't recognize the number, but for some reason, he answered it.

"Yo, cuz, I'm in Blair County Prison. I'm in the receiving room, and I don't have long to talk. I need you to call Jimmy," J.R. started to say.

"I'm already on top of that. I saw ya shit on the news, so I called Jimmy. He said he'll be at the next court hearin'," Reds said.

"A'ight, good lookin'. Look, I can't talk right now, but I'm gonna put you on my visitin' list in the mornin'," J.R. said. He stopped talking for a minute, and asked one of the guards what time visits were the next day. "Visits is from six to eight tomorrow night," J.R. said.

"I'll be there," Reds said then he hung up. Reds hung the phone up and poured himself a glass of Rémy Martin. He drank the whole glass in two big gulps then lay down. A lot of times when people are in bad situations, they get a sudden urge to go to sleep. That's all Reds wanted to do right now, sleep. Things had just taken a turn for the worse.

# 32

Early in the morning, Reds got a call from Sting.

"I'm hungry as shit. Can you bring me somethin' to eat?" Sting asked.

"I gotchu," Reds said.

Reds didn't converse much with Sting; he just hung the phone up. It wasn't that Sting had done anything wrong. It was just that Reds was dealing with a lot mentally. He was busy trying to figure out a way to get J.R. out of this jam. The average person would have just given up because J.R. was already locked up, but Reds had been taught that if you want something bad enough, there's always a way to get it. Reds would find a way to get J.R. out of this. He just needed time to think.

He knew he wouldn't have time to think if he had to keep running shipments to Sting. Reds and Sting had a pretty good relationship established. Sting had proven to be a good ally. Because of the situation that Reds was going through and the way Sting was handling things, Reds decided to give String triple what he normally gave him. Reds figured that this would hold Sting over for a while and give him some time to get this whole J.R. situation in order.

"Merry Christmas," Reds said as he dropped the drugs off to Sting. Reds explained that he was very busy and couldn't afford to be bothered unless it was an emergency. "I'm givin' you a lot more than usual because you haven't let me down yet," Reds said.

"No doubt!" Sting said, hyped from the sight of all the drugs. "I'll call you when I get low again." Sting was glad that Reds trusted him with this much drugs. It was like a showing of appreciation and trust.

As fast as Reds had come, he was gone. Reds dropped the money he collected from Sting at Pearl's house. As he was getting into his car, he got a phone call from Joylin.

"Hey baby! Can I see you?" she asked. Her voice instantly brightened up Reds's day.

"I'm on my way," Reds said with a smile on his face. Reds knew he needed to relax, and who better to do it with than Joylin? She wouldn't pester him or try to find out what was going on. All Joylin would do was chill with him, and that's what Reds needed right now.

As Reds walked into Joylin's apartment, she was making him a plate of rice and beans. They ate and talked about nothing in particular. But Joylin could tell that Reds was stressed. She could hear it in his voice and see it on his face.

"What's wrong, papi?" Joylin asked.

"Street shit. You got any liquor in here?" Reds asked, changing the subject.

"No, but I can go get some," Joylin responded.

"Nah, it's cool. I just need to relax," Reds said.

"Well, why didn't you just say somethin'? I don't need liquor to relax you. All you gotta do is sit back and close your eyes," she said.

Reds lay on the couch and did exactly that. Joylin took Reds's shirt off, his sneakers and socks, then his jeans. "Lay on your stomach," she instructed as she went and grabbed some baby oil.

Reds followed instructions and received a thorough back rub. He was starting to doze off when Joylin flipped him over and started rubbing his chest and stomach. She rubbed him from head to toe. When she was finished, she pulled out Reds's manhood and started sucking it. She started off slowly, then she sped up. She jerked him off while taking him in and out of her mouth. She used her tongue ring to flick circles around the tip of his shaft. In no time, Reds let go in her mouth. Joylin swallowed what Reds spit out, then she laid her head in his lap. She definitely knew how to relax a man. Reds never opened his eyes the whole time Joylin was giving him head. Reds could feel Joylin's naked body lying against him. She felt great.

"Set your alarm clock for five-thirty," Reds instructed.

Joylin set her phone to go off at five-thirty then lay back down. Reds rubbed the inside of her leg for a minute. Joylin opened her legs wide, inviting Reds's fingers to play. Reds rubbed his thumb over her swollen clitoris then slid two fingers inside of her while rubbing her clit.

"Ahhh!" Joylin moaned as she gyrated her hips.

After a few minutes of this, Joylin was shaking. "I'm cummin'," she said softly.

Reds let her ooze all over his hand, then he rubbed it all over her stomach. He kissed the back of her neck then dozed off.

Joylin's alarm woke Reds up at five-thirty. He took a shower and got dressed.

"Thank you, I really needed that. I'll call you later," Reds whispered as he gave Joylin a kiss and palmed her soft behind.

"Any time you need me, I'm here," Joylin said.

Reds grabbed his keys and headed to go see J.R. He arrived at the prison five minutes before six. As soon as Reds walked into the waiting area for the visits, he was swarmed by the female visitors. Reds had sex with most of the women in the waiting area. The ones he didn't have sex with knew of him and wanted to have sex. Most of the women were at the prison to see their man or child's father, but that didn't seem to be important to them at this moment. They wanted to know why Reds hadn't called or where he had been or what he was doing tonight. None of them knew what Reds did for a living. They just assumed he had money because he showed out when in the clubs. Every time Reds had a moment with a woman that made him feel like there was some good in a woman, it would be followed up by a moment like this that would utterly disgust him. Reds took a few numbers, made a few false promises, and then the visitors were let in.

Blair County's visiting room was nothing like Delaware or Chester County's. There was a bunch of booths with plexiglass separating the inmates from the visitors. Reds knew he wasn't going to be able to talk to J.R. like he wanted to because they had to talk over a telephone. J.R. came down to the visiting room using a walker. It crushed Reds to see his cousin like that. They talked for a little while, nothing important, just small stuff. Neither of them knew that the visits would be like this. J.R. needed to talk to Reds, but not like this. Reds put the phone down and mouthed the words, "Can you get a phone in here?"

"Ain't gonna happen," J.R. said into the phone. "They got me pegged as a deranged killer. Ain't none of these guards got no holla for me."

"A'ight, but look, I'm'a do whatever I can to get you out of here," Reds said.

"As far as the law goes, I'm done. The cop is sayin' he pulled me over 'cause I was drivin' erratically. He said he smelled marijuana in the car. That's why he searched it. I gotta holla at Jimmy and see what he thinks.

Get a suit, and find out when Jimmy is coming. I can only have contact visits with Jimmy and/or his secretary," J.R. said.

Reds knew exactly what J.R. was trying to say. "A'ight, I gotchu. I'll be in touch. I got two $500 money orders for you. I'm gonna drop 'em off when I leave. But I gotta go. I need to get out of here before visits are over. These bitches is like vultures on fresh meat," Reds said.

He and J.R. both shared a laugh before he left.

Later on, that week, Jimmy and Reds went to the jail to see J.R. Reds had on a suit and a briefcase. Jimmy showed his ID and told the guard at the door that Reds was his paralegal. The guard let them in without any hassle. They were taken inside the jail and into a small room. Minutes later, J.R. came into the room. He was moving slow and was still using a walker, but he was walking. They all shook hands then sat down.

Jimmy started asking J.R. questions. He looked over the affidavit, then said, "We're going to attack the search. They do a lot of illegal shit out here, but they play dirty, so we're going to have a fight on our hands. Let's just hope that this cop gets in an accident and dies before our preliminary hearing."

"Why?" Reds asked.

"The state needs him to testify as to why he pulled J.R. over. If he doesn't testify, they don't have any probable cause for pulling him over. If they don't have any probable cause, we get the case thrown out," Jimmy said.

Jimmy Dennis was a lawyer by profession, but he was a thug by character. Jimmy was fascinated with the street life. It was situations like this that excited Jimmy. He knew exactly what would be done after he made his latest statement. Jimmy had just put a hit on Officer Moser. Jimmy looked in a folder for a second. "I believe the cop that pulled you over is also the same one that shot you. His name is Officer Matt Moser, and his patrol area is from the UVA, an after-hours club, to the Sheetz on Thirteenth Street," Jimmy said.

"You just earned ya'self a bonus," Reds said.

"I've been paid enough. Don't worry about it. You guys normally make my job pretty easy. Just make sure you do what you got to do in order to get our friend home," Jimmy said.

J.R. had been thinking something similar as to what Jimmy was saying, but now that Jimmy said it, that's what was to happen. Just like that, the meeting was over, and Reds was on a mission.

Reds thought things through during his ride home. Reds had been taught to utilize his assets, and that was exactly what he planned on doing. He was a boss; he wasn't going to do something like kill a cop, but he'd just pay another person to do it. He just had to be extremely careful about who he picked to do the job because this job left no room for error.

Reds went to Pearl's house, picked up his money, then headed back to West Chester. Reds kept the radio and his phone off during the four-and-a-half-hour drive. Reds would use this time to formulate a plan. As he drove, he remembered something that Los had told him. "If you ever have any problems, call me. We are family, your problems are mine," Los had said.

Reds called Los and asked if he could speak to him in person.

"Would you like to come to mi casa for dinner?" Los asked.

"I'd love to," Reds said.

Los gave Reds directions to his home, and Reds told him he'd call when he got close. Reds dropped his money off in West Chester then he headed to New York.

Reds got to Los's mansion and was astonished by the beauty of it. Los's mansion stood behind a large gate, and it had a lot of land surrounding it. It reminded Reds of the White House.

*This is how I'm tryin' to do it,* Reds thought to himself. Reds saw two kids riding four-wheelers on the property. He pressed the intercom and was later greeted by a butler. The butler took Reds in the house to meet with Los.

"Welcome," Los said with his arms open.

"Thank you for havin' me," Reds responded.

"Let me give you a tour, then I'll introduce you to everybody," Los said. He led Reds through the mansion, room after room. The tour took damn near an hour. Los had a movie theater, a weight room, a spa room, tanning rooms, an indoor swimming pool, and a game room. His place made Reds feel like he was watching *MTV Cribs*. Los took Reds into his kitchen were three maids were preparing dinner.

"My two boys are outside riding their four-wheelers, and my wife and daughter are out shopping. I thought they would have been home by now, but I guess not. You will meet them when they arrive. Let's go shoot some pool. Do you play?" Los asked.

"I can shoot," Reds responded.

Reds and Los were shooting their fourth game of pool when a woman that looked like Vida Guerra walked into the room. She was holding a baby in her arms. "We're home," she said.

Los hugged her then gave her a kiss. Reds would have thought she was Los's daughter, but he could tell from the way he kissed her she wasn't. "Reds, I'd like you to meet my wife, Katiana. Kat, this is my friend Reds," Los introduced them.

"Nice to meet chu," Reds said as he looked into her eyes.

Katiana was a woman of extreme beauty. She stood about five-foot-two, and her body was well proportioned. She had a manila complexion with dark brown hair and eyes. Katiana wore a pair of jeans that fit her like they were painted on, and her shirt revealed much cleavage. She was a beauty if Reds ever saw one. She wore no makeup and no jewelry except for two huge diamond earrings and at least a five-karat diamond ring on her finger.

Reds shook her hand, tickled the baby, then went right back to shooting pool. Katiana turned and gave Los a kiss. Reds wanted to look at her ass, but he refrained. He had been taught to never admire another man's lady if that man was family or a friend. After their kiss, Los sent Katiana on her way. After she left, Reds told Los that his daughter was beautiful but said nothing about Katiana. They finished their game then went upstairs to eat.

When they got upstairs, Reds met Los's two sons. Both of which were named Carlos. One was a junior and the other was the third. They looked to be about thirteen or fourteen. Los told Reds that they were from his prior wife. They all sat at a large table and were served. To Reds's surprise, they were served soul food, huge plates of fried chicken, bowls of homemade macaroni and cheese, collard greens, candied yams, and buttermilk biscuits.

"You probably thought you'd be eating beans and rice. Well, I happen to love soul food. I figured you'd enjoy it also," Los said.

"You figured right," Reds responded as he dug in.

As they ate dinner, Katiana pranced around, doing this and grabbing that. It was like she was trying to get Reds to look at her. But Reds never did, not in a lustful manner anyway. Once dinner was over, everybody left the table except for Reds and Los.

"The meal was delicious," Reds complimented.

"Thank my cooks. They made it," Los said with a laugh.

"I do have somethin' I need to talk to you about," Reds said.

"Let's go to the sauna, then we will talk," Los said.

Reds found it a little odd that Los wanted to talk to him in the sauna, but he didn't say anything. They went downstairs, then Los got completely naked and wrapped himself in a towel. Reds stripped down to his boxers and waited for Los to go inside the steam room.

"Please get naked and wrap a towel around yourself," Los said.

"I think I'm good in my boxers," Reds said.

"My friend, I am no homosexual. I ask you to take your clothes off for a reason. I hate to make it seem as if I don't trust you, but you can never be too safe these days. You said you have to talk to me. I'm assuming it's about business. If we are going to talk business, I need to be sure that our ears are the only ears that hear what's being said," Los explained.

"I can respect that," Reds said as he stripped down and wrapped a towel around himself.

They entered the steam room, and Reds explained what had happened in Altoona. "I'll give up all my money to see my family beat this shit," Reds said.

"That says much about you," Los said. "You are a very loyal person, Reds. Your cousin is lucky to have someone like you on his side. I've watched you all day. You didn't bring any guns in my home. You were very respectful, and most importantly, you didn't try to eye-fuck my wife. I tell her to dress and act like that when I have company. I like to see if the men I allow in my home will disrespect me by violating my wife with their eyes. A lot of men haven't been taught the respect that you have. Because of that, they leave my home with a price on their head. If your cousin is in anyway responsible for this, I'd be glad to help him out."

"Thank you. He's very much responsible for the way I am."

"I have a hitman. He's very good. I'll loan you his services for this situation," Los said.

"I really appreciate this," Reds said.

"Are you going to be in Altoona or West Chester?" Los asked.

"Altoona," Reds answered.

"Okay, I'll have him meet you at your home in Hollidaysburg," Los said.

Los's statement caught Reds off guard.

"How do you know I live in Hollidaysburg?" Reds asked.

"It my business to know these things. I know where you live, and so does he," Los said. "He'll be in touch very soon."

Reds thought he was being elusive about his movements. But what

Los just told him showed Reds that he wasn't as good as he thought. Reds left Los's mansion and drove back to his apartment in Hollidaysburg. He watched a movie, then he went to sleep.

Reds woke up around noon and went to take a piss. When he walked into his living room, a skinny white man was sitting on his couch, eating a sandwich.

"What the fuck!" Reds said in a shocked tone.

"All is well. Los sent me," the skinny man said. "I'm here to fix your problem with the law."

"Okay, but how the fuck did you get in here?" Reds asked.

"The same way you did," he answered.

Reds knew he locked his door. He went to the front door.

"I didn't damage your door. I'm a professional," he said. "Now, there's a few things I need to know, and I'll be on my way."

It was eleven o'clock at night. Officer Moser sat in his cruiser, drinking warm coffee. He was parked in a closed garage lot, looking for speeders. There was a call about a domestic dispute on Eleventh Street. Moser radioed in that he was on the call. He put his car in drive and headed to the call. "Another broken home," he said as he pulled off.

Moser pulled up in front of 3201 Eleventh Street and got out of his car. He walked up to the door and was about to knock when he heard a gunshot. Before it even registered, Moser's head exploded all over the front door of 3201. From a block away, Los's hitman laid the .30-30 rifle on the back seat of his stolen car. He covered the gun with a blanket, got in the driver's seat, then pulled off. He dumped the car on the other side of town, put his rifle and his scanner in his car, and left Altoona, never to be seen again.

Over the weekend, things got crazy in Altoona. A police officer had been murdered, so the cops were on a warpath. The chief of police told the news that the police officers of Altoona wouldn't rest until the murderer was captured. They even offered a $25,000 reward for any information leading to the capture of the suspect. On Saturday alone, they raided about ten houses and locked up over fifty people. The cops were sending a clear message: shit rolls downhill. They would apply constant pressure until they got some information. Unfortunately, none of the information was about the murder.

Their tips led them to Fairview Projects. The police were hearing a lot about Fairview being a major distribution center for narcotics. The cops figured they'd go up there, shake a few branches, and see what fell.

Early Sunday morning, Altoona's drug task force was doing surveillance on one of Sting's workers, Shameek. They watched Shameek make sells and go in and out of a certain house all morning. The task force picked Shameek up; when they arrested him, they found heroin on him. They used that to obtain a warrant for the house he was going in and out of. Once the warrant was signed, they raided. The house they hit was only a stash house for money. They didn't find any drugs, but they got a little over $10,000 in cash.

Terry, the lady whose house it was, began talking as soon as the cops said they were going to take her kids. She told the police that the money was picked up every night. She also told them that there was more than one stash house. When they asked who was behind all of this, she told them. "His name is Sting. He's from New York," she said.

Shameek cosigned her story. He not only told the police about everything he knew, but he also showed them were all the houses were. He told the police he had been to Sting's house before and would gladly show them where he lived if they let him walk.

Years back, while Reds was in school, he had learned of a theory called Murphy's law. This theory stated that everything that could possibly go wrong would go wrong. He didn't pay it much attention in school. But as with most things he learned in life, Reds was about to learn what Murphy's law was all about firsthand.

## 33

Sting got the call about fifteen minutes after the stash house got raided. "They got Shameek," one of Sting's female friends in Fairview said. "And they raided one of the stash houses."

Sting hung his phone up, pushed his baby's mom off of him, and got dressed. He didn't know what was going on, but he knew it wasn't good. He didn't think anybody would cooperate with the authorities, but he couldn't rule that one out either. Sting figured it would be a wise move to go get everything out of Fairview just in case people started talking.

Sting drove to Fairview and was going in and out of the stash houses. He'd grab what was in the house and drop it off at his car. Little did Sting know he was being watched. The police had Shameek in an undercover van, identifying people and pointing out stash houses. The cops were planning on taking down the whole projects in one big sweep. When they were all finished there, Shameek was going to show them where Sting lived, and they would take him down too. As Shameek was talking to the head detective, he spotted Sting coming out of one of the stash houses.

"There he go right there!" Shameek said as he pointed to Sting like he was a celebrity.

The cops didn't move immediately. They wanted to see what Sting was doing. They watched him pick up all the drugs and money.

Sting was moving fast but trying not to be obvious about what he was doing. As he made his last pickup, he laughed to himself. "These stupid-ass cops ain't smarter than me. You gotta get up pretty early in the mornin' to get out on me, and I'm up at the crack of dawn," Sting said to himself as he got into his car.

Sting pulled out of Fairview. As soon as he got to the corner, his car was surrounded by police cars. They had watched Sting pick everything up, and when he thought he was making a smooth getaway, they busted him. The police had caught Sting with 3,000 bags of crack, totaling a little more than a kilogram in weight, 6,000 e-pills, 250 bundles of dope, 7 pounds of weed, and almost $55,000 in cash. Altoona police had just made their biggest bust in years. Sting's day had just gotten a lot worse.

Sting was taken into custody and drilled by police. Sting wouldn't say anything at first. But that ended when the cops started talking about his child and child's mother.

"Fuck the code of the streets. You got a kid. Do you really want to leave your kid and its mother out there all alone? You think she's not going to move on? You better start thinking about you and your family. If you don't, nobody else will," the cops said.

"My family don't have nothin' to do with this," Sting said. This was the first time that Sting had spoken since he had been in custody.

The fact that he said something let the cops know they were heating up, so they pressed on. "Oh, yes, they do. We can take your house, take your cars, take all the money in both of your bank accounts. Shit, we can even take your child and lock your lady up for conspiracy. We just caught you with a little over a half a million dollars in drugs, asshole! If you ever want to see your kid or fuck your girl again, you better start talking 'cause as of right now, the only person that's gonna be getting fucked is you," the cop said.

Sting was quiet for a minute. The cop decided to let him think about what he had just said for a while.

"Fine, take the rap for everything. Your son will probably be calling your supplier daddy before the week is over," the cop said as he got up to leave the room.

"His name is Reds," Sting said. "He's the one you want." Sting couldn't risk losing his girl and his baby. Someone had told on him, and Sting wasn't about to go down alone. He figured he'd tell on Reds and then go back to New York where nobody would know what he had done.

"Okay, now we're talking. What's Reds's real name?" the cop asked.

"I don't know," Sting answered.

"Okay, where does he live?" the cop asked.

"I don't know," Sting repeated.

"Where does he hang at?" the cop pressed.

"I don't know!" Sting said, getting frustrated. "All I got is his phone number, and I know he got a cousin named Shontae that lives by the Jaffa."

"Okay, that's a start," the cop said.

Sting went on to tell the cop what Reds looked like and what kind of car he drove. Sting even told the cops about Twan's murder. He said nothing of his involvement in the murder. Instead, he blamed it all on Reds. "He told me that he paid some young kids from Philly to kill Twan and his family, then he sent them back to Philly," Sting said.

"Okay, you just gave me a lot. Let me talk to my boss, and I'll be in touch," the cop said.

"Man, I just told you some heavy shit! Am I gettin' a deal or what?" Sting asked.

"Just be patient. You just did a good thing. If what you said turns out to be true, you'll be with your family a lot sooner than you would have been," the cop said as he walked out.

An hour later, Sting was taken in front of a judge and given a $2,500,000 bail. After that, he was taken to Blair County Prison.

J.R. was sitting in his cell, reading. His cell door opened. J.R. grabbed his cane and went to see why his cell had been hit. He saw that Officer Moser had been killed, so J.R. thought that maybe he had a legal visit. When he got to the front of his cell, J.R. saw Sting walking toward the cell.

"Why they open my door?" J.R. asked.

"I'm ya new celly," Sting replied. "You bangin'?"

"Naw, I ain't into all that," J.R. said as he limped back into the cell.

J.R. sat back on his bed and started reading. He knew it was only a matter of time before he would be released. All he had to do was be patient. J.R. didn't have much to say to Sting. J.R. knew he was on his way out and wasn't trying to make any new friends before leaving.

As Sting was getting unpacked, he noticed that J.R. was basically ignoring him. Sting was an attention whore. He loved for people to grovel over him, so J.R. not paying him any attention only made Sting want to talk more.

"Yo, what chu in for?" Sting asked.

"DUI," J.R. answered.

"Oh, so you on ya way out?" Sting asked.

"Yeah, probably," J.R. said.

"I wish I only had a DUI. These pussies got me in a raid. I'm Sting. You probably heard of me," he said.

"The name don't ring a bell," J.R. said flatly.

"I run Fairview Projects. Faggot-ass cops got one of my workers to tell on me. They caught me with a half a million dollars in work," Sting bragged.

"Nah, I never heard of you," J.R. said.

"That's 'cause I be on some low-key shit. You know the nigga Reds? He get money with me too," Sting said trying to get some recognition.

J.R.'s head popped up. "Yeah, I think I heard of him before," J.R. said. J.R. was all ears now.

As soon as Los's hitman left Reds's apartment, Reds headed to West Chester. He knew that killing a police officer would make things extremely hot, and he didn't want to be anywhere near the heat. Reds thought about warning Sting, but if he did, he'd be implicating himself. *He's smart. He'll figure it out,* Reds thought.

Reds went to Juanita's house. Since he had been in Altoona, Reds hadn't really gotten a chance to spend a lot of time with her. He actually missed Juanita. She was the only person besides J.R. that Reds trusted. He didn't trust her 100 percent, but some trust was better than none. Juanita knew that Reds had money, but she never asked for anything. That was the main reason Reds bought her the house. Reds really loved Juanita, and he believed her when she said she loved him. Reds didn't believe that love lasted forever though, so he refused to commit to her. Reds was afraid of opening his heart to Juanita and she falling out of love before he did. He was playing it safe with Juanita. At least that's what he told himself.

Over the course of the weekend, Reds took Juanita out to eat, shopping, to the movies, bowling, to the casino; you name it—they did it. They also had plenty of sex. Despite what Reds had just gone through with Mia, he didn't wear a condom with Juanita. Her pussy felt too good to wear a condom. Juanita had been having sex with Reds for a while and knew when Reds was about to cum. When Reds would speed his strokes up and his body got tense, Juanita would hold him tight and tell him to cum inside of her. She looked so beautiful saying it that Reds obeyed her request every time. Over the last two days, he had cum inside of her at least ten times.

Sunday night, Reds and Juanita were eating dinner at the Olive Garden. Reds's phone rang. It was Joylin. Reds thought about ignoring it, but he wanted to know what was going on since the cop had been shot.

"Hey baby, how you?" Joylin asked.

"I can't complain. How 'bout ya'self?" Reds asked.

"I'm good. I just wanted to see how you was doin', making sure you didn't get caught up in none of the bullshit," she said.

"What chu talkin' 'bout?" Reds played stupid.

"I thought you watched the news?" Joylin said.

"I do, but I'm not in town right now. I been gone all weekend," Reds responded.

"Well, you picked a damn good time to go," she said.

Reds smiled to himself because he thought he knew what she was talking about. What he was about to hear would make him sick.

"A cop got killed Friday night, and the police been locking people up like crazy. They're raiding and everything," Joylin said.

"Oh, word," Reds said.

"Yeah, you know Sting from up Fairview?" she asked.

"I heard of the dude," Reds said coolly.

"They caught his ass with like a quarter million in cash and a million dollars in drugs," Joylin said. "He can kiss his ass good-bye."

"Damn, that's crazy! But let me call you back. My battery is 'bout to die," Reds said before he hung up.

What Reds had just heard made him dizzy. He looked like he was ready to throw up all over the table.

"Are you okay, baby?" Juanita asked.

"Hell no," Reds said with a dry throat.

"What's wrong?" Juanita asked.

"Leave it alone. I need time to think," Reds said. He motioned for the waiter. "Check please," Reds said. Reds paid for dinner then gave Juanita the keys to the Escalade. "You drive," Reds said.

On the way to her house, Reds threw his Altoona phone out of the window. He was never going back to Altoona again. He didn't know what Sting would say to the police, so he'd play it safe. He was glad J.R. was on his way home. Now was a good time to take a vacation. When they came back from vacation, Reds would find a new town to set up shop. But right now, he needed to think. He told Juanita to take him to his house.

When they got there, he gave her the keys to his Monte Carlo and told her to go home. She didn't know what was going on, but she knew it was serious. She also knew better than to question Reds. She'd give him his space for now. "I'll come by tomorrow. Call me when you wake up. I'll make you breakfast," Juanita said as she gave Reds a kiss.

"Yeah, that'll work," Reds said.

Reds went into his apartment and shot straight to his safe. He grabbed his money counter out of his closet and began counting. When Reds was finished, he knew exactly what he had, six million in his safe and a hundred thousand dollars in a duffle bag. Reds was paranoid. He wanted to get the money out of his house, but where would he put it?

Reds had an idea, but he'd have to wait until tomorrow to do it. For now, he put all of his money inside a treasure chest and boxes. As he was packing his money up, he assessed the situation in Altoona. The more Reds thought, the more certain he was that Sting would talk. Reds didn't really care. Sting didn't know much about him. The only people that knew anything of any importance was Pearl and Shontae. Reds wasn't worried about Pearl, but he wasn't so sure about Shontae. He and Shontae were on the outs, and there was no telling what a woman would do when she was mad at you. The thought of sneaking to Altoona and killing her crossed his mind, but it was too risky. Things in Altoona was scorching hot right now. Reds would just have to hope that Shontae wouldn't say the wrong thing.

After Reds packed his money up, he sat on his couch and strategized. He had enough money to walk away, but he couldn't. Reds was addicted to the money; his greed had overcome him. He thought he had this game all figured out. Reds promised himself that he was going to hustle hard for another year and then he'd consider walking away. If he made six million in a little less than six months, he could have at least ten million by the beginning of next summer even if he slowed down.

Reds sat on his couch and thought himself to sleep.

J.R. spent all day talking to Sting. He wanted to know if Sting was going to talk or not. Just from the little bit J.R. had heard already, he thought Sting was going to tell. Sting was talking like he was only in jail for a weekend or something. He wasn't sounding like a man that had just gotten caught with a half a million dollars' worth of drugs. Even though J.R. had his suspicion, he wanted to be sure he was right before he made his next move.

"Did they grab ya man Reds?" J.R. asked.

"Nah, they ain't catch him yet," Sting replied.

"Oh, so they lookin' for him too?" J.R. pried.

"Yeah, fuck that nigga though. He ain't worried 'bout me. I got a family to take care of. I gotta be there for them. If I do a bid, that nigga ain't gonna send me no money or look out for my folks. If I testify on this nigga, I can go home. I'll take my chick back to New York, and it'll be like this shit never happened. I know if the shoe was on the other foot, he'd tell on me. I gotta do what's best for me," Sting said. "Does that sound crazy?"

"It doesn't really matter what I think. It sounds like you already got cha mind made up," J.R. said.

"Yeah, I got a family to take care of. And if Reds is smart, he'll talk when they catch him," Sting said.

There was a silence in the cell for a minute. J.R. was trying to hide his anger. He knew what he was going to do, but everything had to be right, and now wasn't the right time.

"Yo, I'm'a go call my girl," Sting said.

J.R. loved Reds to death. He was like his little brother. J.R. and Reds had several conversations, and they both knew how much they meant to each other. J.R. would give his life for Reds because he knew Reds would do the same for him. They had already proven this to each other. There was no way J.R. was letting Sting tell on his little cousin. Reds had killed a cop to get J.R. out of jail, so now J.R. would kill Sting to make sure Reds didn't come to jail. J.R. knew that if he did this the right way, he would be able to get maybe a ten-to-twenty-year sentence for killing Sting. He just had to make it look like self-defense. The decision was easy for him to make because he knew Reds would do the same.

When it was time to lock in, J.R. was lying in bed, acting like he was sleeping. Sting came in and lay down. J.R. lay in his bed for hours, waiting. When he was sure that Sting was asleep, he made his move. J.R. had found a piece of metal in the shower on his first day there. He had sharpened it until it looked like an ice pick. He had then made a handle for it with a braided piece of sheet. Since his legs weren't 100 percent, he tucked his weapon in his mattress just in case he needed it one day.

J.R. pulled the shank out of his mattress. He looked at Sting who had his mattress on the floor. Sting was sleeping in his boxers and had no shirt on. J.R. took his boxers off, ripped them in the back, then put them back on. He got up and limped over to Sting's bed. J.R. flopped on him and stabbed him several times. The first blow was to Sting's jugular vein. Blood squirted everywhere.

Sting woke up to a sharp pain in his neck. He was hit fifteen more times. Sting's eyes rolled in the back of his head.

"Only person you gonna be talkin' to is God, pussy," J.R. whispered into Sting's ear.

Those were the last words Sting heard. His body became still, and his bowels released. J.R. rolled around the bed with Sting's body. J.R. had blood all over him. "Get off me! Stop! Stop! No! Help! Help!" J.R. screamed.

Reds woke up the next morning and called Juanita. She came over with eggs, turkey bacon, and Bisquick pancake batter. She went into the kitchen and attempted to make breakfast. As she was mixing the pancake batter, Reds came in the kitchen and grabbed her from behind. He held her tight and kissed her neck as he rubbed his manhood against her backside. As he kissed her neck, he unbuttoned her pants and pulled them down, along with her panties. Reds laid Juanita on the kitchen floor and started eating her pussy. He licked and sucked her clitoris until she exploded in his mouth. Reds then pulled his sweatpants down and slid himself inside of her. She moaned passionately as Reds pushed himself in and out of her love canal. He caressed her body as they made love on the kitchen floor. Juanita loved it when Reds was spontaneous like this.

When they finished, Reds got off the floor and told her he was taking her to breakfast. As they showered, Juanita asked Reds where his sudden urge for sex had come from.

"I just wanted you to know that last night wasn't about you," Reds said. "I really appreciate you givin' me time to collect my thoughts."

"You definitely just thanked me," Juanita said with a big smile.

"After we eat breakfast, do you wanna ride with me to go put some of my dad's stuff in storage?" Reds asked.

"Of course," Juanita responded.

Reds took the boxes and the treasure chest and loaded them into his truck. He also took a few of his father's belongings to make it look good. They went to eat then headed to the storage facility on the west side of town. When they got there, Reds acted like he forgot his ID at the house. "Do you have your ID on you, baby?" Reds asked Juanita.

She gave the storage clerk her ID and got the storage garage in her name. As Reds was unloading the boxes, Juanita tried to grab the treasure chest. She could barely budge it. "What the fuck is in here, babe?" She asked Reds.

"Millions of dollars," Reds said jokingly.

"Yeah right," Juanita shot back.

"Nah, just a bunch of my dad's stuff. I'm not ready to get rid of it. So when I want to remember my pop, I'll come here and go through his stuff," Reds explained.

His answer satisfied her curiosity, so Juanita grabbed the smaller boxes while Reds lugged the treasure chest. When they were finished, Reds went to the front gate and paid for the garage for a year. He was given a lock to secure the garage, then they headed back home. The reason that Reds had the garage put in Juanita's name was so that nothing would be traced back to him.

As Reds and Juanita drove back home, Reds got a call from Jimmy.

"Your cousin has just been charged with another murder," Jimmy informed him.

"What!" Reds responded as his stomach dropped.

"They're saying he killed his cellmate last night. Some guy from New York who was running a drug operation in Altoona. Look, you know I hate phones. Come by the office tomorrow. We'll talk then," Jimmy said.

"I'm close, I'll come by now," Reds said.

"Okay then, get here," Jimmy said before hanging up.

Reds didn't know what to think. It was like shit just kept getting worse for him. He dropped Juanita off then headed to Jimmy's office.

"I'm headed up there in a few hours, I'll know more then. All I know now is what J.R. said over the phone. He said that his cellmate tried to rape him, there was a struggle, J.R. got a hold of his cellmate's shank, and killed him with it," Jimmy explained.

"What the fuck!" Reds said in a baffled tone.

"For all I know, it didn't go down anything like that. I'm just telling you what he said over the phone. He knows not to say the truth over the phone," Jimmy said.

As Jimmy was talking, it hit Reds. The person J.R. had killed was Sting. It was all starting to make sense to him now. Not the part about the rape, but everything else. "I need to talk to J.R.," Reds said. "But I'm not goin' nowhere near Altoona."

"Call my phone at five o'clock sharp. I'll be in the room with J.R. I can put you on the phone with him," Jimmy said.

"That'll work. Okay, now how's shit lookin' as far as the cop case?" Reds asked.

"I guess prayer does work. Officer Moser was killed in the line of duty over the weekend," Jimmy said. "That means the Commonwealth will probably try to use Officer Star, the cop that pulled up for backup, to establish probable cause," Jimmy said.

"Can they do that?" Reds asked.

"No, but in Altoona, they'll try. But I have a trick up my sleeve. I'm going to have so many organizations there and the media. They'll have to throw the case out or risk an investigation for judicial misconduct. Trust me, the last thing Altoona wants is the feds sniffing around. They do too much illegal shit. I'm almost certain they'll throw the case out," Jimmy said.

"Okay, well that's good," Reds said.

"Yeah, but he's going to have to do some time for the jailhouse case. There were only two people in the cell. One of them is dead. As long as the jail or forensics doesn't refute his story, I can get him a deal for involuntary manslaughter. Pennsylvania doesn't have a self-defense law, so I can't get him off," Jimmy said.

"A'ight," Reds said with a sigh. "Keep me posted, and call me with the bill."

"I will do that," Jimmy said. "Now if you'll excuse me, I'm going to get a bite to eat, then I'm headed to see your cousin. Don't forget, five o'clock sharp."

Reds left Jimmy's office and headed to the west side of town. He needed to find some weed to mellow him out.

# 34

Altoona police was getting nowhere with Officer Moser's death. They were, however, gaining grounds on what Sting had told them before his death. Detective Johan had found out where Shontae lived and paid her a visit. Shontae was mad at Reds still, but she also knew Reds was dangerous. The last thing Shontae was about to do was say something that she'd have to testify to later. She saw what happened to Mia on the news. Shontae remembered her from the night Reds went home with her and Amanda. She wasn't sure, but Shontae figured that Reds was somehow behind Mia's murder. Shontae wasn't about to be next on his list of people to kill. She told the detective that she and Reds were cousins. Because of that, she had to tell the detective Reds's real name and where he was from. Detective Johan tried to get more out of her, but she didn't say anything else.

"He's been to my house maybe three times. I don't know what he's doin' up here or how often he's up here," Shontae said.

The wheels in Detective Johan's mind were turning as he listened to Shontae. He remembered that J.R. was from West Chester, and he doubted it was a coincidence. "Do you know Jermaine Richers?" the detective asked.

"Yeah, he's my cousin too," Shontae said.

"Do you know why he may have killed that pregnant girl?" he asked.

"I only know what I saw on the news. I wasn't even aware that Jermaine was in the area before I saw the news," Shontae said.

"Okay, thank you anyway," Johan said as he exited her home. He could tell that Shontae wasn't trying to help him with anything about Reds or J.R. What Shontae didn't know was that she had helped Detective Johan a great deal already. Shontae had just given him a concrete link between J.R. and Reds—they were family.

Next, Detective Johan went to talk to all of Mia's known friends. None of her friends knew anything about J.R., but almost all of them had heard of Reds. It turned out that Mia was telling all her friends how she had gotten pregnant to this guy named Reds. Mia told her friends that she felt like she hit the jackpot because Reds supposedly had a bunch of money. The detective tried to see if anybody knew Reds was a drug dealer, but nobody could say. All everyone said was that Mia said he had a real good job. When the detective talked to her roommate, Amanda, she gave him a little more insight.

"Reds wanted Mia to have an abortion, but she said no," Amanda told the detective.

She gave Detective Johan a telephone number that she had for Reds. This let him know that they were talking about the same person because it was the same number that Sting had given him. The phone would turn out to be untraceable though. It was a prepaid.

By the end of the day, Johan had it all figured out. He thought that Reds wanted Mia to get an abortion, so he wouldn't be tied down. Mia objected because she felt like having a baby to a guy with money was her meal ticket. And when Reds figured out that she wasn't going to get rid of the baby, he got rid of her the same way he got rid of Sting. Now the hard part would be proving it.

Bright and early the next morning, Detective Johan called the West Chester Police Department. As soon as he mentioned Jermaine Richers and Nasir Carter, he was put on the line with Detective Morris who only added fuel to an already-burning fire by telling Detective Johan that he had been after J.R. and Reds for years.

Detective Morris said that both Reds and J.R. were killers, but Reds was also heavy in the drug game. "They're family, but I think that Carter started paying Richers to do his dirty work when he made it big in drug game. I hate those bastards, but I'll tell you this: These two aren't average. They're both highly intelligent," Detective Morris said.

"Yeah, I'd like to have a word with this Carter kid," Detective Johan said.

"Don't waste your time. He has one of the best lawyers in the state, and he won't let you go anywhere near Carter. I told you these guys aren't your ordinary street punks," Morris said.

The two cops talked for a while longer. After Detective Johan was done explaining to Detective Morris what was going on in Altoona, Detective Morris divulged some information to him.

"I have an eyewitness that saw Carter murder a man who turned out to be a federal informant. Once I found out that the man was a federal informant, I turned the case over to them. As I'm listening to what you are saying, I'm thinking you should do the same. The case involves large quantities of drugs and murder for hire. It's a fed case all day. I'd like to get 'em, but the feds may be able to do a better job than we can," Detective Morris explained.

"I just may do that. And thank you for the insight," Detective Johan said before hanging up. After he hung up, he had a whole new outlook on what was going on in Altoona and the people who were behind it.

Reds called Jimmy's phone at five o'clock. He got to speak to J.R., but not like he wanted to because he was on the phone.

"Damn, fam, what the fuck? You was on ya way home," Reds said.

"I had to take one for the team. I'll give my life for my brother as I know you would. Everything else was just for the camera," J.R. said.

When Reds heard that, he knew what happened. He figured that J.R. thought Sting was going to start talking, so he got him out of the way. All the other stuff was just to make it look good. "I love you, cuz," Reds said with tears in his eyes.

"You don't gotta tell me what I already know," J.R. said before he got off the phone.

J.R. could hear that Reds was getting emotional, so he got off the phone before he followed suit. Before Reds hung up, Jimmy got on the phone and told Reds to meet him at the Spare Rib, a bar in West Chester, at eleven o'clock.

Later that night, Reds met Jimmy at the Spare Rib. It was a Monday, so the bar wasn't packed at all. Jimmy explained that as far as it looked, the jail was going along with J.R.'s story about what happened.

"So if they are agreein' that it was self-defense, he should be able to walk," Reds said.

"I told you the state of Pennsylvania doesn't have a self-defense law. I spoke to the DA earlier. He said he doesn't want to talk numbers until the investigation is complete. Like I said before, as long as the forensics doesn't tell another story, I should be able to get him three to six years or something like that," Jimmy said.

"I guess we gotta take the good with the bad," Reds said.

"I'm only gonna charge you $10,000 for the jailhouse case since we're not going to trial," Jimmy said.

"I'll drop it off in the mornin'," Reds said.

They sat in the bar and talked for a little while longer before parting ways for the night.

Reds got a call from Los as he was leaving Jimmy's office the next morning. "I take it you liked my friend's work," Los said.

"Yeah, it was official. I meant to call and thank you, but shit got real crazy since. It ended up costing me a little more than I expected, but I can't complain. I got what I wanted. I just didn't think of the repercussions that would follow," Reds said.

"For every action, there is a reaction," Los said.

"Yeah, I know. I had to get rid of all my employees, so I may be out of business for a while," Reds said.

"I'm sorry to hear that. When you find a new location for your store, call me," Los said.

Los wasn't dumb. He had been in the game for a long time. Reds was too young and made too much money to walk away. The street lifestyle has a gravitating effect on people, especially when they were doing it on Reds's level. Reds was no exception—he'd be back. And when he decided he was ready, Los would be waiting with open arms.

The day of J.R.'s preliminary hearing came, and Jimmy made it a spectacle. Reds wanted to come, but he was afraid to go anywhere near Altoona right now. J.R. didn't need Reds there anyway—Jimmy's friends from Harrisburg and Washington showed up. They all knew J.R. was guilty, but they showed up because Jimmy made large charitable donations to them on a yearly basis. He made those donations just for times like these.

Jimmy understood that the people in power ran the world. There was no such thing as right or wrong. They only used that to control the little people. When it was showtime, all that mattered was who you knew, and Jimmy knew quite a few people of importance. Everybody packed into the back of the courtroom. The news was there, the newspapers, the NAACP, civil rights representatives, even a few people from the Department of Justice were there.

The magistrate was seated. The DA, David Cheeks, stated his name for the record. Jimmy stated his name for the record, then the hearing began.

"Your Honor, the object of this hearing is to establish a prima facie case against my client, Jermaine Richers. However, this is impossible to do because the officer who pulled Mr. Richers over was slain in the line of duty. It's very unfortunate, but the law is clear on this matter. Without the officer that made the stop, probable cause cannot be established. I am respectfully requesting that all charges be dismissed," Jimmy said.

"Your Honor, I have Officer Moser's backup willing to testify today," the district attorney stated.

"Your Honor, it's your duty to dismiss these—" Jimmy started to shout.

"Mr. Dennis, you are not in Chester County. Maybe you tell the judges what to do down there, but not up here. I am fully aware of how to do my job," the judge said, cutting Jimmy off.

The judge was already angry because of the stunt Jimmy had pulled, bringing all this media attention around. Normally, the judge would have waived the case up to the bigger courts, but that couldn't be done today. Today, the judge would have to let a murderer walk free. It wasn't something that he wanted to do, but there was simply too much publicity there. If the judge didn't follow the law, he'd be committing career suicide.

"Yes, Your Honor, I understand, and I apologize," Jimmy said respectfully.

"Mr. Dennis, I don't like this one bit, but you are right. The law is very clear on this type of thing. I am granting your oral motion to dismiss the case," the judge said. "But I will tell you this: Mr. Richers will have his day in court on the day of judgment. And no lawyer, law, or organization will be able to save him."

"Your Honor—" the DA started to say.

"Save it, Mr. Cheeks. The case is being thrown out. As I said earlier, the law is clear on this type of thing," the judge interrupted. "I do understand that Mr. Richers has another preliminary hearing for another murder this afternoon. Is that correct?"

"Your Honor, we may be asking for a continuance on that case. We are considering working out a plea bargain," the DA said.

"Okay, if that's the case, let me know before lunch," the judge said.

The judge called the next case, and just like that, J.R. had beat the Commonwealth of Pennsylvania again.

Detective Johan walked over to the district attorney and asked, "What the fuck was that? You just let that scumbag piece of shit walk on a double murder."

"I didn't do anything. It was the judge's call, and he tossed it. I assume it's because of all the press and organizations here. This guy has a lot of fucking backing—I'll tell you that much," the DA said.

"I got all kinds of information on this guy and his drug-dealing cousin. I think I have a suspect in Officer Moser's murder. I also know that the jailhouse case may have been a hit. What did forensics say?" Detective Johan asked.

"The gun we found in his trunk was brand-new. As far as the jailhouse case goes, forensics can't find anything to dispute this guy's story. I'm going to talk to his lawyer about a plea later today. But if you've got something to support this case being a hit, we can nail this bastard," the DA said.

"I'm not letting you guys fuck anything else up with this guy. I'm going to the feds with this one," Johan said matter-of-factly.

The DA stuffed some papers in his briefcase then stormed off.

The DA walked into the bathroom to take a piss. When he got into the bathroom, he saw Jimmy. He checked to make sure it was only him and Jimmy in the bathroom. "That was a hell of a stunt you pulled today," the DA said.

"That's why I get the big bucks," Jimmy said with a smile.

"I just want you to know that I know all about your client and the things he's into. I had a nice talk with Detective Morris in West Chester. So just to let you know, we're building a case on him for Officer Moser's murder," the DA said, trying to scare Jimmy.

"Don't waste your time. My client was in prison, and unless you have a recorded phone conversation or a letter with him ordering the hit, I'll have it thrown out faster than I had this case thrown out," Jimmy said. "We'll cross that bridge when we get to it. How much time are you offering my client for the jailhouse case?"

"I don't know yet. I'm thinking about playing hard ball," the DA said. The district attorney figured that he'd play a little game of his own in hopes that J.R. would take the first deal he was offered.

"Well, we were thinking three to six years was suitable for involuntary manslaughter," Jimmy said.

"That's not going to happen. Your guy is a murderer," the DA said.

"So let me get this straight," Jimmy said with a puzzled look on his face. "You think my client had Officer Moser killed?"

"That's right," the DA said with a big grin that told Jimmy that the DA thought he had it all figured out.

"So what makes you think that if you don't give him that three-to-six-year deal, we just asked for, he won't have you killed?" Jimmy asked.

"Is that a threat?" the DA asked in an appalled tone.

"Absolutely not. I am an officer of the court. I don't make threats. That's just what I'd be thinking if I were you," Jimmy said before walking out of the bathroom.

The DA stood there for a minute with a stupid look on his face and digested what Jimmy just said.

Jimmy stood in front of the district courthouse and called Reds. He filled Reds in on all that was going on. Reds was ecstatic about J.R. beating the double murder.

"I fuckin' love you, Jimmy! You the best," Reds said.

They talked a little while longer then hung up. As Jimmy was hanging up the phone, the DA came outside and lit up a cigarette.

"The best I can do is offer him five to ten years. But he has to agree to sit down and have an interview with me," he said.

The district attorney had given thought to what Jimmy said, and Jimmy had a point. This case wasn't worth risking his life for. The DA figured he'd give J.R. the deal for the jailhouse case, and that would give the feds time to nail him for what he was about to tell them.

"Let me run it by my client," Jimmy said calmly.

Jimmy walked back inside and pulled J.R. into the attorney-client room. "The DA is offering you five to ten years, but he said the deal is only on the table if you agree to an interview with him," Jimmy said.

"Well, that's not gonna happen. Get the interview dropped, and we got a deal," J.R. said.

"Listen, he said a few things to me that you may want to hear. Shit, I want to hear more. As with any interview, we don't have to talk—just listen. Give him an opportunity to expose himself. This guy thinks he has you figured out, and he wants to brag. Let's see how much he really knows," Jimmy said.

J.R. sat silent for a minute in deep thought. "Okay, get the paperwork drawn up. He got himself an interview," J.R. said.

As Jimmy was getting the paperwork taken care of for the deal, Detective Johan was on the phone with the FBI. He was currently talking to Special Agent Kelly who was the head of Reds's investigation. Detective Johan told Agent Kelly all about what was going on in Altoona.

Agent Kelly hated local police departments. They would always fuck a case up then try to give it to them to fix. Agent Kelly especially disliked Altoona police because they did so much illegal stuff. The feds rarely ever picked a case up from Altoona because it was damned near impossible to get a conviction based on their police work. That's how bad their investigations were. Now here was Detective Johan, giving Agent Kelly a bunch of allegations with no evidence and expecting him to make a bust. "Do you have any hard evidence on these guys?" Agent Kelly asked.

"Not anymore, our informant is dead," Detective Johan answered.

"Any other witnesses that saw them do something?" Agent Kelly followed up.

"Not yet, but we still have an investigation going on," Johan said.

"Okay, well, when you get an informant or something we can use, we'll get involved. If I were you, I'd just worry about Richers. We have Carter booked solid. All we have to do is locate the bastard," Agent Kelly said.

"Okay, thank you," Detective Johan said.

"No, thank you. As I just told you, we were having trouble locating Mr. Carter, but now we know where to look," Agent Kelly said.

"I think with all that's going on right now, he's probably relocated if he's as smart as they say he is," Johan said.

"He's not smart. He's just lucky, but his luck will run out," Agent Kelly said before he hung up. Agent Kelly hated when police called criminals smart. None of them were smart, or they wouldn't be living the type of lifestyle they lived. If they were so smart, Agent Kelly would never catch them, and Agent Kelly always caught his man.

The DA brought the plea paperwork to Jimmy then told him he was ready for the interview. Jimmy had the DA sign the plea then J.R. Then the interview was started. The DA entered the room with a tape recorder. He turned the tape recorder on then started talking.

"Your name is Jermaine Richers. Is that correct?" the DA asked.

"Yes, it is," J.R. responded.

"Do you know Nasir Carter?"

"He's my cousin," J.R. replied calmly.

"Do you know him by the name of Reds?"

"No."

"Okay, before we go any further, you already have your five-to-ten. All that you can do now is help yourself. If you give me the information I need, I can cut your deal in half. So let me ask you again, do you know Nasir Carter as Reds?" the DA asked.

"No," J.R. said flatly.

"Do you know Mr. Carter to be a drug dealer?" the DA asked.

"No."

"Do you know where we can locate Reds?"

"That was a nice try, but I already told you I don't know anybody by the name of Reds," J.R. said with a grin.

The DA was growing frustrated. He could see that J.R. found this to be amusing. "You're not as smart as you think, Mr. Richers. The feds are all over your cousin. I gave you a chance to cut your time in half, but I guess you like jail. Have fun for the next five years," the DA said as he got up and turned the tape recorder off.

"A'ight, hold up," J.R. said.

The DA stopped and looked at him.

"Nah, never mind," J.R. said as he laughed.

The DA stormed out of the room. As soon as the DA was gone, J.R. turned to Jimmy with a look of severity. "Call Reds and tell him to disappear for a while," J.R. instructed.

Jimmy called Reds and told him what had just transpired. "They're asking a lot of questions about you. I think it would be a very wise move for you to disappear for a while," Jimmy said.

Reds wasted no time. He drove to his apartment, packed everything, then headed to Juanita's. "I'm movin' in," Reds said as he walked through the door.

"What's wrong?" Juanita asked.

"Why somethin' gotta be wrong?" Reds asked with a smirk.

"Nigga, I know you. Somethin' is goin' on if you movin' in with me," Juanita said.

"The cops is lookin' for me. I gotta lay low for a while," Reds said in all seriousness.

"Well . . ." Juanita drew her answer out.

Reds looked at her is if she was crazy for even thinking of denying him.

"You know I got chu," Juanita said with a smile. "I was just playin'."

Reds sent Juanita to get his car from his apartment. When she came back, he took her to the tag shop and signed over the truck and car to her. Then Reds sent Juanita to Philly to trade the truck in for whatever she wanted. He stayed at her house and unpacked. Reds didn't like the fact that he had to rely on someone, but he knew that if he had to count on somebody, he could count on Juanita. Other than J.R., she was the only person he trusted. Reds didn't know exactly what the police knew or if they had a warrant for him, but he planned on moving like they did.

The next day, Juanita took the Monte Carlo to the same place she took the truck. She left the Escalade there overnight and promised to return with the Monte Carlo the next day. Juanita traded both the car and the truck for a brand-new midnight blue 2004 Lincoln Navigator. She left it with factory everything. Since Reds told her the cops were looking for him, she didn't want to attract too much attention. She liked that Navigator because it was nice but it wasn't flashy.

When she got home from picking the truck up, Reds was in her room unpacking the last of his things. Juanita walked in the room with a big smile on her face.

"What's up with you?" Reds asked.

"I could get used to this. Comin' home and you bein' here," Juanita said.

"I really appreciate you lettin' me stay here. I want you to know that I will never forget how you holdin' a nigga down," Reds said.

"I do what I do out of love, not because I want recognition," Juanita said. "I don't tell you I love you 'cause it sounds good. I say it 'cause I mean it. Everything I've done for you has been to show you that I'm in ya corner. I don't need ya money, but I still introduced you to my cousin. When you call, I come runnin'. I don't do that because I'm an ugly bitch. I can have whoever I want. It just so happens that the person I want is you. All I want you to do is love me the way I love you."

Reds could hear the emotion in her words. It touched a spot in his heart. He walked over to Juanita and hugged her. "I just don't trust people," Reds said honestly.

"You have to trust me. You trust me with everything else. You might as well trust me with ya heart," Juanita said as she kissed Reds softly on the lips.

Reds and Juanita lay in the bed naked. Reds was in deep thought. He wasn't thinking about what was going on in the streets. He was thinking about what Juanita said. Reds wanted the same thing she wanted, but he was afraid to lay it on the line, and the timing was all wrong. Reds didn't feel like now was a good time for a relationship with all that was going on.

As Reds's mind wandered, he looked at Juanita, who was sleeping on his chest. She looked so beautiful and peaceful. As he looked at her, he couldn't help but to imagine what their baby would look like if he got her pregnant.

Reds's thoughts were interrupted by his phone vibrating. Reds looked at the caller ID and saw it was Jimmy "Anything new?" Reds asked.

"Yeah, and none of it's good. I checked into some things after the shit I heard yesterday. It turns out that the feds have a warrant for your arrest," Jimmy said.

"For what?" Reds asked.

"Murder of a federal informant. If you took what I said about disappearing lightly, you shouldn't have. Get rid of your phone. Don't go home, and call me at the office tomorrow. I should know more by then," Jimmy said as he hung up.

Reds laid in the bed in shock. Just like that, the game had changed from bad to worse.

# 35

Reds had done so much dirt, he had no idea what murder the feds wanted him for. Nice's murder had crossed his mind when he heard *federal informant*, but he was for certain that no one had seen that. As he continued to think, Twan's murder crossed his mind. *Maybe Sting told them that I was responsible for Twan's murder, and he was an informant for the feds*, Reds thought to himself.

The more thoughts that went through Reds' mind, the harder it was for him to pinpoint. There would be no telling until he was arrested for the murder, and he wasn't trying to be arrested, ever. For all Reds knew, Sting could have just put a murder on him, one he didn't even do. *Did J.R. turn on me?* Reds pondered.

He was instantly upset at himself for even thinking something like that. J.R. would never betray him, he hoped. Reds woke Juanita up and asked her to drive his phone to Philly and throw it on the expressway. Juanita asked no questions; she simply got dressed, kissed Reds, then left for Philly.

Reds sat in the house, thinking and drinking. He was careful not to drink too much and get drunk. He just made sure he kept a buzz. Juanita came back home and asked if he wanted to talk. She could tell that something was bothering him, and she wanted him to know that she was there for him. Reds told her what was going on. He didn't want to keep her in the dark. Juanita was super loyal. He at least felt she should know what she was getting herself into.

"We'll get through this," Juanita said as she gave Reds a soft kiss and looked him in his eyes. "Together."

Reds didn't get it. Juanita was either crazy for subjecting herself to this type of danger or she loved Reds even more than he thought. Either way, he appreciated her not turning her back on him. As Reds thought about Juanita, he remembered a conversation he and J.R. had a while back.

"When things are good, our friends know us. When things are bad, we know our friends," J.R. had said.

Nothing could be truer than that statement. Everybody wants to be around when things are good, but it's very seldom that you find someone to go through the rough times with you. Because Reds knew this, he thought that much more of Juanita. Reds was truly happy to have a strong woman like Juanita by his side during this rough time. Normally, Reds would just go seek J.R.'s advice, but J.R. was gone. Reds couldn't talk to him; he would have to get through this one without J.R. It just felt really good to know that Juanita was there to go through it with him.

"Once you get ya money up, you can just go turn ya'self in. You can beat anything if you got enough money. That's what Los always says," Juanita said.

"Listen to you," Reds said with a smile.

"Behind every strong man is a strong woman," Juanita said.

"I heard that. You do have a point though. Money means a lot, but it's not everything. Look at the nigga Big Meech. He gave them white ma'fuckas a quarter billion dollars, and he still went to jail," Reds said.

"How the fuck he give them that much and still do time?" Juanita asked.

"They wanted him, and some in his circle were reckless with what they said over the phone That's why I be by myself, and I eliminate *everything*," Reds said.

"I'm not sure I follow you," Juanita said.

"If I'm drivin' down the street and I come across a wall in the middle of the road, a car can't drive up a wall. So in order for me to get where I'm goin', the wall has to be eliminated. As long as it's still there, I'll always have a problem goin' down that street," Reds said.

"Okay," Juanita responded, letting him know she understood.

"My money is up—that's not the problem. I have to find out what or who the feds have and destroy it. That's the only way I can win against them. But if it is what I think it is, I'll turn myself in. That wall has already been taken care of," Reds said.

Juanita liked it when Reds talked like this. He sounded so powerful.

Nothing turned a woman on like a man with power. "Whatever you need me to do, just let me know, and it's done," Juanita said.

"I'm gonna hold you to that," Reds said as he kissed her on her head.

Morning came, and Reds called Jimmy as soon as he woke up. "What's up?" Reds asked.

"Everybody is being tightlipped about this one. Everything about this case is sealed until you're caught. The only thing that anyone knows is what I told you yesterday," Jimmy said.

"I have a feelin' that this has somethin' to do with the nigga J.R. killed in his cell. If I'm right, that won't hold any weight with him bein' dead, right?" Reds asked.

"They will definitely need more than a dead CI to get a conviction," Jimmy said. "But if I know the feds, they have more than just that."

"So you don't think I should turn myself in?" Reds asked.

"No, wait and see what comes to light. Give me some time. I should be able to find something out," Jimmy said.

"So how much is this gonna cost me?" Reds asked.

"Ahh, for a friend, $50,000. That's a $50,000 flat, no extras for trial or anything," Jimmy said.

"I'll have it dropped off today," Reds said.

"All right, make sure you call me once a week. I'll keep you posted on what I know," Jimmy said.

Reds and Juanita stayed shacked up in the house for about two weeks. From being in Altoona, Reds had learned to lie low, but this was a whole new type of lying low. Reds hadn't been outside in fourteen days; he needed some fresh air. Just a few days prior, Reds had Juanita get a license to carry a firearm and a bounty hunter's license. The bounty hunter's license would allow her to take her gun from state to state. The last thing Reds wanted was to get arrested and have an illegal gun on him. That was just an extra case that he couldn't afford, so he made sure Juanita had things done right.

When Juanita came in from grocery shopping, Reds told her that he needed to get out.

"Where you tryin' to go? Remember you're on the run," Juanita told warned.

"Let's go out to dinner then hit a club. Nothin' 'round here, we can go to Delaware or somethin'," Reds said.

"It's your call," Juanita said.

They put the groceries up, decided what they were going to do for the night, then showered. While they were showering, Reds stood behind Juanita and admired her body. His dick started to get hard as he watched soap run down Juanita's back and down the crack of her ass. Juanita was slim, but her pussy was extra fat. Her legs were slightly bowed, and her ass looked like two nice-sized melons. Reds could see Juanita's pussy from the back. His rock-hard erection poked Juanita in her back.

Over the last two weeks, Reds stopped being aggressive with Juanita during sex. He was very gentle and passionate with her now. Reds hadn't made love to a woman since Maria. He knew that Juanita was taking control of his heart, the same way Maria had. But Reds was tired of fighting it, he admitted to himself that it felt good, and he liked it. Reds pulled Juanita close and kissed her on the nape of her neck. Juanita grabbed his arms and wrapped them around her. Reds held her for a while. He didn't say anything, and neither did she. Reds just kissed her neck and sucked her ears. Juanita moaned softly. Reds took his hand and cupped Juanita's left breast. He rubbed and squeezed it for a minute, then he tugged on her erect nipple. As he did this, his right hand wandered down to her pussy. Reds began to rub on the hood of Juanita's clit, only stopping every so often to slip two fingers inside of her. Juanita was feeling good now. She bent over and started rubbing her ass on Reds' erection.

"Put it in me, papi," Juanita moaned. She used the side of the bathtub to hold her leg up.

Reds knew she wanted him inside of her, but he wasn't finished yet. Reds spread her ass cheeks apart and buried his face in between them. Reds licked Juanita's asshole as he continued to rub her clit.

"Don't stop, baby! I'm cummin'! Oooh, oooh, god! Ahhh, that's it, papi! I love you!" Juanita said as her body released its love juices.

Reds let her thick juice flow in his mouth, then he stood and pushed himself inside of her. They both let out a moan of ecstasy. Juanita reached in between Reds's legs and massaged his balls as he slowly went in and out of her. Juanita must have climaxed three times. No man had ever made her feel the way Reds did.

"Cum inside me, papi. Put it all in me!" Juanita moaned.

Reds's speed began to quicken. Once he felt himself about to let go, he pushed himself as far inside of Juanita as he could. After he came inside of her, he held her tight, leaving himself inside of her until he went completely soft.

Reds turned her around, palmed her ass cheeks, and picked her up.

Juanita wrapped her legs around him. Reds looked Juanita in her eyes and told her that he loved her. Reds thought that Juanita would start crying and get all emotional, but she did just the opposite.

"You gettin' soft," she said as she laughed.

Reds didn't talk much about his feelings, but Juanita wasn't stupid. She could see the change in the way he acted with her. Juanita knew she was close to getting what she wanted—Reds's heart.

# 36

While Reds and Juanita ate dinner, she told Reds that she was pregnant. To Reds's surprise, he was happy about it. When Juanita saw how happy he was, she felt like a ton of bricks had been lifted off of her shoulders. Juanita was fearful of telling Reds about the pregnancy. She wasn't sure how Reds would react because of everything else that was going on. But now that she saw the joy in Reds's face, she felt so much better.

Reds did have mixed emotions about Juanita being pregnant. On one hand, he was afraid that if he got locked up and got some crazy time, he'd be leaving Juanita and the baby on their own. On the other hand, he was extremely happy. Reds saw a lot of good qualities in Juanita, and he knew she would help pass those qualities on to his child. Reds knew that there was a possibility that he ended up going to jail for a long time. If that did happen, he had plenty of money for Juanita and the baby. Also, he'd have a living legacy still on the streets.

Reds didn't show Juanita the discomfort about her being pregnant. He didn't want to ruin the moment. He didn't want her to think that he was displeased with her being pregnant. It wasn't the pregnancy; he was displeased with his predicament during the pregnancy. Some things Reds would just have to deal with himself.

"If it's a boy, I want him to be a junior," Reds said.

"I'm just so happy that you're happy about this too. I kinda felt like I was forcin' this on you," Juanita said with tears in her eyes.

"You thought I didn't know what you wanted? Every time we have sex, you ask me to cum inside of you. I knew what I was doin'," Reds said. "If I'm gonna have a baby, I'm glad it's with you, and not some money-hungry whore. You don't want to know what I did to the last chick I got pregnant,"

Reds said the last part with a devilish smirk that indicated that he was just joking. He liked how he could be honest with a person about something as long as he said it in a certain manner. His remarks would just be laughed off and considered a joke.

"You're so silly," Juanita said.

As they were leaving dinner, Juanita told Reds that she knew of a club that was live. They got to the club, and shit was jumping. Reds wore a dark blue pair of Evisu jeans with the Evisu sign in red on the back, a white and red pair of Jordans, and a red shirt that said "MEET THE DEALER" in white letters. He left his chain at home, but his watch was shining bright. Juanita had on a pair of black Dolce & Gabbana slacks, a white and black striped Dolce & Gabbana button-up, and a black pair of Manolo Blahnik heels. Juanita wore a two-karat diamond earring in each ear. She had her hair straightened and looked magnificent.

The line to get in the club was long, and there weren't any parking spots for at least two blocks. As they approached the club, Juanita changed her mind. "Maybe we should go somewhere else. This line is way too long. We ain't gon' never get in," Juanita said.

"We not waitin' in no fuckin' line," Reds said. He smacked Juanita on her ass and told her to follow him. They walked past everyone in line and went straight to the bouncer.

"How much to get right in, big guy?" Reds asked. "No metal detectors."

Before the bouncer got a chance to answer, a cute brown-skinned chick yelled out, "He can't just be buttin' in line like that!"

"Damn, sis, what's all the hatin' for?" Reds asked as he turned around with a look of disgust on his face. When he saw how pretty she was, he saw an opportunity.

"I'm hatin' 'cause I been waitin' for hours," she shot back.

"Come on, sis, you with us then," Reds said.

The woman quickly jumped out of line and hurried up to where Reds and Juanita were standing. "Thank you," she said as she gave Reds a hug and kiss on the neck.

"How much for me and my two lady friends?" Reds asked again.

"A thousand dollars," the bouncer said.

Reds paid the bouncer, then he, Juanita, and the chick they just met walked around the metal detector and into the club.

"Is I'm rollin' with y'all?" the chick from the line asked.

"What's ya name, ma?" Reds asked.

"Vida," she replied.

"Okay, Vida, you with us tonight," Reds said.

Reds was so busy showing off that he didn't even realize how pissed off Juanita was. Juanita felt disrespected by how Reds was acting. She knew they weren't together, but it felt like they were. Reds had been treating her like royalty as of lately. And since he was happy about the baby, Juanita figured that he was willing to try and be a family. Juanita's feelings were hurt, but she only had herself to blame. Reds had warned her a long time ago not to get territorial on him. Juanita just told herself, *That's what I get for thinking he would change.* But she was still mad at him for sending mixed signals.

Reds told Vida and Juanita that he was going to go get some drinks, then he walked to the bar.

*Why don't you take ya fuckin' lost puppy with you?* Juanita thought to herself.

Reds went to the bar and grabbed a two bottles of Rémy Martin VSOP and a cup of orange juice for Juanita.

While Reds was gone, Vida tried to make conversation with Juanita. "So where are you guys from?" Vida asked.

"Wilmington," Juanita answered. Juanita knew better than to tell Vida the truth.

"I never got your name," Vida said.

"That's 'cause I never gave it," Juanita shot back.

Vida wasn't about to get into a fight with Juanita. She simply rolled her eyes and turned her back to Juanita. *Bitch just mad 'cause I'm cuter than she is,* Vida thought to herself.

Before anything else could be said, Reds had returned with the drinks. He gave Vida a bottle of Rémy and gave Juanita the orange juice. Vida looked at Juanita with a grin because she had gotten a bottle and Juanita only got a cup. Juanita knew what she was thinking, so she grabbed Reds and gave him a tongue kiss. Juanita only did this because she knew if Vida tried to kiss Reds, he'd turn her down. This was Juanita's way of telling Vida that Reds was hers. Reds took Juanita and Vida to the couches that were along the wall.

"Don't you wanna dance?" Vida asked.

"I don't dance, but you can dance on me," Reds responded.

Vida had on a New York Knicks jersey dress and a pair of white, blue, and orange Air Force Ones. Her dress was so tight that Reds could tell that she didn't have anything on under the dress. Vida's hair was short, her lips were full, and she had big brown eyes. On top of all that, she was pretty and thick as hell, just how Reds liked them. Vida reminded Reds of Bird from the movie *Soul Food*.

Vida could tell that Juanita felt some type of way about her being around, so she decided to make her that much angrier. Vida took a swig from the bottle of Rémy Martin then stood in front of Reds. She made her ass cheeks jump one at a time. "You like that?" Vida asked as she looked back at Reds.

Reds didn't hear what she said. The music was too loud. The Clipse song "Grindin'" was blaring out of the speakers. Even if it wasn't, Reds was too busy watching Vida's ass jump. Reds grabbed her by the waist and pulled her down on his lap. Vida began to grind all over Reds.

It took everything Juanita had not to punch Vida and Reds in the face. She wasn't about to make a scene though, so she went on to the dance floor and started dancing. Reds saw her get up, but he didn't stop her. He was too busy with Vida. She grinded on Reds's lap for almost five songs. Reds felt all over her as she swayed her hips from side to side. Vida's ass and titties were so soft that it felt like they were made of cotton.

Reds was hitting the bottle of Rémy hard. He was tipsy and horny as hell. Reds pulled her head close to his mouth. "I felt everything else. Let me see what that pussy feel like," Reds said in her ear.

It was dark in the club, so Vida spread her legs, giving Reds the go-ahead. Reds slid two fingers inside of her. She was already wet. Reds played with her pussy for a while then he pulled his fingers out. He was thinking about taking her to the bathroom and having sex with her. Before Reds proposed this to her, he picked his bottle up and took a drink. When his hand got close to his face, he smelled something foul. Reds sat the bottle back down and smelled his fingers. Without saying a word, he tapped Vida on the shoulder, giving her his fingers to smell.

"What? Chu want me to suck 'em?" Vida asked with a confused look on her face.

"This is all you," Reds said as he put his fingers to her nose.

Vida's pussy smelled like creek water. Without giving her time to respond, Reds pushed Vida off his lap and walked away. Reds could be very ignorant when he drank. He wanted to pour the bottle of Rémy on Vida, but he decided not to waste his liquor on a dirty chick. Reds searched the dance floor for Juanita. He saw her in the corner, giving some short Spanish guy a reenactment of the movie *Dirty Dancing*. Juanita was throwing her ass on him like it was her job. The Spanish guy was feeling all over Juanita.

The sight of this infuriated Reds. He started walking over to them. Juanita saw Reds coming, but she ignored him. The Nelly song "Flap Your Wings" going "Drop down and get cha eagle on" was playing. And that's exactly what Juanita did. She dropped down and got her eagle on. She was dancing like she was auditioning for the video. The Spanish guy and the rest of the dance floor were loving the show Juanita was putting on. This just made Reds angrier. Reds grabbed Juanita by the arm, pulled her up, and yelled in her ear. "You tryna front on a nigga?" Reds shouted with his face broken up.

The Spanish guy didn't know what was going on. All he knew was that he was trying to take Juanita home, so he intervened. He grabbed Reds's shoulder and told him to leave Juanita alone. Reds turned around and looked at the Spanish guy like he was crazy.

"Wrong move," Reds said.

*Spshhhhh!* Reds busted the bottle of Rémy over the Spanish guy's head. The Spanish guy went down, and Reds started stomping him. Juanita was trying to stop Reds, but he was in the zone. Finally, the bouncers came and snatched Reds up like a toddler.

"Pussy, get the fuck off me! You know who the fuck I am? I'll get chu niggas murdered! Get the fuck off me!" Reds yelled.

The bouncers heard Reds's threats. He was only pissing them off even more. They took Reds out back of the club and started pounding on him. Juanita came rushing out and saw what was going on. She yelled for the bouncers to get off of Reds, but they weren't paying her any attention.

"Get the fuck off my man!" Juanita yelled.

"Shut the fuck up, bitch, 'fore we beat ya ass next," the big black bouncer barked.

Juanita knew she was no match for the bouncers. She reached in her purse and grabbed her .38 special. *BOOM! BOOM!*

"I said get the fuck off my man," Juanita said as she held the gun in the air.

The bouncers stopped kicking and punching Reds and put their hands in the air.

"I'm too small to be fightin' you big-ass niggas. But I promise you, if one of y'all hit my man again, I'll shoot the shit outta one of you," Juanita said.

All three bouncers stepped away from Reds. Juanita kept the gun out just in case shit got out of hand again.

"Bring ya stupid ass on," Juanita told Reds.

Reds picked himself up off the ground and walked over to Juanita. Reds's face and ribs were sore from the beating he just took. His pride was also hurt because Juanita had to stop them from damned near killing him.

"Give me the gun, baby, so I can kill these faggot-ass niggas," Reds said.

Juanita ignored him. She started cussing him out in Spanish. She backed out of the alley slowly, with Reds following. Once they got out of the alley, they sprinted to the truck.

Reds and Juanita drove home in silence. Once they got in the house, Reds attempted to check Juanita. "If you ever disrespect me like that again, it'll be you I hit with the bottle," Reds said. "Lettin' that corny-ass nigga feel you up like that and you pregnant with mines. You musta lost ya fuckin' mind."

Juanita went off, throwing anything she could get her hands on at Reds. Reds dipped the first few items, then he bobbed when he should have weaved and got hit in the head with a camcorder. Reds looked at Juanita like she was crazy as he rubbed his head. Reds could feel a knot forming where she hit him. He walked over and slapped the shit out of her. Juanita fell to the ground and touched her lip. It was bleeding.

"Oh, you gon' hit me? Why you ain't hit them niggas that whooped ya ass at the club? All I do for you and you gon' hit me! You a piece of shit! Talkin' 'bout I disrespected you. I only did it 'cause you disrespected me. Got that dirty-ass bitch all in ya fuckin' face and grindin' all on you. Y'all was fuckin' with clothes on! So yeah, I went on the dance floor and gave you a dose of ya own medicine. You got to feel exactly how I was feelin'! If you can do you, I can do me. As long as you respect me, I'll always—and I mean always—respect you. You saw that bitch in the club and forgot about me. I just wanted to let you know that you ain't the only one that can show ya ass," Juanita said.

Reds was at a loss for words. He had never been with a chick like Juanita. She made some very valid points, so good that Reds didn't even have a comeback. He didn't even notice she was mad at the club and she still stopped the bouncers from beating him up. He admired her for that. Reds held out his hand to help Juanita up. She took his hand and stood.

"I'm sorry," Reds said as he gave her a kiss.

"I just want you to know how it works. If you hurt me, I'm'a hurt you," Juanita said.

"I can't do nothin' but respect that," Reds said.

"I know a man is gonna be a man, but I don't wanna know about it. You know how I feel about you. The least you could do is give me that much respect, to flirt with bitches when I'm not around," Juanita said.

"I can do that. But I ain't sharin' mines with nobody," Reds said. "I catch you with another nigga, shit's gonna get ugly."

"Yours?" Juanita asked. "So it's official?"

"What?" Reds responded.

"We're together?" Juanita asked.

"You mean more to me than you could ever know," Reds said.

"So say it," Juanita said.

"What?" Reds asked.

He knew what she wanted; he was just playing with her.

"You know. Say it," Juanita said.

"I love you, baby. If you ain't wifey material, I don't know what is," Reds said.

"You still ain't say it," Juanita said.

"I don't have to say it. You already know what it is. You see what I did to that nigga in the club over you?" Reds asked with a smile.

"I love you, Nasir Carter," Juanita said.

"I love you too. Now let's get some sleep. My body is sore as shit," Reds said as he laughed. "Why you ain't shoot them big-ass niggas?"

"I should've shot you," Juanita said with a laugh.

"Well, in that case, way to control ya'self," Reds shot back.

# 37

Over the next few months, Reds stayed in the shadows. He and Juanita would go out of town three or four times a week. They'd check out a new release at the movies or go out for dinner or he'd take her shopping. They never went anywhere in West Chester due to the fact that the feds had come to town and spoken to a few people in the neighborhood. They just wanted to know if Reds had been seen. They let people know that if they did see him, to call the authorities. The feds only spoke to about eight people, but before the end of the day, everybody in town knew what was going on.

Reds still called Jimmy every week, and every week, there was nothing new about the case being said. Juanita was six months pregnant now and moody as hell. Reds got tired of her mood swings all the time, so he would tell her to go chill with one of her friends or family. He understood that being up under each other all the time wasn't good for their relationship.

Once Juanita started going out more, things got a lot better between them. Juanita would often go to her cousin Lilian's house. Lilian was dating Reds's cousin, Cash. That's where Juanita got all her info from. Lilian and Juanita were like sisters. They talked about everything. Lilian knew that Reds was the father of Juanita's baby and that Reds had bought Juanita the house she lived in. Reds wasn't perfect, but you would never know by the way Juanita talked about him. She had nothing but good things to say about her man. Juanita had told Lilian that she talked to Reds every day, but she said Reds had left town. The only person that knew Reds was living with Juanita was her mom, Lucinda.

Lucinda lived in Puerto Rico. She had recently moved back there. When Juanita finally told her she was pregnant, she decided to come and visit them. Because of this, she was aware of Reds's situation. Lucinda always wanted to take them out or have company over. After a while, they ran out of excuses of why that just couldn't happen, and Juanita told her mom what was going on. Lucinda wasn't thrilled about Reds's situation, but she understood. Her husband, Juanita's father, was doing life in the feds. When Juanita was little, he was caught with a lot of drugs and charged with running a criminal enterprise. Lucinda understood the life Reds lived because she had been a part of it. But that didn't mean she didn't want a better life for her daughter and grandchild. As far as a person, Lucinda loved Reds. He was very respectful. He made her daughter happy. He seemed to be taking good care of Juanita, and he was the reason that Lucinda would be a grandmother soon. Lucinda hoped that Reds never got caught. She didn't want her daughter to go through what she had gone through with her father. The thought of Reds's situation saddened Lucinda because she knew Reds's arrest would happen eventually—nobody could run forever. But under the right circumstances, they could run for a long time.

Juanita came home from Lilian's with a message for Reds. "Cash said you need to call him immediately. Whatever it is, he said it's urgent," Juanita said.

"Well, I don't wanna call 'em 'til tomorrow. If I call tonight, he might figure out that I'm here," Reds said.

As Reds was talking, Juanita looked through the mail. She saw that she had a letter from her mom. She opened it and saw a letter, a birth certificate, and a social security card. She had no idea what the birth certificate and social security card were for, so she just read the letter. When Juanita finished reading the letter, she explained everything to Reds. "Baby, my mom sent you a birth certificate and a social security card," Juanita said.

"For what?" Reds asked with a puzzled look on his face.

"The birth certificate and social security card belongs to a man named Filipe Rivera. My mom said he has never been over here, so you can go get a real state ID or driver's license in his name. You can legally be Filipe Rivera as long as he never comes over here. My mom said she wants to see me happy, and you be a good father, so you better not blow this chance," Juanita explained in a very excited tone.

Reds had an uneasy look on his face.

"What's wrong, baby? You don't look happy," Juanita said.

"I am. I just have to be sure that this will work. I got everything ridin' on this. If I go try to get an ID and this shit ain't 100 percent official, I'm goin' right to jail," Reds said.

"Well, I'll just call her and find out," Juanita said as she picked up the phone. She called her mom and talked for a little while, then she hung up.

"My mom said she wouldn't send you no shit that wasn't a guarantee," Juanita said. "She said it's been done plenty of times before, and nobody has ever had a problem."

"A'ight. We gon' find out. We'll go down there tomorrow," Reds said.

Juanita was super excited. They sat up for most of the night talking about where they planned to live and things like that.

The next morning, Juanita's phone woke them. It was Cash. Juanita talked to him for a minute, then she hung up.

"Cash said to call you right now and tell you to call him," Juanita said.

"A'ight. I'm gonna go down stairs. Call my phone, then we'll three-way him. That way, he doesn't know I'm here," Reds said as he walked out the room.

Juanita called Reds then called Cash. "Cash, I got 'em on three-way," Juanita said before putting the phone down.

"What's good, cuz?" Reds asked.

"Yo, I gotta talk to you in person like right now," Cash said.

"That ain't gonna happen," Reds said.

"I know who told on you," Cash blurted out.

"Meet me at the King of Prussia mall in two hours," Reds said instantly.

"I'll be there," Cash responded.

Reds knew that this could be a setup, so he wanted to make sure it was somewhere that the cops wouldn't be able to fire freely. If it was a setup, Reds planned on killing Cash right in the mall.

"What was that about?" Juanita asked.

"He says he knows who told on me," Reds said.

"Do you believe him?" Juanita asked.

"I don't know, but I definitely wanna find out. If it's a setup, I'm'a kill 'em," Reds said like it was nothing.

This was the first time that Juanita heard Reds talk like that. She was a little shocked, but she had heard stories about him before. Now she assumed the things she heard were true. Juanita was scared of what was going to happen. "Don't go if you don't trust it," Juanita said with tears in her eyes. "Reds, I don't wanna lose you!"

"I gotta find out if this shit is true," Reds said.

"No, the fuck you don't! My mom just sent us all we need. We can go get the ID and get the fuck outta here today," Juanita said now crying.

Juanita was about to have the baby, and there was nothing she wanted more than for Reds to be there when the baby was born. "If you love me and our baby, let's go," Juanita said.

She was crying harder. Juanita felt like she was about to lose one of the most important people in her life. She was pleading with Reds to just listen to her. "We need you!" Juanita said.

Reds didn't say anything for a few seconds. He just looked at Juanita. He was trying to find the right words for what he needed to say. "Because I love you and that baby inside of you, I have to find out what's goin' on. If I just leave, they could always catch me, and I'll have to answer for what they are sayin' I did. If I can eliminate my problem now, when they catch me, there will be nothin' to answer for. I need you to trust me. I'm goin' to make this better," Reds said. "But if somethin' does ever happen to me, make sure you go get all my dad's stuff out of storage. There's a lot of pictures of me and my dad in there. There's also a bunch of stuff about my side of the family that I want our child to know."

Juanita just grabbed Reds and continued to cry uncontrollably. It had sunk in to her that she wasn't going to be able to change Reds's mind. All she could do now was hope that Reds made it back home safe.

Reds drove to King of Prussia mall by himself. Juanita tried to use sex to keep him in the house, but Reds knew what she was trying to do. He made love to her like she wanted, but he had a trick of his own up his sleeve. Reds knew that there was no way in hell Juanita would let him go to the mall by himself. He didn't like what he was going to have to do, but he had to protect her.

When they were finished making love, Reds went into the kitchen and made two glasses of orange juice. On his way back to their bedroom, Reds stopped in the bathroom and put two melatonin pills in Juanita's cup of juice. He stirred it up, then took it to her. As they lay in bed, Juanita drank the juice. Nobody said anything. They just lay there in silence. Juanita had pulled out all of the stops this time. She sexed Reds the best she could, trying to tire him out. As she lay in bed waiting for Reds to doze off, drowsiness hit her like a Mack truck.

Reds could see her fighting the sleep, so he closed his eyes in an attempt to make her feel comfortable going to sleep. His trick had worked. About five minutes after Juanita saw Reds close his eyes, she was out cold. Reds slipped out of the bed, got dressed, and headed for the King of Prussia.

Reds called Cash's cell phone. "Where you at?" Reds asked.

I'm pullin' into the parkin' lot now," Cash said.

"Meet me at the Foot Locker," Reds said.

Reds had his gun on him. He waited for Cash, and after about five minutes, he saw his cousin. Reds's heart was racing. He didn't know if it was a setup or not, but he was definitely about to find out. Reds gave Cash a hug. He felt to see if Cash was wearing a wire while they embraced.

Cash looked at Reds a little funny but didn't say anything about it. Instead, he went right into why he had Reds meet him. "Yo, you know a bitch named Nikki?" Cash asked. "She works out Delaware County."

"Yeah, the bitch a stalker. But what do you know about somebody telling on me?" Reds asked, trying to get past the small talk.

"She the reason you on the run," Cash whispered.

"What the fuck is you talkin' 'bout?" Reds asked.

"I didn't say nothin' to Juanita 'cause shorty said y'all was fuckin' and all that. But she was at the bar the other night, drunk as hell. Somehow your name came up, and the bitch went ballistic. She started sayin' how you tried to front on her after she rode for you, so she told on you. She said that you were gettin' what you deserved. I played along since I heard ya name and asked her about it. She said that she was at the party that you, J.R., and some nigga named Nice threw. She said that you was dissin' her all night in all these other bitches faces. So she followed you to see who you was fuckin' with. You parked on a back street, and that's when you met Nice. She followed y'all, thinkin' that y'all was gonna meet some bitches. She was plannin' on fuckin' up the car y'all was in when y'all went inside of whoever's house. She said she followed y'all out near Widener University and parked like a block away from y'all. That's when she said she saw you kill the nigga Nice. She said that she gave you a chance, and if you would've just been with her, she would've never told. Once you changed your number and she didn't see you around no more, she figured you was with somebody else. Bitch said if wasn't with her, you wasn't gonna be with nobody. I'm assumin' that's when she told the police," Cash said.

Reds was shocked by what he was hearing. He knew Cash wasn't lying because the story was accurate as shit. He still continued to scan the mall to see if he saw anything suspicious. Reds didn't know what to say. He was furious. He wanted to scream, "Why didn't you kill that bitch!"

But he decided to let it go. He stayed silent for a minute and tried to collect his thoughts. Cash knew what Reds was thinking and took his silence as a bad thing. He tried to defend his actions.

"I was gonna shoot the bitch, but I ain't have my gun on me," Cash said.

"It's okay, cuz. You ain't have to bang shorty. The bitch just lyin' on some jealous shit. I didn't kill Nice. He was my man," Reds said.

"A'ight, I just wanted to let you know. I know you layin' low, so I'm gonna let you go. Be safe," Cash said. He gave Reds a hug, then he left.

## 38

It took Reds a few days to track Nikki down. He knew where she worked, so he sat in the parking lot of Delaware County Prison every morning, waiting to see her finish her shift. On the third day, he saw her exit the jail.

Reds followed her to an apartment in West Chester. Reds didn't know if she was visiting or if she had moved there. The last time he heard, she was living in Darby, so he watched and waited. He didn't want to do something right then and there. It was daytime, and nothing was planned. It would be too easy for someone to identify him if he did something now. Reds followed the rule of the three *p*'s: planning and preparation leads to perfection.

Reds watched the apartment for two days. When he was satisfied that Nikki was living there, he mapped out his next move.

It was ten at night, and the street was dark. Reds had been outside of Nikki's apartment for two hours, waiting for her to come out for work, but she never came out. Reds saw her car parked, so he figured it must have been her day off. Reds didn't know exactly what apartment Nikki lived in. He just knew the building. It wasn't like he could just knock on her door and get her to let him in anyway, so he had to think of a way to make her come to him.

After a moment of thought, he knew how he would do it. Nikki always talked about her car. It was her pride and joy. He watched her put her car on alarm every time she got out of it. That would be how he'd get her out in the open.

What Reds didn't know was that Nikki was under twenty-four-hour surveillance by the FBI. Agent Kelly was a very smart man. He had looked over J.R. and Reds's file several times. He knew the rules they played by, and he would use those rules to bring Reds down. Agent Kelly didn't underestimate Reds. It was clear to him that Reds would kill anything that got in his way. Agent Kelly knew that if he threw out some bait, his monster would bite. So Agent Kelly moved Nikki to West Chester and told her to start telling people what she had done. Nikki was afraid at first, but she was assured that she was always being watched, so she went ahead with Agent Kelly's plan.

Nikki was given orders not to leave her apartment unless the agent that was living next door to her was alerted. What they didn't tell Nikki was that Agent Kelly and another agent were parked in a van at the end of the corner of her block just in case of an emergency.

Reds was smart. He should have picked up that this whole thing was too easy. Out of nowhere, Nikki moves to West Chester and starts telling people what she did. But Reds didn't give this any thought. His only focus was killing Nikki. He was furious about what Nikki had done to him, and he wasn't thinking entirely with his head. It was like Reds had tunnel vision; all he could see was him killing Nikki.

Reds slipped out of the truck and walked up to Nikki's car. He pulled her door handle, and the alarm went off. Nikki heard the alarm, looked out the window, then decided to go check on her car. She told the agent that was next door that she was going outside to check on her car because her alarm had gone off. The agent in the apartment radioed to the agents in the van.

"We see what's going on. Stand by. Someone just made her alarm go off. Be advised we may have our suspect. Use extreme caution. This guy's dangerous. I repeat, use extreme caution! Do not let the witness go outside. Perp is on the side of the building," Agent Kelly said into the walkie-talkie.

It was too late. By the time the agent in the apartment got the message, Nikki was already gone.

"Bad-ass kids," Nikki said as she went out the front door.

As soon as Reds heard her voice, he leaped into action. He grabbed Nikki and put his hand over her mouth with one hand and his gun to her head with the other. "You know you 'bout to die, right?" Reds said through clenched teeth.

The agents in the van saw it happen, but it happened so quickly that there was nothing they could do to stop it. They jumped out the van and ran up the block.

"Freeze! FBI!" Agent Kelly yelled from the bottom of the block.

Reds kept Nikki close to him, using her as a shield. He now knew he had been setup. "You stupid-ass bitch! They can't save you!" Reds screamed.

His adrenaline was pumping at maximum capacity now. He heard the front door fly open, and aimed his gun in the direction of the door. When the agent came out of the door with his gun drawn, Reds fired twice. *BOOM! BOOM!*

The agent never saw it coming. He was hit in the neck and face before he knew what was going on. Nikki pissed on herself. The agents that were in the van didn't shoot because they didn't have a clear shot. Reds had Nikki standing in front of him. His arm was wrapped around her neck.

"Put the fucking gun down, Carter! This is over. Nobody else has to get hurt. If you fire another shot, we will kill you. You're outnumbered. Just put the gun down," Agent Kelly said.

Reds was in the zone. He knew it was over. All he could do now was take as many of them with him as he could. Reds fired two shots at Agent Kelly. One shot hit him in the vest. The other hit him in his face.

The female agent that was with Agent Kelly fired three times, hitting Nikki twice in the stomach and Reds in the shoulder. The shot to Reds's shoulder spun him around, forcing him to let go of Nikki. Reds returned fired at the female agent, who had now taken cover behind a car. The agent returned fire, hitting Reds three more times in his chest.

Reds lay on the ground and felt the life leaving his body. He was having trouble breathing, and the bullets he had taken made him feel like his insides were on fire. He heard the sirens and the female agent calling for backup. Reds's ears were ringing from the gunshots, and all he could smell was gunpowder. He tasted blood and began to become dizzy.

"Officers down, officers down!" the agent yelled into the radio.

Reds also heard Nikki coughing up blood, next to him.

*I had a good life, and I'm goin' down in the books as a real nigga. I wouldn't be bitchin' if shit went right, so I won't bitch 'cause things went wrong,* Reds thought to himself. With his last bit of energy, Reds gripped his gun and pointed it at Nikki.

"Triflin'-ass bitch," Reds said as he let three shots rip through her face.

As soon as he started shooting, so did the last FBI agent. She put four more shots in Reds's stomach and chest, killing him.

## Five Months Later

Juanita sealed the envelope with a letter and the pictures that J.R. asked for. Juanita had written to J.R. when Reds first got killed. She knew how tight they were, and she felt like J.R. was the only person that could understand how she was feeling. J.R. had since become like a brother to Juanita, calling and writing all the time. Juanita kept J.R. filled in on what was going on with her and the baby, and J.R. promised he'd be there for them when he got out. They were there for each other during their time of grieving.

Juanita had the money that Reds left in the house, about $40,000, and the money that was in her bank account. She was okay as far as money was concerned, but she was planning on going back to work soon. Juanita felt as though she needed to stay busy to keep her mind off of the hurt. The last few months had been really hard for Juanita, and she was trying to move forward. Juanita was mad at Reds for leaving her alone like this, but he was gone now, and she had a child to raise. She knew she had to put the hurt and the pain away for her to move on, but it was hard. Every time she looked at her son, she saw his father. She still cried many times a day. Juanita loved Reds way more than even she knew.

Her mom came back up from Puerto Rico to help out with the baby, and her cousin Lilian came over often. Juanita was taking slow steps to getting over what happened to Reds, but as with all things, it would take time.

Juanita lay on the floor, playing with her son. Her phone rang. It was Tim, the guy from the storage garage. He informed her that her lease was up. She would have to come pick her things up or rent the storage space longer.

"I'll be there later on today," Juanita said.

So much had been going on that she had completely forgotten about the storage garage. Now that she was thinking about it, she remembered Reds telling her that there were pictures of him and his family there.

"You wanna see pictures of Daddy and Pop-Pop?" Juanita asked her son in a baby voice.

Little Reds just started smiling. When Juanita's mom came home from the store, they went to the storage garage.

When they got there, Juanita showed Tim her ID. "I'm sorry, but a lot has been goin' on. I lost my key. Is there any way you could open the garage for me?" Juanita asked.

"No problem, ma'am," Tim said. He got a pair of bolt cutters, and they headed to Juanita's garage. Tim cut the lock and left Juanita with her belongings. Her mom had parked right in front of the garage space.

"Can I have a minute, Mom?" Juanita asked before she went inside.

"Take your time, baby. Come and get me when you're ready to load the car up," Lucinda responded.

Juanita went in the garage and looked through the boxes. As she moved the clothes that were on the top of the boxes, she saw money. She saw that the first box was filled with money. She didn't waste any time. Juanita went to the next box and the next. She saw that all the boxes were filled with money. She was super excited. Juanita had never seen this much money in her life. She went to the treasure chest and opened it. When she saw what was inside, she damned near fainted. The whole treasure chest was filled with money. Juanita stared at the money and wondered how much it was.

It was then, that she remembered how heavy the treasure chest was when they moved it in. She asked Reds what was inside, and he said, "Six million dollars."

Juanita was so excited she thought she was going to pee on herself. "You weren't lyin', baby," Juanita said as she jumped up and down. "I love you, Nasir Carter!"

Maybe her mind was playing tricks on her because she was so happy, but she swore she heard Reds's voice say, "I love you too, ma."

# STRICTLY BUSINESS

*Thanks for the love & support!!*